Translated from the Italian by Judith Landry

I MALAVOGLIA
(The House by the Medlar Tree)

Giovanni Verga

with an introduction by
Eric Lane

D1341546

DEDALUS

Eastern Arts
Board Funded

Published in the UK by Dedalus Ltd.,
Langford Lodge, St. Judith's Lane, Sawtry, Cambs, PE17 5XE.

UK ISBN 1 873982 13 5

Distributed in the United States by Subterranean Company, P.O. Box 160,
265 South Fifth Street, Monroe, Oregon 97456.

Distributed in Australia & New Zealand by Peribo Pty Ltd.,
58 Beaumont Road, Mount Kuring-gai, N.S.W. 2080.

Distributed in Canada by Marginal Distribution,
Unit 102, 277 George Street North, Peterborough, Ontario, KJ9 3G9.

Publishing History
First published in Italy in 1881
First published by Dedalus in 1985
Reprinted in 1987
New B. Format edition in 1991
Reprinted in 1998

Translation copyright © Dedalus 1985
Introduction copyright © Eric Lane 1985

Printed in Finland by Wsoy

This book is sold subject to the condition that it shall not, by way of trade or
otherwise, be lent, re-sold, hired out, or otherwise circulated without the
publisher's prior consent in any form of binding or cover other than in
which it is published and without a similar condition including this
condition being imposed on the subesequent purchaser.

AC.I.P. listing is available for this title on request.

The Translator

Judith Landry was educated at Somerville College, Oxford where she obtained a first class honours degree in Italian and French. She combines a career as a translator of fiction, art and architecture with part-time teaching at the Courtauld Institute, London.

Her translations include *The Devil in Love* by Jacques Cazotte, *Smarra and Trilby* by Charles Nodier and *The Weeping Woman on the Streets of Prague* by Sylvie Germain.

INTRODUCTION

Luigi Capuana, the novelist and critic, hailed "I MALAVOGLIA" as the arrival of the modern novel in Italy. The rest of the critics and the Italian reading public disliked Italy's first modern novel intensely. It was set in the back of beyond, Sicily, and was about illiterate fishermen, written in a style totally at odds with the literary style fashioned by Manzoni. It had nothing to recommend it to the bourgeoisie of the cities and was soon forgotten. The publication of Mastro Don Gesualdo and Verga's play, "Cavalleria Rusticana", established Verga's reputation and fortune in Italy. By the time of his death he was the great old man of Italian letters, his reputation now based on the once despised, "I Malavoglia".

The preoccupation with heredity and fatalism given to Victorian society by the advent of Darwinism, the arrival of the modern world of railways, telegraphs, taxation and revolution in an enclosed, and hitherto cut off society, with the originality of the style and content makes "I Malavoglia" a powerful literary work, but any critic who dwells on these features misses the essential strength of the novel; its overwhelming emotional content. This is a book which brings the tears gushing into the eyes as the reader is drawn into the Homeric world of Aci Trezza. The elements, combine with Fate and the hubris of young 'Ntoni to bring about the downfall of the noble Malavoglia family. Padron 'Ntoni is a hero fit for a Greek tragedy, who fights nobly against insuperable odds to keep his family afloat, only to see everything he believes in submerged as he dies in a hospital bed.

Even today the epic qualities of 'I Malavoglia" haunt the imagination of the reader, while the modernity of the novel has but passing interest. What Verga intended as a sincere and dispassionate study of society will live forever as a lyrical testimony to the indomitable spirit of the individual engaged in a fight he cannot win.

* * *

The novel is set in the Sicily of the 1860's, shortly after its conquest by Garibaldi from the Bourbons, and its annexation to the new Kingdom of Italy. The aspirations for a better life created by the charismatic Garibaldi, and the replacement of the despotic and backward rule of the Bourbons from Naples, with the constitutional monarchy of Piedmont, were soon disappointed. The new Kingdom had as little to offer to the agrarian masses of Sicily as the dynasty it had deposed. Unification led to the bankruptcy of the protected and inefficient Southern industries, higher taxes, compulsory national service, and the arrival of an industrialized world which Sicily was not prepared for. The opportunities for self-advancement became less rather than more and the gap between the rulers, the Northern monarchy of Savoy, and the ruled Sicilians became even greater, and there were rebellions in the island in favour of the deposed Bourbons.

This aspiration for betterment caused by the arrival of the railways, the telegraphy system, the opportunity given by national service to see how others lived in the city is at the heart of the novel. 'Ntoni of padron 'Ntoni is conscripted, and after a spell in Naples returns a new man — life has to be different, even if he is not sure in what way. In Visconti's 1947 film of the novel, "La Terra Trema", it is clear what the solution is, increased class consciousness but in the Sicily of 1860's there is no solution. You must accept your lot, as not to do so, will lead only to despair. Life might be hard, but least it is clear, and the novel lays great stress in belonging, whether to a village, a family, or a trade. To go outside your environment as 'Ntoni does cannot bring anything better, and will only make it impossible to return, as he and Alfio Mosca learn. As in Hardy and the French Naturalist novels heredity, fate, social determinism, which had penetrated into literature from the works of Darwin, provide the structure of the novel. People might go to Alexandria, in Egypt, or Naples in search of their fortune, but there is no mass exodus to America as a solution to poverty and centuries of neglect. Verga wrote "I

Malavoglia" during 1878-81 while thousands went in search of a better life to America, but he deliberately set it in the pre-emigration period, providing his characters with no escape.

The Malavoglias are victims of progress, and the restoration of the house by the Medlar Tree and their boat is only possible by turning against progress and returning to the time honoured values of the grandfather, the family pulling together, each one helping the other, like the five fingers of the hand, with the interests of the family greater than those of any individual member. The religion of the family is vindicated at the end, when the worldy wise 'Ntoni wants nothing better than to stay, now that he knows everything, but cannot, his example having brought shame on his family.

Although it is young 'Ntoni's inability to do his share which leads to the collapse of the Malavoglia family it is aided and abetted by the grandfather's moral code. It is the grandfather who speculates in the cargo of lupins, which brings about the death of Bastianazzo, and the debt to zio Crocifisso. It is also the grandfather who accepts to pay when he doesn't have to, because despite what the law says, it is clear to him and Maruzza what is right and wrong. The spectacle of the Malavoglia scrimping and saving to pay the usurer, zio Crocifisso, for a cargo of lupins which were rotten when he sold them to the Malvoglia family, and losing everything while they do this is at the heart of the novel. There is no criticism of the usurer, as his values are those of the village and of society, while the Malavoglia lose their house and possessions, and must leave at night in shame. This is very much the survival of the fittest, with evolution feeling no compassion for the defeated, however noble. It is this which gives the novel its epic intensity.

* * *

Verga intended "I Malavoglia" to be the first in a cycle of five novels in which he would study society and man's innate aspirations for something more. The second novel, "Mastro Don Gesualdo", gives us the self-made man whose social pretentions brings about his downfall as his money is insufficient to bring about his acceptance in the rigid structure of 19th c Sicily. The next novel, "La Duchessa di Leyra" was begun but never finished, so Verga's study of society was limited to the fishermen of Aci Trezza and an enriched peasant. It is in the small enclosed world of Aci Trezza that Verga is most eloquent. Although ostensibly a narrow canvas, the whole of the world is found within its pages, with a penetration and insight and harmony not to be found anywhere else in Verga's work. We are taken inside the mind and the soul of the characters, so that we believe that we are there watching as a bystander, and not the beneficiaries of the author's narration.

The language of the book is strange, whether in the original Italian or the English of the translation. It is not there to be transposed elsewhere, it is unique and fashioned to represent the enclosed world of Aci Trezza and nowhere else. It is literary, but distorted to reflect the dialect and speech patterns of the fishermen, with the expressions and proverbs restricted to the elements, the sea, the land and the everyday objects of the peasant and the fishermen. There is a lot of direct speech, the character speaking for themselves, and even more indirect speech, with statements seemingly coming from someone, but no one in particular. This is what a lot of the critics refer to as the mystic village chorus. What in Joyce becomes interior monologue is supplied externally by comments which sound like a villager speaking. This degree of dialogue, whether direct and indirect, gives the novel great freshness and vividness, and makes us feel we are one of the mystic chorus, abiding our turn to have our say. It is this feeling of being part, if only as a bystander which pulls at the heartstrings of the reader, and makes "I Malavoglia" so unforgettable. It is a world where everyone knows everyone else, where people are referred to as uncle, neighbour or cousin, and the sight of a strange face is a cause for suspicion. But it is a world where the stranger is entering, and there is nostalgia for the past. The social order is changing and even in Aci Trezza, people can be conscripted to fight in unknown wars and new taxes be imposed.

What represents the past are the proverbs which give the

wisdom of the ancients, tried and trusted statements which do not lie, and have withstood the test of time. There is no need to think, as the proverb has done it for you, with the neighbours exchanging proverbs of an evening. It is only the new men like the apothecary who need to think and argue, as they wish for a different world. For padron 'Ntoni it has all been said before, and it is just a case of finding the right proverb or saying. When padron 'Ntoni loses his wits after an accident at sea, his proverbs become meaningless. The wisdom of the past has no function now, with 'Ntoni in prison and Lia living immorally in the city.

* * *

Italian literature, which was during the Renaissance the world's greatest literature, declined during the Counter Reformation, and by the 19th c was very second rate. Verga had very little of a narrative tradition to follow. There was Foscolo's "Le Ultime Lettere di Jacopo Ortis", written in the romantic style of the early Goethe. A generation later Manzoni produced "I Promessi Sposi", a historical novel in the grand manner, full of, for the time, realism, psychological perception, with two peasants for its heroes. Idealized and over didactic as it is, it ranks as one of the great achievements of Italian literature, and gave a model which many followed.

Verga began as a romantic novelist, writing novels of passion set in the city. His main influence were the Bohemian poets whom he frequented in Milan. These earlier novels are not read today. It was when Verga forsook the decadence of the town for the struggle for existence going on in his native Sicily that he found his voice as a writer. His florid prose style became shaped into an economical and sharply tuned tool. In 1874 he wrote "Nedda", his first attempt at a realist story set in Sicily. Other short stories followed, including "Fantasticheria", which became the model for "I Malavoglia". Influenced by French Naturalism, and Flaubert's ideas of impersonalness of the author, and the novels of Zola, Verga produced Italy's first modern novel.

Eric Lane

CAST OF CHARACTERS

The Malavoglia family :

Padron 'Ntoni
Bastianazzo (Bastiano), his son
Comare Maruzza, called La Longa, wife of Bastianazzo

Bastianazzo & Maruzza's children

Padron 'Ntoni's 'Ntoni
Comare Mena(Filomena), called Saint Agatha
Luca
Alessi (Alessio)
Lia (Rosalia)

Other inhabitants of Aci Trezza

Uncle Crocifisso (Crucifix), also called Dumbell, the money lender
Comare La Vespa(Wasp), his niece

Don Silvestro , town clerk
Don Franco, pharmacist
La Signora (The Lady), his wife
Don Giammaria, the priest
Donna Rosalina, his sister
Don Michele, customs sergeant
Don Ciccio, the doctor
Dr. Scipioni, the lawyer
Mastro Croce Calla , called Silkworm and Giufa (puppet), mayor and mason
Betta ,his daughter
Padron Fortunato Cipolla, owner of vineyards, olive groves and boats
Brasi Cipolla, his son

Comare Sister Mariangela, called Santuzza, tavern keeper
Uncle Santoro, her father
Nunziata, later Alessi's wife
Compare Alfio Mosca, carter
Mastro Turi Zuppido(Lame), caulker
Comare Venera, called La Zuppidda, his wife
Comare Barbara, their daughter
Compare Tino (Agostino) Piedipapera (Duckfoot), middleman
Comare Grazia Piedipapera, his wife
La Locca (The Madwoman), sister of Uncle Crocifisso
Menico, her elder son
" La Locca's son", her younger son

Cousin Anna
Rocco Spatu, her son
Mara, one of her daughters
Comare Tudda (Agatuzza)
Comare Sara (Rosaria), her daughter
Compare Mangiacarrube, his daughter

Mastro Vanni Pizzuto, barber
Massaro Filippo, farmer
Mastro Cirino, sexton and shoemaker
Peppi Naso, butcher
Uncle Cola, fisherman
Barabba, fisherman
Compare Cinghialenta, carter

Explanation of Italian terms

padron -self employed man
mastro -master craftsman
compare(male) - close neighbour
comare (female) -close neighbour

Note : In the small enclosed world of Aci Trezza, neighbours are often
referred to as uncle or cousin.

AUTHOR'S PREFACE

This story is the honest and dispassionate study of the way in which the first strivings after well-being might possibly be born, and develop, among the humblest people in society; it is an account of the sort of disquiet visited upon a family (which had lived relatively happily until that time) by the vague desire for the unknown, the realization that they are not well-off, or could be better.

The mainspring for the human activity which produces the stream of progress is here viewed at its source, at its humblest and most down-to-earth. The mechanism of the passions which are vital to such progress in these low realms is less complicated, and can thus be observed with greater accuracy. One has simply to allow the picture its pure, peaceful tones, and its simple design. This search for betterment eats into the heart of man, and as it spreads and grows, it also tends to rise, and follows its upward movement through the social classes. In *I Malavoglia* we still have merely the struggle to fulfil material needs. When these are satisfied, the search becomes a desire for riches, and is to be embodied in a middle-class character, *Mastro-don Gesualdo*, set within the still restricted framework of a small provincial town, but whose colours are beginning to be more vivid, and whose design is broader and more varied. It then becomes aristocratic vanity in *La Duchessa de Leyra*; and ambition in *L'Onorevole Scipioni*, culminating in *L'Uomo di Lusso* (The Man of Luxury) who combines all these yearnings, all these vanities, all these ambitions, to embrace and suffer them, to feel them in his blood and to be consumed by them. As the sphere of human actions broadens out, the mechanism of the passions becomes more complicated; the various characters do indeed emerge as less genuine but more eccentric, because of the subtle influence which upbringing exerts on them as well as the considerable component of artificiality to be found in civilized society. Language too tends to become more individual, to be embellished with all the half-tones which express half-feelings, with all the devices of the word which may give emphasis to the idea, in an era which, as a rule of good taste, insists on a pervasive formalism to mask a uniformity of feelings and ideas. In order for the artistic reproduction of these settings to be accurate, the norms of this analysis have to be scrupulously observed: one has to be sincere in order to show forth the truth, since form is as inherent in subject-matter as any part of the subject-matter itself is necessary to the explanation of the general argument.

The fateful, endless and often wearisome and agitated path trod by humanity to achieve progress is majestic in its end result, seen as a whole and from afar. In the glorious light which clothes it, striving, greed and egoism fade away, as do all the weaknesses which go into the huge work, all the contradictions from whose friction the light of truth emerges. The result, for mankind, conceals all that is petty in the individual interests which produce it; it justifies them virtually as necessary means to the stimulating of the activity of the individual who is unconsciously co-operating to the benefit of all. Every impulse towards this intense universal activity, from the search for material well-being to the loftiest ambitions, is justified by the mere fact that it works towards the goal of this ceaseless process; and when one knows where this immense current of human activity is tending, one certainly does not ask how it gets there. Only the observer, himself borne along by the current, as he looks around him, has the right to concern himself with the weak who fall by the wayside, with the feeble who let themselves be overtaken by the wave and thus finish the sooner, the vanquished who raise their arms in desperation, and bow their heads beneath the brutal heel of those who suddenly appear behind, to-day's victors, equally hurried, equally eager to arrive, and equally certain themselves to be overtaken to-morrow.

I Malavoglia, Mastro-don Gesualdo, L'Onorevole Scipioni

and *L'Uomo di lusso* are so many vanquished whom the current has deposited, drowned, on the river bank, after having dragged them along, each with the stigmata of his sin, which should have been the blazing of his virtue. Each, from the humblest to the highest, has played his part in the struggle for existence, for prosperity, for ambition — from the humble fisherman to the *parvenu*, to the intruder into the upper-classes and to the man of genius and firm will, who feels strong enough to dominate other men, to seize for himself that portion of public consideration which social prejudice denies him because of his illegitimate birth and who makes the law, despite himself being born outside the law; and to the artist who thinks he is following his ideal when he is in fact following another form of ambition. The person observing this spectacle has no right to judge it; he has already achieved much if he manages to draw himself outside the field of struggle for a moment to study it dispassionately, and to render the scene clearly, in its true colours, so as to give a representation of reality as it was, or as it should have been.

Milan, 19 January 1881

CHAPTER I

At one time the Malavoglia had been as numerous as the stones on the old Trezza road; there had been Malavoglia at Ognina too, and at Aci Castello, all good honest sea-faring folk and, as is often the case, quite the opposite of their nick-name, which means 'men of ill-will'. Actually, in the parish records they were called Toscano, but that didn't mean any-thing because they had always been known as the Malavoglia from generation to generation, ever since the world began, in Ognina, in Trezza and in Aci Castello, and they had always had sea-going boats and a roof over their heads. But now the only ones left in Trezza were padron 'Ntoni and his family from the house by the medlar-tree, who owned the *Provvidenza* which was moored on the shingle below the public wash-place, next to zio Cola's boat *Concetta* and padron Fortunato Cipolla's fishing-boat.

The squalls which had scattered the other Malavoglia had passed without doing much harm to the house by the medlar-tree and the boat moored below the wash-place; this miracle was explained by padron 'Ntoni who would show his clenched fist, which looked as if it were carved out of walnut wood, and would say that the five fingers of a hand had to pull together to row a good oar, and also that 'little boats must keep the shore, larger ships may venture more.'

And padron 'Ntoni's little family was indeed like the fingers of a hand. First there was padron 'Ntoni himself, the thumb, the master of the feast, as the Bible has it; then his son Bastiano, called Bastianazzo or big Bastiano because he was as large and solid as the Saint Christopher painted under the arch of the town fishmarket; but large and solid as he was, he did his father's bidding like a lamb, and wouldn't have blown

1

his own nose unless his father said to him 'blow your nose', and indeed he took La Longa as his wife when they said to him 'Take her'. Then came La Longa, a short person who busied herself weaving, salting anchovies and producing children, as a good housewife should; then came the grandchildren in order of age: 'Ntoni, the eldest, a great layabout of twenty or so, who still got the odd slap from his grandfather, and the odd kick lower down to redress the balance if the slap had been too hard; Luca, 'who had more sense than his elder brother,' as his grandfather used to say; Mena (short for Filomena) nicknamed Saint Agatha because she was always at her loom and, the saying goes, 'a woman at her loom, a chicken in the hen-run and mullet in January are the best of their kind;' Alessi (short for Alessio), a snotty-nosed brat who was the image of his grandfather; and Lia (Rosalia) who was too young to be fish, flesh or good red herring. On Sundays, when they went to church one behind the other, they were quite a troupe.

Padron 'Ntoni also knew certain sayings and proverbs which he had heard the old folks use, and he felt the old folks' sayings were tried and true: a boat couldn't go without a helmsman, for instance; if you wanted to be Pope, first you had to be sexton; a cobbler should stick to his last, a beggar could never be bankrupt and a good name was better than riches, he said. He had quite a stock of such prudent sayings.

This was why the house by the medlar-tree flourished, and padron 'Ntoni passed for a sensible fellow, to the point where they would have made him a town councillor if don Silvestro, the town clerk, had not put it about that he was a rotten diehard, a reactionary who approved of the Bourbons and was plotting for the return of King Francis II, so that he could lord it over the village as he lorded it in his own home.

But padron 'Ntoni didn't know the first thing about Francis II, and simply minded his own business, and used to say that some must watch while some must sleep, because Old Care has a mortgage on every Estate.

In December 1863 'Ntoni, the eldest grandchild, was called up for naval service. So padron 'Ntoni rushed to the village bigwigs, who are the people who can help in such cases. But don Giammaria, the parish priest, told him he'd got his just deserts, and that this was the result of that fiendish revolution they had brought about by hanging that tri-coloured bit of flag from the belltower. While don Franco the chemist began to snicker, and promised him gleefully that if they ever managed to get anything like a republic under way, everyone connected with conscription and taxes would be given short shrift, because there wouldn't be any more soldiers, but everyone would go to war, if need be. Then padron 'Ntoni beseeched him for the love of God to have the republic come quickly, before his grandson 'Ntoni went for a soldier, as though don Franco had it all buttoned up; and indeed the chemist finally ended up by losing his temper. While don Silvestro the town clerk split his sides laughing at these discussions, and finally told padron 'Ntoni that a certain sum slipped into a certain pocket, on his advice, could produce a defect in his grandson that would get him exempted from military service. Unfortunately the boy was conscientiously built, as they still make them at Aci Trezza, and when the army doctor looked at the strapping lad before him, he told him that *his* defect was to be set like a column on great feet that resembled the shovel-like leaves of a prickly pear; but such shovel-feet are better than neat-fitting boots on the deck of a battleship on a rough day; and so they took 'Ntoni without so much as a 'by your leave'. When the conscripts were taken to their barracks at Catania, La Longa trotted breathlessly alongside her son's loping stride, busily urging him to keep his scapular of the Virgin Mary always on his chest, and to send news every time anyone he knew came home from the city, and he needn't worry, she would send him the money for the writing paper.

His grandfather, man that he was, said nothing; but he too felt a lump in his throat, and he avoided his daughter-in-law's gaze, as if he were annoyed with her. So they went back to Aci Trezza in silence, with their heads down. Bastianazzo had hastily tidied up the *Provvidenza* so as to go and wait for them at the top of the street, but when he saw them coming along like that, all crestfallen and with their boots in their hands, he didn't have the heart to open his mouth, and went home with

3

them in silence. La Longa immediately rushed to shut herself straight in the kitchen, as though she couldn't wait to be alone with her pots and pans, and padron 'Ntoni said to his son: 'Go and have a word with the poor creature, she can't take any more.'

The next day they all went back to the station at Aci Castello to see the convoy of conscripts on their way to Messina, and they waited over an hour behind the railings being jostled by the crowd. At last the train came, and they saw all those boys flapping their arms about, with their heads sticking out of the train windows, like cattle on their way to market. There was so much singing, laughing and general din that it was almost like the feast day at Trecastagni, and amid the hubbub and racket the earlier sense of pain was almost forgotten.

'Goodbye, 'Ntoni!' 'Goodbye, mother!' 'Goodbye, and remember what I told you.' And there at the roadside was Sara, comare Tudda's girl, apparently cutting grass for their calf; but comare Venera, known as 'la Zuppidda', the lame, was spreading the rumour that in fact she had come to say goodbye to padron 'Ntoni's 'Ntoni, who she used to talk to over the garden wall, she herself had seen them as sure as she would wind up before God her maker. Certain it is that 'Ntoni waved goodbye to Sara, and she stood there with her sickle in her hand staring at the train until it moved off. La Longa felt she personally had been cheated of her own good-bye; and for a long time afterwards, every time she met Sara in the square or at the wash-place, she turned her back on her.

Then the train had left, whistling and roaring in such a way as to drown everyone's songs and goodbyes. And when the onlookers had gone their own ways, there was just a group of women left, and the odd poor soul who carried on standing up against the railings without quite knowing why. Then gradually even they ambled off, and padron 'Ntoni, guessing that his daughter-in-law must have a bitter taste in her mouth, treated her to two *centesimos* worth of lemon water.

To comfort La Longa, comar Venera la Zuppidda came out with: 'Now you may as well resign yourself — for five years you'll just have to act as though your son were dead, and shut him out of your mind.'

But they continued to think about him, in the house by the medlar-tree, sometimes because of an extra bowl that La Longa kept coming across when she set the table, sometimes because of a running bowline for securing the rigging which 'Ntoni could do better than anyone else, or when a rope had to be pulled as taut as a violin string, or a hawser hauled up by hand when you really needed a winch. Between his puffings and pantings, his grandfather would interpolate remarks like 'Here's where we could do with 'Ntoni,' or 'I haven't got that boy's wrist, you know.' And as his mother plied her comb rhythmically across her loom she would remember the pounding of the engine which had taken her son away, a pounding which had stayed with her, amid all that bewilderment, and whose insistent beat seemed to be with her still.

His grandfather had some odd ways of comforting himself, and others: 'After all, let's be honest: a bit of soldiering will do that boy good. He always did prefer loafing about of a Sunday to using that good pair of arms of his to earn an honest crust.'

Or: 'When he's tasted the salt bread you eat elsewhere, he'll stop complaining about the soups he gets at home.'

At last 'Ntoni's first letter arrived from Naples, and it set the whole neighbourhood buzzing. He said that the women in those parts wore silken skirts which swept the ground, and that on the quay you could watch Pulcinella, and they sold pizza at two centesimos, the sort rich people ate, and that you couldn't exist without money, it wasn't like being at Aci Trezza, where you couldn't spend a brass farthing unless you went to Santuzza's wine shop. 'We'd better send that greedy boy some money to buy himself some pizza,' said padron 'Ntoni grudgingly; 'It's not his fault, that's just how he is; he's like a codfish, which would swallow a rusty nail given a chance. If I hadn't held him at the font with my own arms, I'd swear don Giammaria had put sugar in his mouth instead of salt.'

When comare Tudda's Sara was at the wash-place, the Mangiacarrubbe girl kept saying:

'I can just imagine it! Women dressed in silks simply waiting to get their hands on padron 'Ntoni's 'Ntoni. They don't have that kind of booby there.'

The others guffawed, and from then on the more disgruntled girls called him the booby.

'Ntoni also sent a photograph of himself, all the girls at the wash-place had seen it, because comare Tudda's Sara let them pass it round from hand to hand, under their aprons, and the Mangiacarrubbe girl was sick with jealousy. He looked like the archangel Michael in flesh and blood, with those feet of his resting on the carpet, and that curtain at his head, like the one behind the Madonna at Ognina, and so handsome, sleek and clean that his own mother wouldn't have recognised him; and poor La Longa couldn't see enough of the carpet and the curtain and that column against which her son was standing so stiffly, with his hand scratching the back of a fat armchair; and she thanked God and his saints that they had placed her son in the midst of all that finery. She kept the portrait on the chest-of-drawers, under the glass dome with the statue of the Good Shepherd — to whom she told her beads — said la Zuppidda, and she thought she'd got a real treasure there on that chest-of-drawers, while in fact sister Mariangela la Santuzza had another one just like it, for anyone who cared to look, given her by compare Mariano Cinghialenta, and she kept it nailed on the counter in the wine-shop, behind the glasses.

But after a bit 'Ntoni got hold of a lettered comrade, and then he let fly with complaints about the wretched life he led on board ship, his superiors, the discipline, the thin soup and tight shoes. 'That letter isn't worth the twenty centesimos it cost to send,' grumbled padron 'Ntoni. La Longa lost patience with all those scrawls, which looked like fish-hooks and couldn't possibly say anything good. Bastianazzo shook his head as if to say no, it wasn't right, if it had been him he would have covered that paper with cheerful things only, to make people feel better — and he thrust out a finger as thick as a rowlock pin — if only out of consideration for La Longa, who couldn't seem to resign herself, and was like a mother cat that has lost her kittens. Padron 'Ntoni went in secret to have the letter read out to him by the chemist, and then by don Giammaria, who was a man of the opposite persuasion, so as

6

to hear both sides, and when he was convinced that the letter was indeed as it had first seemed, he repeated to Bastianazzo and his wife:

'Didn't I say that that boy ought to have been born rich, like padron Cipolla's son, so he could scratch his stomach all day long without doing a hand's turn?'

Meanwhile it had been a bad year and fish had virtually to be given away like alms, now that Christians had learned to eat meat on Fridays like so many Turks. Furthermore there weren't enough hands left at home to manage the boat, and at times they had to take on Menico della Locca, or someone else. Because the king's trick was to take boys away for conscription when they were ready to earn their own bread; but as long as they were a drain on family resources, you had to bring them up yourself, so they could be soldiers later; and in addition to all this Mena was nearly seventeen and was beginning to turn young men's heads when she went to mass. 'Man is fire, and woman the straw; the devil comes, and blows.' That was why the family from the house by the medlar-tree had to sweat blood to keep the boat seaworthy.

So, to keep things going, padron 'Ntoni had arranged a deal with zio Crocifisso Dumb-bell, a deal in connection with some lupins which were to be bought on credit and resold at Riposto, where compare Cinghialenta had said there was a boat loading up for Trieste. Actually the lupins were not in the peak of condition; but they were the only ones in Trezza, and the artful Dumb-bell also knew that the *Provvidenza* was wasting good sun and water moored up there by the washplace, not doing anything; that was why he persisted in acting dumb. 'Eh? Not a good deal? Leave it then! But I can't make it one *centesimo* less, so help me God!' and he shook his head in such a way that it did indeed resemble a bell without a clapper. This conversation took place at the door of Ognina church, on the first Sunday in September, the feast of the Virgin Mary, and all the people from the nearby villages were there, including compare Agostino Piedipapera, or Duckfoot, who was so bluff and blithe that he managed to bring about an agreement on the price of two *onze* and ten per *salma*, to be paid on the never at so much a month. Things

7

always turned out like that for zio Crocifisso, he could always be wheedled into agreeing because, like some girls, he couldn't say no. 'That's it. You simply can't say no when you should,' sniggered Piedipapera, 'You're like those . . .' and he said what he was like.

When La Longa heard about the deal with the lupins, after supper, when they were sitting chatting with their elbows on the tablecloth, her mouth fell open; it was if she could feel that huge sum of forty *onze* weighing physically on her stomach. But women have no business sense, and padron 'Ntoni had to explain to her that if the deal went well they would have bread for the winter, and ear-rings for Mena, and Bastiano would be able to go to Riposto and back in a week, with Menico della Locca. Meanwhile Bastiano was snuffing out the candle without saying a word. That was how the lupin deal came about, and with it the voyage of the *Provvidenza*, which was the oldest of the village boats but which had a lucky name anyhow. Maruzza still felt black at heart, but she kept quiet, because it wasn't her business, and she quietly went about organizing the boat and everything for the trip, the fresh bread, the pitcher with the oil, the onions and the fur-lined coats stowed under the footrest and in the locker.

The men had been up against it all day, what with that shark zio Crocifisso, who had sold them a pig in a poke, and the lupins, which were past their prime. Dumb bell said he knew nothing about it, honest to God. 'What's been agreed is fair indeed,' was his contribution. And Piedipapera fussed and swore like a maniac to get them to agree, insisting heatedly that he had never come upon such a deal in his whole life; and he thrust his hands into the pile of lupins and showed them up to God and the Virgin, calling upon them as witnesses. Finally, red, flustered and beside himself, he made a last desperate offer, and put it to zio Crocifisso who was still acting dumb and to the Malavoglia who had the sacks in their hands: 'Look. Pay for them at Christmas, instead of paying so much a month, and you'll save a *tari* per *salma*. Now can we call an end to it?' And he began to put the lupins into the sacks: 'In God's name, let's call it a day!'

The *Provvidenza* set sail on Saturday towards evening, and

the evening bell should already have rung, though it hadn't, because mastro Cirino the sexton had gone to take a pair of new boots to don Silvestro the town clerk; that was the time of evening when the girls clustered like a flock of sparrows around the fountain, and the evening star was already shining brightly, so that it looked like a lantern hanging from the *Provvidenza's* yard. Maruzza stood on the seashore with her youngest child in her arms, not saying a word, while her husband unfurled the sail, and the *Provvidenza* bobbed like a young duckling on the waves which broke around the fangs of rock offshore.

'When the north is dark and the south is clear, you may set to sea without any fear,' padron 'Ntoni was saying from the shore, looking towards Etna which was all black with clouds. Menico della Locca, who was in the *Provvidenza*, shouted something, but the sea swallowed it. 'He said you can give the money to his mother, la Locca, because his brother is out of work,' added Bastianazzo, and this was the last word they heard him speak.

CHAPTER II

The whole village was talking of nothing but the lupin deal, and as La Longa came home with Lia in her arms, the neighbours stood on their doorsteps to watch her pass.

'What a deal!' bawled Piedipapera, clumping along with his twisted leg behind padron 'Ntoni, who had gone to sit down on the church steps, alongside padron Fortunato Cipolla and Menico della Locca's brother, who were enjoying the cool of the evening. Old zio Crocifisso was squawking like a plucked fowl, but there was no need to worry, the old man had plenty of feathers to spare. 'We had a hard time of it, didn't we, padron 'Ntoni?' — but he would have thrown himself off the top of those sharp rocks for padron 'Ntoni, as God lives, and zio Crocifisso paid heed to him, because he called the tune, and quite a tune it was, more than two hundred *onze* a year! Dumb-bell couldn't blow his own nose without Piedipapera.

La Locca's son, overhearing mention of zio Crocifisso's wealth — and zio Crocifisso really was his uncle, being la Locca's brother — felt his heart swell with family feeling.

'We're related,' he would say. 'When I work for him by the day he gives me half-pay, and no wine, because we're relatives.'

Piedipapera snickered. 'He does that for your good, so as not to get you drunk, and to leave you the richer when he dies.'

Compare Piedipapera enjoyed speaking ill of people who cropped up in conversation; but he did it so warmly, and so unmaliciously, that there was no way you could take it amiss.

'Massaro Filippo has walked past the wine shop twice,' he would say, 'and he's waiting for Santuzza to signal to him to

10

go and join her in the stable, so they can tell their beads to-gether.'

Or he might say to La Locca's son:

'Your uncle Crocifisso is trying to steal that smallholding from your cousin la Vespa; he wants to pay her half of what it's worth, by giving her to understand that he's going to marry her. But if she manages to get something else taken from her too, you can say goodbye to any hope of that inherit-ance, along with the wine and the money that he never gave you.'

Then they started to argue, because padron 'Ntoni main-tained that when all was said and done, zio Crocifisso was a decent member of the human race, and had not thrown all judgment to the dogs, to consider going and marrying his brother's daughter.

'How does decency come into it?' retored Piedipapera. 'He's mad, is what you mean. He's swinish rich, while all la Vespa has is that pocket-handkerchief smallholding.'

'That's no news to me,' said padron Cipolla, swelling like a turkey-cock, 'it runs along the side of my vineyard.'

'Do you call that couple of prickly pears a vineyard?' countered Piedipapera.

'There are vines among those prickly pears, and if St. Francis sends us rain, it will produce some fine grape must, you'll see. The sun set behind the clouds to-day — that means wind or rain.'

'When hidden by cloud the sun goes to rest, then you may hope for a wind from the west,' specified padron 'Ntoni.

Piedipapera couldn't bear that pontificating pedant padron Cipolla, who thought he was always right just because he was rich, and felt that he could force those who were less well off than himself to swallow his rubbish wholesale.

'One man's meat is another man's poison,' he went on. 'Padron Cipolla is hoping for rain for his vineyard, and you're hoping for a west wind for the *Provvidenza*. A rippling sea means a fresh wind, as the proverb has it. The stars are all out to-night, and at midnight the wind will change; listen to it blowing.'

You could hear carts passing slowly by on the road. 'There

11

are always people going about the world, day and night,' compare Cipolla then observed.

And now that you couldn't see either land or sea any more, it seemed as if Trezza were the only place in the whole world and everyone wondered where those carts could be going at that hour.

'Before midnight the *Provvidenza* will have rounded the Capo dei Mulini,' said padron 'Ntoni, 'and then this strong wind won't be against her any more,'

All padron 'Ntoni thought about was the *Provvidenza*, and when he wasn't talking about his own affairs he made no more contribution to the conversation than a discarded broom handle.

So Piedipapera said to him, 'You ought to go and join the chemist's lot, they're discussing the pope and the king. You'd cut a fine figure there. Listen to them bellowing.'

The chemist held forth at the door of his shop, in the cool, with the parish priest and one or two others. As he knew how to read, he would read the newspaper aloud to the rest, and he also owned the history of the French Revolution, which he kept to hand, under the glass mortar, and that was why he quarrelled all day long with don Giammaria, the parish priest, to pass the time, and this made them almost ill from bad temper; but they wouldn't have lasted a day without seeing each other. Then on Saturdays, when the newspaper arrived, don Franco would actually run to half an hour's candle, or even an hour, at the risk of being scolded by his wife, so as to parade his ideas and not just go to bed like a dumb beast, like compare Cipolla or compare Malavoglia. And during the summer there wasn't even any need for the candle, because you could stay out at the front door under the lamp, when mastro Cirino lit it, and sometimes don Michele, the customs guard, would come along too; and so would don Silvestro, the town clerk, pausing for a moment or two on his way home from his vineyard.

Then, rubbing his hands, don Franco would say that they were quite a little Parliament there, and he would go and settle in behind the counter, running his fingers through his bushy beard with a special sly smile as though he wanted to eat a man for breakfast, and at times he would let slip the odd brief phrase to the public, getting up on his short legs, so that you could tell he was shrewder than the others, and indeed he induced in don Giammaria a feeling of such intense gall that he found him quite unbearable, and would spit assorted Latin tags in his direction. Whereas don Silvestro relished the bad blood they generated, by trying fruitlessly to square the circle; at least he didn't get riled, as they did, and that, as they said in the village, was why he owned the finest small-holding in Trezza — where he had arrived barefoot, as Piedi-papera pointed out. He set them one against the other, and then cackled fit to burst, just like a hen.

'There's don Silvestro laying another egg,' La Locca's son observed.

'And they're golden eggs he lays down there at the Town Hall,' said Piedipapera.

'Hm,' padron Cipolla said sharply, 'not all that golden. Comare Zuppidda wouldn't give him her daughter's hand in marriage.'

'That means that mastro Turi Zuppiddo prefers the eggs from his own hens,' replied padron 'Ntoni. And padron Cipolla nodded in agreement.

'Birds of a feather flock together,' added padron Malavo-glia.

Then Piedipapera retorted that if don Silvestro had been content to flock together with birds of his own sort, he would be holding a spade instead of a pen to this day.

'Would you give your grand-daughter Mena to him?' padron Cipolla asked finally, turning to padron 'Ntoni.

'What's bred in the bone will not out in the flesh.'

Padron Cipolla carried on nodding, because in fact there had been some talk between him and padron 'Ntoni of marrying Mena to his son Brasi, and if the lupin deal went well, Mena would have her dowry in ready cash, and the matter could be promptly wrapped up.

'A girl's worth lies in her upbringing, and the quality of the hemp lies in the spinning,' said padron Malavoglia after a bit, and padron Cipolla confirmed that everyone in the village felt that la Longa had known how to bring up her daughter, and

13

everyone who passed down the little street at that hour, hearing the clicking of Saint Agatha's loom, agreed that comare Maruzza hadn't wasted her efforts in that direction.

When she arrived back home, la Longa had lit the lamp and had sat down on the balcony with her winder, filling up the spools she would be needing for her week's weaving.

'You can't see comare Mena, but you can here her at her loom day and night, like Saint Agatha,' the neighbours would say.

'That's what girls should be brought up to do,' Maruzza would reply, 'instead of standing at the window. A woman at the window is a woman to be shunned.'

'But you do sometimes catch a husband that way, with all those men passing by,' observed cousin Anna from the doorstep opposite.

Cousin Anna was in a position to know about such things; because her son Rocco, that great dolt, had let himself be ensnared by the Mangiacurrubbe girl, a brazen-faced starer out of windows if every there was one.

Hearing conversation in the street, comare Grazia Piedipapera came out on to her doorstep as well, with her apron full of the beans she was shelling, and started complaining about the mice which had riddled her sack as full of holes as a sieve, and seemed to have done it on purpose, as though they were blessed with human judgment; and at that the conversation became general, because Maruzza too had suffered a lot of damage from those dratted little beasts! Cousin Anna's house was teeming with them since her cat had died, an animal which had been worth its weight in gold and which had been killed by a kick from compare Tino. Grey cats were the best mousers, and as elusive as the eye of your needle. Nor should you open the door to cats at night, because an old woman from Aci Sant'Antonio had been killed that way, as the thieves had stolen her cat three days earlier and then brought it back to her half dead with hunger, mewing piteously in front of her door; and the poor woman didn't have the heart to leave the dumb creature out on the street at that hour, and had opened the door, and that was how the thieves had got into her house.

Nowadays mischief-makers got up to all kinds of tricks;

and at Trezza you saw faces which had never been seen there before, on the cliffs, people claiming to be going fishing, and they even stole the sheets put out to dry, if there happened to be any. Poor Nunziata had had a new sheet stolen that way. Poor girl! Imagine robbing her, a girl who had worked her fingers to the bone to provide bread for all those little brothers her father had left on her hands when he had upped and gone to seek his fortune in Alexandria in Egypt. Nunziata was like cousin Anna, when her husband had died and left her with that brood of children, and Rocco, the largest of the little ones, not even knee-high. Then cousin Anna had had to bring up that great shirker, just to see him stolen from her by the Mangiacarrubbe girl.

Then into the midst of this chatter walked la Zuppidda, the wife of Turi the caulker, who had been at the end of the alley; she always appeared to put her oar in, like the devil in the litany, so that no one ever knew where she had popped up from.

'Anyhow,' she now muttered, 'your son Rocco didn't help you, and if he did earn a penny he'd go straight to the wine shop and spend it on drink.'

La Zuppidda knew everything that went on in the village and that was why people said she went around barefoot all day, acting the informer with the excuse of her spindle, which she always held up in the air so that it wouldn't whirr on the cobbles. She always spoke the gospel truth, this indeed was her mistake, and that was why her comments were far from welcome, people said that she had the devil's own tongue in her mouth, the kind of tongue that leaves a track of spittle. 'A sour mouth spits forth gall,' and her mouth tasted bitter indeed because of her Barbara whom she had not managed to marry of, and she wanted to give her to the son of King Victor Emanuel himself, for all that.

'A fine piece, the Mangiacarrubbe girl,' she continued, 'a brazen-faced minx, who has had the whole village passing under her window.' A woman at a window is a woman to be shunned, and Vanni Pizzuto used to take her prickly pears stolen from massaro Filippo's the greengrocer, and they ate them together in the vineyard, among the vines, under the almond tree, she herself had seen them. And Peppi Naso, the butcher, after a sudden pang of jealousy brought on by compare Mariano Cinghialenta, the carter, had had the bright idea of dumping the horns of all the animals he'd slaughtered into her doorway, since people had said that he used to go and preen under the Mangiacarrubbe girl's window.

But cousin Anna, that happy soul, smiled through it all.

'Don Giammaria says you're committing a mortal sin by speaking ill of your neighbour!'

'Don Giammaria would do better to preach to his sister donna Rosolina,' retorted la Zuppidda, 'and not let her carry on with don Silvestro when he happens to pass by, or with don Michele the sergeant, thirsting for a husband as she is, and so old and fat, poor thing!'

'God's will be done,' concluded cousin Anna. 'When my husband died, Rocco was no taller than this distaff and his little sisters were all smaller than he was. But did I lose heart for that? Problems are something you get used to, they help you get down to work. My daughters will do as I have done, and as long as there are slabs in the wash-place, we won't lack for the bare essentials. Look at Nunziata, she has more sense than many an old woman, and manages to bring up those little ones as though she'd given birth to them.'

'By the way, where is Nunziata?' asked la Longa of a crowd of tattered urchins who were whimpering on the doorstep of the little house opposite; they set up a chorus of wailing at mention of their sister's name.

'I saw her going out on the *sciara*, the lava field, gathering broom, and your Alessi was there too, walking with her,' said cousin Anna. The children were quiet for a moment, and then all began to grizzle in unison, and the least tiny of them, who was perched on a large stone, said after a bit.

'I don't know where she is.'

The neighbourhood women had come out, like slugs after the rain, and you could hear a continuous chattering from one doorway to the next, all along the lane. Even Alfio Mosca's window was open, Alfio Mosca, that is, who had the donkey cart, and from it came a strong smell of broom. Mena had left her loom and come out on the balcony as well.

'Oh, Saint Agatha,' exclaimed the neighbours; and every-one was glad to see her.

'Aren't you thinking of marrying off your Mena?' la Zuppidda asked comare Maruzza in a low voice. 'She'll be eighteen at Easter; I know because she was born the year of the earthquake, like my Barbara. Anyone who is interested in my Barbara must first suit me.'

At that point a rustle of branches was heard down the street, and Alessi and Nunziata arrived, barely visible under the bundles of broom, they were so small.

'Oh Nunziata!' called the neighbours. 'Weren't you afraid out on the *sciara* at this hour?'

'I was there too,' said Alessi.

'I stayed out late with comare Anna at the wash-place, and I didn't have any wood for the fire.'

The young girl lit the lamp and moved quickly about, pre-paring things for supper, while her little brothers trailed after her up and down the room, so that she looked for all the world like a hen with her chicks. Alessi had removed his load, and was gazing gravely from the doorway, with his hands in his pockets.

'Oh Nunziata,' called Mena from the balcony, 'when you've put the water on to boil, come over here for a bit.'

Nunziata left Alessi to keep an eye on the fire, and ran to perch on the balcony alongside Saint Agatha, so that she too could have a moment of well-earned rest.

'Compare Alfio Mosca is cooking his beans,' observed Nunziata after a pause.

'You're two of a pair, neither of you has anyone at home of an evening to make your soup for you when you come home tired.'

'Yes, that's true; and he even know how to sew and wash, and he mends his own shirts' — Nunziata knew everything about her neighbour Alfio, and she knew his house like the back of her hand. 'Now,' she would say, 'he's going to get wood; now he's seeing to his donkey' — and you could see the light in the courtyard, or in the shed. Saint Agatha would laugh, and Nunziata would say that all he lacked to be a thorough-going woman was a skirt.

'Anyway,' concluded Mena, 'when he marries, his wife will go around with the donkey cart, and he will stay at home and mind the children.'

In a huddle in the street, the mothers too were talking about Alfio Mosca, and even la Vespa swore she wouldn't have wanted him for a husband, according to la Zuppidda, because la Vespa had her own precious smallholding, and if she decided to marry, she certainly wouldn't want someone whose only possession was a donkey cart: 'your cart is your bier,' says the proverb. She had set her sights on her zio Crocifisso, her uncle, the cunning little piece.

Privately, the girls took Mosca's part agains that vicious Vespa; and personally Nunziata flinched at the scorn they heaped upon compare Alfio, just because he was poor, and had no one in the world, and suddenly she said to Mena; 'If I were grown up I would have him, if I were told to.'

Mena had been about to say something; but she suddenly changed the subject.

'Will you be going into town for the All Souls' Day fair?'

'No, I can't leave the house empty.'

'We'll being going, if the lupin deal goes well; grandfather said so.'

Then she thought for a moment, and added:

'Compare Alfio Mosca usually goes too, to sell his walnuts.'

And they both fell silent, thinking of the All Souls' Day fair, where Alfio went to sell his walnuts.

'Zio Crocifisso, all meek and mild as he is, is going to get his hands on la Vespa,' said cousin Anna.

'That's just what she'd like,' la Zuppidda promptly retorted, 'that's *just* what she'd like, to have him get his hands on her. As it is she's always hanging around the house, like the cat, with the excuse of bringing him choice morsels, and the old man doesn't refuse, after all he's got nothing to lose. She's fattening him up like a pig, with all that coming and going. I'm telling you, la Vespa wants him to get his hands on her!'

Everyone had their contribution to make on the subject of zio Crocifisso, who was always bleating and groaning like Christ crucified between the thieves, and yet he had pots of money, because one day when the old man had been ill, la Zuppidda had seen a coffer under the bed as long as your arm.

La Longa felt the forty *onze* from the lupin debt weighing her down, and changed the subject, because even walls have ears, and you could hear zio Crocifisso talking nearby with don Giammaria, as they walked through the square, so that even la Zuppidda broke off the vituperations that she was casting in his direction, to greet him.

Don Silvestro was cackling away, and his way of laughing got on the chemist's nerves, though in fact the chemist had never been endowed with much patience anyway, and he left that virtue to donkeys and people who were satisfied with the revolution as it stood.

'Precisely, you've never had any patience, you wouldn't know where to put it,' don Giammaria shouted at him; and don Franco, who was a small man, would rise to the bait and address rough words to the priest, words which could be heard from one end of the square to the other, in the dark. Dumb-bell, hard as stone, was shrugging his shoulders, and took care to repeat guardedly that it didn't matter a hoot to him, he minded his own business. 'And don't tell me it's not your business if nobody pays a penny towards the Brotherhood of the Good Death,' don Giammaria said to him. 'When it's a question of putting their hands into their pockets, people become a pack of heathen, worse than the chemist, and cross to the other side when they see the Brotherhood's coffers!'

From his shop don Franco sniggered aloud, trying to imitate don Silvestro's maddening laugh. But the chemist was one of Them, as everyone knew; and don Giammaria shouted to him from the square: 'You'd find the money all right, if it were for schools and lamps!'

The chemist held his tongue, because his wife had appeared at the window; and when he was far enough away not to fear being overheard by don Silvestro, the town clerk, who also pocketted a bit of a salary as an elementary school teacher, zio Crocifisso said that it didn't matter to him.

But in his day they hadn't had all those lamps, nor all those schools; you didn't force the horse to drink, and everyone was the better off for it.

'You never went to school; but you can manage your business.'

'And I know my catechism,' added zio Crocifisso, to return the compliment.

In the heat of the dispute don Giammatria, missed his usual way across the square almost tripped and, God forgive him, let slip a bad word.

'If only they'd light their precious light, at least!'

'In this day and age you have to look after yourself,' zio Crocifisso pronounced.

Don Giammaria tugged him by the sleeve of his jacket every time he wanted to say something disparaging about this person or that, in the middle of the square, there in the dark; about the lamplighter who stole the oil, about don Silvestro who turned a blind eye to it, about the catspaw of a mayor who let himself be led by the nose. Now that he worked for the municipality, mastro Cirino was a most unreliable sexton, ringing the angelus only when he had nothing else to do, and the communion wine he purchased was reminiscent of the kind which Jesus Christ had had on the cross, it was a real sacrilege. Dumb bell kept on nodding out of habit, though it was completely dark and they couldn't see each other at all, and don Giammaria reviewed his victims one by one, saying that so and so was a thief, so and so a villain, so and so a fire-brand.

'Have you heard Piedipapera talking with padron Malavoglia and padron Cipolla? He's another of the gang, I tell you! A rabble-rouser, with that lame leg!' And when he saw him hobbling across the square he gave him a wide berth, but followed him with a suspicious stare, to find out what he might be up to hobbling along like that. 'He's got the devil's own foot,' he would mutter. Zio Crocifisso shrugged his shoulders and repeated that he was a decent fellow, and wouldn't be drawn. 'Padron Cipolla, now there's another idiot and a windbag! letting himself be swindled by Piedi-papera . . . and padron 'Ntoni will be falling for it too, before long . . . you have to be prepared for anything in this day and age!'

20

Decent folk minded their own business, zio Crocifisso repeated. Meanwhile compare Tino was holding forth like a statesman seated on the steps of the church; 'Now you listen to me: before the revolution it was quite another matter. Now the fish have got wise to things, let me tell you!'

'No, no, the anchovies sense the north-easter twenty-four hours before it arrives,' replied padron 'Ntoni; 'that's how it's always been; the anchovy has more sense than the tunny. Now they are fishing them out in shoals beyond the Capo dei Mulini, with fine-meshed nets.'

'I'll tell you what the matter is,' compare Fortunato suggested. 'It's those wretched steamers coming and going, and stirring up the water with their wheels. What can you expect, the fish take fright and move off. That's what it is.'

La Locca's son was listening open-mouthed, and scratched his head. 'Well done,' he said after a moment. 'If that were true, the steamers would have scared the fish away at Syracuse too, or Messina. But they bring fish from there on the railway by the ton.'

'Sort it out yourselves then,' said padron Cipolla, nettled. 'It's not my problem, I couldn't care less. I've got my small-holding and my vines to bring in my daily bread.'

And Piedipapera administered a firm clout to la Locca's son, to teach him manners. 'Blockhead! Hold your tongue when your elders are talking!'

The young lout went off bawling and hitting his head with his clenched fists, because everyone took him for a blockhead just on account of being la Locca's son. Sniffing the air, padron 'Ntoni commented:

'If the north-wester doesn't start up before midnight, the *Provvidenza* will be able to round the Cape.'

From the top of the belltower came the slow, sonorous tolling of the bell. 'One hour after sunset,' said padron Cipolla.

Padron 'Ntoni crossed himself and said:

'Peace to the living and rest to the dead.'

'Don Giammaria is having fried vermicelli for supper to-night,' observed Piedipapera sniffing in the direction of the windows of the priest's house. Don Giammaria, passing by

21

on his way home, even condescended to greet him, because as
things were going you had to humour those doubtful characters; and compare Tino, whose mouth was still watering,
shouted after him:

'Eh! fried vermicelli to-night, don Giammaria!'

'Did you hear him? Right down to what I eat!' grumbled
don Giammaria between his teeth. 'They even keep a tally on
the number of mouthfuls eaten by God's servants! all out of
hatred for the church!' and coming face to face with don
Michele, the customs man, who went around with his pistol
on his stomach and his trousers tucked into his boots, looking
for smugglers: 'But they don't begrudge that lot their mouthfuls, oh dear no!'

'I like that lot,' said Dumb bell. 'I like them mounting
guard over decent folks' possessions.'

'The tiniest prompting, and he'd join the gang too,' don
Giammaria said to himself, knocking at his door. 'Gang of
thieves,' and he carried on grumbling, with the knocker in his
hand, listening warily to the footsteps of the sergeant as they
died away in the darkness, in the direction of the wine shop,
and brooding on what might take him towards the wine shop
when he was mounting guard over decent folks' interests!

But compare Tino knew why don Michele was going to
guard decent folks' interests over near the wine shop, because
he had lost several nights' sleep lying in wait behind the
nearby elm to find out precisely that. 'He goes there for a
private chat with zio Santoro, Santuzza's father,' was his
comment. 'Those government idlers have to play the spy, and
know everybody's business, in Trezza and everywhere else,
and zio Santoro, blind as he is, like a bat in the sunlight on the
door of the wine shop, knows everything that goes on in the
village, and could call us by name just from hearing our footsteps. The only time he doesn't hear is when massaro Filippo
goes to tell his beads with Santuzza, and he's a sterling guard,
better than if you put a handkerchief over his eyes.'

Hearing one hour after sunset strike, Maruzza had rushed
homewards to lay the table; gradually the neighbours had
thinned out, and as the village itself was gradually falling
asleep, you could hear the sea snoring nearby, at the bottom

of the little street, and every so often it heaved a sigh, like someone turning over in his bed. Only down at the wine shop did the din continue, and you could hear the bawling of Rocco Spatu, who treated every day as if it were a Sunday.

'Compare Rocco is a happy soul,' said Alfio Mosca from the window of his house after a while, when it had seemed as though no one were there.

'Oh, are you still there, compare Alfio?' said Mena, who had stayed out on the balcony waiting for her grandfather.

'Yes, I'm here, comare Mena; I'm eating my soup here, because when I see you all at table, with the lamp, I don't feel so alone, and loneliness takes away your appetite.'

'*You're* not a happy soul, then?'

'You need a lot of things to make you happy.'

Mena said nothing, and after another pause Alfio added: 'To-morrow I'm going into town with a load of salt.'

'Will you be going to the All Souls' Day fair as well?'

'I'm not sure; this year those few walnuts that I have are rotten.'

'Compare Alfio is going to town to look for a wife,' said Nunziata from the door opposite.

'Is that true? asked Mena.

'Well, comare Mena, if that was all there was to it I'd be glad to take a girl from my own village, without having to go anywhere else to look for one.'

'Look at all those stars winking up there,' said Mena after a bit. 'They say that they are souls from Purgatory, on their way to Paradise.'

'Listen,' said Alfio to her after they had looked at the stars for a bit too; 'you're Saint Agatha — if you happen to dream a lucky number in the state lottery, tell me, and I'll put my shirt on it, and then I'll be able to think about taking a wife.'

'Good night,' said Mena.

The stars winked harder than ever, as if they were catching fire, and the Three Kings shone over the rocks with their arms folded, like St. Andrew's Cross. The sea snored quietly away at the bottom of the little street, and every so often you heard the noise of the odd cart passing by in the darkness, jolting over the cobbles, and going about the world which is

23

so big that if you were to walk and walk for ever, day and night, you'd never get there, and there were actually people who were going around the world at that hour, and who knew nothing about compare Alfio, or the *Provvidenza* at sea, or the All Souls fair; as Mena thought on the balcony as she waited for her grandfather.

Before shutting the door, her grandfather went out on to the balcony another couple of times, to look at the stars which were twinkling so unnecessarily brightly, and then he muttered: 'Salt sea, salt tears.'

Rocco Spatu was singing himself hoarse at the door of the wine shop, in front of the little light. 'Happy souls are always singing,' concluded padron 'Ntoni.

CHAPTER III

After midnight the wind began to raise merry hell, as if all the cats in the village were on the roof, shaking the shutters. You could hear the sea lowing around the tall rocks so that it seemed as if the cattle from the Sant' Alfio market were gathered there, and day broke as black as a traitor's soul. A bad September Sunday, in short, that sort of treacherous September day which suddenly throws up a storm, like a rifle shot among the prickly pears. The village boats were drawn up on the beach, and well-moored to the boulders below the wash-place; and the local children were amusing themselves shouting and whistling whenever they saw the odd tattered sail pass by in the distance, in all that wind and mist, as though they were being driven along by the devil himself; but the women crossed themselves, as if they could clearly see the poor folk who were in those boats.

Maruzza la Longa said nothing, as was only right, but she couldn't be still for a moment, and kept going hither and thither though the house and the courtyard, like a hen when it is about to lay an egg. The men were at the wine shop, or in Pizzuto's barber's shop, or under the butcher's awning, pensively watching it pour down. The only people on the beach were padron 'Ntoni, because of that load of lupins he had at sea, along with the *Provvidenza* and his son Bastianazzo to boot, and la Locca's son, though **he** had nothing to lose, and all he had in the boat with the lupins was his brother Menico. Padron Fortunato Cipolla, while he was being shaved in Pizzuto's barber's shop, said that he didn't give two brass farthings for Bastianazzo and the load of lupins.

'Now they all want to play the dealer and get rich quick,' he said, shrugging; 'and they try to shut the stable door after the horse has gone.'

There was a crowd in Santuzza's wine shop: there was that drunkard Rocco Spatu, who was bawling and spitting fit for ten, compare Tino Piedipapera, mastro Turi Zuppiddo, compare Mangiacarrubbe, don Michele the customs man, with his trousers tucked into his boots and his pistol slung across his stomach, as though he were likely to go looking for smugglers in that weather, and compare Mariano Cinghialenta. That mammoth mastro Turi was jokingly dealing his friends punches that would have brought an ox to its knees, as though he still had his caulker's mallet in his hands, and them compare Cinghialenta started shouting and swearing, to show that he was a true red-blooded carter.

Zio Santoro, crouched under that bit of shelter, in front of the doorway, waited with his outstretched hand for someone to pass, so that he could ask for alms.

'Between the two of them, father and daughter,' said compare Turi Zuppiddo, 'they must be making a fine living, on a day like this, when so many people come to the wine shop.'

'Bastianazzo Malavoglia is worse off than he is, at this moment,' replied Piedipapera, 'and mastro Cirino can ring the bell for mass as hard as he pleases, the Malavoglia won't be going to church to-day; they're turning their backs on God, because of that cargo of lupins they've got at sea.'

The wind sent skirts and dry leaves swirling, so that Vanni Pizzuto, razor poised, would hold whoever he was shaving casually by the nose, to turn to look at the passers-by, and put his hand on his hips, with his hair all curly and shiny as silk; and the chemist stood at the door of his shop, wearing that awful great hat which gave the impression of acting as an umbrella, and pretending to have a serious discussion with don Silvestro the town clerk, so that his wife couldn't order him into church by force; and he snickered at this ruse, winking at the girls who were tripping along through the puddles.

'To-day,' Piedipapera was saying, 'padron 'Ntoni wants to play the heathen, like don Franco the chemist.'

'If you so much as turn your head to look at that impudent don Silvestro, I'll give you a slap right here where we stand,' muttered la Zuppidda to her daughter, as they were crossing the square. 'I don't like that man.'

At the last toll of the bell, Santuzza had put the wine shop into her father's care and had gone into church, bringing the customers behind her. Zio Santoro, poor man, was blind, and it was no sin for him not to go to mass; that way no time was wasted in the wine shop, and he could keep an eye on the counter from the doorway, even though he couldn't see, because he knew the customers one by one just by their footsteps, when they came to drink a glass of wine.

'Santuzza's stockings,' observed Piedipapera, as Santuzza was picking her way past on tiptoe, dainty as a kitten, 'come rain or shine, Sntuzza's stockings have been seen only by massaro Filippo the greengrocer; and that's the truth.'

'There are little devils abroad to-day,' said Santuzza crossing herself with holy water. 'It's enought to drive you to sin.'

Nearby, la Zuppidda was gabbling Hail Maries, squatting on her heels and darting poisonous glances hither and thither as though she were in a fury with the whole village, and telling anyone who would listen: 'Comare la Longa isn't coming to church, even though her husband is at sea in this storm! Small wonder the good Lord is punishing us!' Menico's mother was there too, even though all she was good for was watching the flies go by!

'We should pray for sinners as well,' said Santuzza. 'That's what pure souls are for.'

'Yes, like the Mangiacarrubbe girl is doing, all pious behind her shawl, and goodness knows what vile sins she causes young men to commit.'

Santuzza shook her head, and said that when you're in church you shouldn't speak ill of your neighbour. 'The host has to smile at all comers,' replied la Zuppidda, and then, in la Vespa's ear: 'Santuzza is concerned that people are saying that she sells water for wine; but she would do better to think about not causing Filippo the greengrocer to commit a mortal sin, because he has a wife and children.'

'Myself,' replied la Vespa, 'I've told don Giammaria that I don't want to carry on in the Daughters of Mary, if they keep Santuzza on as leader.'

'Does that mean you've found a husband?' asked la Zuppidda.

'I have not found a husband,' snapped back la Vespa waspishly. 'I'm not one of those women who bring a string of men after them right into church, with polished shoes, or big paunches.'

The one with the paunch was Brasi, padron Cipolla's son, who was the darling of mothers and daughters alike, because he owned vines and olive groves.

'Go and see if the boat is properly moored,' his father said to him, making the sign of the cross.

No one could help thinking that that wind and rain were pure gold for the Cipolla family; that is how things go in this world, and once reassured that their boat was well-moored, they were rubbing their hands in glee at the storm; while the Malavoglia had turned quite white and were tearing their hair, because of that cargo of lupins they had bought on credit from zio Crocifisso Dumb bell.

'Shall we face facts?' snapped la Vespa. 'The really unlucky man is zio Crocifisso, who sold the lupins on credit.'

'If you give credit without a pledge, you'll lose your friend, the goods and the edge.'

Zio Crocifisso was kneeling at the foot of the altar of Our Lady of Sorrows, with plenty of beads to hand, and intoning the little verses in a nasal whine which would have melted the heart of Satan himself. Between Hail Maries there was talk of the lupin deal, and the *Provvidenza* which was on the high seas, and la Longa who had five children to look after.

'In this day and age,' said padron Cipolla, shrugging, 'nobody is content with their lot, and everybody wants to take heaven by storm.'

'The fact is,' concluded compare Zuppiddo, 'that this is a bad day for the Malavoglia.'

'Myself,' added Piedipapera, 'I wouldn't like to be in compare Bastianazzo's shoes.'

Dusk fell cold and gloomy; occasionally there was a gust of north wind, which brought down a little burst of fine, silent rain; it was one of those evenings when, if your boat was in harbour with its belly in the dry sand, you could enjoy seeing the pot steaming in front of you, with your child between your knees, listening to the woman padding about the house behind you. Layabouts preferred to spend that Sunday in the wine shop, and it looked as if Sunday was going to run into Monday, too, in the wine shop, and even the doorposts were warmed by the flames from the fire, so much so that zio Santoro, posted out there with his hand outstretched and chin on his knees, had drawn in a bit, to warm his old back up a little.

'He's better off than compare Bastianazzo, at this moment,' repeated Rocco Spatu, lighting his pipe at the door.

And without any more ado he put his hand into his pocket, and splashed out to the tune of two *centesimos* of alms.

'You're wasting your money thanking God you're safe at home,' Piedipapera told him. 'There's small danger that you'll end up like Bastianazzo.'

Everyone showed their appreciation of this sally, and then they looked from the doorway down to the sea, as black as the *sciara*, without saying another word.

Padron 'Ntoni had wandered around aimlessly all day, as though he had St. Vitus' dance, and the chemist asked him if he were taking an iron cure, or just going for an idle stroll in that bad weather. 'Some providence, eh, padron 'Ntoni?' But the chemist was godless, everyone knew that.

La Locca's son was outside there with his hands in his pockets because he hadn't got a penny to his name, and he said:

'Zio Crocifisso has gone to look for padron 'Ntoni with Piedipapera, to get him to say that he bought the lupins on credit in front of witnesses.'

'That means he thinks they're in danger, along with the *Provvidenza*.'

'My brother Menico is with compare Bastianazzo on the *Provvidenza* too.'

'Well done — what we were saying was that if your brother doesn't come back, you will be head of the household.'

'He went because zio Crocifisso would only pay him half wages too, when he sent him out with the fishing boat, whereas the Malavoglia are paying him in full.' And when the others sniggered, he just stood their slack-jawed.

At dusk Maruzza had gone to wait on the *sciara* with her younger children, because you could see quite a large stretch of sea from there, and she shuddered and scratched her head without a word when she heard it roar like that. The baby was crying and the poor creatures looked like lost souls, all alone on the *sciara*, at that hour. The baby's crying gave her a pang, poor woman, it struck her as a bad omen; and she couldn't think what to come up with to quieten her, and sang her little songs in an unsteady voice which had a quiver of tears about it too.

On their way from the wine shop with their oil pitchers or wine flasks, the neighbours stopped to have a word with la Longa as though nothing were wrong, and the odd friend of her husband Bastianazzo, compare Cipolla, for instance, or compare Mangiacarrubbe, coming over to the *sciara* to take a look at the sea and find out what sort of mood the old moaner was falling asleep in, asked la Longa about her husband, and stayed with her a bit to keep her company; smoking their pipes in silence right under her nose, or talking among themselves in low voices. Frightened by these unaccustomed attentions, the poor creature gazed at them in distress and clutched her child to her, as though they wanted to steal it away. At last the toughest or most compassionate of them took her by the arm and led her home. She let herself be led, calling desperately upon the holy Virgin in a vain attempt at consolation. Her children followed her, clinging to her skirts as though they were afraid that something might be stolen from them too. As they passed in front of the wine shop, all the customers came to the door amidst all the smoke, and fell silent as they watched her go by, as though she were already a curiosity.

'Requiem aeternam,' zio Santoro mumbled under his breath, 'that poor Bastianazzo always gave me charity when padron 'Ntoni left him a penny in his pocket.'

The poor creature still didn't realise that she was a widow, and kept calling stumblingly upon the Virgin to succour her.

A group of neighbourhood women were waiting for her in front of her balcony, chatting in low voices amongst themselves. When they saw her appear at the end of the street, comare Piedipapera and cousin Anna went towards her, their hands folded, without saying a word. Then she dug her nails into her hair with a desperate cry and ran to hide away in the house.

'What a disaster,' they were all saying on the street. 'Boat, cargo and all. More than forty *onze* of lupins!'

CHAPTER IV

The worst thing was that the lupins had been bought on credit, and zio Crocifisso said that fine words buttered no parsnips; and he was as ungiving as a dumb bell, which was how he got his name, because he became pig-headed and mulishly obstinate when anyone tried to repay him with chatter, and he would say that credit always led to trouble. He was a good enough fellow, and lived by lending money to his friends, and had no other job, and that was why he hung around all day long with his hands in his pockets, or leant up against the wall of the church, wearing that ragged jacket of his looking for all the world like a pauper; but he had money, and to spare, and if anyone went to ask him for twelve *tari* he would lend them immediately and with security; because 'giving credit without a pledge, loses you friends, the goods and the edge,' and it would be understood that the money would be repaid by Sunday, in good, hard money, and with one extra *carlino*, as was only fair, because 'interest knows no friendship'. He would buy up all the catch at one go, at a discount, when the poor devil who had done the fishing needed the money fast; but they had to weigh it out on his scales, which were as false as Judas, according to certain habitual malcontents who said they had one arm longer than the other, like Saint Francis; and he would also advance the expense for the crew, if they wanted, and take back no more than the money advanced, and the price of a couple of pounds of bread per head, and a drop of wine, and he didn't want anything more, because he was a good Christian and would have to account to God for his doings in this world. In a word he was a godsend to those in distress, and he also dreamed up a hundred ways of helping his neighbours out, and without being a seafaring man himself he had boats, and tackle, and everything, for people who didn't have any, and he loaned them out, making do with a third of the catch, plus the share for the boat, which counted as a member of the crew, and for the tackle, if they wanted that loaned too, and in the end the boat ate up all the profit, so that people called it the devil's boat. And when they asked him why he himself didn't risk his skin like everyone else, but took the lion's share of the catch without any danger to himself, he would reply: 'Now just a minute: what if something were to happen to me at sea, God forbid — if I were to leave my carcass there, who would look after my business?' He minded his own affairs, and would have loaned out the shirt on his back; but then he wanted to be paid, and without any shilly-shallying; and it was pointless to quibble, because he was deaf, and short of brain-power into the bargain, and all he could say was 'what's been agreed is fair indeed' and 'you will know the good payer on the promised day.'

Now his enemies were openly enjoying his discomfiture because of those lupins the devil had snatched away from him; and he even had to say the *de profundis* for Bastianazzo's soul, when they held the funeral, along with the other members of the Confraternity of the Good Death, with that foolish hood on his head.

The windows of the little church glittered, and the sea was smooth and gleaming, so that it no longer seemed the same water which had stolen la Longa's husband from her; and that was why the members were in a hurry to get it all over with, and each go off about their own business, now that the weather was set fair again.

This time the Malavoglia were there, squatting in front of the bier, the floor awash with all their weeping, crying as though the dead men were really between those four boards, clutching those lupins which zio Crocifisso had sold them on credit because he had always known padron 'Ntoni to be a decent man; but if they wanted to cheat him out of what was rightfully his, with the excuse that Bastianazzo had been drowned, then they were cheating Christ himself, as sure as God exists; because that credit was as sacred as the consecrated host, and he would hang those five hundred lire at the feet of Christ crucified; but by heaven, padron 'Ntoni would go to prison if necessary! The law is the law even in Trezza!

Meanwhile don Giammaria was hastily flicking the water sprinkler over the coffin, and mastro Cirino began to go around snuffing out the lights. The members of the Confraternity hastily leapt over the benches with their hands high, to take off their hoods, and zio Crocifisso went to give a pinch of snuff to padron 'Ntoni, to give him heart, because after all when you're a decent fellow you leave a good name behind you and gain a place in paradise — this was what he had said to anyone who asked him about his lupins: 'I'm all right with the Malavoglia because they're decent folk and they don't want to leave compare Bastianazzo in the devil's hands'; padron 'Ntoni could see with his own eyes that things had been done without penny-pinching, in honour of the dead man; and the mass cost so much, so much for the candles, and so much for the funeral — he added it up on thick fingers stuffed into cotton gloves, and the children stared open-mouthed at those things for their father which cost so much: the coffin, the candles, the paper flowers; and seeing all the lights, and hearing the organ play, the baby began to gurgle cheerfully.

The house by the medlar tree was full of people; and as the proverb says, 'Sad is that house which people visit because of the husband.' And seeing those little Malavoglia on the doorstep with their dirty faces and hands in their pockets, the passers by shook their heads and said: 'Poor comare Maruzza! Now troubles are beginning for her and her family!'

All their friends brought something along, as is the custom, pasta, eggs, wine and all manner of good things, and you would have had a job to eat through it all, and even compare Alfio Mosca had come with a chicken in each hand. 'Take them, gnà Mena,' he said, 'I would gladly have taken your father's place, I swear. At least I wouldn't have caused anyone any sorrow, and no one would have wept.'

Leaning against the kitchen door, with her face in her apron, Mena felt her heart beating so hard that it seemed about to fly out from her breast, like those poor creatures she held in her hand. St. Agatha's dowry had gone down with the *Provvidenza*, and everyone who was visiting the house by the medlar tree believed that zio Crocifisso would sink his claws into it.

Some people had been perched on the high-backed chairs, and they went off again without so much as opening their mouths, like the real idiots they were; but anyone who could string two words together tried to hold a scrap of conversation, to ward off desolation, and somewhat distract those poor Malavoglia who had been crying like fountains for two days. Compare Cipolla was saying how the price of anchovies had gone up two *tari* a barrel, which might interest padron 'Ntoni, if he still had anchovies to sell; he himself had prudently kept back a hundred barrels or so; and they also spoke of compare Bastianazzo, God bless him, no one would ever have thought it, a man in the prime of life and bursting with health, poor fellow!

Then there was the mayor, mastro Croce Callà, also known as 'Silkworm' and 'stooge,' along with the town clerk don Silvestro; and he was sitting with his nose in the air, so that people said he was sniffing the wind to know which way to turn, and he turned his head from one person to another as they spoke, as if he really were looking for mulberry leaves, and wanted to eat their words, and when he saw the town clerk laughing, he would laugh too.

To amuse the company don Silvestro drew the conversation around to compar Bastianazzo's death duty; and in this way he included a funny story he had heard from his lawyer, and which he had found so amusing, when it was thoroughly explained to him, that he never failed to drag it into conversation every time he was at a funeral visit.

'At least you have the satisfaction of being related to Victor Emanuel, since you'll have to give him his share too.'

Everyone split their sides with laughter, and indeed there is no funeral gathering without laughter, just as there is no wedding without tears.

The chemist's wife looked down her nose at this uproar, and kept her gloved hands on her stomach, and put on a long face, as people do in the big cities in such circumstances, so that people fell silent at the mere sight of her, as though the dead man were there in person, and that was why she was known as 'the Signora.'

Don Silvestro was flirting with the women, constantly on the move with the excuse of offering seats to new arrivals, to make his polished shoes squeak. 'They ought to burn the lot of them, those tax people,' grumbled comare Zuppidda, as yellow as if she'd eaten lemons, and she said it right in don Silvestro's face, as though he were the tax man. She knew quite well what certain penpushers wanted, people with no socks inside their polished shoes, who tried to wheedle their way into people's houses to gobble up the dowry along with the young lady: 'I don't want you, my beautiful, I want your money.' That was why she had left her daughter Barbara at home.

'I don't like those sort of faces.'

'You're telling me,' exclaimed padron Cipolla; 'they flay me alive like St. Bartholomew.'

'By God,' exclaimed mastro Turi Zuppiddo, clenching a threatening fist which resembled his great caulker's mallet. 'It's going to end badly with these Italians.'

'You be quiet,' said comare Venera sharply, 'you know nothing.'

'I'm just repeating what you said, that they'd take the shirt off our backs,' mumbled compare Turi, crestfallen. Then to cut things short Piedipapera said quietly to padron Cipolla: 'You ought to take comare Barbara, to console yourself; in that way mother and daughter could both be put out of temptation's way.'

'It's a dirty business,' exclaimed donna Rosolina, the priest's sister, red as a turkey cock and fanning herself with her handkerchief; she went on to complain about Garibaldi who was putting on taxes, and nowadays you could hardly live any more, and no one got married any longer. What did this matter to donna Rosolina, at this stage? whispered Piedipapera. And now donna Rosolina was telling don Silvestro about the weighty matters she had in hand: ten lengths of warp threads on the loom, vegetables to be dried for the winter, the tomato preserve to be made, and she had a secret all her own to keep it fresh all winter. A house without a woman was doomed to disaster; but that woman had to have practical good judgment, and not be one of those flipperti-jibbets who do nothing but preen themselves, with lots of hair and little brain, so that a poor husband might sink to the bottom, like compare Bastianazzo, god bless him. 'Lucky man,' sighed Santuzza, 'he died on a holy day, the eve of the feast of the sorrows of Mary Virgin, and he is praying up there for us sinners, among the angels and saints in paradise.' 'The properer the man, the worse luck', the proverb goes. He was a good man, the sort who mind their own business, and don't waste time speaking ill of this person or that, and sinning against his neighbour, as so many do.

Then Maruzza, seated at the foot of the bed, pale and dishevelled as a rag that had been through the wash, so that she looked like Our Lady of Sorrows herself, began to cry all the harder, with her face in the pillow, and padron 'Ntoni bent in two and looking at least a hundred, gazed and gazed at her, shaking his head, and didn't know what to say, because of the pain of Bastianazzo so sharp in his heart, as if a shark were gnawing at it.

'Santuzzaa had a honeyed tongue,' observed comare Grazia Piedipapera.

'If you're running an inn,' replied Zuppidda, 'you have to be like that. Those who don't know their trade must shut up shop, and those who can't swim must sink.'

La Zuppidda had had all she could take of Santuzza's honeyed behaviour, which was such that even the Signora turned round to talk with her, with her pursed mouth, without taking any notice of the others, wearing those gloves of hers as if she were afraid of soiling her hands, with her nose all wrinkled, as though the others stank worse than sardines, while in fact the person who stank was Santuzza, of wine and all kinds of other filth, despite that scapular she was wearing, and the medal of the Daughter of Mary almost bouncing off her arrogant chest. Of course they understood one another because trade is a great bond, and they made money in the same way, by cheating their neighbour, and selling dirty water as if it were gold, and they neither of them gave a damn about taxes, oh dear no!

'Now they're probably going to tax salt too,' added compare Mangiacarrubbe. 'The chemist said so, it's in the paper. So that will be the end of salt anchovies, and we may as well burn our boats in the fireplace.'

Mastro Turi the caulker was about to raise his fist and pitch in with a curse, but he looked at his wife and fell silent, biting back his words.

'What with the bad season we've got ahead of us,' added padron Cipolla, 'with no rain since St Clare's Day, if it hadn't been for that last storm when the *Provvidenza* was lost, which was truly a godsend, you would have been able to cut hunger with a knife this winter!'

Everyone told their own troubles, partly to console the Malavoglia, who weren't the only people to have problems. 'The world is full of sorrows, and some have more than others, like everything else,' and the people who were outside in the courtyard were looking at the sky, because another drop of rain wouldn't have come amiss. Padron Cipolla personally knew why it never rained now as it used to do. 'It never rains nowadays because they've put up that dratted telegraph wire, which attracts all the rain and draws it away.' Then compare Mangiacarrubbe and Tino Piedipapera stood open-mouthed, because indeed there were telegraph posts right there on the Trezza road; but as don Silvestro began his farmyard cackling, padron Cipolla got up from the wall in a fury, and expressed irritation with those ignorant people whose ears were as long as a donkey's. Didn't they know that the telegraph carried news from one place to the next; it did this because there was a sort of juice inside the wire like the sap in a vine tendril, and in the same way it drew water from the clouds and carried it away, to where it was needed more; they could go and ask the chemist, he had said so; and this was why they had passed a law saying that anyone breaking a telegraph wire should go to prison. Then don Silvestro did not know what more to say, and he held his tongue.

'Holy saints! We ought to cut down all those telegraph poles and throw them on the fire,' began compare Zuppiddo, but no one paid him any attention, and they peered into the vegetable patch, to change the subject.

'A fine bit of land,' said compare Mangiacarrubbe; 'when it's properly tended, it provides vegetables for soup the whole year round.'

The Malavoglia's house had always been one of the most important in Trezza; but now, after the death of Bastianazzo, and with 'Ntoni doing his soldiering, and Mena to be married off, it was letting in water from all sides.

Anyhow, what could the house be worth? Everyone craned their necks to look over the wall of the vegetable patch and gave an appraising look, to reckon it up at a glance. Don Silvestro knew better than anyone else how things stood, because he had the deeds, in the office in Aci Castello.

'Do you want to bet twelve *tari* that all that glitters is not gold?' he said; and he showed everyone a new five *lire* piece.

He knew that the house had a rateable value of five *tari* a year. Then they all began to tot up how much the house could be sold for, with the vegetable patch and everything.

'Neither the house nor the boat can be sold, because they are part of Maruzza's dowry,' said somebody else, and everyone got so worked up that they could be heard in the room where they were mourning the dead man. 'Quite so,' said don Silvestro, delivering his bombshell. 'It's part of the dowry.'

Padron Cipolla, who had exchanged the odd word with padron 'Ntoni about marrying Mena to his son Brasi, shook his head and held his peace.

'So,' continued compare Turi, 'the real victim is zio Crofifisso, who won't get the credit on his lupins.'

They all turned towards Dumb bell, who had come along too, out of tact, and was sitting quietly in a corner, to hear what they were saying, with his mouth open and his nose in the air, so that he seemed to be counting how many tiles and rafters there were on the roof, as though wanting to assess the value of the house. The more curious craned their necks from the doorway, and winked at one another glancing in his direction. 'He looks like the bailiff making a distraint,' they sniggered.

The neighbours who knew about the discussions between

padron 'Ntoni and compare Cipolla said that now comare Maruzza would have to be helped over her grief, and conclude that marriage of Mena's. But at that moment Maruzza had quite other matters on her mind, poor creature.

Padron Cipolla turned his back on them coldly without a word; and after everyone had gone away, the Malavoglia were left alone in the courtyard. 'Now,' said padron 'Ntoni, 'we are ruined, and it is as well for Bastianazzo that he knows nothing of it.'

At those words first Maruzza, and then all the others started crying again, and the children, seeing the grown ups cry, started to wail too, although their father had been dead for three days. The old man wandered hither and thither, not knowing what he was doing; but Maruzza did not stir from the foot of the bed, as though she had nothing more to do. When she did utter a word, she would repeat it, gazing fixedly, and it seemed as though she had nothing else in her mind at all. 'Now there's nothing more for me to do!'

'No!' replied padron 'Ntoni, 'that's not so, we must pay the debt to zio Crocifisso, so that there is no excuse for people to say that when a decent man becomes poor, he becomes a rogue.'

And the thought of the lupins thrust the thorn of Bastianazzo deeper into his heart. The medlar tree loosened its grip on its withered leaves, and the wind drove them around the courtyard.

'He went because I sent him,' padron 'Ntoni would say over and over, 'like the wind sending those leaves blowing over the ground, and if I'd told him to throw himself off the rocks with a stone round his neck, he would have done so without a word. At least he died when the house and the medlar tree were still his, down to the last leaf; and I, an old man, am still here. 'Long life knows long misery.' '

Maruzza said nothing, but she had a single thought fixed in her head, which kept hammering at her and gnawing at her heart, and that was to know what had happened on the fateful night, because if she closed her eyes she seemed still to see the *Provvidenza* down there towards the Capo dei Mulini, where the sea was glassy and dark blue and dotted with boats, which looked like so many gulls in the sun, and you could count them one by one, zio Crocifisso's, compare Barabba's, the *Concetta* belonging to zio Cola, and padron Fortunato's fishing boat, a sight to make the heart ache. And you could hear mastro Turi singing like a mad thing with those ox's lungs of his, while thumping away with his caulker's mallet, and there was a smell of tar coming from the beach, and the linen that cousin Anna was beating on the stones of the wash place, and you could even hear Mena crying quietly away in the kitchen.

'Poor thing,' murmured her grandfather, 'the house has fallen about your ears too, and compare Fortunato went off so coldly, without saying a word.'

And one by one he touched the implements which were lying in a heap in the corner, with shaking hands, as old people do; and seeing Luca dressed in his father's jacket which they had put on him, and which came down to his ankles, he said to him: 'That will keep you warm, when you go to work; because now we must all help each other to pay off the lupin debt.'

Maruzza stopped her ears with her hands so as not to hear la Locca who was perched on the balcony, outside the door, shrieking from dawn to dusk, with that cracked voice of hers, demanding that they give her son back, and she wouldn't listen to reason.

'She does that because she's hungry,' said cousin Anna at last; 'now zio Crocifisso has it in for all of them because of the lupin deal, and he won't give her anything. I'll go and take her something now, and then she'll go away.'

Cousin Anna, poor creature, had left her linen and the girls to come and give comare Maruzza a hand — because it was as though Maruzza were ill, and if they had left her to her own devices she wouldn't even have remembered to light the fire, and put on the pot, and they would all have died of hunger. 'Neighbours must be like the tiles on a roof, and send the water over one from the other.' Meanwhile those children's lips were pale with hunger. Nunziata helped too, and Alessi, his face grubby from all the crying that he had done, seeing his mother weep, kept an eye on the little ones, so that they shouldn't always be under people's feet, like a brood of chicks, because Nunziata wanted to have her hands free.

'You know your business,' cousin Anna said to her; 'and you'll have your dowry right there in your own hands, when you're grown up.'

CHAPTER V

Mena had no idea that they wanted to marry her to padron Cipolla's Brasi to help her mother get over her grief, and the first person to mention it to her, some time later, was compare Alfio Mosca, by the gate to the vegetable patch, when he was coming back from Aci Castello with his donkey cart. Mena said that it just wasn't true; but she was embarrassed, and while he was explaining how and when he had heard this news from la Vespa, at zio Crocifisso's house, she suddenly became quite red in the face.

Compare Mosca too looked distraught, and seeing the girl like that, with that black handkerchief round her neck, he started to fiddle with the buttons on his jerkin, and would have paid good money to be transported elsewhere. 'Listen, it's no fault of mine, I heard in in Dumb bell's courtyard, while I was chopping up the carob tree that was brought down in the storm on St. Clare's day, do you remember? Now zio Crocifisso gets me to do his odd jobs for him, because he doesn't want any more to do with la Locca's son, after the other brother got involved in the wretched lupin business.' Mena had her hand on the gate latch but she couldn't bring herself to open it. 'And anyhow if it wasn't true, why have you gone so red?' She couldn't say, in all conscience, and kept fiddling with the latch. She knew the fellow by sight only, that was all. Alfio reeled off a long list of Brasi Cipolla's possessions; after compare Naso the butcher, he passed for the village's biggest catch, and the girls feasted their eyes on him. Mena stood there listening wide-eyed, and then marched off abruptly with a firm goodbye, and went into the vegetable patch. Alfio, furious, ran off to complain to la Vespa who had fed him such lies, just to make him quarrel with people.

'It was zio Crocifisso who told me,' replied la Vespa. 'I don't tell lies.' 'Lies, lies,' grumbled zio Crocifisso. 'I wouldn't damn my immortal soul for that lot. I heard it with these very ears. I also heard that the *Provvidenza* is part of Maruzza's dowry, and the house has a rateable value of five *tari*.'

'Never mind, we'll see. Sooner or later we'll see whether you're lying or not,' continued la Vespa, lolling to and fro as she leant against the doorpost, with her hands behind her back, watching him with those devouring eyes of hers. 'You men are all the same, untrustworthy.'

Sometimes zio Crocifisso would go deaf, and instead of swallowing the bait he changed the subject entirely, and began to talk about the Malavoglia who were thinking about marriage, but not paying any heed at all to that matter of the forty *onze*.

'Look here,' la Vespa snapped out at last, losing her patience, 'if they were to listen to you, nobody would even think about getting married.'

'I don't care about whether people marry or not. I want my rightful deserts, that's all that matters to me.'

'It may be all that matters to you, but some people have other concerns, do you hear? Not everyone behaves as you do, putting things off from one day to the next.'

'And what might you be in such a rush about?'

'Unfortunately, I *am* in a rush. *You've* plenty of time; But do you really think that other people want to wait until they're as old as St Joseph, to get married?'

'It's been a bad year,' said Dumb bell, 'and this is no time to think of such things.'

Then la Vespa stuck her hands on her hips and let fly with her stinging tongue.

'Now here is what I've come to say to you. When all is said and done, I have my property, and thanks to God I have no need to go begging for a husband, as well you know. And if it weren't for your having put that bee in my bonnet with your flattery, I could have found a hundred husbands, Vanni Pizzuto and Alfio Mosca, and cousin Cola, who was tied to

44

my apron strings before he went as a soldier, and he wouldn't have let me so much as bend down to tie up a shoelace. All simmering with impatience, and they wouldn't have kept me hanging on for so long, from Easter to Christmas, as you have done!'

This time zio Crocifisso put his hand to his ear, so as to hear properly, and he began to soothe her with fine words. 'Yes, I know you're a sensible girl, that's why I'm so fond of you, and I'm not one of those men who run after you to get their hands on your smallholding, which they would then drink away at Santuzza's wine shop.'

'It's not true that you're fond of me,' and she carried on, fending him off with her elbows, 'if it were true, you'd know what you ought to do, and you'd see that that's all I'm thinking about.'

She turned her back on him angrily, and unintentionally knocked against him with her shoulder. 'But you don't give a hang about me.' Her uncle was offended at this slanderous accusation. 'You're saying this to lead me into sin,' he began complainingly. He not care about his own flesh and blood? because she *was* his own flesh and blood, like the small-holding — which had always been in the family, and would have remained in it, if his brother, God rest his soul, had not bethought himself to marry and bring la Vespa into this world; and that was why she had always been the apple of his eye, and he had always considered her welfare. 'Listen,' he said to her, 'I thought of handing you over the Malavoglia debt, in exchange for the smallholding — it's forty *onze*, and it could be as much as fifty, with expenses and interest, and you stand to get the house by the medlar tree, which could be better for you than the smallholding.'

'You can keep your house by the medlar tree,' snapped la Vespa. 'I'm sticking to my smallholding, and I know what to do with it.'

Then zio Crocifisso too became angry, and told her that he knew what she wanted to do with it, she wanted to let it slip into the clutches of that down-and-out Alfio Mosca, who had been giving her the sheep's eye for that smallholding, and he didn't want to see Mosca around the house and courtyard any

45

more, because when all was said and done he had human blood in his veins too.

'So now you're going to put on a jealous act,' exclaimed la Vespa.

'Of course I'm jealous,' retorted zio Crocifisso, 'jealous as anything'; and he felt like paying someone five *lire* to break Alfio Mosca's bones.

But he didn't do so because he was a good Christian with the fear of God in him, and in this day and age anyone who is a decent fellow gets swindled, good faith being lodged in simpleton street, where they sell you enough rope to hang yourself, and this was proved by the fact that he had marched back and forth in vain in front of the Malavoglia's house, so that people actually began to laugh, and said that he was making a 'pilgrimage' to the house by the medlar tree as people make a votive offering to the Madonna of Ognina. The Malavoglia repaid him with much cap doffing; and when they saw him looming into sight at the end of the lane, the children ran off as if they'd seen the bogy man; but so far none of them had spoken to him about the money for the lupins, and All Souls' Day was almost upon them, and meanwhile padron 'Ntoni was thinking of marrying off his granddaughter.

He went to let off steam with Piedipapera, who had got him into that scrape, as he told other people; but others said that he went there just to gaze at the house by the medlar tree, and la Locca, who was always hanging about there because they had told her that her Menico had gone out in the Malavoglia's boat and she thought she might still find him there, began to howl like a crow of doom as soon as she saw her brother Crocifisso, and this upset him more than ever. 'She'll drive me to sin yet,' he muttered.

'It isn't All Souls' Day yet,' replied Piedipapera waving his arms; 'be patient. Do you want to suck padron 'Ntoni dry? You haven't lost anything yet, because the lupins were all rotten, as well you know.'

But he knew no such thing; all he knew was that his peace of mind was in God's hands. And the Malavoglia children didn't dare play on the balcony when he walked past Piedipapera's door.

And if he met Alfio Mosca with his donkey cart, and Alfio too doffed his cap, while looking quite brazen, Dumb bell felt his blood boil, out of jealousy about the smallholding. 'He's hoodwinking my niece to steal my smallholding,' he grumbled to Piedipapera. 'What a wastrel. All he can do is wander about with that donkey cart, which is all he's got. A dead beat. A rascal who puts it about that he's in love with that ugly mug of that hideous witch of a niece of mine, all for love of her property.' And when he had nothing else to do he would go and plant himself in front of Santuzza's wine shop, near zio Santoro, who seemed just another poor soul like himself, and he didn't go there to spend a brass farthing on wine, but would whinge and whine like zio Santoro, as if he too wanted alms; and he would say: 'Listen, compare Santoro, if you see my niece la Vespa around this way when Alfio Mosca comes to bring your daughter Santuzza a cartload of wine, keep an eye on what they get up to together;' and zio Santoro with his beads and sightless eyes, said yes, he shouldn't worry, he was there for that very reason, and not a fly passed by without his noticing; and indeed his daughter Mariangela used to ask him why he got involved in Dumb bell's affairs, saying that he never spent any decent money at the wine shop, and he stood in the doorway for nothing.

But Alfio Mosca wasn't thinking of la Vespa, and if he had anyone in his thoughts at all it was rather padron 'Ntoni's comare Mena, whom he saw every day in the courtyard or on the balcony, and if he heard the cackling of the two hens he had given her, he felt something within him, and it seemed to him as if he himself were in the courtyard of the house by the medlar tree, and if he had not been a poor carter, he would have asked for St Agatha's hand in marriage, and carried her away in his donkey cart. Whenever he thought of all this, he felt he had so many things there in his head to tell her, and when he saw her his tongue was tied and he discussed the weather, or the cartload of wine he had taken to Santuzza, or the donkey which could pull four quintals better than a mule, poor animal.

Mena stroked the poor animal, and Alfio smiled as if she were stroking him. 'Ah! If my donkey were yours, comare

Mena.' Mena shook her head and her breast swelled as she reflected that it would have been better if the Malavoglia had been carters, then her father wouldn't have died like that.

'The sea is salt,' she said, 'and the sailor dies in the salt sea.'

Alfio, who was in a hurry to unload Santuzza's wine, could not make up his mind to get up and go, and stood there chatting about what a fine thing it was to be an innkeeper, a trade where you always made money, and if the price of wine must went up all you had to do was add more water to the barrels. That was how zio Santoro got rich, and now he asked for alms as a pure pastime.

'And do you earn good money, with cartloads of wine?' asked Mena.

'Yes, in the summer, when you can go by night as well; then I make a decent day's living. This poor animal earns its keep. When I've put aside a bit of money I'll buy a mule and be able to be a real carter, like compare Cinghialenta.'

The girl was all ears for what compare Alfio was saying, and meanwhile the grey olive tree was rustling as if it were raining and scattering the road with little dry crumpled leaves. 'Now winter is coming, and I shan't be able to do that again before the summer,' observed compare Alfio. Mena kept her eyes on the shadows of the clouds which were running over the fields and scattering like the leaves of the grey olive tree; that was how the thoughts ran in her head, and she said to him: 'compare Alfio, did you know, that story about padron Fortunato Cipolla's son is quite untrue, because first we have to pay off the debt for the lupins?'

'I'm pleased about that,' replied Mosca, 'because that way you won't be leaving the neighbourhood.'

'Soon 'Ntoni will be back from military service, and we'll ill work to pay off the debt, with grandfather and all the others. Mother has taken in cloth to weave for the Signora.'

'Being a chemist is no bad thing either,' observed Mosca.

At that point comare Venera Zuppidda appeared in the lane, spindle in hand. 'Oh goodness,' exclaimed Mena, 'people are coming,' and she rushed inside.

Alfio whipped the donkey, and wanted to be off too. 'Oh compare Alfio, what's the hurry?' asked la Zuppidda; 'I wanted to ask you whether the wine you're delivering to Santuzza is from the same cask as last week's.'

'I don't know; they give me the wine in barrels.'

'Hers was fit for making salads,' replied Zuppidda, 'real poison; that's how Santuzza got rich, and to cheat the world at large she's hung the scapular of the Daughter of Mary from her chest! That scapular covers a multitude of sins. In this day and age, that's the way you have to behave. If you don't, you just move crabwise, like the Malavoglia. They've pulled up the *Provvidenza*, have you heard?'

'No, I haven't been around, but comare Mena didn't know anything about it.'

'They brought the news just now, and pa`ron 'Ntoni ran straight to the Rotolo, to see her being towed towards the village, and it was as though the old man had new legs. Now they've got the *Provvidenza*, the Malavoglia will get their feet again, and Mena will be marriageable once more.'

Alfio said nothing, because Zuppidda was staring at him with her little yellow eyes, and he said that he was in a hurry to go and deliver the wine to Santuzza. 'He won't say anything to me,' grumbled Zuppidda. 'As if I hadn't seen them with my own eyes. They're trying to hide the sun with a net.'

They had towed the *Provvidenza* to shore all shattered, just as they had found her beyond the Capo dei Mulini, with her nose amid the rocks, and her back in the air. The whole village, men and women, had immediately run to the shore, and padron 'Ntoni, mingling with the crowd, was there as well, just like the other lookers-on. Some even gave a kick at the *Provvidenza's* belly, and the poor old man felt that kick as though it were to his own stomach. 'Providential for you, what?' don Franco said to him, having come down in shirt sleeves, with his awful old hat on his head and pipe in his mouth, to have a look along with the rest.

'Now all she's good for is burning,' concluded padron Fortunato Cipolla; and compare Mangiacarrubbe, who was in the trade, volunteered the information that the boat had sunk all at once, and without those in her having been able to say so much as 'Christ, help me!' because the sea had swept away sails, yards, oars and everything; and it had not left a single wooden peg holding firm.

'This was where father sat, where there's the new rowlock,' said Luca, who had climbed on to the edge, 'and the lupins were under there.'

But there was not a single lupin left, for the sea had washed everything out, swept everything clean. That was why Maruzza had not even left the house, and she never wanted to see the *Provvidenza* again as long as she lived.

'Her belly is sound, and something can still be done with her,' mastro Zuppiddo the caulker pronounced finally, and he too gave her a few kicks with his great feet. ' A few planks, and I could have her back at sea for you. She'll never be a boat for strong tides, a sideways wave would knock the bottom out of her like a rotten barrel. But she could still serve for longshore fishing, in good weather.' Padron Cipolla, compare Mangiacarrubbe and compare Cola stood listening without saying a word.

'Yes,' said padron Fortunato gravely at last.

'Rather than throw her on the fire . . .'

'I'm delighted,' said zio Crocifisso who was there taking a look too, with his hands behind his back. 'We're good Christians, and must rejoice in our neighbours' good fortune; the proverb says 'it's an ill wind that blows nobody any good,'.

The Malavoglia children had settled in the *Provvidenza*, along with the other village children who wanted to climb in too.

'When we've patched up the *Provvidenza* good and proper,' said Alessi, 'she'll be just like zio Cola's *Concetta*;' and they too puffed and panted, pushing and pulling the boat to mastro Zuppiddo's door, where there were big stones to hold the boats, and the tub for the tar, and a pile of ribs and planking leaning against the door.

Alessi was for ever scuffling with the boys who wanted to climb on to the boat and help to blow into the fire under the tar cauldron, and when they gave him a good thrashing he would threaten, snivelling the while:

'Soon my brother 'Ntoni will be back from military

service.'

And indeed 'Ntoni had managed to obtain his discharge, although don Silvestro the town clerk had assured them all that if he stayed on for another six months, his brother Luca would be exempted from conscription. But 'Ntoni didn't want to stay on even another week now that his father was dead; Luca would have done the same, and he had had to weep over his misfortune alone, when they brought him the news about his father, and he would have liked to drop everything then and there, if it hadn't been for those brutes of superiors.

'Myself,' said Luca, 'I'll gladly go for a soldier instead of 'Ntoni. That way, when he comes back, you'll be able to put the *Pròvvidenza* to sea again, and we won't need to take on anyone extra.'

'He's a Malavoglia through and through,' commented padron 'Ntoni exultantly. 'Just like his father Bastianazzo, whose heart was as big as the sea, and as good as God's mercy.'

One evening, after the boats had returned, padron 'Ntoni arrived at the house all breathless, and said: 'The letter's here; compare Cirino gave it to me just now, while I was taking the fish traps to the Pappafave.' La Longa went white as a sheet, and they all rushed into the kitchen to see the letter.

'Ntoni arrived with his beret at a rakish angle and a shirt with the five pointed military star, and his mother couldn't get enough of touching it, and trailed after him amidst all the friends and relatives while they were coming back from the station; and then the house and the courtyard were suddenly filled with people, just like when Bastianazzo had died, all that time back, and now no one thought about that any more. There are some things that only old people think about, as though it were yesterday — and indeed la Locca still hung around outside the Malavoglia's house, leaning up against the wall, waiting for Menico, and she turned her head this way and that down the little road, at every step she heard.

CHAPTER VI

'Ntoni had arrived on a holiday, and he went from door to door greeting friends and neighbours, so that everyone stood looking at him as he passed; his friends followed after him, and the girls came to stand at the window; but the only one not in evidence was comare Tudda's Sara.

'She's gone to Ognina with her husand,' Santuzza told him. 'She married Menico Trinca, who was a widower with six children, but stinking rich. She married him within a month of his wife's death, and the bed was still warm, God forgive them!'

'A widower is like a person who goes off soldiering,' added Santuzza. 'A soldier's love it does not last, at the beat of a drum his love is past.' ' And then, the *Provvidenza* had been lost.

Comare Venera, who had been at the station when padron 'Ntoni's 'Ntoni had left, to see whether comare Tudda's Sara had gone to say goodbye to him, because she had seen them talking over the vineyard wall, wanted to get a good look at 'Ntoni's face when he received this news. But time had gone by for 'Ntoni too and, as they say, 'out of sight, out of mind.' And now 'Ntoni wore his beret at a rakish angle, like a real man of the world. 'Compare Menico is aiming to die a cuckold,' he said to comfort himself, and she liked that, the Mangiacarrubbe girl, who had called him 'booby', and now that she saw what kind of a booby he was, she would willingly have exchanged him for that good-for-nothing Rocco Spatu, whom she'd taken up with because there was no one else.

'I don't like those flippertigibbets who carry on with two or three boys at a time,' said the Mangiacarrubbe girl, pulling the corners of her scarf over her chin and looking all demure.

'If I loved someone, I wouldn't exchange them for Victor Emanuel, or Garibaldi, you wait and see!'

'I know who you're interested in,' said 'Ntoni with his hand on his hip.

'Of no you don't, compare 'Ntoni, and what you've heard is gossip. If you happen to pass my door some day, I'll tell you all about it.'

'The Mangiacarrubbe girl has set her sights on padron 'Ntoni's 'Ntoni, and that's a bit of good luck for cousin Anna,' said comare Venera.

'Ntoni went off all arrogant, rolling his hips, with a band of friends in tow, and he would have liked every day to be Sunday, so that he could parade his star-covered shirt; that afternoon they amused themselves having a good punch-up with compare Pizzuto, who wasn't afraid of God himself, although he'd never done military service, and he went sprawling on the ground in front of the wine shop, with a bloody nose; whereas Rocco Spatu was stronger, and had 'Ntoni down on the floor.

'Holy Virgin,' exclaimed the bystanders. 'That Rocco is as strong as Turi Zuppiddo. If he chose to work, he could certainly earn his bread.'

'I know how to use this fellow,' said Pizzuto brandishing his razor, so as not to appear the loser.

In a word, 'Ntoni enjoyed himself the whole day long; but that evening, while they were sitting chatting around the table, and his mother was asking him about this and that, and the younger ones, half-asleep, were gazing at him wide-eyed, and Mena was touching his beret and shirt with the stars, to see how they were made, his grandfather told him that he had found him a job by the day on compare Cipolla's fishing boat, and well-paid too.

'I took them on out of charity,' padron Fortunato would say to anyone who cared to listen, sitting outside the barber's shop. 'I took them on out of the goodness of my heart, when padron 'Ntoni came to ask me, under the elm tree, if I needed men for my boat. Now I never need men; but a friend in need is a friend indeed, and padron 'Ntoni is so old anyway, that you're really wasting your money! . . .'

'He's old but he knows his trade,' replied Piedipapera; 'you're not wasting your money; and his grandson is a boy anyone would envy you.'

'When mastro Bastiano has put the *Provvidenza* in order, we'll fit out our boat, and then we won't need to go out to work by the day,' padron 'Ntoni would say.

In the morning, when he went to waken his grandson, it was two hours before dawn, and 'Ntoni would have preferred to stay under the covers a little longer; when he went out yawning into the courtyard, Orion was still high towards Ognina, with his legs in the air, and the Pleiades were sparkling to the other side of the sky, which was swarming with stars which looked for all the world like the sparks running over the black bottom of a frying pan. 'It's just like being in the navy,' grumbled 'Ntoni. 'This wasn't worth coming home for.'

'You be quiet — your grandfather is getting the tackle ready and he got up a good hour before us,' said Alessi. But Alessi was just like his father Bastianazzo, God rest his soul. Their grandfather was coming and going in the courtyard with the lantern; outside you could hear people going down to the sea, and knocking from one door to another to waken their companions. But when they reached the beach, in front of the black sea where the stars were reflected, and which was snoring quietly on the shingle, and they saw the lanterns on the boats dotted here and there, even 'Ntoni felt his heart swell.

'Ah,' he exclaimed, lifting his arms. 'It's good to come home. We know each other, the beach and I.' And padron 'Ntoni had already said that a fish can't live out of water, and the sea waits patiently for those who are born to fish.

In the boat they teased him because Sara had jilted him, while they took in the sails, and the *Carmela* swung gently round, with the nets behind her like a snake's tail. 'Pork meat and soldiers have short spans,' the proverb says; this was why Sara jilted him.

'Woman will be faithful to man when the Turk becomes Christian,' added zio Cola. 'I'm not short of girl friends,' replied 'Ntoni; 'in Naples they ran after me like pet lambs.'

'In Naples you wore proper clothes, and a cap with the name of your ship, and shoes on your feet,' said Barabba.

'Are there beautiful girls in Naples, as there are here?'

'The girls here can't hold a candle to the girls in Naples. I saw one with a silk dress and red ribbons in her hair, and an embroidered bodice, and golden epaulets like the captain's. A fine figure of a girl, taking her employer's children for a walk, and that was all she had to do.'

'It must be some life around those parts,' commented Barabba.

'You on the left! Stop rowing,' shouted padron 'Ntoni.

'By the blood of Judas! you're taking us into the nets,' zio Cola began to shriek from the tiller. 'Now just stop that jabbering; are we here for our health, or to do a job?'

'It's the swell which is pulling us back,' said 'Ntoni.

'Ease off on your side, you bastard,' Barabba shouted at him, 'you're making us waste the day, with those fancy queens you've got on your mind.'

'Damn it,' said 'Ntoni with his oar poised in the air, 'if you say that again I'll lay into you with this.'

'What's all this now?' called zio Cola sharply from the tiller; 'is this the sort of thing you learned on military service, not to take criticism?'

'I'll be going then,' replied 'Ntoni.

'Be off if you like, padron Fortunato can find someone else for his money.'

'The servant needs patience, and the master prudence,' said padron 'Ntoni.

'Ntoni carried on rowing, grumbling the while, because he couldn't storm off on foot, and to make the peace compare Mangiacarrubbe said that it was time for breakfast.

At that moment the sun appeared, and everyone was ready for a good swig of wine, because the air had turned chill. Then the lads began chewing, with the flask between their legs, while the fishing boat heaved gently amid the broad circle of corks.

'A kick up the backside for whoever talks first,' said zio Cola.

Everyone began to chew like oxen, to avoid getting that

kick, looking at the waves approaching from the open sea, and rolling in without breaking, green wineskins which, even on a sunny day, put you in mind of the black sky and slate-coloured sea.

'Padron Cipolla will have a few things to say this evening,' said zio Cola sharply; 'but it's not our fault. You don't catch fish when the sea is rough!'

First compare Mangiacarrubbe landed him a hefty kick, because zio Cola, who had made the rule, had been the first to talk; and then he answered: 'Still, now that we're here, let's wait a bit before pulling the nets in.'

'And the swell is coming from the open sea, which is good for us,' added padron 'Ntoni.

'Ahi,' grumbled zio Cola the while.

Now that the silence was broken, Barabba asked 'Ntoni Malavoglia to give him a cigar butt.

'I haven't got one,' said 'Ntoni, forgetting the previous dis-agreement, 'but I'll give you half of mine.'

Seated on the bottom of the boat, with their backs to the seat and hand behind their heads, the men were singing popular songs, each on his own behalf and quite softly, so as not to fall asleep, because their eyes were closing under the bright sunlight; and Barabba clicked his fingers as the mullet jumped out of the water.

'They haven't got anything else to do,' said 'Ntoni, 'so they pass the time by jumping.'

'It's good, this cigar,' said Barabba; 'did you smoke cigars like this in Naples?'

'Oh yes, dozens of them.'

'Look, the corks are beginning to sink,' observed compare Mangiacarrubbe.

'Do you see where the *Provvidenza* went down with your father?' said Barabba; 'over there at the Cape, where there's that sunlight on those white houses, and the sea looks all gold.'

'The sea is salt and the sailor dies at sea,' was 'Ntoni's reply.

Barabba passed him his flask, and then they began to grouse in low voices about zio Cola, who was merciless with the men in his fishing boat, as though padron Cipolla were there to see that they were doing and what they were not doing.

'All to make him think that the boat couldn't move without him,' added Barabba. 'Copper's nark.'

'Now he'll say that it was *his* skill that caught us the fish, with this rough sea. Look how the nets are sinking, you can't see the corks any more.'

'Hey boys,' shouted zio Cola, 'shall we pull in the nets? When the swell gets here it will pull them out of our hands.'

'Ohi. Oohi,' the crew men began to shout, passing the rope to one another.

'Saint Francis help us,' exclaimed zio Cola, 'I can hardly believe we've taken this many fish with this swell.'

The nets were swarming and sparkling in the sun as they emerged from the water, and the whole of the bottom of the boat seemed full of quicksilver. 'Padron Fortunato will be pleased,' murmered Barabba, red and sweating, 'and he won't resent the three *carlini* he gives us for our day's work.'

'Just our luck,' added 'Ntoni, 'to break our backs for other people; and then when we've put a bit of money together, the devil comes and takes it.'

'What are you complaining about?' asked his grandfather, 'doesn't compare Fortunato pay you a day's wages?'

The Malavoglia were working desperately to make money in all sorts of ways. La Longa took in the odd *rotolo* of cloth to weave, and also did people's washing at the wash place; padron 'Ntoni and his grandsons hired themselves out by the day, helped one another as best they could, and when the sciatica bent the old man like a nail, he stayed in the courtyard mending the nets and the fish traps and tidying up the tackle, because he knew every aspect of his trade. Luca went to work on the railway bridge for fifty *centesimi* a day, although his brother 'Ntoni said that it wasn't worth the shirts he ruined carrying stones in a basket, but Luca didn't care about his shoulders, let alone shirts, and Alessi went collecting crayfish along the rocks, or worms for bait, which were sold at ten *soldi* a *rotolo*, and sometimes he went as far as Ognina and the Capo dei Mulini, and came back with his feet in shreds. But compare Zuppiddo took good money every Saturday, for patching up the *Provvidenza*, and it took all those mended fish traps, all those stones from the railway, that ten *soldi* of bait and the cloth for bleaching, with water up to one's knees and the sun beating down overhead, to make the forty *onze* needed! All Souls' Day had come and gone, and zio Crocifisso did nothing but walk up and down the little street with his hands behind his back, looking for all the world like the basilisk.

'This business is going to end up with the bailiffs,' zio Crocifisso would say to don Silvestro and don Giammaria the parish priest.

'There won't be any need of a bailiff, zio Crocifisso,' padron 'Ntoni told him when he came to hear what Dumb bell was saying. 'The Malavoglia have always been decent folk, and they don't need any bailiffs.'

'That's neither here nor there,' replied zio Crocifisso with his shoulders against the wall, beneath the roof of the court-yard, while they were piling up his vine shoots, 'All I know is, I must be paid.'

At last, through the good offices of the parish priest, Dumb bell agreed to wait until Christmas to be paid, accepting as interest the seventy-five *lire* which Maruzza had put together *soldo* by *soldo* in the stocking hidden under the mattress.

'That's how things go,' grumbled padron 'Ntoni's 'Ntoni; 'we work day and night for zio Crocifisso, and then when we've put a few *lire* together, Dumb Bell comes and takes it from us.'

Padron 'Ntoni and Maruzza comforted themselves by building castles in the air for the summer, when there would be anchovies to be salted, and prickly pears at ten a *grano*, and they made great plans to go fishing for tuna and swordfish, where you could get a good day's pay, and by then mastro Turi would have set the *Provvidenza* to rights. Chins cupped in their hands, the boys listened attentively to those discussions, which took place on the balcony, or after supper at table; but 'Ntoni, who had been away and knew the world better than the others, got bored listening to that babbling, and preferred to go and hang around the wine shop, where there were so many people doing nothing, and zio Santoro among them, who was as badly off as you could be, did the light job of stretching out his hand to whoever passed by, mumbling Hail Maries the while; or he went to compare Zuppiddo's, with the excuse of seeing how the *Provvidenza* was getting on, to have a chat with Barbara, who came to put kindling under the cauldron, when compare 'Ntoni was there. 'You're always busy, comare Barbara,' 'Ntoni said to her, 'and you're the mainstay of the family; that's why your father doesn't want to marry you off.'

'He doesn't want to marry me off to unsuitable parties,' answered Barbara. 'Birds of a feather flock together, and people should stick to their own kind.'

'I'd stick to your kind, by the holy Virgin, if you wanted, comare Barbara . . .'

'What are you saying, compare 'Ntoni? Mother is spinning in the courtyard, she can hear every word.'

'I was talking about those green sticks, which won't burn. You leave it to me.'

'Is it true that you come here to see the Mangiacarrubbe girl, when she comes to the window?'

'I come here on quite different business, comare Barbara. I come here to see how the *Provvidenza* is coming along.'

'She's coming along well, and my father said that you will have her in the water by Christmas Eve.'

During the nine days before Christmas, the Malavoglia spent all their time coming and going from mastro Zuppiddo's courtyard. Meanwhile the whole village was preparing for the celebrations; each house decorated its images of the saints with branches and oranges, and the children trooped after the bagpipes which were played in front of the niches with their lit-up saints, outside the doorways. Only in the house by the medlar tree did the statue of the Good Shepherd remain unlit, while padron 'Ntoni's 'Ntoni strutted here and there, and Barbara Zuppidda said to him:

'I hope at least that you'll remember that it was I who melted down the pitch for the *Provvidenza*, when you're at sea?'

Piedipapera maintained that all the girls were wild about

'Ntoni.

'I'm the person who's wild,' whinged zio Crocifisso. 'I'd like to know where they are going to get the money for the lupins from, if 'Ntoni gets married, let alone having to give Mena a dowry, with the rates to be paid on the house, and all those complications of the mortgage which cropped up at the last minute. Christmas is here, but I still haven't seen the Malavoglia.'

Padron 'Ntoni went back into the square, or under the shelter, to look for him, and said: 'What do you expect me to do if I haven't got the money? You can't get blood out of a stone! Wait until June, if you're willing to do me that favour, or take the *Provvidenza* and the house by the medlar tree. I haven't anything else.'

'I want my money,' repeated Dumb bell, his back to the wall. 'You said that you were decent folk, and that you wouldn't make me idle offers about the *Provvidenza* and the house by the medlar tree.'

He had put body and soul into the whole business, and lost sleep and appetitite over it, and couldn't even let off steam by saying that the whole matter would end with the bailiffs, because padron 'Ntoni would immediately send don Giammaria or the town clerk to ask for mercy, and they wouldn't let him back on to the square, for his own affairs, without trailing after him, so that everyone in the village said that the money involved was devil's money. He couldn't let off steam with Piedipapera because Piedipapera immediately piped up that the lupins had been rotten, and that he had merely been the broker. 'But he could do that much for me,' Dumb bell suddenly said to himself and couldn't sleep any longer that night, so pleased was he with his brain wave, and he went to find Piedipapera as soon as it was light, and indeed Piedipapera was still stretching and yawning in his doorway. 'What you must do is pretend you're taking over my credit,' he told him, 'that way we can send the bailiff to the Malavoglia and they won't tell *you* you're acting the usurer, nor that it's devil's money.' 'Did you have that bright idea last night?' sniggered Piedipapera, 'that you should wake me at dawn to tell me about it?'

'I also came to tell you about those vine shoots; if you want them, you can come and get them.' 'Then you can send for the bailiff,' replied Piedipapera, 'but you're responsible for the expenses.' Comare Grazia, good woman that she was, had come out specially in her nightdress to ask her husband what zio Crocifisso had come to chat with him about: 'You leave those poor Malavoglia alone, they've got enough problems as it is.' 'You get on with your spinning,' said compare Tino. 'Women are long of hair and short of judgment,' and he hobbled away to drink absinthe with compare Pizzuto.

'They want to give that family a bad Christmas,' murmered comare Grazia with hands folded.

In front of each house every little shrine was decorated with branches, and oranges, and in the evenings the candles were lit, when they came to play the bagpipes, and they sang the litany in such a way that the festive spirit seemed to be abroad everywhere. The children played at their Christmas version of fivestones, using hazel nuts, and if Alessi paused to watch them in a business-like fashion, they said to him: 'You go away, if you haven't any hazelnuts to play with. Now they're taking your house away, too.'

And indeed on Christmas Eve the bailiff came specially for the Malavoglia, in a carriage, so that the whole village was in uproar; and he deposited an official document on the chest of drawers, by the statue of the Good Shepherd.

'Did you see, the bailiff has come for the Malavoglia?' said comare Venera. 'Now they're in a pretty pickle.'

Then her husband, who could hardly believe he had been right, began to clamour tumultuously.

'Ye holy saints in Paradise, I said I didn't want 'Ntoni hanging around the house.'

'You be quiet, you know nothing,' snapped la Zuppidda. 'This is women's business. This is how girls get married, otherwise they are left hanging around for you to trip over, like old saucepans.'

'This is some time to talk of marriage when the bailiff has called.'

'Did you know that the bailiff was going to come? You're always yapping about things after they've happened, but you don't lift a finger to stop them happening. Anyhow, the bailiff doesn't eat people'.

It is true that the bailiff doesn't eat people, but the Malavoglia reacted as if disaster had suddenly struck, and they were in the courtyard, sitting in a circle, looking at each other, and the day the bailiff called, there were no meals at all in the Malavoglia household.

'Damn it,' exclaimed 'Ntoni. 'We're sitting ducks, and now they've sent in the bailiff to wring our necks.'

'What shall we do?' asked la Longa.

Padron 'Ntoni didn't know, but at last he forced himself to take up that horrible official document and went to look for zio Crocifisso with his two older grandsons, to tell him to take the *Provvidenza*, which mastro Bastiano had just patched up, and the poor fellow's voice trembled as it had done when his son Bastianazzo died. 'I know nothing about it,' Dumb bell replied. 'It's nothing to do with me any more. I've sold my credit to Piedipapera, and from now on you'll have to deal with him.'

As soon as Piedipapera saw the little procession, he began to scratch his head. 'What do you expect me to do?' he said. 'I'm a poor devil and I need that money, and I wouldn't know what to do with the *Provvidenza* because that's not my trade; but if zio Crocifisso wants, I'll help you to sell her. I'll be right back .'

Those poor creatures sat waiting there on the wall, and they hadn't the heart to look one another in the eye; but they cast long glances on to the road where they expected Piedipapera to appear, and finally he did, walking very slowly — though when he wanted to, he could hobble along pretty speedily on that twisted leg of his. 'He says she's useless as an old shoe, and he wouldn't know what to do with her,' he shouted from a distance. 'I'm sorry, but I couldn't do anything.'

So the Malavoglia went home clutching the official document.

But something had to be done, because they had heard that if that paper lay around on the chest of drawers, it would devour the chest of drawers, the house and the lot of them.

'Here's where we need advice from don Silvestro the town clerk,' Maruzza suggested. 'Take him these two hens, and he will have something to tell you.'

Don Silvestro said that there was no time to lose, and he sent them to a good lawyer, doctor Scipioni, who lived on via degli Ammalati in Catania opposite zio Crispino's stables, and he was young, but he had enough patter in him to make mincemeat of all old lawyers who wanted five *onze* just to open their mouths, whereas he made do with twenty five *lire*.

The lawyer, Scipioni, was busy making cigarettes, and he had them come and go two or three times before he gave them a hearing; the best part was that they made up quite a little procession, one behind the other, and la Longa went there too, with her child in her arms, to help state the case, and they wasted the whole day like that. Then when the lawyer had read the papers, and had managed to glean something from the garbled answers which he had painfully to extract from padron 'Ntoni, while the others were perched on their chairs without daring to breath, he began to laugh with all his might, and the others laughed with him, without knowing why, just to get their breath back. 'Nothing,' replied the lawyer, 'there's nothing you need do'; and as padron 'Ntoni was about to repeat that the bailiff had come, 'Let the bailiff come once a day if he wants, the creditor will soon get tired of paying for him. They can't take anything from you, because the house is part of the dowry, and we'll make a claim for the boat in mastro Turi Zuppiddo's name. Your daughter-in-law has nothing to do with the purchase of the lupins.'

The lawyer carried on talking without so much as spitting, or scratching his head, for more than twenty five *lire* worth, so that padron 'Ntoni and his grandchildren felt their mouths watering with eagerness to get a word in too, to blurt out that fine defence which they felt swelling within them; and they went off stunned, overwhelmed by all those reasons they now had, mulling over the lawyer's jabber and gesticulating to it all along the street. Maruzza hadn't gone this time, and when she saw them arriving red-faced and bright-eyed, she felt a great weight lifting from her too, and her face cleared as she waited for them to tell her what the lawyer had said. But no one said a word and they just stood there looking at each other.

'Well?' asked Maruzza at last, dying of impatience.

'Nothing! There's nothing to be afraid of,' padron 'Ntoni replied calmly.

'And the lawyer?'

'Yes, the lawyer said there was nothing to be afraid of.'

'But what exactly did he say?' insisted Maruzza.

'Well, he knows how to put things. A most impressive man. Those twenty five *lire* were well spent.'

'But what did he say?'

Grandfather looked at grandson, grandson at grandfather and back again.

'Nothing,' said padron 'Ntoni at last. 'He said we should do nothing.'

'We don't pay him anything,' added 'Ntoni more boldly, 'because they can't take either the house or the *Provvidenza* from us. We don't owe him anything.'

'And the lupins?'

'That's true! What about the lupins?' repeated padron 'Ntoni.

'The lupins? . . . we didn't steal his lupins . . . we haven't got them in our pockets; and zio Crocifisso can't take anything from us; the lawyer said so, and that zio Crocifisso will pay the expenses.'

A moment of silence followed; meanwhile Maruzza did not seem convinced.

'So he said not to pay?'

'Ntoni scratched his head, and his grandfather added:

'It's true, he gave us the lupins, and we must pay for them.'

There was no more to be said. Now that the lawyer wasn't there, they had to be paid for. Shaking his head, padron 'Ntoni murmured:

'We've always paid what we owe. Zio Crocifisso can take the house, and the boat, and everything — we've always paid our debts.'

The poor old man was confused; but his daughter-in-law was crying in silence into her apron.

'Then we must go to don Silvestro,' concluded padron

'Ntoni.

And with one accord grandfather, daughter-in-law and grandsons trooped once more to the town clerk, to ask him what they ought to do to pay the debt, without zio Crocifisso sending more official documents, which devoured house, boat and the lot of them along with it. Don Silvestro, who knew about the law, was passing his time constructing a cage-trap which he wanted to give to the Signora's children. He didn't behave like the lawyer, and he let them talk and talk, while he carried on with his cage. At last he came up with what was needed: 'Well now, if gnà Maruzza would set her mind to it, everything could be sorted out.' The poor woman could not imagine what she should set her mind to. 'You must set your mind to a sale,' don Silvestro told her, 'and give up the dowry mortgage, even though it wasn't you who bought the lupins.' 'We all bought the lupins,' murmured la Longa, 'and the Lord has punished us all together by taking away my husband.'

Seated motionless on their chairs, those poor ignorant things looked at one another, and meanwhile don Silvestro was laughing at them behind their backs. Then he sent for zio Crocifisso, who came chewing on a dry chestnut because he had just finished eating, and his little eyes were even brighter than usual. At first he didn't want to listen at all, and said that it wasn't his business any more. 'I'm like a handy wall, everyone leans on me and uses me as they choose, because I can't talk like a lawyer, and state my case; somehow my property seems like stolen property, but what they are doing to me is tantamount to what they did to Christ on the cross;' and he went on grumbling and complaining with his shoulders to the wall and hands stuffed into his pockets; and you couldn't even understand what he was saying, because of the chestnut he had in his mouth. Don Silvestro sweated through a whole shirt to get it into zio Crocifisso's head that when all was said and done the Malavoglia could not be said to be swindlers, if they wanted to pay the debt, and the widow was giving up her right to the mortgage. 'The Malavoglia are quite happy to pay all they can in order to avoid a quarrel; but if you put them with their backs to the wall, they too will begin sending official documents, and that's that. In short you have to have a bit of charity, in Christ's name. What's the betting that if you carry on digging in you heels like a mule, you'll get nothing at all?'

Then zio Crocifisso replied: 'When you talk to me like that, I don't know what to say,' and he promised to talk to Piedipapea. 'I'd make any sacrifice for the sake of friendship.' Padron 'Ntoni could vouch that he would so such and such a thing, for the sake of friendship; and he offered him his snuff box, patted the baby and gave her a chestnut. 'Don Silvestro knows my soft spots; I can't say no. This evening I'll have a talk with Piedipapera, and tell him to wait until Easter; as long as comare Maruzza sets her mind to it.' Comare Maruzza didn't know what she was supposed to set that mind of hers to, but she said she'd set it to it straight away, anyway. 'Then you can send for those beans you asked me for, and plant them,' zio Crocifisso said to don Silvestro, before going off.

'Fine, fine,' said don Silvestro. 'I know your heart is as big as the sea, for your friends.'

Piedipapera didn't want any talk of delay in front of people: and he shrieked and tore his hair, asking whether they wanted to get him into a strait jacket, and to leave him without bread for the winter, him and his wife Grazia, having persuaded him to take over the Malavoglia debt, and he'd said goodbye to five hundred good solid *lire* that he had taken out of his own mouth in order to give them to zio Crocifisso. His wife Grazia, poor thing, stared in amazement, because she didn't know where he had got this money from, and put in good words for the Malavoglia, who were decent folk, and everyone in the neighbourhood had always known them as such. Now zio Crocifisso too was taking the Malavoglia's part. 'They said they will pay, and if they can't pay they'll leave you the house. Gnà Maruzza will set her mind to that too. Don't you know that in this day and age you have to do what you can to get your just deserts?' Then Piedipapera threw on his jacket and went off swearing, saying they could do as they wanted, zio Crocifisso and his wife, since he counted as nothing in his own house.

CHAPTER VII

That was a bad Christmas for the Malavoglia; at that very same time Luca drew his conscription number, the sort of low number that the poor devil always gets, and he went off to do his soldiering without anyone doing much weeping and wailing, because by now they were used to that sort of bad luck. This time 'Ntoni went with his brother, with his cap low over one ear, so that it seemed as if it were he who was going, and he told him there was nothing to it, and he too had done his military service. That day it was raining, and the road was one great puddle.

'I don't want you to come with me,' Luca kept saying to his mother; 'anyhow the station is a long way away.' And he stood at the doorway watching it pour down on the medlar tree, with his little bundle under his arm. Then he kissed his grandfather and his mother on the hand, and hugged Mena and the little ones.

So la Longa watched him go off under the umbrella, and all his relatives with him, jumping over the cobbles of the little street which was one great puddle, and the boy, who was as sensible as his grandfather, had tucked up his trousers on the balcony, although he wouldn't be wearing them any more, now that they were giving him soldiers clothes.

'This one won't be writing for money, when he's away,' thought the old man; 'and if God gives him long life, he will set the house by the medlar tree to rights again.' But God did not give him long life, for the simple reason that he was that sort of person; and when later, the news came that he was dead, la Longa was left with the hurtful memory that she had let him leave in the rain, and hadn't gone with him to the station.

'Mother,' said Luca turning round, because it broke his heart to leave her there standing so quietly on the balcony, like Our Lady of Sorrows; 'when I come back I'll let you know beforehand, and you can all come and meet me at the station.' And Maruzza remembered those words until her dying day; and until that same day she carried that other thorn thrust deep into her heart, the fact that her boy hadn't been present at the rejoicings that went on when they put the *Provvidenza* to sea again, and the whole village was there, and Barbara Zuppidda had appeared with her broom to sweep away the shavings. 'I'm doing this for love of you,' she had told padron 'Ntoni's 'Ntoni; 'because it's your *Provvidenza*.'

'With that broom in your hand you look like a queen to me,' replied 'Ntoni. 'There is no housewife in Trezza to touch you.'

'Now you're taking away the *Provvidenza*, you won't be coming around this way any more, compare 'Ntoni.'

'Oh yes I shall. Anyway, this is the shortest way to the *sciara*.'

'You'll come here to see the Mangiacarrubbe girl, because she comes to stand at the window when you pass by.'

'I leave the Mangiacarrubbe girl to Rocco Spatu. I've other fish to fry.'

'You must have so many girls to think about, girls from outside the kingdom, haven't you?'

'There are beautiful girls here too, comare Barbara, as well I know.'

'Really?'

'Upon my word!'

'What should you care?'

'I do care, most definitely! but they don't care about me, because they've got ladykillers parading under their windows, ladykillers with polished boots!'

'I pay not the slightest heed to polished boots, by the Virgin of Ognina! Mother says polished boots serve no purpose but to eat up our dowry, and everything else besides; and one fine day she wants to come into the street with her spindle in her hand, and have it out with that don Silvestro, if he doesn't leave me in peace.'

'Do you really mean that, comare Barbara?'

'I do indeed!'

'I'm glad to hear that,' said 'Ntoni.

'Listen, what about going to the *sciara* on Monday, when my mother goes to market?'

'On Monday my grandfather won't let me draw breath, now that we're putting the *Provvidenza* to sea again.'

The moment the mastro Turi had said that the *Provvidenza* was ready, padron 'Ntoni went to fetch her with his grandsons, and all his friends, and as she went on her way towards the beach, she tottered over the stones as if she were seasick, there amid the crowd.

'Give her here,' compare Zuppiddo shouted, loudest of all; but the others sweated and shouted as they pushed her on the slipway, when the boat jolted on the stones. 'Let me do it; or else I'll take her up in my arms just like that.'

'Compare Turi actually could do just that, with those arms of his,' some people said. Or: 'Now the Malavoglia are back in the saddle again.'

'That devil compare Zuppiddo has got magic in his hands,' they exclaimed. 'She really did look like an old boot, and see what he's done with her.'

And indeed now the *Provvidenza* seemed a different boat, gleaming with new pitch, and with that fine red stripe round her side, and St Francis on the stern with his beard that looked like cotton wool, so that even la Longa felt more kindly towards the *Provvidenza*, for the first time since the boat had returned without her husband, and had made peace with her out of fear, now that the bailiff had been.

'Long live St Francis,' everyone shouted when they saw the *Provvidenza* go by, and la Locca's son shouted louder than any of them, because he hoped that now padron 'Ntoni might take him on too by the day. Mena had come out on to the balcony, and was crying once again, this time for joy, and even la Locca got up and went along with the crowd, behind the Malavoglia.

'Oh comare Mena, this must be a fine day for all of you,' said Alfio Mosca from his window opposite; 'you must feel as I shall feel when I get my mule!'

'And will you sell your donkey?'

'What else can I do? I'm not rich like Vanni Pizzuto; if I

were, in all conscience, I wouldn't.'

'Poor creature.'

'If I had to feed another mouth, I'd rather take a wife, and not be alone, like a dog,' said Alfio, laughing.

Mena didn't know what to say, and at last Alfio added:

'Now that you've got the *Provvidenza* at sea again, they'll marry you off to Brasi Cipolla.'

'Grandfather hasn't said anything about it.'

'He will. There's plenty of time. So many things will happen between now and your marriage, and goodness knows what roads I'll travel with my cart! They say that there's work for everyone on the railway beyond the city, on the plain of Catania. Now Santuzza has come to an arrangement with massaro Filippo for the new grape must, and I shan't have anything to do here.'

But although the Malavoglia were in the saddle once again, padron Cipolla continued to shake his head, and went round proclaiming that theirs was a horse without legs; he knew where the weak spots were, hidden under the new pitch.

'A patched up *Provvidenza*,' sniggered the chemist, 'syrup of althea and mucilage of gum arabic, stuck together like our constitutional monarchy. You'll see, they'll even make padron 'Ntoni pay property tax on her.'

'They'll make us pay for the very water we drink. Now they say that they're going to put a tax on pitch. That's why padron 'Ntoni was in such a hurry to get his boat done; although in fact mastro Turi is still owed fifty *lire* by him.'

'The only one with any sense is zio Crocifisso, when he sold Piedipapera the credit for the lupins.'

'Now, if the Malavoglia have more bad luck, Piedipapera will take the house by the medlar tree; and the *Provvidenza* will go back to compare Turi.'

Meanwhile the *Provvidenza* had slid into the sea like a duck, with her beak in the water, and was wallowing in it, enjoying the cool, rocking gently in the green sea which slopped around her sides, and the sun danced on her paint-work. Padron 'Ntoni enjoyed the sight too, hands behind his back, and legs apart, frowning slightly as sailors do when they squint against the sun, which was a fine winter sun, and the fields were green, the sea was glittering and the endless sky was deep blue. So the warm sun and the kind winter mornings become so again even for eyes which have wept, and which have found them the colour of pitch; and everything is born anew, like the *Provvidenza*, and all she needed was a bit of paint and pitch, and a few planks, for her to seem brand new, and the only ones who don't see anything anew are those eyes which have stopped weeping, and are closed in death.

'Compare Bastianazzo wasn't here to see this rejoicing,' Maruzza thought to herself as she went backwards and forwards in front of her loom, arranging the weft threads, because her husband had made the framework and crossbars with his own hands, on Sundays or when it was raining, and he himself had set them there in the wall. Everything in that house still spoke to her of him, and his oil cloth was there in a corner, and his almost new shoes under the bed. While she smeared the threads with size, Mena too felt black at heart, thinking of compare Alfio, who was going off to Bicocca, and was going to sell his donkey, poor beast! because young people have short memories, and eyes which look only towards the dawning day; and it is only the old who look westward, those who have seen the sun set so many times.

'Now that :hey've got the *Provvidenza* at sea again,' said Maruzza at last, seeing her daughter looking thoughtful, 'your grandfather :as started to talk to padron Cipolla; I saw them together this morning from the balcony, in front of Peppi Naso's shed.'

'Padron Fortunato is rich and has nothing to do, and stands in the square all day long,' replied Mena.

'Yes, and his son Brasi has considerable property. Now that we have our boat, and our men won't have to go out by the day, we too will be out of the wood; and if the souls in Purgatory help us to repay the lupin debt, we'll be able to start thinking about other matters. Your grandfather is well aware of things, don't you worry, and he won't let you feel you've lost a father, because he is like another father to you.'

Soon afterwards padron 'Ntoni arrived, laden with nets so that he looked like a mountain, and you couldn't see his face.

'I went to get them from the fishing boat,' he said, 'and we must look at the mesh, because to-morrow we're going to fit out the *Provvidenza*.'

'Why didn't you get 'Ntoni to help you?' said Maruzza by way of reply, pulling from one side, while the old man turned round in the middle of the courtyard like a wool winder, to unravel the endless nets, and he looked like a snake and its tail. 'I left him over there, with mastro Pizzuto. Poor boy, he has to work the whole week! And it's warm even in January with that bit of gear on your shoulders!'

Alessi laughed at his grandfather, seeing him so red and bent like a fish hook, and his grandfather said to him: 'Look, that poor Locca is out there; her son is in the square doing nothing, and they haven't got any food.' Maruzza sent Alessi to la Locca, with a few beans, and the old man wiped the sweat away with his shirt sleeve and added: 'Now that we've got our boat, if we make it as far as the summer, with God's help, we'll repay our debt.' That was all he could say, and he gazed at his nets, sitting under the medlar tree, as if he saw them all full.

'Now we must stock up with salt, before they put the tax on it, if indeed they're going to,' he said with his hands under his armpits. 'We'll pay compare Zuppiddo the first money we get because he's promised to provide me with kegs on credit.'

'There are five *onze* from Mena's cloth in the chest of drawers,' added Maruzza.

'Good! I don't want any more debt with zio Crocifisso, I couldn't bring myself to do that after the lupin business; but he could give us thirty *lire* for the first time we went out to sea with the *Provvidenza*.'

'You leave him be,' exclaimed la Longa, 'zio Crocifisso's money brings bad luck! I heard the black hen crowing this very night!'

'Poor creature,' said the old man smiling, as he saw the black hen walking in the courtyard with her tail in the air and her comb over her ear, as if it had nothing to do with her. 'She lays an egg every day.'

Then Mena spoke up, standing in the doorway. 'There's a basket full of eggs,' she added, 'and on Monday, if compare

Alfio goes to Catania, you could get him to sell them in the market.'

'Yes, that all helps with the debt,' said padron 'Ntonî 'but all of you ought to eat the odd egg, when the mood takes you.'

'Well the mood doesn't take us,' replied Maruzza, and Mena added 'If we eat them, compare Alfio won't have any to sell in the market; now we'll put ducks' eggs under the sitting hen, and the chicks will sell at eight *soldi* a piece.' Her grandfather looked her in the eye and told her that she was a real Malavoglia.

The fowl were flapping in the dust of the courtyard, and the broody hen, all dazed, with her comb drooping, was shaking her beak in a corner; along the wall, more cloth was hanging for bleaching in the sun, under the greenery of the plants in the vegetable patch, weighed down by stones. 'It all brings in money,' repeated padron 'Ntoni; 'and with God's help, they won't need to evict us from our own house. 'East, west, home's best.' '

'Now the Malavoglia will have to pray to God and St Francis for the catch to be good,' Piedipapera was saying.

'Yes, what with catches as they are,' exclaimed padron Cipolla, 'and they seem to have thrown the cholera into the sea for the fish, into the bargain.'

Compare Mangiacarrubbe nodded, and zio Cola returned to the subject of the salt tax they wanted to introduce, after which the anchovies could relax, with no more fear of the steamboat wheels, because no one would go and fish for them any more.

'And they've dreamt up something else,' added mastro Turi the caulker, 'a tax on pitch.' Those who didn't care about pitch said nothing but Zuppiddo carried on shrieking that he would shut up shop, and anyone who needed their boat caulking would have to use their wife's chemise as oakum. Then there was a wave of shouting and swearing. At this juncture the engine whistle sounded, and the great railway coaches emerged suddenly out of the slope of the hill from the hole they had made in it, smoking and clamouring like the very devil. 'Here we go,' said padron Fortunato; 'the railway on the one hand and the steamers on the other. Life at

Trezza has become impossible, upon my soul!'

In the village all hell broke loose when they wanted to put a tax on pitch. Zuppidda, foaming at the mouth, went up on to the balcony and began to proclaim that this was another of don Silvestro's dastardly deeds, since he wanted to ruin the village, because they hadn't wanted him for a husband for Barbara; neither she nor her daughter even wanted the man in the wedding procession. When comare Venera talked about the husband her daughter would be taking, you would have thought that she herself was the bride. Mastro Turi would shut up shop, she said, but she would like to see how people would manage to get their boats to sea, and they would be reduced to devouring each other for want of bread. Then the neighbourhood women came to their doorsteps with their distaffs in their hands, bawling that they wanted to kill the lot of them, those tax people, and set fire to all their vile papers, and the place where they kept them. As they came back from the sea, the men left their tackle to dry, and stood at the windows to watch the revolution their wives were bringing about.

'All because padron 'Ntoni's 'Ntoni is back,' continued comare Venera, 'and he's always here, hanging on to my daughter's apron strings. Now don Silvestro doesn't like those cuckold's horns. And if we won't have him, what can he hope for? My daughter is my affair, and I can give her to whomsoever I please. I gave a clear no to mastro Callà when he came with the message, zio Santoro saw me too. Don Silvestro gets that stooge of a mayor to do anything he wants; but I don't give a damn about the mayor and his town clerk. Now they are trying to get us to shut up shop all because I won't let my possessions be grabbed by any Tom, Dick or Harry! What a crowd, eh? why don't they put a tax on wine, or on meat, since no one eats it? but massaro Filippo wouldn't like that, out of love for Santuzza, and they're both in a state of mortal sin, and she wears the scapular of a Daughter of Mary to hide her dirty deeds, and that old cuckold zio Santoro sees nothing. Everyone feathers their own nest, like compare Naso, who's fatter than his own pigs! Fine councillors we have! Now we're going to have to make mincemeat of the whole rotten bunch.'

Mastro Turi Zuppiddo was stumping about on the balcony clutching his mighty implements, wanting to draw blood, and not even chains would have held him back. Fury was spreading from one doorstep to the next like the waves of the sea in a storm. Don Franco was rubbing his hands, with his awful great hat, and saying that the people were rearing their heads at last; and when he saw don Michele pass by, with his pistol slung over his stomach, he laughed right in his face. Gradually the men too had allowed themselves to become heated by their womenfolk, and were seeking each other out in order for their tempers to mount; and they wasted their day hanging around the square with their hands under their arm-pits and mouths agape, listening to the chemist who was holding forth in a low voice, so that his wife upstairs shouldn't hear him, saying that the people should rise up in revolt, if they weren't fools, and not take any notice of the tax on salt or the tax on pitch, but a clean sweep was needed, and the people should be king. But some people sneered and turned their backs on him, saying that he was the one who wanted to be king, and that he was involved in the revolution to reduce poor people to starvation. And they preferred to go off to Santuzza's wine shop, where there was good wine which went to your head, and compare Cinghialenta and Rocco Spatu got angry enough for ten. Now that the business of the taxes was under discussion once again, there would be more talk of that next tax on 'hair', as they called the tax on beasts of burden, and of raising the tax on wine. By Christ! This time it would end badly, by the Virgin!

The good wine loosened tongues, and loose tongues make you thirsty, and for the moment they hadn't raised the tax on wine; and those who had drunk waved their fists in the air, with their shirt sleeves rolled up, and got worked up against the very flies as they flew.

'This is a real windfall for Santuzza,' they said. La Locca's son, who had no money for drink, was there outside the door-way, shouting that he would prefer to die, now that zio Crocifisso didn't want him even on half pay, because of his brother Menico who had been drowned along with the lupins. Vanni Pizzuto had shut up shop, because no one went to get shaved any more, and he carried his razor in his pocket, and poured out curses from a distance, and spat on people who were only going about their business, with their oars over their shoulders, shrugging.

'They're all swine, and they don't give a fig about their country,' bawled don Franco, puffing on his pipe as though he wanted to devour it. 'People who wouldn't lift a finger for their country.'

'You let them talk away,' said padron 'Ntoni to his grandson, who wanted to break his oar over the heads of anyone who called him a swine; 'they don't get us any bread with their chatter, nor do they reduce our debt by a single *soldo*.'

Zio Crocifisso, who was the sort of person who minds his own business, and lets his wrath simmer within him, for fear of something worse, when they drew blood from him with their taxes, was now no longer to be seen on the square, leaning against the wall of the belltower, but stayed holed up in his house, reciting paternosters and Hail Maries to cool his anger at all those loudmouths, people who wanted the village put to fire and sword, and went around ransacking anyone who had two beans to rub together. 'He's quite right,' they said in the village, 'because he must have pots of money. Now he's even got the five hundred *lire* from the lupins which Piedipapera gave him!'

But la Vespa, whose wealth was all in land, so that she had no fear that it would be stolen from her, went round shouting on his behalf, waving her hands in the air, as black as a smoking coal and with her hair loose in the wind, saying that they ate her uncle alive every six months, with the land tax, and she would gouge out the collector's eyes with her own hands, if he came back again. Now she was constantly buzzing round comare Grazia, cousin Anna and the Mangiacarrubbe girl, first with one excuse and then another, to see how compare Alfio was getting on with St Agatha, and she would have liked to wipe out St Agatha along with all the other Malavoglia; and that was why she went around saying that it wasn't true that Piedipapera had acquired the credit on the lupins, because Piedipapera had never had five hundred *lire* in his life, and the Malavoglia still had zio Crocifisso's foot on their necks, and he would crush them like ants, he was so rich, and she had been wrong to turn him down, for the love of someone who had only a donkey cart, while zio Crocifisso loved her as the apple of his eye, although at that moment he wouldn't even open the door to her, for fear that people might force their way in to put the place to fire and the sword.

Anyone who had anything to lose, like padron Cipolla or massaro Filippo the greengrocer, stayed holed up in their houses, with the doors well bolted, and didn't so much as put their noses outside; this was how Brasi Cipolla earned himself a hefty swipe from his father, when he had found him at the courtyard door staring into the square like a codfish. The big-wigs lay low during the storm, and didn't show themselves, not even the real blockheads, and left the mayor with his nose in the air looking for the mulberry leaf again.

'Don't you see that they are treating you as a puppet?' his daughter Betta said to him, her hands on her hips. 'Now that they've landed you in this trouble they're turning their backs, and leaving you to splash through the mire; that's what happens when you let yourself be led by the nose by a troublemaker like don Silvestro.'

But don Silvestro said that it was his daughter Betta who played the mayor, whereas mastro Croce Callà just wore the trousers by mistake. In this way, what with the two of them, poor Silkworm was between hammer and anvil. Now that the squall had come, and everyone was leaving him to curry favour with that mad beast, the mob, he no longer knew which way to turn.

'What does it matter to you?' Betta shouted at him. 'You do just as the others do; and if they won't have a tax on pitch, don Silvestro will manage to find something else.'

But don Silvestro was firmer; he carried on walking about, with that brazen face of his; and when they saw him, Rocco Spatu and Cinghialenta hurried back into the wine shop in order not to do something drastic, and Vanni Pizzuto swore hard, touching the razor inside his trouser pocket.

Without taking a blind bit of notice, don Silvestro went off to have a chat with zio Santoro, and put two *centesimi* into his open hand!

'Heaven be praised,' exclaimed the blind man, 'this must be don Silvestro the town clerk, because none of the others gives a *centesimo* of alms to the souls in Purgatory, they just come here to shout and hammer their fists on the benches and shriek that they want to kill the mayor and the town clerk and the whole lot of them; that's what Vanni Pizzuto said, and Rocco Spatu and compare Cinghialenta. Vanni Pizzuto has started to go barefoot, so as not to be recognised; but I recognise him all the same, because he drags his feet, and raises the dust, like when the sheep go past.'

'What's all this to you?' his daughter asked him, as soon as don Silvestro had gone off. 'This doesn't concern us. The wine shop is like a sea port, people come and go, and you have to be friendly with everyone and faithful to no one; that is why we have one soul apiece, and everyone has to look after their own interests, and not make rash judgments about their neighbour. Compare Cinghialenta and Spatu spend money with us. I'm not defending Pizzuto who sells absinthe and tries to take our customers from us.'

Then don Silvestro went to call by to see the chemist, who stuck his beard in front of him and told him that it was time to call it a day, and turn everything upside down, and make a clean sweep.

'What do you bet this time it will end badly?' don Silvestro kept on, putting two fingers into the small pocket of his jerkin, to bring out the new twelve *tari* piece. 'No taxes are enough taxes, and one day or another they really will have to scrap the lot. There's got to be a change of tune with Silkworm, because he's under the thumb of his daughter, who plays the mayor; massaro Filippo doesn't give a hang, and padron Cipolla had the cheek not to want to be mayor even if they slaughtered him. They're just a bunch of reactionaries; numbskulls who say white to-day and black to-morrow, and the last one to speak is always right. It's all very well for people to squeal about this government, which is sucking us dry worse than a leech; but the money has to come from somewhere, people have to produce it either out of conviction or by force. What we need is a thinking man, a liberal mayor

78

like yourself.'

Then the chemist began to say what he would do, and how he would sort everything out; and don Silvestro stood listening to him in silence, and so attentive you'd have thought it was a sermon he was listening to. They would also have to think about re-electing the Council; they didn't want padron 'Ntoni, because he was queer in the head, and this was because of the death of his son Bastianazzo — there was a man of judgment, if he had been alive — and then he had got his daughter-in-law involved in debt with the business of the lupins, and had left her with next to nothing. If he were to run the town's affairs in the same way! . . .

But meanwhile the Signora had appeared at the window, so that don Franco changed the subject, and shouted: 'Fine weather we're having eh?' winking at don Silvestro, to let him know what he really wanted to say. 'There's no trusting the aims of a man who's afraid of his wife,' don Silvestro thought to himself. Padron 'Ntoni was among those who shrugged and went off with oars over their shoulders; and he told his grandson to mind his own business, because 'Ntoni wanted to rush out into the square too and see what was happening.

'You mind your own business, because everyone of them is out for himself, and our main concern is with our debt.'

Compare Mosca too was among those who minded their own business, and went his way quietly, with his cart, among the people who were shouting or brandishing their fists.

'Will it matter to you if they put a tax on hair?' asked Mena, when she saw him coming up, with the donkey all panting, its ears laid flat against its head. 'It certainly will, but you just have to plod on to pay it; otherwise they'll take the hair and the donkey along with it, and the cart into the bargain!'

'People are saying that they want to kill the lot of them, heaven help us! Grandfather has told us to keep the door shut, and not open until he's back. Will you still be going away to-morrow?'

'I'll be getting a cartload of lime for mastro Croce Callà.'

'What are you going to do that for? You know he's the mayor, and they'll be after you too.'

'He says he cannot help it; he's a builder, and he's got to see to that wall along the vineyard for massaro Filippo, and if they don't put the tax on pitch, don Silvestro will think of something else.'

'I told you that it was don Silvestro's doing,' exclaimed la Zuppidda who was still there with her distaff in her hand, blowing on the fire. 'This is the work of thieves and people who have nothing to lose, and who don't pay the tax on pitch, because they've never had so much as a chair leg at sea. It's don Silvestro's fault,' she carried on bawling throughout the village, 'and that trouble-maker Piedipapera, who hasn't got any boats, and lives off his neighbour, and is just a cat's paw for other people. And just listen to this: it's not true that he's bought the credit off zio Crocifisso. It's a put-up job between the two of them, to screw those poor people. Piedipapera has never seen five hundred *lire* in his life.'

To hear what was being said about him, don Silvestro often went to buy the odd cigar in the wine shop, and then Rocco Spatu and Vanni Pizzuto came out swearing; or he would stop to chat with zio Santoro, on his way home from the vineyard, and that was how he came to hear of the whole story of Piedipapera's feigned taking over of the debt; but he was a Christian with a stomach as deep as a well, and he stowed everything away in it. He knew his business, and as Betta welcomed him with her mouth agape worse than a rabid dog, and mastro Croco Callà had let slip that he didn't give a hang, he replied that they could bet on it that he would drop them, and he didn't show his face in the mayor's house again; that way they themselves could work out how to get out of that mess, and Betta would no longer have the opportunity to tell him openly that he wanted to ruin her father Callà, and that his advice was the advice of a Judas, who had bartered Christ for thirty pieces of silver, and that he wanted to bring down the mayor for his own ends, and act the cock of the roost in the village. So that on Sunday when the council was to meet, don Silvestro plonked himself in the main room of the town hall, where the National Guard used to be, and calmly started sharpening the pens, in front of the pine table, to pass the time, while la Zuppidda and the other women bawled in the street, spinning in the sunshine, and wanted to tear the eyes out of every man jack of them.

When they ran to call him from the wall of massaro Filippo's vineyard, Silkwork slipped on his new jacket, washed his hands, brushed himself down from the lime but wouldn't budge unless they called on don Silvestro for him first. In vain Betta berated him and pushed him out of the door, telling him that he'd made his bed and now he had to lie on it, and that he should let other people take the action provided they left him to be mayor. This time mastro Callà had seen that crowd outside the town hall, with their distaffs in their hands, and he dug his feet in worse than a mule. 'I'm not going unless don Silvestro comes,' he repeated, eyes bulging. 'Don Silvestro will find some way out!'

'I'll find you a way out,' replied Betta. 'So they don't want a tax on pitch? Well then, leave things as they are.'

'Wonderful! And where do I get the money from?'

'Where from? Get the money from the people who've got it, zio Crocifisso, for instance, or padron Cipolla, or Peppi Naso.'

'Wonderful! They're the councillors!'

'Then dismiss them and get some others; in any case they won't be able to keep you on as mayor when no one else wants you. You have to satisfy the majority.'

'That's just how women think! As though it were they who keep me where I am. You know nothing. The councillors elect the mayor and they're the people who have to be the councillors, them and no one else. What do you expect? Beggars from the streets?'

'Then let the councillors be and dismiss the town clerk, that troublemaker don Silvestro.'

'Wonderful, and then who will be town clerk? who knows the ropes? You or I, or padron Cipolla, even though he pours out opinions worse than a philosopher.'

Then Betta was stumped at last, and she gave vent to her spleen by unleashing all manner of insults against don Silvestro, who was the boss of the village, and had them all in his pocket.

'Wonderful,' repeated Silkworm. 'Look, if he's not there I don't know what to say. I'd like to see you in my shoes.'

81

At last don Silvestro arrived, with a face harder than a wall, hands behind his back, and humming a little tune. 'Come now, don't lose heart, mastro Croce, the world won't collapse for so little!' Mastro Croce let himself be led away by don Silvestro, to be seated at the pine council table, with the ink-well in front of him; but the only councillors there were Peppi Naso the butcher, all greasy and red-faced, and afraid of no one in the whole world, and compare Tino Piedipapera. 'He has nothing to lose!' shouted la Zuppidda from the doorway, 'and he comes here to suck the blood of us poor people worse than a leech, because he acts the cat's paw for this person or that in their dirty deeds. What a pack of thieves and murderers!'

Although he would have liked to play the cool customer because of the dignity of his office, Piedipapera finally lost patience and rose up on his crooked leg, shouting to mastro Cirino, the municipal attendant who was responsible for good order, and had a cap with red on it for that reason when he wasn't being the sexton too: 'Get that loudmouth there to shut up!'

'Quite so — it would suit you if no one spoke, eh, compare Tino?'

'As if everyone didn't know what you're up to, shutting your eyes when padron 'Ntoni's 'Ntoni comes to talk to your daughter Barbara.'

'You're the one who shuts their eyes, you old cuckold! when your wife acts the go-between for la Vespa, who comes to hang around your doorway every morning looking for Alfio Mosca, and you play gooseberry. A fine carry-on! But compare Alfio doesn't want to know, I can tell you; he's dreaming of padron 'Ntoni's Mena, and you lot are wasting the oil in your lamps, whatever la Vespa may say.'

'I'll come and give you a good thrashing,' threatened Piedipapera, and began hobbling around the pine table.

'To-day things will end badly,' muttered that parrot mastro Croce.

'Come now, what sort of carry-on is this? Do you think you're on the public square?' shrieked don Silvestro. 'I'll throw all you women out if you're not careful. I'll soon sort this all out.'

Zuppidda wanted to hear nothing of sorting things out, and she threw herself at don Silvestro, who pushed her out, pulling her by the hair, and then took her aside behind the gate of the smallholding.

'Well then, what is it that you want?' he asked her when they were alone, 'what does it matter to you if they put a tax on pitch? do you or your husband pay it, maybe? or is it the people who have their boats mended, who pay it? You listen to me: your husband is a fool to turn against the town hall and make all this uproar. Now they will have to elect new councillors, instead of padron Cipolla and massaro Mariano, who are useless, and your husband could be put forward.'

'I know nothing about that,' replied la Zuppidda, suddenly calming down. 'I don't meddle in my husband's affairs. I know he's gnawing his hands with rage. I can't do anything except go and tell him, if it's certain.'

'Go and tell him, it's as certain as God exists, I tell you! Are we decent folk or not, by heavens?'

La Zuppidda ran off to get her husband, who was cowering in the courtyard carding tow, pale as death, and he wouldn't come out for love or money, shouting that they would cause him to commit some dreadful deed, by God!

Before opening the council, and seeing what the nets held, they would still have to wait for padron Fortunato Cipolla and massaro Filippo the greengrocer, who didn't seem to be showing up, so that people began to get irritated, and indeed the neighbourhood women had begun spinning, along the low wall of the smallholding.

At last they sent word that they weren't coming because they were busy; and the council could decide about the tax without them, if they wanted. 'Just what my daughter Betta said,' grumbled mastro Croce, the man of straw.

'Then get your daughter Betta to help you,' exclaimed don Silvestro. Silkworm did not utter a breath and continued to grumble in a strangled voice.

'Now,' said don Silvestro, 'you'll see that the Zuppiddos will come of their own accord, to tell me they're letting me take Barbara, but I'll play hard to get.'

The session was disbanded without anything being concluded. The town clerk wanted a bit of time to ponder; in the meantime midday had struck and the women had hurried home. When they saw mastro Cirino closing the door and putting the key in his pocket, the few who remained also went about their business here and there, chattering about the insults that had flown between Piedipapera and Zuppidda.

That evening padron 'Ntoni's 'Ntoni too heard about those words, and by Christ, he wanted to show that fellow Piedipapera that he had done his military service! He met him just as he was coming in from the *sciara*, near the Zuppiddos' house, with that fiend's foot of his, and he began to tell him where he got off, that he was a swine and should think twice before speaking ill of the Zuppiddos and what they did, because it was none of his business. Piedipapera couldn't contain himself. 'So you think you've come back from so far just to act the braggart round here, do you?'

'I came to give you a thrashing, if you say anything more.'

At these shouts people had come to their doorways, and a big crowd had gathered; so that they scrapped for real, and Piedipapera, who was no stranger to the fist fight, let himself fall to the ground in a huddle with 'Ntoni Malavoglia, and that way at least it didn't matter what sort of legs you had, and they thrashed around in the mud, hitting out at each other and biting like Peppi Naso's dogs, so much so that padron 'Ntoni's 'Ntoni had to rush into the Zuppiddo's courtyard, because his shirt was all torn, and Piedipapera was led home as bloody as Lazarus.

'Now look here,' shrieked comare Venera again after they had banged the door in the neighbours' faces, 'kindly note that in my own house I am mistress to do just as I please. I can give my daughter to whomsoever I want.'

All red in the face, the girl had run into the house, with her heart beating like that of a day-old chick.

'They half pulled your ear off,' said compare Turi, carefully pouring water over 'Ntoni's head. 'Compare Tino bites worse than a Corsican dog!.

'Ntoni still had blood all over his face, and was burning to do something rash.

'Listen, comare Venera,' he then said in front of everybody, 'personally, if I can't have your daughter, I won't
marry anyone.' And the girl was listening from the other
room. 'This isn't the moment for such talk, compare 'Ntoni;
but if your grandfather agrees, I for my part would have you
rather than Victor Emanuel himself.' Meanwhile compare
Zuppiddo was sitting silent, and handed him a piece of towel-
ling to dry himself; so that evening 'Ntoni went home well
pleased.

But when they heard about the fight with Piedipapera, the
poor Malavoglia were expecting the bailiff to arrive from one
moment to the next to come and drive them out of their
house, since Easter was approaching, and they had hardly got
together half of the debt, and that with great difficulty.

'See what happens when you hang around houses where
there are marriageable girls,' said la Longa to 'Ntoni. 'Now
everyone is talking about your affairs. And I'm sorry for
Barbara.' 'And *I'll* marry her, 'Ntoni replied.

'You'll marry her?' exclaimed his grandfather.

'And what about me? When your father took a wife, and she
was the woman whom you see there, he came to consult me
first. Your grandmother was alive then, and he came to talk to
me about things in the vegetable patch, under the fig tree. But
now such things aren't done, and old people count for
nothing. Once there used to be a saying, 'an old person's word
is the best insurance'. Your sister Mena has to marry first, do
you realise that?'

'What a life I lead,' 'Ntoni began to shout, tearing his hair
and stamping his feet. 'Working all day long! Never going to
the wine shop! and not a penny in my pocket! And now I've
found the right girl, I can't have her. Why did I ever come
back from military service?'

'Listen,' his grandfather said to him, rising with difficulty
because of the pains in his back. 'The best thing you can do
now is to go to sleep. This isn't the sort of discussion to have
in front of your mother!'

'My brother Luca is better off than I am, being a soldier,'
grumbled 'Ntoni as he went off.

CHAPTER VIII

Luca, poor lad, was neither better off nor worse; he was
doing his duty, as he had at home, and he made the best of a
bad job. He didn't write often, it's true — the stamps cost
twenty *centesimi* — nor had he yet sent his portrait, because as
a small boy he had been teased for having sticking out ears;
but instead of that he put the odd five *lire* note in his letters,
which he managed to set aside by doing odd jobs for the
officers.

As his grandfather had said: 'First Mena must marry.'
They weren't actually talking about it yet, but they thought of
it all the time, and now that they had the odd something set
aside in the chest of drawers to pay the debt, padron 'Ntoni
calculated that with the salting of the anchovies they could
pay Piedipapera, and the house would be unencumbered for
his grand-daughter's dowry. That was why he sometimes
chatted with padron Fortunato on the sea shore, in low
voices, while they were waiting for the boats to come in, or
sitting in the sun in front of the church, when there were no
people around. Padron Fortunato didn't want to go back on
his word, if the girl had a dowry, particularly since his son
Brasi was giving him more than his fair share of worry,
running after girls who had nothing, like the dolt he was.

'You may know the man by his word, and the ox by its
horns,' he would say.

Mena often felt sick at heart while she wove, because girls
have a seventh sense, and now that her grandfather was constantly out conversing with compare Fortunato, and talking
about the Cipolla family often at home, she had that same
image always before her eyes, as if that lad compare Alfio were
stuck on to the wood of the loom, along with the pictures of

the saints. One evening she waited until late to see compare Alfio coming home with his donkey cart; she had her hands under her apron, because it was cold and all the doors were closed, and there wasn't a living soul all up and down the lane; so she said good evening to him from the doorway.

'Will you be going off to Bicocca on the first of the month?' she asked him at last.

'Not yet, no; I've still got over a hundred cartloads of wine for Santuzza. After that, God will provide.' Then she didn't know what to say, and compare Alfio busied himself in the courtyard unharnessing the donkey, and hanging the tackle on the hook, and coming and going with the lantern. 'If you go to Bicocca there's no knowing when we shall meet again,' Mena said at last, in a voice that was barely audible.

'Now why is that? Are you going away too?'

The poor creature didn't answer for a bit, although it was dark and no one could see her face. Every so often you could hear the neighbours talking behind their closed doors, and children crying, and the noise of the bowls, when they were eating, so that no one could hear them either. 'Now we've got half the money we need for Piedipapera, and when we've salted the anchovies we'll have the other half too.'

On hearing this Alfio left the donkey in the middle of the courtyard and came out on to the road. 'So they'll be marrying you off after Easter?' Mena didn't answer. 'I told you so,' added compare Alfio. 'I saw padron 'Ntoni talking to padron Cipolla.'

'It's all in God's hands,' Mena then said. 'I wouldn't mind getting married, as long as they let me stay on here.'

'It must be a fine thing,' added Mosca, 'when you are as rich as padron Cipolla's son, who can take any wife and can live anywhere he chooses!'

'Goodnight, compare Alfio,' Mena then said, after another short spell of gazing at the lantern hanging on the gate, and at the donkey cropping the nettles along the wall. Compare Alfio said goodnight too, and went back to putting the donkey in the stable.

'That brazen-faced St Agatha,' muttered la Vespa, who was at the Piedipaperas at all times of the day with the excuse

87

of borrowing knitting needles, or presenting them with the odd handful of beans she had picked in her smallholding, 'that brazen-faced St Agatha is for ever hanging round compare Alfio. She doesn't leave him a moment to draw breath! It's shameful!' and she carried on grousing in the road, while Piedipapera shut the door, sticking his tongue out after her. 'La Vespa is as angry as a wasp in July,' compare Tino sniggered.

'What does it all matter to her?' asked comare Grazia.

'It matters to her because she has it in for anyone who gets married, and she's got her eye on Alfio Mosca.'

'You ought to tell her that I don't like playing gooseberry. As if people couldn't see that she comes here for compare Alfio, and then la Zuppidda goes around spreading the word that it suits us to play the part.'

'La Zuppidda would do better to worry about her own affairs, because there's plenty to worry about! what with that nonsense of discussing marriage with padron 'Ntoni's 'Ntoni, while the old man and the rest of them are raising hell and don't want to hear anything about it. To-day I spent a good half-hour enjoying the scene between 'Ntoni and Barbara, and my back still hurts from being crouched against that wall, to hear what they were saying. 'Ntoni had slipped away from the *Provvidenza*, with the excuse of going to get the big harpoon for the grey mullet; and he said to her: 'If my grandfather is against it, how shall we manage?' 'We'll manage by running away together, and once we've done that they'll have to think about marrying us, they'll be forced to agree to it,' she replied; and her mother was there behind the wall listening, I'll bet my eye teeth. A fine figure that witch cuts! Now I feel like setting the whole village cackling. When I told him, don Silvestro said that he felt he could make Barbara drop into his arms like a ripe pear. And don't put the latch down, I'm expecting Rocco Spatu to come and have a word with me.'

To get her to drop into his arms, don Silvestro had cooked up a trick so cunning that not even the friar who gives out lottery numbers could ever have conceived of it. 'What I need,' he had said, 'is for everyone who is trying to take her from me to be out of the way. When she has no one else to marry, then she will have to beseech me, and I'll drive a hard bargain, like they do at the market, when buyers are scarce.'

Among those who were trying to take Barbara from him had been Vanni Pizzuto, when he went to shave mastro Turi who had sciatica, and also don Michele, who was bored with strutting around with his pistol slung over his stomach doing nothing, when he wasn't behind Santuzza's counter, and making eyes at the pretty girls, to wile away the time. At first Barbara had responded to these come-hither looks, but when her mother had told her that they were all spongers and scroungers, police spies rather than anything else, and that all foreigners should be whipped, she had slammed the window in his face, all moustachioed and braided-capped as he was, and don Michele had fumed and fretted, and carried on walking up and down the street out of sheer spite, twirling his moustache, with his cap over his eye. Then on Sundays he wore his hat with the feather, and would deliver a very nasty look from Vanni Pizzuto's shop, while the girl was going to mass with her mother. Don Silvestro too took to having himself shaved with the other people who were waiting to go to mass, and warming himself at the brazier for the hot water, and exchanging jokes. 'That Barbara has got her eye on 'Ntoni Malavoglia,' he said. 'What's the betting he collars her? You can see he's all set to wait for her, lounging about with his hands in his pockets.'

Then Vanni Pizzuto left don Michele with the soap all over his face, and went to the door:

'What a fine figure of a girl, by the Virgin! The way she walks with her nose in her shawl, so that she looks just like a spindle! And to think that that dunderhead 'Ntoni Malavoglia will get her all for himself!'

' 'Ntoni won't be getting her if Piedipapera intends to be paid, let me tell you. The Malavoglia will have other worries, if Piedipapera takes the house by the medlar tree.'

Vanni Pizzuto resumed possession of don Michele's nose. 'What do you say, don Michele? You've been after her too. But she's the sort of girl who makes you eat gall.'

Don Michele said nothing, but he brushed himself down,

curled his moustaches and put on his hat in front of the mirror. 'You need something more than hats with feathers for that girl,' sniggered Pizzuto.

At last, on one occasion, don Michele said:

'If it weren't for my hat with the feather, by Christ, I'd show that lout of a Malavoglia how I go about things.' Don Silvestro was thoughtful enough to go and tell 'Ntoni Malavoglia everything, including the fact that don Michele the sergeant was the fighting kind, and would probably want to have things out with him.

'I'll laugh in the face of that moustachioed sergeant,' replied 'Ntoni. 'I know why he's annoyed with me; I'll let him off this time, but if he has any sense he'll stop spoiling his shoes by constantly walking up and down in front of la Zuppidda's place, with his braided cap, as though he had a crown on his head; because people don't give a hoot about him or his cap.'

And if he met him he would look him in the eye, narrowing his gaze as a red-blooded young man who has been a soldier should do, and not let his cap be snatched away amidst the crowd. Don Michele carried on walking down the little road out of pigheadedness, so as not to seem beaten by 'Ntoni, because he would have snapped him up like bread, if he hadn't been for that hat with a feather.

'They're eating each other alive,' said Vanni Pizzuto to anyone who came to have a shave, or to buy cigars, or fishing bait, or small bone buttons. 'One of these days 'Ntoni Malavoglia and don Michele are going to snap each other up like bread! It's only that blessed hat with a feather which is tying don Michele's hands. He'd pay Piedipapera anything to get that fathead 'Ntoni out of the way.' So much so that la Locca's son, who spent the whole day wandering around with his arms dangling at his side, began to trail after them to see how it would all end.

When he went to have a shave and heard that don Michele would have given anything to have 'Ntoni Malavoglia out of the way, Piedipapera swelled up like a turkey cock, because that implied that he was held in some regard in the village.

As Vanni Pizzuto kept telling him: 'The sergeant would

pay any amount of money to have the Malavoglia in his clutches as you have. So why did you let 'Ntoni off so lightly over that punch up?'

Piedipapera shrugged and carried on warming his hands at the brazier. Don Silvestro began to laugh, and answered for him:

'Mastro Vanni Pizzuto would like to use Piedipapera's paw to get his chestnuts out of the fire for him. As you know, comare Venera doesn't want any truck with foreigners or people in braided caps; so when she has got rid of 'Ntoni Malavoglia, there would be only him left to fool around with the girl.'

Vanni Pizzuto said nothing, but he chewed over this all night.

'That might be no bad thing,' he pondered to himself. 'The important thing is to grab Piedipapera by the horns, and on the right day.'

The right day arrived, and just in time, one evening when Rocco Spatu didn't show up and Piedipapera came two or three times, late, to ask about him, white-faced and looking distraught, and the customs guards had been seen rushing about busily this way and that, with their noses to the ground like hunting dogs, and don Michele along with them with his pistol on his stomach and his trousers tucked into his boots. 'You could do don Michele a great favour, by getting 'Ntoni Malavoglia out of his way,' Pizzuto repeated to compare Tino, when the latter went to stick himself in the darkest corner of the little shop to buy a cigar. 'You'd do him a famous favour, and then he really would be your friend for life.'

'A fine thing that would be,' sighed Piedipapera, who was short of breath that evening, and he said no more.

In the night shots were heard towards the Rotolo, and along the whole plain, so that it sounded like quail-hunting. 'Quails my foot,' murmured the fishermen sitting up in their beds to listen. 'Those are two-footed quails, the sort that bring sugar and coffee, and contraband silk handkerchieves. Last night don Michele was going about with his trousers in his boots and his pistol slung on his stomach!'

91

Piedipapera was in Pizzuto's shop having a little drink, before dawn, and the lantern was still burning outside the door; but this time he looked like a dog with its tail between its legs, he wasn't telling the usual funny stories and he was asking people what all that racket had been about, and had they seen Rocco Spatu and Cinghialenta, and he doffed his cap to don Michele, who had swollen eyes and dusty boots, and he did his best to pay for the sergeant's drink. But don Michele had already been to the wine shop where Santuzza, pouring him a glass of her good wine, had said: 'What have you been doing, risking your skin, you fool? Don't you know that if you get killed, you'll drag others into the grave with you?'

'You don't seem to set much store by my duty, do you? If I had caught them red-handed to-night there would have been plenty in it for us, damn it!'

'If they want you to believe that it was massaro Filippo trying to smuggle his wine in, don't you believe them, by this blessed scapular I'm wearing so unworthily on my chest. That's a pack of lies told by brazen people without consciences, who would damn their own souls in their eagerness to harm their neighbours.'

'No, I know what it was! It was silk handkerchieves and coffee and sugar, more than a thousand *lire's* worth of goods, by the Virgin, which slipped through my fingers like eels; but I've got them in my sights, the whole gang, and another time they won't get away with it.'

Then Piedipapera said to him: 'Have a drink, don Michele, it'll do your stomach good, with all that sleep you've lost.'

Don Michele was in a bad mood, and he huffed and puffed.

'He's asking you to have one, so have one,' added Vanni Pizzuto. 'If compare Tino is paying, it means he's got money, and to spare. And he *has* got money, the cunning devil! In fact he has taken over the debt from the Malavoglia; and now they're repaying him with beatings.'

Here don Michele allowed himself to laugh a little.

'By the blood of Judas,' exclaimed Piedipapera, banging his fists on the counter, and pretending to get into a real rage now. 'I don't need to send that lout 'Ntoni to Rome, to make

92

him do penance!'

'Bravo,' said Pizzuto encouragingly. 'I certainly wouldn't have let it pass. Eh, don Michele?'

Don Michele gave a grunt of approval. 'I'll see about cutting 'Ntoni and all his family down to size,' threatened Piedipapera. 'I have no wish to be the laughing stock of the whole village. You can rest assured of that, don Michele!'

And he went off hobbling and swearing as though he were blind with fury, muttering to himself:

'You have to keep the lot of them sweet, those narks'; and pondering on how to keep them sweet he went to the wine shop, where zio Santoro told him that neither Roccu Spatu nor Cinghialenta had been seen, so he went to cousin Anna, who had not slept, poor thing, and was standing at the door looking first in one direction and then the other, pale and distraught. There he also met la Vespa who was coming to see whether comare Grazia had a little yeast, by any chance.

'I've just met compare Mosca,' she said, for something to say. 'He hadn't got his cart with him, and I'll warrant he was going to hang about on the *sciara*, behind St Agatha's vegetable patch. 'Loving your neighbour is a fine thing indeed, you see each other often and to travel there's no need.' '

'A fine saint to pin up on the wall, that Mena!' la Vespa began to bawl. 'They want to give her to Brasi Cipolla, and she carries on flirting all over the place. What a disgraceful business!'

'You leave her be! That way people will know what sort of a person she is, and their eyes will be opened. But doesn't compare Mosca know she's been promised to compare Cipolla?'

'You know what men are like, if there's some little flirt with an eye on them they all run after her just for the joy of it. But then, when they want to start something serious, they need the kind of girl I have in mind.'

'Compare Mosca ought to take someone like you.'

'For the moment, I'm not thinking about marriage; but certainly he'd be well-suited with me. Anyway, I've got my smallholding, and no one can lay their hands on that, whereas the house by the medlar tree could be blown away at the first

93

chill wind. We'll see what's what, when the trouble starts.'

'You leave her be! Fair weather is followed by foul, and the lightweights get blown away like dead twigs. To-day I have to talk to your uncle Dumb bell about you-know-what.'

Dumb bell was all too willing to talk about the never-ending affair, and 'long things turn into snakes . . .' Padron 'Ntoni kept repeating that the Malavoglia were decent folk, and would pay, but he would like to know where they were going to get that money from. In the village they already knew what everyone owned, down to the last *centesimo*, and those ever so decent Malavoglia would never be able to raise the sum between now and Easter, even by selling their souls to the Turks; and to take over the house by the medlar tree would require a lot of red tape, and don Giammaria and the chemist were right when they talked of the government being a thief; as true as his name was zio Crocifisso, he was angry not only with the people who fixed the taxes, but also with the people who objected to them, and who turned the whole village upside down to such a degree that a decent fellow could no longer sit quietly in his own house with his own possessions, and when they came to ask him if he would like to be mayor, he had answered: 'That's a fine question. And who would look after my business? I'll look after my own affairs.' Meanwhile padron 'Ntoni was thinking of marrying off his granddaughter, because they had seen him going around with padron Cipolla — zio Santoro had seen them — and they had also seen Piedipapera playing the go-between for la Vespa and acting for that starveling Alfio Mosca, who wanted to get his hands on her smallholding. 'I tell you, he'll get his hands on it,' said Piedipapera shouting in his ear to convince him. 'It's all very well huffing and puffing around the house. Your niece is crazy about him, always trailing after him. I can't shut the door in her face, when she comes to chat with my wife, just for your sake, after all she is your niece and flesh of your flesh.'

'Some consideration you show for me! Such consideration that you're making me lose my smallholding!'

'Of course you'll lose it! If the Malavoglia girl marries Brasi Cipolla, compare Mosca will be helpless, and he'll take la Vespa and the smallholding and have done with it once and for all!'

'The devil can take her, for all I care,' exclaimed zio Crocifisso at last, dazed by compare Tino's babble. 'I don't give a hang; what I do mind about more than anything is the sins that witch has made me commit. I want my property, which I earned with the sweat of my brow, as true as Christ's blood in the chalice at mass, and yet you'd think it was stolen property, the way everyone seems to be dicing for it, compare Alfio, la Vespa and the Malavoglia. I'm going to start a lawsuit, and take the house.'

'You're the boss. If you tell me to start proceeding, I'll do so right away.'

'Not yet. We'll wait for Easter; 'you may know the man by his word and the ox by its horns'; but I want to be paid down to the last brass farthing, and I won't listen to any talk of postponement.'

Easter was indeed now approaching. The hills were covered in green again, and the prickly pears were once again in flower. The girls had sown the basil in their window-boxes, and white butterflies came to settle on it; even the poor broom on the *sciara* had its own pale little flowers. In the morning, on the roofs, the green and yellow tiles smoked, and the sparrows twittered until sunset.

The house by the medlar tree, too, had a cheerful air about it once again; the courtyard was swept clean, the tools were standing in good order along the wall or hanging from hooks, the vegetable patch was green with cabbages and lettuces and the bedrooms so open and full of sun that it too seemed pleased with life, and everything told you that Easter was on its way. The old people sat out at their doorways towards mid-day, and the girls sang at the wash place. The carts started to pass by at night again and once again in the evening there was a hum of people chatting in the little street.

'Comare Mena is going to be married,' people said. 'Her mother is working on her trousseau.'

Time had passed and time carries away cruel things as well as kind ones. Now comare Maruzza was busy cutting and sewing garments, and Mena didn't even ask who they were for; and one evening they had brought Brasi Cipolla into the house, with padron Fortunato his father, and the whole family. 'Here's padron Fortunato comé to pay you a visit,' said padron 'Ntoni, ushering them in, as though no one knew anything about it, while wine and toasted chick peas had been prepared in the kitchen, and women and children were dressed in their best. Mena really did look like St Agatha, with that new dress and her black handkerchief on her head, so that Brasi couldn't take his eyes off her, like the basilisk, and was sitting perched on that chair, with his hands between his legs, rubbing them from time to time in sheer glee. 'He has come with his own son Brasi, who is a grown man now,' added padron 'Ntoni.

'That's right, boys grow up and elbow their fathers into the grave,' replied padron Fortunato.

'Now drink a glass of wine with us — it's good wine,' added la Longa, 'and those chick peas were roasted by my daughter. I'm sorry, I wasn't expecting you, and I can't offer you anything that is really worthy of you.'

'We were just passing by,' answered padron Cipolla, 'and we said: 'let's go and call on comare Maruzza.' '

Brasi filled his pockets with chick peas, staring at the girl, and then the children pillaged the tray, though Nunziata with the baby in her arms vainly tried to hold them at bay, speaking in a low voice as if she were in church. Meanwhile the old people had begun to talk among themselves, under the medlar tree, and the neighbourhood women formed a circle and sang the girl's praises, saying what a good housewife she was, keeping the house as clean as a new pin. 'A girl's worth lies in her upbringing, and the quality of hemp lies in the spinning!'

'Your granddaughter too has grown up,' observed padron Fortunato, 'and it must now be time for her to marry.'

'If the good Lord sends us a good match, we would like nothing better,' replied padron 'Ntoni.

'Marriages and bishoprics are made in heaven,' added la Longa.

'A good horse does not lack for a saddle,' concluded padron Fortunato; 'a girl like your Mena will not lack for takers.'

Mena sat near the young man, but she didn't raise her eyes from her apron, and Brasi grumbled, when he went off with his father, that she hadn't offered him the plate with the chick peas.

'You mean you wanted more?' padron Fortunato thundered at him, when they were some way off; 'all we could hear was you munching, as if you were a mule with a sack of oats! Look, you've got wine on your trousers, Brasi, and ruined me a new suit!'

Delighted, padron 'Ntoni was rubbing his hands and saying to his daughter-in-law: 'I can hardly believe we're home and dry, with God's help! Mena won't lack for anything, and now we'll sort out our little affairs, and you'll remember how your old father-in-law used to say that laughter and tears go hand in hand.'

That Saturday, towards evening, Nunziata came to get a handful of beans for her children, and said: 'Compare Alfio is off to-morrow. He's taking out all his things.'

Mena went pale and stopped spinning.

The light was on in compare Alfio's house, and everything was topsy turvy. He came to knock on their door soon afterwards, and he too had an odd look on his face, and fiddled with the knots of the whip he held in his hand.

'I've come to say goodbye to you all, comare Maruzza, padron 'Ntoni, the children, and you too, comare Mena. The Aci Catena wine is finished. Now Santuzza has started taking wine from massaro Filippo. I'm going to Bicocca, where there's work I can do with my donkey.'

Mena said nothing; only her mother opened her mouth to answer: 'Will you wait for padron 'Ntoni? he'll want to say goodbye to you.'

Compare Alfio perched uncomfortably on the chair, with his whip in his hand, and looked around, at those parts of the room not containing Mena.

'So when will you be back?' asked la Longa.

'Heaven only knows. I go where my donkey takes me. I'll stay away as long as I have work; though I'd prefer to come right back here, if I had any way of earning a living.'

'Look after yourself, compare Alfio. They tell me people

97

are dying like flies at Bicocca, of malaria.'

Alfio shrugged, and said that there was nothing he could do about it.

'I don't want to go,' he repeated, looking at the candle. 'Have you nothing to say to me, comare Mena?'

The girl opened her mouth once or twice to say something, but her courage failed her.

'You too will be leaving the district, now that you're getting married, added Alfio. 'The world is like a stable, some come and some go, and gradually everyone will have changed places, and nothing seems the same.' As he said this he rubbed his hands and laughed, but with his lips and not from his heart.

'Girls,' said la Longa, 'go where God sends them. At first they have no worries or cares, and when they go out into the world they begin to know its sorrows and its disappointments.'

After padron 'Ntoni and the children had come home, compare Alfio couldn't bring himself to leave, and he hung about at the doorway, with his whip under his arm, shaking hands with this person and that, even with comare Maruzza, as you do when you are about to leave for a distant place and don't know whether you're ever going to be seeing each other again: 'Forgive me if I haven't always been all I should.' The only person who didn't shake his hand was St Agatha, who was sitting in a corner, near her loom. But that is how girls have to behave, as everyone knows.

It was a fine spring evening, with the moonlight in the streets and on the courtyards, the people at their doorsteps and the girls walking by arm in arm, singing. Mena too came out arm in arm with Nunziata, feeling she would stifle in the house.

'Now we won't see compare Alfio's light in the window any more, of an evening,' said Nunziata, 'and the house will be shut up.'

Compare Alfio had loaded most of his poor possessions on to the cart, and was putting what little hay was left in the manger into a sack, while his bean soup was cooking.

'Will you be leaving before daybreak?' asked Nunziata at

98

the entrance to the courtyard.

'Yes, I've a long way to go, and that poor animal will have to have a bit of a rest during the day.'

Mena said nothing, leaning against the door post to look at the loaded cart, the empty house, the half-made bed and the pan boiling on the stove for the last time.

'Are you there too, comare Mena?' Alfio exclaimed as soon as he saw her, and left what he was doing.

She nodded, and meanwhile Nunziata had run to skim the saucepan which was boiling over, like the good housewife she was.

'That's good, then I can say goodbye to you,' said Alfio.

'I came to say goodbye to you,' she said, with a knot in her throat. 'Why are you going to Bicocca if there's malaria there?'

'Why am I going? That's a good question. Why are you marrying Brasi Cipolla? You do what you can, comare Mena. If I had been able to do what I wanted, you know quite well what I would have done . . .'

She looked at him and he looked at her, their eyes bright. 'I'd have stayed here, where the very walls know me, and I know where to put my hands, and indeed I could even drive the donkey by night; and I'd have married you, comare Mena, for I've had a place for you in my heart for quite a time now, and I'd have taken you with me to Bicocca, and everywhere else I went. But there's no point in talking about this now, and you have to do what you can. Even my donkey goes where I make it go.'

'Goodbye then,' said Mena; 'I too feel as if I had a thorn inside me . . . and now that I shall always see this window closed, I'll feel as if my heart is closed too, and that window closed on top of it, as heavy as a wine cellar door. But that is God's will. Now I'll say goodbye and be off.'

The poor creature was crying quietly, with her hands over her eyes, and she went off together with Nunziata to cry under the medlar tree in the moonlight.

CHAPTER IX

Neither the Malavoglia nor anyone else in the village knew what Piedipapera was concocting with zio Crocifisso. On Easter Day padron 'Ntoni took the hundred *lire* from the chest of drawers and put on his new jacket to go and take them to zio Crocifisso.

'Is that the lot?' zio Crocifisso asked.

'Well, it couldn't be the lot, zio Crocifisso; you know what it takes to earn a hundred *lire*. But 'something is better than nothing,' and 'the person who pays a first instalment is not a bad payer.' Now the summer is coming, and with God's help we'll pay the lot.'

'Why are you telling me all this? You know it's nothing to do with me, but with Piedipapera.'

'It comes to the same thing, because when I see you I still feel that I owe you the money. Compare Tino won't say no, when you tell him you want to wait till the Madonna of Ognina.'

'This isn't even enough for the expenses,' repeated Dumb bell, tossing the money in his hand. 'You go and ask him if he'll wait, it's not my business any more.'

Piedipapera began to swear and dash his cap to the ground, in his usual way, saying that he had no bread to eat, and couldn't wait even until Ascension Day.

'Listen, compare Tino', padron 'Ntoni said to him with his hands clasped as though he were in the presence of God Himself. 'If you don't wait until St John Day, now that I am about to marry off my grand-daughter, you might as well give me a stab in the back right now.'

'Heavens alive,' shrieked compare Tino, 'you're forcing me to do something I can't do,' and he cursed the day and the hour when he got himself involved in this mess, and went off tearing his old cap.

Padron 'Ntoni arrived home quite pale, and said to his daughter-in-law: 'I did it, but I had to beg him as if he were

God Almighty,' and the poor fellow was still all a-tremble. But he was pleased that padron Cipolla should know nothing about it, so that his grand-daughter's wedding hadn't gone up in smoke.

On the evening of Ascension Day, while the children were jumping around the bonfires, the neighbourhood women had come together again outside the Malavoglia's balcony, and even comare Venera la Zuppidda arrived to hear what was being said, and to make her own contribution. Now that padron 'Ntoni was marrying off his granddaughter, and the *Provvidenza* was seaworthy once more, everyone had a welcome again for the Malavoglia, who knew nothing of what Piedipapera was hatching, and nor indeed did comare Grazia his wife, who chatted with comare Maruzza as though her husband were hatching nothing at all. 'Ntoni would go every evening to chat with Barbara, and he had confided in her that his grandfather had said that Mena must marry first. 'And then it's my turn,' added 'Ntoni. So Barbara sent Mena a gift of basil, all decorated with carnations, and a fine red bow, which was an invitation to become special friends; and everyone made a fuss of St Agatha, and her mother had even taken off her black handkerchief, because when there is a wedding in the offing it is bad luck to wear mourning; and they had even written to Luca, to tell him that Mena was getting married.

Only Mena, poor thing, seemed less cheerful than the rest, and it was as though her heart spoke to her and made her see everything in black, while the fields were all dotted with little gold and silver stars and the children were making garlands for Ascension Day, and she herself had gone up the ladder to help her mother hang them at the door and windows.

All the doors had flowers on them, and only compare Alfio's door, black and dilapidated, remained closed, and there was no longer anyone to hang the Ascension Day flowers on it.

'That little flirt St Agatha,' la Vespa went round saying, foaming at the mouth, 'has sent compare Alfio packing from the village, with all her words and deeds.'

Meanwhile St Agatha had been dressed in her new dress

and they were waiting for St John's Day to take the little silver sword from her hair, and to part it on her forehead, before going into church, so that when they saw her pass everyone said how lucky she was.

But her mother, poor thing, did feel a deep sense of joy, because her daughter was going to be part of a family where she would want for nothing, and in the meanwhile she was completely absorbed in her cutting and sewing. Padron 'Ntoni wanted to be involved too, when he came home at night, and he would hold the cloth and the skein of cotton, and every time he went into town he would bring back some little thing. With the fine weather he felt a return of courage, and the children were all earning, some more and some less, and the *Provvidenza* earned her keep too, and they reckoned that with God's help on St John's Day they would be out of difficulties. Then padron Cipolla spent whole evenings sitting on the steps of the church disussing the achievements of the *Provvidenza* with padron 'Ntoni. Brasi kept wandering up and down the Malavoglia's little street in his new suit, and soon afterwards the whole village learned that that Sunday comare Grazia Piedipapera herself was going to part the bride's hair, and take out the little silver sword, because Brasi Cipolla's mother was dead, and the Malavoglia had invited Grazia Piedipapera in order to ingratiate themselves with her husband, and they also invited zio Crocifisso, and the whole neighbourhood, and all their friends and relatives, with no thought of the cost.

'I'm not going,' muttered zio Crocifisso, to compare Tino, with his back against the elm, in the square. 'I've had to down enough rage over them, and I don't want to be driven crazy. You go though — it's nothing to you, and it's not your property that's involved. There's still time for the bailiff; the lawyer said so.'

'You're the boss, and I'll do as you say. Now that Alfio Mosca has gone away, it's not so important to you. But you'll see, as soon as Mena is married, he'll come back here and lay hands on your neice.'

Comare Venera la Zuppidda raised hell because they had invited comare Grazia to part the bride's hair, while it should have fallen to her, since she was about to become an in-law of the Malavoglia, and her daughter had become special friends with Mena with the gift of basil, and indeed she had very promptly sewn Barbara a new dress, and wasn't expecting that slight at all. In vain 'Ntoni begged and beseeched her not to take offence at that minor matter, and let things pass. Comare Venera, hair all neatly combed but hands covered in flour, because she had started kneading dough, just to show that she didn't care about going to the Malavoglia's gathering, answered:

"You wanted Grazia Piedipapera? Have her then; it's either her or me! There's no room for both of us.'

Everyone knew quite well that the Malavoglia had chosen comare Grazia because of that money they owed her husband. Now they were hand in glove with compare Tino, ever since padron Cipolla had got him to make peace with padron 'Ntoni's 'Ntoni in Santuzza's wine shop, over the business of the fist fight.

'They're licking his boots because they owe him that money for the house,' Zuppidda would mutter. 'They owe my husband fifty *lire* for the *Provvidenza*, too. And to-morrow I'll get them to hand over.'

'Leave them be, mother, leave them be,' begged Barbara. But she too was in a sulk, because she hadn't been able to wear her new dress, and she almost regretted the money spent for the basil she had sent to comare Mena; and 'Ntoni, who had come to get them, was sent away all crestfallen, so that his new jacket seemed suddenly to fall limply from his very shoulders. Then while they were putting the bread into the oven, mother and daughter stood looking out from the courtyard, listening to the babble going on in the Malavoglia's house, because the voices and laughter could be heard right where they were, to annoy them still further. The house by the medlar tree was full of people, as it had been when compare Bastianazzo died, and Mena, without her little silver sword and with her hair parted on her forehead, looked quite different, so that all the neighbourhood women crowded round her, and you couldn't have heard a cannon shot for the babble and festivity. Piedipapera seemed to be positively tickling the women, he was so witty, while the lawyer was drawing up the documents, because there was still time to call in the bailiff, zio Crocifisso had said so; even padron Cipolla let himself go to the extent of telling some jokes, at which only his son Brasi laughed; and everyone talked at the same time, while the children fought over the beans and chestnuts between the grown-ups' legs. Even la Longa, poor thing, had forgotten her sorrows in her delight; and padron 'Ntoni sat on the wall nodding sagely, and laughed to himself.

'Don't you give a drink to your trousers like last time, *they're* not thirsty' said compare Cipolla to his son, and he also said he felt in better fettle than the bride herself and wanted to dance the *fasola* with her.

'Well, there's no place for me here, I might as well go home!' said Brasi who wanted to tell his own jokes, and who was annoyed that they left him alone in a corner like a dunderhead, and not even Mena paid him any attention.

'The party is for comare Mena,' said Nunziata, 'but she's not as cheerful as the rest of them.'

Then cousin Anna pretended the jug had slipped from her hand, with a drop of wine still in it, and she began to shout that where there were shards, there there was good cheer, and that spilt wine meant good luck.

'I nearly ended up with wine on my trousers this time too,' grumbled Brasi, who was watchful after his previous mishap with the suit.

Piedipapera had seated himself astride the wall, with his glass between his legs, so that he seemed like the boss, because of that bailiff he could send in, and he said: 'Not even Rocco Spatu is in the wine shop, to-day all the merry-making is here, and it's like being at Santuzza's place.'

'It's far better here,' commented la Locca's son, who had brought up the rear, and they had asked him in so he could have a drink too. 'They don't give you anything at Santuzza's if you go there without any money.'

From his wall Piedipapera was watching a small group of people who were talking among themselves near the fountain, looking as solemn as if the end of the world were at hand. At the chemist's there were the usual loafers, mumbling their orisons to each other with the newspaper in their hands, or waving wildly in each other's faces, chattering, as though they wanted to pick a quarrel; and don Giammaria was laughing and taking a pinch of snuff, and you could see how delighted he was from quite a long way off.

'Why haven't the priest and don Silvestro come?' asked Piedipapera.

'I mentioned it to them too, but they must have other things to do,' replied padron 'Ntoni.

'They're there, in the chemist's shop, as though the man who predicts the lottery numbers were there. What the devil has happened?'

An old woman went shrieking through the square, and tearing her hair, as though they had brought her bad tidings; and in front of Pizzuto's shop there was the sort of crowd you get when a donkey collapses in front of a cart, and everyone pushes forward to see what has happened, and even the idle women were peering from a distance open-mouthed, without daring to go any closer.

'Personally, I'm going to see what's happened,' said Piedipapera, and he got slowly down from the wall.

Amidst that group, instead of a fallen donkey, there were two soldiers with bags on their shoulders and bandaged heads, who were coming home on leave. Meanwhile they had stopped at the barber's to have a glass of absinthe. They said that a great sea battle had been fought, and that ships as big as the whole of Aci Trezza had gone down, brim full of soldiers; in short a whole rigmarole, so that it seemed as though they were telling the story of Orlando and the paladins of France on the front at Catania, and the people stood listening with their ears flapping, thick as flies.

'Maruzza la Longa's son was on the *Re d'Italia* too,' commented don Silvestro, who had come up to listen.

'I'm going to tell my wife,' said mastro Turi Zuppiddo immediately, 'because I don't like long faces between friends and neighbours.'

But meanwhile la Longa remained blissfully ignorant, poor thing, and she was laughing and enjoying herself among friends and relatives.

The soldier carried on chatting with anyone who would listen, making play with his arms like a preacher. 'Yes, there were Sicilians there too; there were people from all over. But in any case when the alarm is sounded on the gundeck, you don't have much thought for where people come from, and rifles all speak the same way. They're all good lads! and with plenty of guts. Listen, when you've seen what these eyes have seen, and how those boys did their duty, you can wear this cap over your ear, by the Virgin Mary!'

The young man's eyes were shining, but he said it was nothing, it was because he'd been drinking. 'She was called the *Re d'Italia*, a ship like no other, all armoured — if you can imagine a corset like you women wear, but a corset of iron, that's what she had, so that you could fire cannon shots on her without doing any damage. She went to the bottom in a moment, and she was lost to sight for the smoke, which was like the smoke of twenty brick kilns, can you imagine?'

'There was chaos in Catania,' added the chemist. 'Everyone was crowding around the people who were reading the papers, it was like a party.'

'The papers are just so many printed lines,' pronounced don Giammaria.

'They say it's been a bad business; we've lost a great battle,' said don Silvestro. Padron Cipolla too had come up to see what the crowd was about. 'Do you believe all this?' he sniggered at last. 'It's just talk to make people pay out a *soldo* for the paper.'

'But everyone says we've lost!'

'What?' asked zio Crocifisso, putting his hand to his ear.

'A battle.'

'Who has lost it?'

'Me, you, Italy, everyone, in fact,' answered the chemist.

'I haven't lost anything,' said Dumb bell shrugging; 'now it's compare Piedipapera's business, and he can deal with it,' and he looked towards the house by the medlar tree where they were making merry.

'You know what it's like?' concluded padron Cipolla, 'it's like when the Aci Trezza town council was fighting for land with the Aci Castello town council. What good did it do us, you and me?'

'It *did* us some good,' exclaimed the chemist, red in the face. 'It did . . . what boors you are . . . '

'Those who will suffer are all the poor mothers,' somebody hasarded; zio Crocifisso, who wasn't a mother, shrugged his shoulders.

'I'll tell you what it's like in two words,' the other soldier went on meanwhile. 'It's like at the wine shop, when people get worked up and throw plates and glasses amidst all the smoke and shouting. You've seen that? Well, that's just what it's like. At first, when you're on the barricading with your rifle in your hand, in all that great silence, all you hear is the pumping of the engine, and it seems to you that that sound is happening to you, in your own stomach: nothing more. Then, at the first cannon shot, and as the pandemonium begins, you want to start dancing too, and chains wouldn't hold you back, like when the violin starts in the wine shop, after you've eaten and drunk, and you stick out your rifle wherever you see anything human at all, amid the smoke. On land it's quite another thing. A *bersagliere* who was coming back with us to Messina was telling us that you can't hear the crack of gunshots without feeling your feet tingling with the desire to rush forward with your head down. But the *bersaglieri* aren't sailors, and they can't imagine how you manage to stay in the rigging with your foot steady on the rope and your hand steady on the trigger, despite the pitching of the ship, while your mates are falling around you like rotten pears.'

'Heavenly Virgin,' exclaimed Rocco Spatu. 'I'd like to have been there too, to give them a taste of my fists.'

All the others stood listening, all agog. The other young man then told them how the *Palestro* had blown up — 'burning like a pile of wood, when she passed near us, and the flames were as high as the foremast peak. But all those boys were at their posts, on the gundeck or on the topgallant bulwark. Our commander asked whether they needed anything. 'No thanks very much,' they replied. Then she went to Larboard and no one saw her again.'

'This business of being roasted to death doesn't sound so

good,' concluded Rocco Spatu, 'but I'd have liked the fighting part.' And as she was going back to the wine shop Santuzza said to him:

'Tell them to come along here, those poor lads, they must be thirsty, after all that journeying, and they could do with a bit of decent wine. That Pizzuto poisons people with his absinthe, and he doesn't mention it at confession. Some people have their consciences behind their backs, poor things!'

'They strike me as so many madmen,' said padron Cipolla, blowing his nose thoughtfully. 'Would you get yourself killed if the king told you to go and do so for his sake?'

'Poor things, it's not their fault,' observed don Silvestro. 'They have to, because behind every soldier there is a corporal with a loaded gun, and his whole job consists in keeping an eye on the soldier to see if he's trying to escape, and if he does the corporal shoots him worse than a little garden warbler.'

'Oh, I see! What a business!'

The whole evening there was laughing and drinking in the Malavoglia's courtyard, under a fine moon; and later, when everyone was tired, and slowly chewing over the roasted beans, and some were even singing quietly, with their backs to the wall, they began to tell the news which the two discharged soldiers had brought to the village. Padron Fortunato had left early, and had taken away Brasi with his new suit.

'Those poor Malavoglia,' he said when he met Dumb bell on the square. 'May Heaven spare them! They've got the evil eye upon them.'

Zio Crocifisso kept silent and scratched his head. Now it was not his business any more, he had washed his hands of it. Now it was Piedipapera's lookout; but he was sorry, in all conscience.

The next day the rumour began to go round that there had been a battle at sea towards Trieste between our ships and those of the enemy, though no one even knew who they were, and a lot of people had died; some told the story one way and some another, in dribs and drabs; swallowing their words.

The neighbourhood women came with their hands under their aprons to ask whether comare Maruzza's Luca had been there, and they stood and looked at her all eyes before going off again. The poor woman began to sit around in the doorway, as she did every time something awful happened, turning her head this way and that, looking from one end of the street to the other, as though she were expecting her father-in-law and the children back from sea earlier than usual. Then the neighbours asked her if Luca had written, or whether she hadn't heard from him for a long time. In fact she hadn't thought about letters, and she couldn't sleep the whole night, and in her mind she was down there, in the sea towards Trieste, where the disaster occurred; and she could see her son before her, pale and motionless, looking at her with such staring shining eyes, and just saying yes, yes, like when they had sent him to do his soldiering — so that she too felt a thirst upon her, an unspeakable burning. Amidst all the stories which were going the rounds in the village, and which they had come to tell her, one remained with her in particular, of one of those sailors, whom they fished up after twelve hours, when the sharks were about to devour him, and in the middle of all that water he was dying of thirst. When she thought about that man who was dying of thirst in the midst of that water, la Longa couldn't help going to drink from the jug for minutes on end, as though that thirst had been within herself, and she opened her eyes wide in the darkness, where the image of that fellow was forever imprinted.

But with the passing of the days, no one talked about what had happened any more; but as the letter didn't seem to be arriving la Longa had no interest either in working or in staying indoors: she wandered continually from door to door, as though she were looking for some kind of answer. 'Ever seen a cat which has lost its kittens?' said the neighbours. But the letter didn't come. Padron 'Ntoni didn't go to sea either and stayed hanging around his daughter-in-law's skirts like a puppy dog. People told him to go to Catania, which was a big place, and they would be able to tell him something there.

In that big place the poor old man felt worse than if he'd been at sea at night, without knowing which way to turn the rudder. At last they had the goodness to tell him that he should go to the harbour master, since he probably knew the news. There, after having sent him from pillar to post, for a bit, they began to leaf through certain sinister looking books, running their fingers down the list of the dead. When they came to one name la Longa, who hadn't heard properly because her ears were ringing, and she was listening as white as the paper itself, slumped gently to the floor, more dead than alive.

'It happened over a month ago,' added the clerk, closing the register. 'At Lissa; didn't you know?'

They took la Longa back home on a cart, and she was ill for several days. From then onwards she was seized with a great devotion for Our Lady of Sorrows, on the altar of the little church, and it seemed to her that that long body stretched out on his mother's knee, with its black ribs and knees red with blood, was the image of her Luca, and she herself felt all those silver swords of the Madonna planted in her own heart. Every evening, when they went to benediction, and as compare Cirino rattled the keys before shutting up, the old women saw her still there, in the same spot, having fallen to her knees, and they called her Our Lady of Sorrows, too.

'She's right,' they said in the village. 'Luca would soon have been back, and he would have worked for his thirty *soldi* a day. It never rains but it pours.

'Have you seen padron 'Ntoni?' added Piedipapera; 'after that tragedy with his grandson he looks just like an owl. Now the house by the medlar tree is letting in water from all sides, like an old boot, and every decent man has to look to his own.'

La Zuppidda was in a permanent sulk, muttering that now the whole family would be dependent on 'Ntoni! Now a girl would think twice before taking him as a husband.

'What have you got against that poor man?' asked mastro Turi.

'You keep quiet, you understand nothing,' his wife shrieked at him. 'I don't like such messes. Go and get working; this isn't your business,' and she sent him out of the door with his arms dangling at his side and his great caulker's mallet in his hand.

Sitting on the parapet of the terraces and stripping the dry leaves off the carnations, with her mouth set, Barbara proferred the comment that 'married couples and mules like to be alone,' and that 'there's little love lost between mother-in-law and daughter-in-law.'

'When Mena is married,' answered 'Ntoni, 'grandfather will give us the upstairs room.'

'I'm not used to being in an upstairs room, like the doves,' Barbara snapped back, so that her father, who after all was her father, said to 'Ntoni, looking around him while they walked down the little street: 'She'll become just like her mother, Barbara will; you'll have to be firm with her right from the start, otherwise you'll end up with the pack saddle on, just like me.'

But comare Venera had pronounced. 'Before my daughter goes to sleep in the dovecote we'll need to know who the house is going to, and I want to see how this lupin business will end.'

How it ended was that this time Piedipapera wanted to be paid, by Christ! St. John's Day had come, and the Malavoglia started to talk again of giving part payments, because they hadn't got all the money, and they hoped to get together the sum with the olive harvest. He had taken that money out of his own mouth, and he had no bread to eat, as sure as God exists! He couldn't get by until the olive harvest.

'I'm sorry, padron 'Ntoni,' he had said; 'but what can I do? I have to consider my own interest. Charity begins at home.'

'The year will soon be over,' added zio Crocifisso, when he was alone grumbling with compare Tino, 'and we haven't seen a ha'porth of interest: those two hundred *lire* will barely cover expenses. You'll see, when the olive harvest comes they'll tell you to wait till Christmas, and then till Easter. This is how families meet their downfall. But I've earned my property with the sweat of my brow. Now one of the family is in heaven, the other wants to get his hands on la Zuppidda; they can't keep that shattered boat afloat, yet they're trying to marry off the girl. All they think about is marriage; it's an obsession, like with my niece la Vespa. Now that Mena is getting married, you'll see how comare Mosca will come

111

back, to grab la Vespa's smallholding.'

Finally they blamed the lawyer, who persisted in writing endless letters before sending in the bailiff.

'It must have been padron 'Ntoni who told him to go slow,' added Piedipapera; 'you can buy ten *rotoli* of lawyers with one *rotolo* of fish.'

This time he had broken in earnest with the Malavoglia, because la Zuppidda had gone to remove comare Grazia's washing from the side of the wash place and had put her own there; the sort of offensive behaviour which makes your blood boil; la Zuppidda dared to do this because she was backed up by that goon 'Ntoni Malavoglia, who was a noted bully. A pack of swine, those Malavoglia, and she didn't want even a distant glimpse of those mugs of theirs that that other mug don Giammaria had christened with his damned holy water.

Then the red tape began to fly, and Piedipapera said that the lawyer couldn't have been sufficiently satisfied with padron 'Ntoni's present to allow himself to be bought, and that proved what a stingy band they were, and whether you could believe them when they promised to pay. Padron 'Ntoni started rushing to the town clerk again and to Scipioni the lawyer; but the lawyer just laughed in his face, and told him that 'fools should stay at home,' that he shouldn't allow his daughter-in-law to 'set her mind to it' and that he had made his bed and now he would have to lie on it. 'The stumbler may not call for help.'

'Now you listen to me,' don Silvestro put it to him. 'You're better off giving him the house, otherwise you'll lose the *Provvidenza* too in expenses, let alone your peace of mind; and you'll waste your earning time too, coming and going to that lawyer.'

'If you hand over the house without a fuss,' Piedipapera said to him, 'we'd leave you the *Provvidenza*, so you'll always be able to earn your bread, and you'll be self-employed still, and there won't be any bailiffs with documents.'

Compare Tino hadn't an ounce of gall in him, and he spoke to padron 'Ntoni as if it were nothing to do with him, putting his arm around his neck, and saying: 'Look, my friend, I feel worse about this than you do, throwing you out of your own

112

house, but what can I do? I'm just a poor devil; I took those five hundred *lire* from my own mouth, and charity begins at home. In all conscience, if I were rich like zio Crocifisso I wouldn't so much as mention it.'

The poor man didn't have the courage to tell his daughter-in-law that they should go without a struggle, after they had been there so long, and it was almost as if they were having to leave the village, and go into exile, or were like those who had left and had been supposed to come back, but then hadn't, and Luca's bed was still there, and the nail where Bastianazzo used to hang up his jacket. But in the end they had to take all those poor household belongings down from their places and go off with them, and each one left a mark where it had been, and the house seemed a different place, without them. They took their things away at night, to the little house which they had rented from the butcher, as though the whole village didn't know that the house by the medlar tree belonged to Piedipapera now, and that they had had to leave it; but at least no one saw them with their belongings in their arms.

When the old man pulled out a nail, or took a small table from its usual position in the corner, he gave a little shake of the head. Then they all sat down on the mattresses which were piled up in the middle of the room, to rest a little and they looked around to see if they had forgotten anything; but padron 'Ntoni soon got up and went into the courtyard, into the open air.

But there was straw scattered everywhere there too, and broken pieces of pot, shattered lobster pots and, in one corner, the medlar tree, and the vine over the door, all tendrils. 'Let's go,' he said. 'Let's go, children. What difference does it make whether it's to-day or tomorrow! . . . ' and still he didn't move.

Maruzza was looking at the courtyard door through which Luca and Bastianazzo had gone, and the little street down which her son had walked with his trousers tucked in, while it was raining, and then vanished from sight under his oilskin. And Alfio Mosca's window was closed too, and the vine was hanging from the courtyard wall, tugged at by every idle passer-by. Everyone had something to look at in that house, and as he was leaving the old man put a surreptitious hand on the battered door which, as zio Crocifisso had said, needed a couple of nails and a solid bit of wood.

Zio Crocifisso too had gone to have a look, along with Piedipapera, and they were talking out loud in the empty rooms, so that the words could be heard as though they were in church. Compare Tino had been unable to survive by living on thin air until that day, and had had to sell everything back to zio Crocifisso, to get his money back.

'What can I do, compare Malavoglia?' he said to him, putting his arms round his neck. 'You know I'm a poor devil, and five hundred *lire* means something to me. If you'd been rich I would have sold it to you.' But padron 'Ntoni couldn't bear going round the house like that, with Piedipapera's arm around his neck. Now zio Crocifisso had come with the carpenter and builder, and all kinds of people who were sauntering hither and thither through the rooms as though they were in the square, and saying: 'You could do with some tiles here, a new beam here, the shutter needs mending here,' as though they owned the place; and they also said that the house should be whitewashed, and then it would look like another house altogether.

Zio Crocifisso was scuffling through the straw and broken shards, and even picked up a piece of what had been Bastianazzo's hat, and threw it into the vegetable patch, where it might serve as manure. Meanwhile the medlar tree still rustled gently, and the garlands of daisies, shrivelled by now, were still hanging at the door and windows, as they had been hung on Ascension Day.

La Vespa had come to see too, with her knitting at the neck of her dress, and was poking through everything, now that it all belonged to her uncle. 'Blood is thicker than water,' she said loudly, so that even the deaf man might hear. 'I care about my smallholding.' Zio Crocifisso let her speak on and didn't seem to hear, now that compare Alfio's door was there for all to see, with its great bolt. 'Now that compare Alfio's door is bolted, you can set your heart at rest, and I'm not thinking of him, as you can imagine,' said la Vespa into zio Crocifisso's ear.

'My heart *is* at rest,' he answered. 'Don't you worry.'

From then onwards the Malavoglia didn't dare show themselves in the streets or in church on Sundays, and they went all the way to Aci Castello for mass, and no one greeted them any more, not even padron Cipolla who went round saying: 'Padron 'Ntoni shouldn't have played that trick on me. It's tantamount to deceiving your neighbour, if they involved his daughter-in-law's affairs in the lupin debt.'

'Just what my wife says,' added mastro Zuppiddo. 'She says that now even dogs avoid the Malavoglia.'

But that bird brain Brasi stamped his feet and wanted Mena, whom he had been promised, like a child at the toy stand in a fair.

'Do you think I stole your property, you blockhead', his father said to him, 'to be willing to throw in your lot with someone who has nothing?'

They had even taken away Brasi's new suit, and he gave vent to his feelings by going and digging out lizards on the *sciara*, or sitting astride the wall at the wash place, and swore not to lift a finger again, not even if they killed him, now that they wouldn't give him his wife, and they had even taken away his wedding suit; luckily Mena couldn't see him dressed as he was, because the Malavoglia too were always behind closed doors, poor things, in the little house belonging to the butcher which they had rented, in the strada del Nero, near the Zuppiddos, and if he chanced to see them in the distance, Brasi ran to hide behind the wall, or among the prickly pears.

Cousin Anna, who saw everything from the beach where she would lay out cloth, said to comare Grazia: 'Now that poor St Agatha will stay at home, like a pot hanging on the wall, exactly like my daughters who have no dowry.'

'Poor thing,' replied comare Grazia, 'and they had even parted her hair.'

But Mena was quite happy, and she had put the little silver sword back into her hair of her own accord, without saying anything. Now she had so much to do in the new house, where everything had to be found a new place, and you could no longer see the medlar tree and the door of cousin Anna's and Nunziata's kitchen. Her mother feasted her eyes on her, while she worked beside her, and seemed almost to caress her with the tone of her voice, when she said: 'Pass me the scissors,' or 'hold my skein,' because she felt for her daughter in her very bowels, now that everyone was turning their backs on them; but the girl sang like a starling, because she was eighteen years old, and at that age if the sky is blue it shines through your eyes, and the birds sing right in your heart. In any case she had never had any feeling for that fellow, she told her mother in a low voice, while they were laying out the threads. Her mother was the only person who had seen into her heart, and who had let a kind word fall amidst all that distress. 'If only compare Alfio were here, he wouldn't turn his back on us. But when the new wine is ready, he'll come back too.'

The neighbourhood women, poor things, hadn't turned their backs on the Malavoglia either. But cousin Anna was so busy, with all she had to do to keep her head above water with her daughters, who were still on her hands just like unused saucepans, and comare Piedipapera was ashamed to show herself because of that trick that compare Tino had played on the poor Malavoglia. She had a good heart, gnà Grazia, and she didn't go along with her husband when he said that she should leave them be, because they had neither king nor kingdom, and anyway what were they to her? The only person they saw from time to time was Nunziata, with the little one in her arms, and all the others trailing behind; but even she kept herself to herself.

And that is how the world goes. It is each man for himself: as comare Venera said to padron 'Ntoni's 'Ntoni, charity begins at home. 'Your grandfather gives you nothing, what obligation have you towards him? If you marry, you'll set up on your own, and what you earn will go towards your own home. 'God blessed a hundred hands, but not all in the same dish'.'

'That's a fine way of looking at things,' answered 'Ntoni. 'Now that my family is in trouble, you tell me to desert them along with the rest! How will my grandfather keep the *Provvidenza* going and find food for them all, if I leave him?'

'Then sort it out among yourselves,' exclaimed la

Zuppidda, turning her back to him to go and poke around in the drawers, or in the kitchen, throwing things into confusion in order to seem to be doing something, so as not to look him in the eye. 'My daughter's not stolen property! One could turn a blind eye if you had nothing, because you're young, and you've always got your health, so you can work, and you're in a good line of business, especially since husbands are scarce now, with that fiendish conscription which whisks all the young men out of the village; but if the dowry you're given has to be pocketted by your whole family, that's another matter! I only want one husband for my daughter, not five or six, and I don't want to make two families dependent on her.'

Barbara, in the other room, pretended not to hear, and carried on firmly with her woolwinding. But as soon as 'Ntoni appeared on the threshold she lowered her eyes to the spools, and her face lengthened too. So that the poor lad went yellow and green and a hundred colours, and didn't know what to do, because Barbara had him ensnared like a sparrow with those great dark eyes of hers, and she said to him: 'That means that you don't love me as much as you love your own family!' and began to cry into her apron when her mother wasn't there.

'Hang it all,' exclaimed 'Ntoni, 'I'd rather go back to soldiering!' And he tore his hair and pummelled his head, but he couldn't resolve himself to take the right decision, like the real oaf that he was. 'Well then,' said la Zuppidda, 'birds of a feather must flock together.' And her husband repeated: 'I told you to steer clear of the whole thing!' 'You go and get on with your work,' she replied, 'because you know nothing about it.'

Everytime he went to the Zuppiddo's house, 'Ntoni found long faces, and gnà Venera continued to reproach him for the fact that the Malavoglia had invited Grazia Piedipapera to comb Mena's hair — 'and a fine job she made of it!' — in order to lick compare Tino's boots, because of those few pennies owing on the house; but he'd taken the house all the same, and had left them stripped to their undergarments like the infant Jesus.

'Do you think I don't know what your mother Maruzza

said all that time when she had her nose in the air — that Barbara wasn't right for her son 'Ntoni because she had been brought up as a lady, and didn't know what was needed to be a good sailor's wife. They told me at the wash place, comare Mangiacarrubbe and gnà Cicca.'

'Comare Mangiacarrubbe and gnà Cicca are two old gossips,' answered 'Ntoni, 'and they were just irritated that I didn't marry the Mangiacarrubbe girl.'

'You can have her as far as I'm concerned. And what a bit of luck for *her*!'

'If you say that to me, comare Venera, it is tantamount to telling me not to set foot in your house again.'

'Ntoni wanted to act the man, and didn't show himself around there for two or three days. But little Lia, who knew nothing of such chatterings, continued to go and play in comare Venera's courtyard, as they had accustomed her to doing, when Barbara gave her prickly pears and chestnuts, because she loved her brother 'Ntoni, and now they didn't give her anything any more; and la Zuppidda would say to her: 'Is it your brother you've come looking for? Your mother is afraid they'll steal him from you!'

And comare la Vespa would go into the Zuppiddos' courtyard too, with her knitting at her neck, saying inflammatory things about men, who were worse than dogs. And Barbara would say pointedly to the little girl: 'I know I'm not as good a housekeeper as your sister!' and comare Venera would conclude: 'Your mother is a washerwoman, and instead of twittering about other people's doings at the wash place, she would do better to give a rinse to that few ha'porth worth of a dress you've got on.'

Much of this went over the little girl's head; but what little she did answer annoyed la Zuppidda, and led her to say that it was her mother Maruzza who put her up to it and sent her round there on purpose to annoy her, so that finally the little girl stopped going there, and gna Venera said it was better like that, then they wouldn't come to the house snooping, still afraid of being robbed of that precious nincompoop of theirs.

Things reached a point where comare Venera and la Longa no longer talked to one another, and if they saw each other in church they turned their backs on one another.

'Soon they'll be getting out the brooms,' said the Mangia-carrubbe girl gleefully, 'or my name isn't Mangiacarrubbe. That business of la Zuppidda and the Booby is a fine carry on.'

Usually the men don't meddle in such women's quarrels, otherwise matters would go from bad to worse and might end up with knives; but after they have put the brooms out, and given vent to their fury by swearing, and tearing each other's hair, neighbourhood women are immediately reconciled, and hug and kiss each other, and stand at their doorways talking just like before. And 'Ntoni, bewitched by Barbara's eyes, had gone back on the sly to stand under her window, to make up, but gnà Venera felt like throwing the bean water over his head, sometimes, and even her daughter shrugged her shoulders, now that the Malavoglia had neither king nor kingdom.

And she said as much to his face, finally, to rid herself of the whole matter, because the lad was always standing outside her door like a puppy dog, and would make her lose such chances as she had, if ever anyone else might have the intention of passing that way with her in mind.

'Come now, compare 'Ntoni, the fish in the sea are for those who can eat them; let's just resign ourselves and think no more about it.'

'You may be able to resign yourself, comare Barbara, but as for me, 'love cannot be compelled.''

'Just you try — you'll find you can do it as well as the next man. You loose nothing by trying. I wish you well and all good luck, but now leave me to my own affairs, because I'm already twenty two.'

'I knew you were bound to say that to me when they took the house away from us, now that everyone is against us.'

'Listen, compare 'Ntoni, my mother may come in from one moment to the next, and it wouldn't be right for her to find you with me.'

'Yes, that's true; now that they've taken away the house by the medlar tree, it's not right.' He felt heavy at heart, poor 'Ntoni, and didn't want to leave her like that. But she had to go and fill the jug at the fountain, and said goodbye to him, running off swiftly and swinging her hips bravely — she was called Zuppidda, the lame, because her father's grandfather had broken his leg in a cart accident at the feast of Trecastagni, but Barbara had two fine legs of her own and no mistake about it.

'Goodbye, comare Barbara,' the poor fellow answered, and thus they let bygones be bygones and he went back to rowing like a galley slave, from Monday to Saturday, and he was tired of being driven mad for nothing, because when you have nothing it is pointless to slave away from morning to night, and not find even a dog who welcomes you, and that was why he had had a belly full of that life; he would have preferred really to do nothing, to stay in bed malingering, like when he was fed up of military service, and his grandfather didn't examine him as carefully as the doctor on the frigate. 'What's the matter?' he asked him.

'Nothing, that's what. The matter is that I'm a poor devil.

'And what can you do about that? We have to live as we were born.'

Unwillingly he allowed himself to be loaded up with tackle worse than some poor donkey, and the whole day long he didn't open his mouth except to grumble or to swear: 'People who fall in the water are bound to get wet.' If his brother happened to sing, while they were under sail, 'yes, yes, sing on. When you're old, you'll bark like grandfather, too,' he would snap.

'Well, you won't gain anything by barking now,' the boy replied.

'You're right — since life is so good.'

'Good or not, it's our own doing,' said his grandfather.

In the evening he ate his soup in a sulk, and on Sundays he went to hang around the wine shop, where all people had to do was laugh and enjoy themselves and forget about the next day when they would have to go back to doing what they had done the whole week; or he would stay for hours on end sitting on the church steps, with his chin cupped in his hand, watching people go by, musing about those trades where you have nothing to do.

At least on Sundays he enjoyed those things in life which

are free — the sun, standing with your hands tucked beneath your armpits doing nothing, and then he was irritated even by the effort of thinking about his condition, by wanting those things he'd seen as a soldier and with whose memory he used to wile away the time on working days. He liked to stretch out like a lizard in the sun and do nothing more. And when he met carters who were sitting on their shafts, he would mutter that theirs was a fine trade, going around in a carriage all day, and if he saw some poor old woman pass by, coming back from town, bent under her load like a tired donkey and complaining as she went, as old people do:

'I wish I could be doing what you're doing, my sister,' he would say to comfort her. 'When all's said and done, it's really like taking a stroll.'

CHAPTER X

'Ntoni's fate was to take a stroll on the sea every blessed day, a back-breaking stroll with oars. But when the sea was rough, and threatened to swallow them up in a single gulp — then, the *Provividenza*, and everything else besides — then the boy had a courage that was bigger than the sea itself.

'It's the Malavoglia blood,' said his grandfather; and he was a sight to see, on the rigging, with his hair whistling in the wind, while the boat leapt over the breakers like a lovesick mullet.

Old and patched up as she was, the *Provvidenza* often ventured out to sea, lured by the prospect of that bit of a catch, now that there were so many boats scouring the sea. Even on those days when the clouds were low, towards Agnone, and the horizon bristling with black dots to the east, you could always see the *Provvidenza's* sail like a pockethand-kerchief, far away on the leaden-looking sea, and everyone said that padron 'Ntoni's family were troubling trouble. Padron 'Ntoni would reply that what he was looking for was bread, and when the corks disappeared one by one, in the open sea which was as green as grass, and the little houses of Trezza blurred into a white splodge, and all you could see was water, he could begin to chat with his grandsons out of sheer contentment, and then in the evening la Longa and all the others would be there waiting for them on the shore, when they saw the sail peeking out from between the tall rocks, and they too would be able to look at the catch leaping in the fish baskets and filling the bottom of the boat like so much silver; and before anyone could open their mouths, padron 'Ntoni would say, 'a hundred kilos,' and he wouldn't be so much as a *rotolo* out; and they would talk about it all evening, while the women ground the salt between the stones, and they would count the barrels one by one, and zio Crocifisso came to see how they had done, to make his offer blind, and Piedipapera shouted and swore to get the right price, but in those circumstances Piedipapera's shouts were a joy to hear, because you mustn't bear people grudges in this world, and then la Longa would count out the money Piedipapera brought in a handkerchief penny by penny in front of her father-in-law, and say: 'This is for the house! and this is for the household expenses.' Mena too helped grind the salt, and arrange the barrels, and now she was once again wearing her dark blue dress and the coral necklace they had had to give to zio Crocifisso as a pledge; now the women could go to mass in the village again, so that it didn't matter if the occasional young man cast looks in Mena's direction, now that her dowry was being built up once again.

'As far as I'm concerned,' said 'Ntoni, wielding his oar gently, so that the current wouldn't carry them out of the circle of nets, 'so far as I'm concerned, all I want is for that horror Barbara to have to gnaw her elbows when we've got things sorted out, and to have to regret having slammed her door in my face.'

'The pilot in the dangerous seas is known', answered the old man. 'When we're back to where we were, everyone will be pleased to see us, and will open their doors to us again.'

'The people who haven't slammed their doors in our faces,' added Alessi, 'are Nunziata, and cousin Anna.'

'A friend in need is a friend indeed. That's why the good Lord helps Nunziata and Anna, with all those mouths they have to feed.'

'When Nunziata goes out to get wood on the *sciara*, or if her bundle of cloth is too heavy, I help her too, poor thing,' said Alessi.

'*Now* will you help by pulling on this side, because St Francis is being bounteous.' The boy pulled and dug in his feet, and puffed and panted as though he were doing it all himself. Meanwhile 'Ntoni was singing, stretched out on the footrest with his arms beneath his head, watching the white seagulls flying against the boundless deep blue sky, and the

Provvidenza bobbed on the green waves, which came from as far away as the eye could see.

'How come the sea is sometimes green, sometimes dark blue, sometimes white and then black as the *sciara*, and not always the same colour like the water that it is?' asked Alessi.

'It's the will of God,' replied his grandfather. 'That way the sailor knows when he can put to sea without fear, and when it's better not to go.'

'Those gulls have a fine life, flying about up there, and out of danger if the sea is rough.'

'But they don't get anything to eat either, poor things.'

'So everyone needs good weather, just like Nunziata who can't go to the fountain if it's raining,' concluded Alessi.

'Good weather and bad weather, neither kind will last forever,' observed the old man.

But when the weather was bad, or the mistral was blowing, and the corks were dancing on the water all day long, as though they were listening to the violin, or the sea was as white as seething milk, or rippling as though it were boiling, then it was another kettle of fish altogether, and 'Ntoni had no desire to sing, with his greatcoat over his nose, and he had to bail the water out of the *Provvidenza* and it seemed endless, and his grandfather would calmly say: 'when wind is in the east, it's neither good for man or beast,' or 'rain comes scouth when the wind's in the south', as though they were there to have lessons in proverbs; and when he stood assessing the weather from the window with his nose in the air of an evening, he would use those same blessed proverbs to say that when the moon was red there would be a wind, and when it was bright, it would be calm; and when it was pale, it would rain.

'If you know it will rain, why are we going to sea to-day?' 'Ntoni would ask him. 'Wouldn't it be better to stay in bed for for another couple of hours?'

'When ther ṣ water from heaven, there are sardines in the nets,' the old man would reply. 'Ntoni would rant and rave, knee deep in water.

'This evening,' his grandfather said to him, 'Maruzza will have a fire ready for us, to dry us out.'

And that evening at dusk, as the *Provvidenza*, with her belly full of God's bounty, was returning home, with her sail billowing like donna Rosolina's skirt, and the lights of the houses winking one by one behind the tall black rocks, so that it seemed as though they were calling one another, padron 'Ntoni pointed to the fine fire which was flaming in la Longa's kitchen, at the back of the little courtyard in the stradduccia del Nero, because the wall was so low that you could see the whole house from the sea, with the little lean-to for the hens, and the oven to the other side of the door. 'You see, la Longa has a fire waiting for us!' he said jubilantly; and la Longa was waiting for them on the shore with the baskets ready, and when they had to take them back empty they didn't feel like chatting, but if there actually weren't enough baskets, and Alessi had to run home to fetch more, his grand-father would put his hands to his mouth to call: 'Mena, oh Mena,' and Mena knew what that meant, and they all trooped out, Mena, Lia and even Nunziata, with all her little ones behind her — then there was merriment, and no one took any notice of the cold, and the rain, and they would stand in front of the fire and chat until late about the blessed bounty sent by St Francis, and what they would do with the money.

But they were risking their lives making that desperate play for the odd *rotolo* of fish, and on one occasion the Malavoglia were a hair's breadth from losing their lives for love of gain, like Bastianazzo, while they were off Agnone, towards evening, and the sky was so dark you couldn't even see Etna, and the wind was blowing in gusts as though it could speak.

'Foul weather,' said padron 'Ntoni. 'To-day the wind is swinging faster than a silly girl's fancy, and the sea looks like Piedipapera when he's cooking up some vile trick.'

The sea was the colour of the *sciara*, although the sun had not yet gone down, and sometimes it boiled all round them like water in a saucepan.

'Now the seagulls must all be asleep,' observed Alessi.

'They must already have lit the Catania lighthouse,' said 'Ntoni, 'but you can't see anything.'

'Keep the tiller to the north-east, Alessi,' ordered his grandfather. 'In half-an-hour's time you won't be able to see anything at all, it'll be worse than being in an oven.'

'We'd be better off in Santuzza's wine shop on a filthy night like this.'

'Or safely asleep in your bed, don't you mean?' answered his grandfather. 'Then you ought to be a town clerk, like don Silvestro.'

The poor old man had barked all day because of his pains. 'There's a change in the weather,' he would say, 'I can feel it in my bones.'

Suddenly it had become so dark that you couln't see even to swear. Only the waves, when they passed the *Provvidenza*, shone as if they had eyes and wanted to eat her up; and no one dared utter a word any longer, in the midst of that sea which was lowing on all sides.

'I have a feeling', 'Ntoni said suddenly, 'that this evening's catch is going to have to go to the devil.'

'You hush,' his grandfather said to him, and his voice made them feel as small as children, there on the seat where they sat.

You could hear the wind hissing in the *Provvidenza*'s sails, and the rope singing like a guitar string. Suddenly the wind began to whistle like a steam engine when it comes out of the hole in the hill, above Trezza, and a wave came out of nowhere unexpectedly, and made the *Provvidenza* creak like a sack of walnuts, and threw her into the air.

'The sail! Down with the sail,' shouted padron 'Ntoni. 'Cut it, quick!'

With the knife between his teeth, 'Ntoni was clinging to the lateen yard like a cat and, standing on the edge to counter-balance the weight, he let himself dangle over the sea which was howling greedily beneath him.

'Hold firm,' his grandfather shouted to him amid the racket of the waves, which seemed to want to pluck him off, and which suddenly hurled the *Provvidenza* and everything else into the air, making the boat list heavily to one side, so that the water inside her was up to their knees. 'Cut it, quick,' his grandfather repeated.

'Hell's bells', exclaimed 'Ntoni. 'If I cut it, what shall we do when we need to sail?'

'This is no moment for curses, we're in God's hands!'

Alessi was clinging to the tiller, and on hearing his grandfather's words he began to shriek for his mother.

'Now stop that,' his brother shouted at him with the knife between his teeth. 'Stop that or I'll give you a kick, and how!'

'Now cross yourself, and be quiet,' repeated his grandfather. So the boy no longer dared to breath a word.

Suddenly the sail fell all of a piece, so taut had it been, and 'Ntoni gathered it instantly and tied it down tightly.

'You know your trade like your father,' his grandfather said to him, 'and you're as much a Malavoglia as any of them.'

The boat straightened up and took a great bound forward; then she proceeded to somersault through the waves.

'This way with the tiller; you need a firm hand now,' said padron 'Ntoni; and although the boy was clinging to it like a cat, some large waves banged the tiller up against both their chests.

'The oar,' shouted 'Ntoni, 'use your oar, Alessi, you're no baby. Now oars are more important than the tiller.'

The boat creaked under the powerful effort of that pair of arms. And Alessi too, standing braced against the footrest, put all he had into pulling the oars, as best he could.

'Hold steady,' his grandfather shouted to him, though you could hardly hear from one end of the boat to the other, for the whistling of the wind. 'Hold steady, Alessi!'

'Yes, grandfather, yes,' replied the boy.

'Are you afraid?' 'Ntoni asked him.

'Of course not,' his grandfather answered for him. 'But we should commend our souls to God.'

'Jesus Christ,' exclaimed 'Ntoni, his chest heaving, 'here you need arms made of iron like a steam engine. The sea is getting the better of us.'

His grandfather was silent and they stopped to listen to the storm.

'Mother is probably down on the shore watching out for us,' Alessi then said.

'Never mind mother,' said his grandfather, 'it's best not to think of her.'

'Where are we?' asked 'Ntoni after another pause,

wheezing with exhaustion.

'In God's hands,' answered his grandfather.

'Leave me to cry then,' said Alessi, who couldn't take any more. And he began to shriek and call for his mother aloud, in the midst of the noise of the wind and the sea; and no one dared to scold him any longer.

'You can bleat all you like, but no one can hear you, and you'd do better to keep quiet,' his brother said to him at last in a changed voice, so that he himself hardly recognised it. 'Be quiet, it isn't any good crying like that now, either for you or for anyone else.

'The sail,' ordered padron 'Ntoni; 'the tiller into the wind to the north-east, and God's will be done.'

The wind hampered matters, but in five minutes the sail was unfurled, and the *Provvidenza* began to leap over the waves, bowing from one side to another like an injured bird. The Malavoglia stood to one side, clinging to the edge; and at that moment no one breathed, because when the sea utters in that way human beings daren't open their mouths.

All padron 'Ntoni said was: 'They'll be telling their beads for us there now.'

And they said no more, running with the wind and waves, in the darkness which had come upon them all of a sudden, as black as pitch.

'The light on the quay,' shouted 'Ntoni, 'can't you see it?'

'To starboard,' shouted padron 'Ntoni, 'to starboard! It's not the quay light. We're going on to the rocks. Take in the sail.'

'I can't,' said 'Ntoni, his voice stiffled by storm and effort, 'the sheet is wet. The knife, Alessi, quick!'

'Cut then, and fast!'

At that moment there was a sudden splintering sound: the *Provvidenza,* which had been bowed to one side, shot up like a spring, and almost threw the lot of them into the sea; yard and sail fell on to the boat, broken as a bit of straw. Then a voice was heard moaning, like someone at death's door.

'Who is it? Who's shouting?' asked 'Ntoni, using teeth and knife to cut the cord at the edges of the sail, which had fallen on to the boat along with the mast and was covering

everything. Suddenly a gust of wind took it right away and
carried it off, hissing. Then the two brothers were able
completely to free the stump of the yard and throw it into the
sea. The boat righted itself, but not so padron 'Ntoni, nor did
he answer 'Ntoni when he called him. Now, when sea and
wind shriek together, there is nothing more frightening than
not receiving an answer to your own call.

'Grandfather,' Alessi shouted too, and as they heard
nothing, the hair stood up on the two brothers' heads. The
night was so black that you couldn't see from one end of the
Provvidenza to the other, so that Alessi actually stopped crying from sheer shock. Their grandfather was stretched out on
the bottom of the boat, his head broken. 'Ntoni finally felt his
way towards him and thought he was dead, because he wasn't
breathing or moving at all. The tiller kept banging hither and
thither, while the boat first leapt into the air, then plum-
metted into the abyss.

'Blessed St Francis of Paola, help us,' the two boys
shrieked, now that they didn't know what else to do.

St Francis in his mercy heard them, as he was going
through the storm to the help of his devotees, and he laid his
cloak beneath the *Provvidenza*, just as she was about to break
open like a nutshell on the *scoglio dei colombi*, below the
customs' look-out point.

The boat bounded over the rock like a colt, and then ran
aground sharply, nose downwards. 'Courage,' the guards
shouted to them from the shore, and ran this way and that
with their lanterns, throwing out ropes. 'We're here! Keep
going!' At last one of the ropes fell athwart the *Provvidenza*,
which was trembling like a leaf, and right across 'Ntoni's face
worse than a whiplash, but at that moment it felt better than a
caress.

'Throw it here,' he shouted, grasping the rope as it ran
rapidly through his hands, ready to slip away altogether.
Alessi too clung on with all his strength, and somehow they
managed to wrap it round the tiller once or twice, and the
customs guards pulled them to shore.

But padron 'Ntoni still gave no sign of life, and when they
put the lantern up to his face they saw that it was streaked

with blood, so that they all thought he was dead, and his grandsons began to tear their hair. But after a couple of hours don Michele, Rocco Spatu, Vanni Pizzuto and all the loafers who had been in the wine shop when they heard the news came running, and they got him to open his eyes by dint of cold water and a lot of rubbing. When he realised where he was, the poor old man asked them to carry him home on a ladder, because it was less than an hour to Trezza.

Shrieking on the square and beating their breasts Maruzza, Mena and the neighbours saw him arriving like that, stretched out on the ladder and as white as a corpse.

'It's nothing,' don Michele assured them, leading the crowd, 'a mere nothing,' and he rushed to the chemist for medicinal vinegar. Don Franco came in person holding the little bottle in his hands, and Piedipapera, comare Grazia, and the Zuppiddos, padron Cipolla and the whole neighbourhood came rushing up too, into the strada del Nero, because on such occasions all quarrels are forgotten, and even la Locca came along, because she always went wherever there was a crowd, whenever she heard bustle in the village, day or night, almost as though she no longer ever slept and was permanently waiting for her Menico. So people crowded into the little street outside the Malavoglia's house, as though there were a dead man there, and cousin Anna had to shut the door in people's faces.

'Let me in,' shouted Nunziata, banging on the door, having come running up half-dressed. 'Let me see what is going on at comare Maruzza's.'

'What was the point of sending us for the ladder, if you don't let us into the house to see what's up?' yelled la Locca's son.

Zuppidda and the Mangiacarrubbe girl had forgotten all the insults they had exchanged, and were chatting outside the door, with their hands under their aprons. 'That's what it's like in that business, you end up paying with your life,' said Zuppidda, 'and if you marry your daughter with seagoing folk one day or the next you'll have her coming home a widow, and with orphans into the bargain, and if it hadn't been for don Michele there wouldn't be a single male

Malavogia left to-night.' The best thing seemed to be one of those who did nothing and earned their daily bread all the same, like don Michele, for instance, who was bigger and fatter than a cleric, and always wore fine cloth, and got fat on half the village, and everyone pandered to him; even the chemist, who wanted to get rid of the king, bowed and scraped to him, with his nasty great black hat.

'It's nothing,' don Franco came out and said; 'we've bound him up; but now he has to run a fever, or he's a dead man.'

Piedipapera wanted to go and see too, because he was almost like one of the family, and padron Fortunato, and anyone else who could elbow their way in.

'I don't like the look of him,' pronounced padron Cipolla, shaking his head. 'How do you feel, compare 'Ntoni?'

'This is why padron Fortunato didn't want to give his son to St Agatha,' Zuppidda commented meanwhile, left in the doorway as she was. 'That wretched man has a sixth sense.'

And la Vespa added: 'Property at sea is writ on water.' Landed property is what you need.'

'What a night for the Malavoglia,' exclaimed comare Piedipapera. 'All the disasters for this house happen at night,' observed padron Cipolla, as he left the house with don Franco and compare Tino.

'All because they were trying to earn an honest crust, poor things,' added Grazia.

For two or three days padron 'Ntoni was more dead than alive. The fever had come, as the chemist had said, but it had come on so strongly that it almost carried the sick man off. The poor fellow no longer complained, lying in his corner, and when Mena or la Longa took him something to drink he clutched the jug with trembling hands, as though they were trying to snatch it from him.

Don Ciccio came in the mornings, tended the wounds, felt his pulse, had him put out his tongue and then went off shaking his head.

One night they even left the candle alight, when don Ciccio had shaken his head particularly firmly; la Longa had put the image of the Virgin beside him, and they were telling their beads by the sick man's bed, and he wasn't even breathing and didn't even want any water, and no one went to sleep, so that Lia was practically dislocating herself yawning, she was so sleepy. The house had an ominous silence about it, so that the carts passing on the road made the glasses dance on the table, and caused the people watching over the sick man to start; and the whole of the next day went by like this, too, and the neighbours stood on the doorstep, chatting among themselves in low voices, keeping an eye on everything through the doorway. Towards evening padron 'Ntoni asked to see his family one by one, and his eyes were dull, and he asked what the doctor had said. 'Ntoni was at the bedside, crying like a child, for he was a good lad at heart.

'Don't cry like that,' said his grandfather. 'Don't cry. You're the head of the household now. Remember that you have others dependent on you, and do as I have done.'

The women began to cry, with their hands in their hair, hearing such talk, even little Lia, since women have no judgement in such circumstances, and they didn't notice that the poor man was becoming distressed at seeing them despair, as if he were about to die. But he continued weakly:

'Don't spend too much on the funeral when I'm gone. The Lord knows we can't afford much, and he'll be satisfied with the rosary that Maruzza and Mena will say for me. You, Mena, always do as your mother has done, for she has been a good woman, and she too has seen her share of troubles; and keep your sister under your wing, as the hen does with her chicks. As long as you help one another, things won't seem so bad. Now 'Ntoni is a grown man, and soon Alessi will be able to help you, too.'

'Don't talk like that,' the weeping women begged, as though he were dying of his own free will. 'For pity's sake don't talk like that.' He shook his head sadly, and answered:

'Now that I've said what I wanted to say, my mind is at rest. I'm old. When the oil runs out, the light fades. I'm tired.'

Later he called 'Ntoni again, and said to him:

'Don't sell the *Provvidenza*, old though she is, or you'll be forced to do day labouring, and you can't imagine how hard that is, when padron Cipolla and zio Cola say they don't need anyone for Monday. And the other thing I wanted to say to you, 'Ntoni, is that when you've put a few pennies aside the first thing you must do is marry off Mena, and give her a man from the trade her father plied, but a good fellow; and I also wanted to tell you that when you've married off Lia, too, if you have any savings, put them aside and buy back the house by the medlar tree. Zio Crocifisso will sell it to you, if he makes a profit, because it has always belonged to the Malavoglia, and your father went from there to die, and Luca too, God bless his soul.'

'Yes, grandfather, yes,' promised 'Ntoni weeping. Alessi was listening too, as solemn as though he were a grown man.

The women thought that the sick man was delirious, hearing him talking on like that, and put moistened cloths on his forehead.

'No,' said padron 'Ntoni, 'I'm not delirious. I want to say everything I have to tell you before I go.'

Meanwhile you could hear the fishermen beginning to call one another from one doorway to the next, and the carts started trundling down the road again.

'In two hours it will be day,' added padron 'Ntoni, 'and you can go and call don Giammaria.'

Those poor folk waited for day as you wait for the Messiah, and kept going to the window to see if dawn were breaking. At last the little room began to whiten and padron 'Ntoni said again:

'Now go and get the priest; I want to confess.'

Don Giammaria came when the sun was already high, and when they heard the bell ringing down the strada del Nero, the neighbourhood women came to see the viaticum being taken to the Malavoglia, and they all went in, because you cannot shut the door in people's faces where the Lord is walking, so that those poor creatures, seeing the house so full, didn't even dare to cry and despair, while don Giammaria was muttering away, and mastro Cirino was putting the candle under the sick man's nose, so stiff and yellow he looked like a candle himself.

'He looks like the patriarch St. Joseph in person, laid out on that bed with that long beard. Lucky him,' exclaimed

Santuzza, who had set down jugs and all, and always went where she felt the presence of the Lord.

'Like a crow,' as the chemist said.

Don Ciccio arrived while the parish priest was still there with the holy oil, and indeed he almost turned his donkey's head and went off again.

'Who said there was any need for the priest? Who asked for the viaticum? It's for us doctors to say when it's time for that; and I'm surprised at the priest coming without the certificate. Now listen here: there's no need for any viaticum. He's better, I tell you!'

'It's a miracle worked by our Lady of Sorrows,' exclaimed la Longa; 'the Virgin has given us a miracle, because the Lord has visited this house once too often!' 'Ah blessed Virgin,' exclaimed Mena with her hands clasped. 'Ah holy Virgin, you have shown us mercy.' And everyone wept with relief, as though the sick man were in a state to step straight back on to the *Provvidenza*.

Don Ciccio went off grumbling:

'That's all the thanks I get. If they survive, it's the Virgin's doing; if they croak, it's my fault!'

The neighbourhood women were waiting at the door to see the dead man pass, because they had been thought to be coming to get him from one moment to the next.

'Poor thing,' they muttered too. 'That man has a tough hide; he's got nine lives, like a cat. You listen to what I'm telling you,' said Zuppidda hectoringly. 'I tell you, he'll outlive us all.' The women made as if to touch wood.

'I'm protected by being a Daughter of Mary,' and la Vespa even kissed the medal on her scapular. 'Fee fie foe fum, thunder in the air means sulphurous wine,' Zuppidda added.

'At least you have no children to marry off, as I have, which means I would cause serious problems if I were to go under the sod.' The others laughed, because la Vespa had only herself to marry off, and she couldn't manage even to do that.

'As far as that's concerned, padron 'Ntoni would cause the most problems of all, because he's the pillar of the household,' replied cousin Anna.

'That nincompoop 'Ntoni isn't a child any longer.' But

134

they all shrugged. 'If the old man dies, you'll see how that household will crumble.'

At this point Nunziata came running up, with her pitcher on her head.

'Make way, they're waiting for water at comare Maruzza's. And if my children start to play around, they'll leave everything all over the road.'

Lia had taken up a position in the doorway, all proud and saying to the neighbours:

'Grandfather is better, don Ciccio says he's not going to die quite yet,' and she could hardly believe her luck when the women stood there listening to her as though she were a grown women. Alessi too came out and said to Nunziata:

'Now that you're here, I'll go and have a quick look at what's happening to the *Provvidenza.*'

'That lad has more sense than his older brother,' said cousin Anna.

'They'll give don Michele a medal for having thrown a rope to the *Provvidenza,*' said the chemist. 'And then there's a pension. That's how they spend people's money.'

In don Michele's defence, Piedipapera went round saying that he had deserved it, both medal and pension, because he had thrown himself knee deep into the water, with those great boots, to save the Malavoglia's lives, which was quite something: three people! And he had been within inches of losing his own life, and everyone was talking about it, so that on Sunday, when he put on his new uniform, the girls feasted their eyes on him, gazing at him to see if he had a medal.

'Now that she has got that great Malavoglia idiot out of her mind, Barbara Zuppidda will take a more kindly interest in don Michele,' Piedipapera went round saying. 'I've seen her with her nose between the shutters when he passes by.'

And don Silvestro, hearing this, said to Vanni Pizzuto:

'A fine advantage you've gained yourself, getting padron 'Ntoni's 'Ntoni out of the way, now that Barbara has her eye on don Michele!'

'If she has, she'll soon take it off again, because her mother won't have anything to do with policemen, or spongers, or foreigners.'

135

'You'll see. Barbara is twenty three, and if she gets it into her head that by waiting for a husband she'll start to moulder, she'll take him by hook or by crook. I'll bet you twelve *tari* that they're still talking to one another from the window,' and he pulled out the new five *lire* bit.

'I won't bet anything,' replied Pizzuto, shrugging, 'I don't give a hang.'

The people who were standing around listening, Piedipapera and Rocco Spatu, choked themselves laughing.

'I'll take you on for nothing,' added don Silvestro, suddenly good-humoured; and he went off with the others to chat with zio Santoro, in front of the wine shop.

'Listen, zio Santoro, do you want to win twelve *tari*?' and he brought out the new coin, although zio Santoro couldn't see it —

'Mastro Vanni Pizzuto wants to bet twelve *tari* that now don Michele the sergeant will go and talk with Barbara Zuppidda, of an evening. Do you want to win those twelve *tari*?'

'Holy souls in Purgatory,' exclaimed zio Santoro kissing his rosary; he had been listening intently with his sightless eyes; but he was ill at ease; and his lips were twitching like a hunting dog's ears when it scents quarry.

'They're friends, don't worry,' added don Silvestro smirking. 'It's compare Tino and Rocco Spatu,' added the blind man, after a moment's concentration.

He knew everyone who went by, by the sound of their steps, whether they wore shoes or went barefoot, and he would say:

'That's compare Tino', or: 'that's compare Cinghialenta.' And since he was always there, telling jokes with this person or that, he knew everything that was happening in all the village; so to lay his hands on those twelve *tari*, as the children came to get their wine for supper, he called them:

'Alessi, or Nunziata, or Lia,' and then asked: 'Have you seen don Michele? Does he go down the strada del Nero?'

As long as it had been necessary, 'Ntoni, poor lad, had run hither and thither eagerly, and he too had torn his hair. Now that his grandfather was better, he wandered round the village, with his hands under his armpits, waiting to be able to take the *Provvidenza* to mastro Zuppiddo again to have her patched up; and he went to the wine shop to have a chat, since he hadn't a penny to his name, and told people how he had looked death in the eye, and that was how he passed his time, chatting and hawking. And when he had been offered the odd glass of wine, he expressed anger towards don Michele, who had stolen his beloved, because he had asked Nunziata if don Michele ever went down the strada del Nero.

'By the blood of Judas, if I can't get my revenge for this dishonour, my name isn't 'Ntoni Malavoglia!'

People enjoyed making him full of gall, and so they offered him drinks. While she rinsed out the glasses, Santuzza turned away so as not to hear the curses and swear words they uttered; but hearing talk of don Michele, she steeled herself and stood listening wide-eyed. She too had become curious, and was all ears when they talked, and she would give presents of apples and green almonds to Nunziata's little brother, or Alessi, when they came for wine, to find out who had been seen in the strada del Nero. Don Michele swore black and blue it wasn't true, and often of an evening, when the wine shop was already shut, you could hear all hell breaking loose behind closed doors.

'Liar,' shouted Santuzza. 'Murderer! Thief! Unbeliever!'

The result was that don Michele no longer went to the wine shop, and had to make do with buying wine and drinking it in Pizzuto's shop, alone with his bottle, in order to avoid trouble.

Instead of being pleased that another dog had thus been removed from that bone that was Santuzza, massaro Filippo preferred mild words and tried to get them to make up, so that the whole thing became hopelessly confused. But it was a waste of time.

'Can't you see that he's lying low and not showing his face here any more?' exclaimed Santuzza. 'That is a sign that the thing is absolutely true! No! I don't want to hear any more about it, even if I have to shut the wine shop and start to do knitting!'

Then massaro Filippo looked sour with anger and he went

to beg and beseech don Michele, in the guard's room, or in Pizzuto's shop, to make up that quarrel with Santuzza, after all they had been friends; and now people would talk — and he embraced him and tugged him by the sleeve. But don Michele dug his feet in like a mule, and said no. And those who were present, savouring the scene, observed that massaro Filippo cut a fine figure, as sure as God exists!

'Massaro Filippo needs help,' said Pizzuto. 'That Santuzza would devour the Cross itself!'

Then one fine day Santuzza put on her shawl and went to confession, although it was Monday, and the wine shop was full of people. Santuzza went to confession every Sunday and stayed for an hour with her nose to the grille of the confessional, rinsing out her conscience, which she liked to keep cleaner than her glasses. But that time donna Rosolina, who kept a jealous eye on her the brother the priest, and who also confessed often in order to see what he was up to, was left astounded, there where she was, waiting on her knees, that Santuzza should have such a lot on her mind, and she noticed that her brother the priest blew his nose more than five times.

'What was up with Santuzza to-day for her to take so long?' she asked don Giammaria when they were at table.

'Nothing, nothing,' replied her brother, stretching his hand out towards the plate. But she knew his weak point, leaving the lid on the tureen, and tormented him with questions, so that at last the poor fellow had to say that his lips were sealed, and as long as he was at table he sat with his nose in his plate, and gobbled the maccheroni as if he hadn't seen food for two days, so that it almost choked him, and he grumbled to himself because people would simply never leave him alone. After the meal he took his hat and his cloak, and went to pay a visit to Zuppidda.

'There must be something behind all this,' donna Rosolina muttered. 'There must be some very dirty business between Mariangela and Zuppidda, something he can't talk about because of the seal of confession.' And she went to the window to see how long her brother would stay in comare Venera's house.

Zuppidda was incensed on hearing what suor Mariangela

138

was telling her through don Giammaria, and she went out on to the balcony and yelled that she didn't want other people's second-hand goods, and Santuzza would do well to heed that! And if she saw don Michele going down her road she would gouge out his eyes with the distaff she had ready to hand, despite the pistol he wore across his stomach, because she wasn't afraid of pistols or of anyone, and she wouldn't give her daughter to anyone who ate the king's bread and played the policeman, and he was in mortal sin with Santuzza into the bargain, don Giammaria had told her so under the seal of the confessional but she turned a blind eye to the seal of the confessional when her Barbara was involved — and she swore so much that la Longa and cousin Anna had to close the door so that the little girls shouldn't hear; and her husband mastro Turi too, not to be outdone, bawled:

'If they involve me, I'll do something I'll regret, by God! I'm not afraid of don Michele, or massaro Filippo, or all Santuzza's mob!'

'Be quiet,' comare Venera contradicted him promptly. 'Haven't you heard that massaro Filippo isn't involved with Santuzza any more?'

The others carried on saying that Santuzza had massaro Filippo to help her say her prayers, Piedipapera had seen him.

'Nice work! Massaro Filippo needs help too,' repeated Pizzuto.

'Haven't you seen him coming to beg and beseech don Michele to help him?'

In the chemist's shop don Franco called people in just so he could cackle about the matter.

'I told you so, didn't I? They're all the same, those pious folk! With the devil under their skirts! Now that they're giving don Michele a medal, they can hang it up along with the Daughter of Mary medal that Santuzza's got.' And he poked his head out of the doorway to see if his wife was at the window upstairs. 'Eh! Church and barracks! Throne and altar! Always the same story, you mark my words!'

He wasn't afraid of the sabre and the holy water sprinkler; and he didn't give a hang about don Michele, and indeed he read him a lecture about his behaviour when the Signora wasn't at the window and couldn't hear what was being said in the chemist's shop; but donna Rosolina gave her brother a good ticking off, as soon as she came to hear that he had got himself into that scrape, because sabre-bearers have to be kept sweet.

'Sweet my eye,' replied don Giammaria. 'The people who are taking the bread from our very mouths? I've done my duty. I don't need them. If anything, it's they who need us.'

'At least you ought to say that Santuzza sent you, under the seal of the confessional,' maintained donna Rosolina, 'then you wouldn't have to arouse bad feelings.'

But she went round mysteriously telling all the neighbourhood women and men that it was under the seal of the confessional, when they came buzzing round her wanting to know how the business had come out into the open. Ever since he had heard don Silvestro say that he wanted to have Barbara fall for him like a ripe pear, Piedipapera had gone round whispering:

'This is all don Silvestro's doing, because he wants Barbara to fall for *him.*'

And he said it so often that it reached the ear of donna Rosolina, while she was making the tomato preserve, with her sleeves tucked up, and she exerted herself defending don Michele to people, so that it should be known that they personally didn't wish don Michele ill, although he was a government man; and she said that man is a hunter, and Zuppidda ought to think about looking after her daughter herself, and if don Michele had other involvements this concerned him and his conscience alone.

'This is don Silvestro's doing, because he wants Zuppidda for himself, and he's bet twelve *tari* that he can make her fall for him,' la Vespa told her, while she was helping donna Rosolina to make the tomato preserve; she had come to beg don Giammaria to drum some scruples into the head of that scoundrel zio Crocifisso, because it was harder than a mule's. 'Doesn't he see that he has one foot in the grave?' she said. 'Does he want to die with this on his conscience too?'

But hearing this story about don Silvestro, donna Rosolina

suddenly changed her tune, and began to hold forth with her ladle in the air, as red as her tomato preserve, against men who flatter marriageable girls, and those gossips who stand at windows to hoodwink such men. Everyone knew what sort of a flirt Barbara was; but it was surprising that even someone like don Silvestro should fall for it, because he seemed a man of judgement, and no one would have expected such a betrayal from him; whereas in fact he was looking for trouble with Zuppidda and don Michele, while he had good luck within his grasp, and was letting it go. In this day and age, to know a man you have to eat through a full seven *salme* of salt.

But don Silvestro was seen around arm in arm with don Michele, and no one dared to say a word to their faces about the rumours which were going around. Now donna Rosolina slammed the window in his face, when the town clerk stood gazing upwards from the door of the chemist's shop, and didn't even turn her head when she put the tomato preserve in the sun on the little terrace; then once she went to confess at Aci Castello, because there was something she couldn't confess to her brother, and as it happened she met don Silvestro by chance, just as he was coming back from the vineyard.

'Fancy seeing you,' she began to say, pausing to draw breath, because she was all red and flustered. 'You must have weighty matters on your mind, not to remember old friends.'

'I have nothing on my mind, donna Rosolina.'

'I have been told that you have, and such nonsense it is that it would really weigh you down, if it were true.'

'Who says so?'

'The whole village is talking about it.'

'Let them talk. Anyway, as it happens, I do just as I wish; and if I'm weighed down, as you put it, that's my affair.'

'Much good may it do you,' said donna Rosolina all red in the face. 'It seems to me that these worries are starting to affect you right now, if you answer me in this fashion, and indeed I didn't expect it, because I always thought you were a man of judgement; forgive me if I was mistaken. This is tantamount to saying that 'water afar quenches not the fire,'

141

and 'good weather and bad weather, neither weather lasts for ever.' But don't forget that the proverb says: 'Better the devil you know' and 'handsome is as handsome does.' Enjoy Zuppidda in peace, because it doesn't mean a thing to me. And for all the gold in the world I wouldn't want people to say of me the things they say of your Zuppidda.'

'Don't you worry, donna Rosolina — by now there's nothing anyone *could* say about you.'

'At least people don't say that I wolf up half the village; do you understand me, don Silvestro?'

'Let them say what they wish, donna Rosolina. 'He who has a mouth may eat, and he who doesn't may die.' '

'And they don't say of me what they say of you, either, that you're a defrauder!' continued donna Rosolina, green as garlic. 'Do you understand me, don Silvestro? and one can't say as much of everyone. When you can spare them, I'd be glad of those twenty five *onze* I lent you. I don't steal money, as some people do.'

'Don't you worry, donna Rosolina, I didn't say that you stole your twenty five *onze*, and I shan't go telling your brother, don Giammaria. It doesn't matter to me whether you got them out of the household expenses or not; all I know is, I don't owe you them. You told me to invest them for your dowry, if anyone were to take you in marriage, and I put them in a Bank on your account, in my name, so that the matter shouldn't be discovered by your brother, who would ask where the money came from. Now the Bank has gone bankrupt. What fault is it of mine?'

'You swindler!' Donna Rosolina spat in his face, foaming at the mouth. 'You trickster! I didn't give you that money to put in a bank that would go bankrupt. I gave it to you to cherish as if it were your own!'

'But I did, I did,' answered the town clerk, so brazenly that donna Rosolina turned her back to him so as not to explode with rage, and she went back to Trezza dripping like a sponge, in the heat of the day, with her shawl on her back. Don Silvestro stood there sneering, in front of the wall of massaro Filippo's vegetable patch, until she had rounded the corner, muttering to himself:

142

'I don't care what they say.'

And he was right not to care what they said. They said that if don Silvestro had got it into his head to get Barbara to drop into his arms, then drop she would, such an arrant rascal was he! But they doffed their caps to him, and his friends nodded in his direction, when he went to chat in the chemist's shop.

'You're a masterful fellow!' don Franco said to him, patting his shoulder. 'A real feudal lord! You're the man of destiny, sent down to earth to prove once and for all that the old society must be flushed out!' And when 'Ntoni came to get his grandfather's medicines he would say:

'You're the people. As long as you behave like patient donkeys, you'll get beaten.'

To change the subject, the Signora, who was knitting behind the counter, asked how his grandfather was getting on. 'Ntoni didn't dare open his mouth in front of the Signora, and went off mumbling, with the glass in his hands.

His grandfather was better now, and they put him in the doorway, in the sun, wrapped up in a cloak, with a handkerchief on his head, so that he looked like someone who had returned from the dead, and people used to go and look at him out of curiosity; and the poor old man nodded to this person and that, and smiled, he was so pleased to be there, in his cloak, at the doorway, with Maruzza spinning at his side, the sound of Mena's loom behind him inside, and the hens scratching in the street. Now that he had nothing else to do, he learned to know the hens one by one, and watched what they were doing, and spent the time listening to the neighbour's voices, saying:

'That's comare Venera scolding her husband,' or 'That's cousin Anna coming back from the washplace.' Then he would watch the shadow of the houses lengthening, and when the sun had gone from the doorway, they put him against the wall opposite, so that he was like mastro Turi's dog, who always followed the sun to stretch out in.

At last, he began to be on his feet again, and they took him down to the seashore, because he liked to doze among the stones, nears the boats, and he said that the smell of the salt water did him good; and he passed the time watching the

143

boats, and hearing how other people's days had gone. The men, while they were busy about their own affairs, proferred him the odd word, saying, to comfort him:

'This means there's oil in the old lamp yet, eh, padron 'Ntoni?'

In the evening, when the whole family was at home, with the door closed, while la Longa told her beads, he liked seeing them all there, and gazed at each one of them in turn, and looked at the walls of the house, and the chest with the statuette of the Good Shepherd, and the little table with the light on it;

'I can't believe I'm still here, with all of you,' he would say.

La Longa said that fear had caused a great mix up in her blood and in her head, and that now she didn't seem to have those two poor dead souls before her eyes any longer; whereas until that day they had been like two thorns in her breast, so that she had gone to confess the matter to don Giammaria. But the confessor had given her absolution, because with misfortunes this is what happens, one thorn drives out another, and our Lord doesn't choose to thrust them all in at the same time, because you would die of heartbreak. Her son and husband were dead; she had been driven from her home; but now she was glad that she had managed to pay the doctor and the chemist, and didn't owe anyone anything any more.

Gradually their grandfather began to ask for something to do, saying he couldn't sit like that without doing anything. He mended nets; and wove fish traps; then, leaning on his stick, he began to go as far as mastro Turi's courtyard to see the *Provvidenza*, and stayed there enjoying the sun. Finally he actually went in the boat with his grandsons.

'Just like a cat,' said Zuppidda, 'with nine lives.' La Longa had even put a little bench at the door, and sold oranges, nuts, hard-boiled eggs and black olives.

'Soon she'll be selling wine, too,' said Santuzza. 'I'm delighted, because they're God-fearing people.' And padron Cipolla shrugged his shoulders when he went down the strada del Nero, past the house of those Malavoglias, who now wanted to launch themselves as shopkeepers.

Trade was going well because the eggs were always fresh,

so that now that 'Ntoni hung around the wine shop, Santuzza sent to Maruzza for olives, when there were good drinkers who weren't thirsty. Thus penny by penny they paid mastro Turi Zuppiddo, and had the *Provvidenza* patched up once again, so that now she really did look like an old shoe; but at the same time they put the odd *lira* aside. They had purchased a good stock of barrels, and the salt for the anchovies, if St. Francis were to send good luck, the new sail for the *Provvidenza*, and they had put a bit of money aside in the chest of drawers.

'We're like ants,' said padron 'Ntoni; and he counted the money every day, and then went to amble past the medlar tree, with his hands behind his back. The door was closed, the sparrows were twittering on the roof, and the vine swayed gently in the window. The old man climbed on to the wall of the vegetable garden, where they had sowed onions which were like a sea of white plumes, and then he would run after zio Crocifisso, saying a hundred times:

'You know, zio Crocifisso, if we manage to get that money together for the house, you must sell it to us, because it has always belonged to the Malavoglia'.

' 'Home is home, though it be never so homely,' and I want to die where I was born. 'Happy is the man who dies in his own bed.' ' Zio Crocifisso said yes grudgingly, so as not to compromise himself; and he had a new tile put on the roof, or a trowel-full of lime on the courtyard wall, so that the price would rise. Zio Crocifisso would reassure him, telling him not to worry.

'The house won't run away. All you need to do is keep your eye on it. Everyone keeps their eyes on things that matter to them.' And once he added:

'Aren't you going to marry off your Mena now?'

'I'll marry her off when God wills,' replied padron 'Ntoni; 'if it were up to me I'd marry her off to-morrow.'

'If I were you I'd give her to Alfio Mosca, he's a good boy, honest and hard-working; and he's looking for a wife all over the place, that's his only fault. Now they say he'll come back to the village, and I'd say he's tailor-made for your grand-daughter.'

145

'Didn't they say he wanted to take your niece la Vespa?'

'You too!' Dumb bell began to shout. 'Who says so? That's all gossip; he wants to get his hands on my niece's smallholding, that's what he wants. A fine business, eh? What would you say if I sold your house to someone else?'

Here Piedipapera, who was always hanging around the square, and as soon as two or three people were having a discussion he tried to muscle in to act the broker, promptly poked his nose in as well.

'Now la Vespa has Brasi Cipolla on her hands, since the marriage with St. Agatha went up in smoke, I've seen them with my own eyes, going together along the path by the stream; I'd gone there to look for two smooth stones for the plaster for that leaking trough. And she was acting so coy, the little flirt! with the corners of her handkerchief over her mouth, and saying to him:

'By this blessed medal I've got here, it's not true. Pooh! You make me sick when you talk to me about that doting old uncle of mine!' She was talking about you, zio Crocifisso; and she let him touch her medal, and you know where she keeps it!' Dumb bell was acting dumb, and shaking his head, dumbfounded. Piedipapera went on:

'And Brasi said: 'So what shall we do?' 'I don't know what you're going to do,' answered la Vespa, 'but if it is true that you love me, you won't leave me in this state, because when I don't see you my heart feels as if it's split in two, like two segments of orange, and if they marry you to someone else I swear by this blessed medal I have here, that you'll see something serious happen in this village, and I'll throw myself into the sea with all my clothes.' Brasi scratched his head, and went on:

'As far as I'm concerned, I want nothing more; but what will my father do?'

'Let's leave the village,' she said, 'as if we were man and wife, and when the damage is done, your father will have to say yes. He has no other sons and he doesn't know who to leave his property to.' '

'Pretty goings on, eh,' Zio Crocifisso started to shriek, forgetting that he was deaf.

'That witch has the devil tweaking her under her skirts! And to think that they wear the holy medal of the Virgin round their necks! Padron Fortunato will have to be told, and no two ways about it. We have our standards, don't we? If padron Fortunato doesn't keep a watch out, that witch of a niece of mine will quite simply rob him of his son, poor thing!'

And he ran off down the street like a mad man.

'I beg of you, don't say that I saw them,' shouted Piedipapera, in pursuit. 'I don't want to put myself in the wrong with that viper of a niece of yours.'

In an instant zio Crocifisso had the whole village topsy turvy, and he even wanted to send the guards and don Michele to put la Vespa into custody; after all, she was his niece, and it was his duty to take care of her; and don Michele was paid for that, to watch over decent folks' interests. People enjoyed seeing padron Cipolla running this way and that with his tongue lolling, and they relished the fact that that great ninny of a son of his should have got tangled up with la Vespa, while it seemed that not even Victor Emanuel's daughter was good enough for him, because he had jilted the Malavoglia girl without even so much as a by your leave.

But there had been no black handkerchief for Mena, when Brasi jilted her; indeed now she had started to sing again while she was at her loom, or helping to salt anchovies on fine summer evenings. This time St. Francis really had sent good luck. There had been an anchovy season such as had never been seen, real bounty for the whole village; the boats returned laden, with the men singing and waving their caps from afar, to signal to the women as they waited with their babies in their arms.

The retailers came in crowds from the town, on foot, on horseback, by cart, and Piedipapera didn't have time to scratch his head. Towards evensong there was a positive market on the seashore, and shouts and racketting of all kinds. In the Malavoglia's courtyard the light stayed on till midnight, almost like a party. The girls sang, and the neighbours came to help, because there was enough for everyone to earn something, and there were four rows of barrels all ready lined up along the wall, with their stones weighing down on top.

'This is when I'd like Zuppidda here,' exclaimed 'Ntoni, sitting on the stones so that he too could make weight, with his hands under his armpits.

'Now you can see that we too are doing all right, and we don't give a hang about don Michele and don Silvestro!'

The retailers pursued padron 'Ntoni waving their money. Piedipapera tugged him by the sleeve, saying to him:

'Now is the time to make a profit.' But padron 'Ntoni held out. 'We'll talk about it at All Saints; then the anchovies will get a better price. No, I don't want any deposits, I don't want to tie my hands! I know how things go.' And he brought down his fist on the barrels, saying to his grandchildren:

'This represents your house, and Mena's dowry. 'A man's home is his castle.' St. Francis has granted my prayers and allowed me to close my eyes content.'

At the same time they had laid in all the purchases for the winter, grain, beans and oil; and they had given the deposit to massaro Filippo for that bit of wine they had on Sundays.

Now they were no longer so worried; father-in-law and daughter-in-law resumed their counting of the money in the stocking, of the barrels lined up in the courtyard, and made their calculations to see how much was still needed for the house. Maruzza knew that money sou by sou, the money for the oranges and the eggs, what Alessi had brought back from the railway, what Mena had earned at her loom, and she would say that there was some from everybody.

'Didn't I say that the five fingers of the hand have to pull together to row a good oar?' padron 'Ntoni would repeat. 'We're nearly there now.' And then he would sit in a corner conferring with la Longa, and glancing towards St. Agatha who, poor thing, was only talked about by other people 'because she had neither mouth nor will of her own' and simply concentrated on working, singing to herself as birds do in their nests before dawn; and only when she heard the carts go by, in the evening, did she think of compare Alfio Mosca's cart, which was going round the world, though there was no guessing quite where; and then she would stop singing.

Throughout the village all you could see was people with their nets around their necks, and women sitting on doorsteps pounding tiles; and there was a row of barrels in front of each door, so that just to walk down the street was a treat for the nose, and right from a mile outside the village you could sense that St. Francis had sent bounty; people talked of nothing except pilchards and brine, even in the chemist's shop where they set the world to rights after their own fashion; and don Franco wanted to teach them a new method of salting anchovies, which he had read about in books. When they laughed in his face, he started to shout:

'You're just like cattle, you are! and you want progress! and the republic!' People turned their backs on him, and left him there shrieking like a loon. Ever since the world began anchovies have been made using salt and ground tiles.

'The usual story! That's how my grandfather did it,' the chemist continued to shout after them. 'All you need to be donkeys is a tail! What can you do with people like this? and they make do with mastro Croce Callà, that nodding idiot, because he has always been the mayor; and they'd be quite capable of telling you that they don't want a republic because they've never had one!' He then repeated all this to don Silvestro, in connection with certain discussions they had had in private, although don Silvestro hadn't uttered, it's true, but he had listened intently. And it was known that he was on bad terms with mastro Croce's Betta, because she wanted to act the mayor, and her father had allowed himself to be led by the nose, so that to-day he said one thing and to-morrow another, just as Betta had wanted. And all he could say was:

'I'm the mayor, by Jove!' as his daughter had taught him; and she would rest her hands on her hips when talking with don Silvestro, saying reproachfully:

'Do you think they will always let you lead that poor dear father of mine by the nose, to do your bidding and guzzle up the lot of them? because even donna Rosolina is going round saying that you're gnawing away at the whole village! But you won't eat me, because I'm not obsessed with marriage, and I look after my father's affairs.'

149

Don Franco declared that without new men you couldn't achieve anything, and it was pointless to go running to the big wigs, like padron Cipolla, who told you that by the grace of God he was quite well set up and didn't need to act the unpaid public servant at all; or like massaro Filippo who thought of nothing except his smallholdings and his vines, and who paid attention only when there was talk of putting a tax on wine must.

'Old-fashioned folk,' don Franco concluded with his beard in the air. 'People at home with cliques and factions. In this modern age you need new men.' 'We'll send off to the kiln for another batch,' quipped don Giammaria.

'If things went as they should, we'd be swimming in gold,' said don Silvestro; and that was all he would say.

'You want to know what we need?' said the chemist, in a low voice, casting a glance towards the back of the shop. 'We need people like us!'

And after having whispered this secret in their ear, he ran on tiptoe to stand at the doorway, with his beard in the air, rocking to and fro on his short legs with his hands behind his back.

'Fine people they would be,' muttered don Giammaria. 'You'll find as many as you need in Favignana, or the other prisons, without having to go to any kiln. Go and tell Tino Piedipapera, or that drunkard Rocco Spatu, they are all in favour of the ideas of your time! All I know is that I've been robbed of twenty five *onze*, and nobody has gone to Favignana! Typical of these new times and new men!'

At that moment the Signora came into the shop, with her knitting in her hand, and the chemist promptly swallowed what he was about to say, and carried on muttering into his beard, while pretending to look at the people who were going to the fountain. At last, seeing that everyone had fallen suddenly so silent, don Silvestro said loudly and clearly that the only new men were padron 'Ntoni's 'Ntoni and Brasi Cipolla, because *he* wasn't in awe of the chemist's wife.

'You keep out of this,' the Signora then rebuked her husband; 'it's not your business.'

'I'm not saying anything,' replied don Franco, smoothing

150

his beard.

Now that he had the upper hand, with don Franco's wife there, so that he could throw stones from behind the wall, the parish priest amused himself by irritating the chemist.

'A fine lot, your new men! Do you know what Brasi Cipolla is doing, now that his father is after him to pull his ears because of la Vespa? He's scuttling around hiding all over the place like a naughty schoolboy. Last night he slept in the sacristy; and yesterday my sister had to send him a plate of maccheroni when he was hiding in the chicken run because the great idiot hadn't eaten for twenty four hours and was all over little chickens! And 'Ntoni Malavoglia, he's another fine new man! His grandfather and all the rest of them sweat away to get back on their feet again; but whenever he can skive off with an excuse, he goes sauntering round the village, standing around outside the wine shop, just like Rocco Spatu.'

The council dissolved as it always did, without concluding anything, because everyone kept to their own opinions, and furthermore on that occasion the Signora was there, so that don Franco couldn't give vent to his feelings in his own way.

Don Silvestro was cackling away, and as soon as the conversation broke up he too went off, with his hands behind his back and his head teeming with thoughts.

'Just look at don Silvestro, he's so much more sensible than you,' the Signora said to her husband, while he was shutting up shop. 'He's a man with conviction, and if he has something to say he shuts it inside himself and doesn't utter a word. The whole village knows he swindled twenty five *onze* out of donna Rosolina, but no one will say as much to his face, not to a man like that! But you will always be the kind of fool who can't mind his own business; one of those asses who bray at the moon! a great chatterbox!' 'But what have I done, damn it?' whinged the chemist, walking up the stairs behind her holding the lamp. Did she know what he had said? He did not usually venture on his endless ramblings in front of her. All he knew was that don Giammaria had gone off crossing himself over the square and muttering that they were a fine race of new men, like that 'Ntoni Malavoglia, ambling round the village at this hour!'

151

CHAPTER XI

Once, on his amblings, 'Ntoni Malavoglia had seen two young men who had set sail a few years earlier from Riposto in search of their fortunes, and who were now coming back from Trieste, or perhaps Alexandria, the one in Egypt, anyhow from a long way off, and they were spending at the wine shop more freely than compare Naso, or padron Cipolla; they would sit astride the tables and tell jokes to the girls, and they had silk handkerchieves in every jacket pocket; so that the whole village was in a state of ferment.

The only people at home that evening when he returned were the women, who were changing the brine in the barrels, and chatting in groups with the neighbours, sitting on the stones; and meanwhile they were passing the time by telling stories and riddles, just about good for the children who were listening wide-eyed, half-dazed with sleep. Padron 'Ntoni was listening too, keeping an eye on the dripping of the brine and nodding approval at those who told the best stories, and at the children who showed as much judgement as the adults in explaining the riddles.

'The really good story,' 'Ntoni then said, 'is the one about the foreigners who arrived to-day, with so many silk handkerchieves it hardly seems possible; and they don't even look at their money when they take it out of their pockets. They've travelled half the world, they say, and Trezza and Aci Castello put together are nothing in comparison. I've seen as much too; and out there people spend their time enjoying themselves all day long, instead of sitting around salting anchovies; and the women are dressed in silk and laden with more rings than the Madonna of Ognina, and they go around the streets stealing all the handsome sailors.'

The girls blinked, and padron 'Ntoni too pricked up his ears, as when the children explained the riddles:

'When I'm grown up,' said Alessi, who was carefully emptying the barrels and passing them to Nunziata, 'if I get married, I want to marry you.'

'There's plenty of time,' said Nunziata, very gravely.

'There must be big cities like Catania; the sort of place where you get lost if you don't know them; and you feel stifled always walking between two rows of houses, without seeing sea or countryside.'

'Cipolla's grandfather has been there too,' added padron 'Ntoni; 'and he got rich there. But he didn't come back to Trezza, and he just sends money to his children.'

'Poor thing,' said Maruzza.

'Let's see if you can guess this one,' said Nunziata; 'two shiners, two prickers, four hooves and one licker.'

'An ox,' said Lia quick as a flash.

'You already knew it, you got there so fast,' said her brother.

'I'd like to go there too, like padron Cipolla's father, and get rich,' added 'Ntoni.

'You leave all that be,' said his grandfather, pleased because of the barrels he could see in the courtyard.

'Now there are anchovies to be salted.' But la Longa looked at her son with a heavy heart, and said nothing, because every time there was talk of leaving, a picture of those had had never returned loomed up before her eyes.

The rows of barrels were lining up nicely against the wall, and as each one was put in its place, with the stones on top, padron 'Ntoni would say:

'There's another one ready! And by All Saints' Day they'll all mean money.'

Then 'Ntoni laughed, like padron Fortunato when you talked to him about other people's property.

'Big money,' he said scathingly; and he went back to thinking about those two foreigners who were going hither and thither, and stretching out on the wine shop benches, and ringing their change in their pockets. His mother looked at him as though she could read his thoughts; and the jokes they were telling in the courtyard didn't raise a smile in her.

'The person who eats these anchovies,' began cousin Anna, 'will be the son of a crowned king, as fair as the sun, who will walk for a year, a month and a day, with his white horse; until he arrives at an enchanted fountain of milk and honey; there, getting down from his horse to drink, he will find my daughter Mara's thimble, carried there by the fairies when she was filling her jug; and as he drinks out of Mara's thimble, the king's son will fall in love with her; and he will walk for another year, a month and a day until he arrives in Trezza, and the white horse will take him right to the wash place, where my daughter Mara will be rinsing out the washing; and the king's son will marry her and put the ring on her finger; and then he will put her on the back of his white horse, and carry her off to his kingdom.'

Alessi was listening open-mouthed, as though he could see the king's son on the white horse, carrying Anna's Mara behind him.

'And where will he take her?' Lia asked.

'Far away, to his kingdom beyond the sea; the kingdom from which you never return.'

'Your daughter hasn't a ha'porth of dowry, and that's why the king's son won't come and marry her,' said 'Ntoni; 'in fact they'll turn their backs on her, as they do with people who have nothing.'

'That's why my daughter is working here now, after having spent all day at the wash place, to earn her dowry. Isn't it, Mara? At least if the king's son doesn't come, someone else will. Even I know that that is how the world goes, and we have no right to complain. Why didn't you fall in love with my daughter, instead of with Barbara, who is as yellow as saffron? It was because of her smallholding, wasn't it? and when misfortune caused you to lose your own possessions, it was only natural that Barbara should drop you.'

'You put up with everything,' replied 'Ntoni sulkily, 'and they're right to call you a 'happy soul.'

'And if I weren't, what good would that do? When you haven't got anything, the best thing is to go off, like compare Alfio Mosca did.'

'That's what I say,' exclaimed 'Ntoni.

'The worst thing,' said Mena at last, 'is to leave your own village, where even the stones know you, and it must be a heartbreaking thing to leave them all behind you on the road. 'East, west, home's best.' '

'Good for you, St. Agatha,' said her grandfather firmly. 'That's sensible talk.'

'Yes,' snarled 'Ntoni, 'and in the meantime, when we've sweated and strained to make our nest, we'll be short of things to put on our bread; and when we've managed to get back the house by the medlar tree, we'll have to carry on working our guts out from Monday to Saturday; and it will never end.'

'So you want to stop working? What would you rather do? play the lawyer?'

'I don't want to play the lawyer,' grumbled 'Ntoni, and went off to bed in a bad temper.

But from then on he thought of nothing except that trouble-free existence which other people led; and of an evening, to avoid their insipid chatter, he sat himself on the doorstep with his shoulders to the wall, watching people pass by, and digesting his hard lot; at least like that he was resting, ready for the next day, when he would go back to doing the same old thing, just like Mosca's donkey, which would draw its breath as soon as it saw its owner reaching for the pack saddle, waiting to be harnassed.

'Donkey flesh,' he would grumble; 'that's what we are: labouring flesh.' And it was quite clear that he was tired of that dreary life, and wanted to go off and make his fortune, like the others; so that his mother, poor thing, stroked his shoulders and caressed him with the tone of her voice, and with her tear-filled eyes, peering at him fixedly so as to read what was written inside his head and to touch his heart. But he said no, it would be better for him and for them; and when he came back they would all be happy. The poor woman didn't close an eye all night, and soaked her pillow with tears. Finally padron 'Ntoni noticed, and called his grandson outside, beside the little shrine, to ask him what was wrong.

'Come on, what's brewing? Tell your grandfather now.'

'Ntoni shrugged; but the old man kept on nodding his

155

head, and spitting, and scratching his head as he searched for words.

'Oh, you've got something cooking, my boy! Something new.'

'What's cooking is that I'm a poor devil, that's what's cooking!'

'What's new about that? Didn't you know? That's what your father was, and your grandfather before him.' 'He who is content in his poverty is wonderfully rich.' 'Better to be content than to lament.' '

'Some comfort that is!'

This time the old man found words quickly, because he felt his heart on his lips:

'At least don't say as much in front of your mother.'

'My mother . . . would have done better never to have borne me.'

'Yes,' agreed padron 'Ntoni, 'yes, she would, if it means that you're talking like this today.'

For a moment 'Ntoni didn't know what to say.

'Well,' he said at last, 'I'm doing it for you, for her, for all of us. I want to make my mother rich, that's what I want to do. Now we're leaving no stone unturned for the house and Mena's dowry; and then Lia will be growing up, and if by chance we have a bad year, we'll still be in dire poverty. I don't want to carry on like this. I want to change my life, for myself and all of you. I want us to be rich, mother, you, Mena, Alessi and everyone.'

Padron 'Ntoni eyes widened, and he chewed over those words, as if he couldn't quite swallow them.

'Rich,' he said, 'rich. And what will we do when we're rich?'

'Ntoni scratched his head, and he too started to think what they would do.

'We'll do what other people do . . . nothing, that's what we'll do . . . we'll go and live in the town, and eat pasta and meat every day.'

'You go and live in the town if you want to. I want to die where I was born;' and thinking of the house where he had been born, and which was no longer his, he let his head droop

156

on to his chest.

'You are a boy, and you know nothing . . . you know nothing! You'll see what it's like when you can no longer sleep in your own bed; when the sun no longer comes in through your window. You'll see! You listen to an old man' The poor fellow was coughing fit to choke, with his back all bent, and shaking his head sadly:

' 'East, west, home's best.' Do you see those sparrows? They've always made their nests there, and they'll carry on doing so — and they don't want to go away.'

'I'm not a sparrow. I'm not a creature like them,' answered 'Ntoni. 'I don't want to live like a dog on a chain, like compare Alfio's donkey, or mule on a chain pump, always keeping the wheel turning, I don't want to die of hunger in a corner, or be swallowed up by sharks.'

'You should rather thank God, who caused you to be born here; and think twice before going off to die far from the stones which know you. 'Better the devil you know.' You're afraid of work, you're afraid of poverty; and I have neither your strength nor your health, but I'm not afraid, you'll see. 'The pilot in the dangerous seas is known'. You're afraid of having to earn the bread you eat, that's what it is! Your great grandfather, God rest his soul, left me the *Provvidenza* and five mouths to feed, I was younger than you are and I wasn't afraid; and I did my duty without complaining; and I still do; and I pray God to help me carry on doing it as long as I've got breath in my body, as your father did, and your brother Luca, God rest his soul — he wasn't afraid to go and do his duty; and as your mother did, too, poor woman, locked away amidst these four walls; you've no idea of the tears she has shed, the tears she's shedding now because you want to leave; and in the morning your sister finds the sheets all wet. But she holds her tongue and doesn't come out with any of these things that come into *your* head; and she too has worked away like some poor ant; she'd done nothing else all her life, until it fell to her lot to cry too much, right from when she was giving you the breast, and you couldn't even button up your trousers; because then the temptation of exercising your legs one in front of the other and going about the world like a

157

gypsy hadn't even entered your head.'

In the end 'Ntoni began to cry like a child, because basically the boy had a heart as good as bread; but the next day he started off again. In the morning he unwillingly let himself be loaded up with tackle, and went off to the sea grumbling:

'Just like compare Alfio's donkey! at first light I crane my neck to see if they're coming to saddle me up.' After they had cast the nets, he left Alessi to move the oar gently so as to keep the boat steady, and put his hands under his armpits to gaze into the distance, to where the sea ended, and there were those big cities where you didn't do anything except walk up and down and do nothing; or he would think of the two sailors who had come back from so far, and who had now been gone for some time; but it seemed to him that they had nothing else to do except wander the world, from one wine shop to another, spending the money they had in their pockets. In the evening, after having tidied up the boat and tackle, his family left him to wander around like a stray dog, so as not to have to look at that long face of his.

'What's wrong, 'Ntoni?' la Longa asked him, gazing timidly into his face, with her eyes bright with tears, because the poor creature guessed what was wrong. 'Tell your own mother.' He wouldn't answer; or he answered that nothing was wrong. But at last he did tell her what was wrong, that his grandfather and the others had it in for him, and he had had enough. He wanted to go and seek his fortune, like all the others.

His mother listened to him, and she didn't dare open her mouth, with her eyes full of tears, so much did what he was saying hurt her, and he cried and shuffled his feet and tugged at his hair. The poor thing would have liked to speak, and throw her arms around him and cry too, so as not to let him go; but whenever she started to say anything, her lips would tremble and she couldn't utter a word.

'Listen,' she said at last, 'you go, if you want to go, but you won't find me here when you come back, because now I feel old and tired, and I don't think I'm going to be able to take this last blow.'

'Ntoni tried to reassure her, said that he would come back loaded with money and they would all be happy. Maruzza shook her head sadly, still looking into his eyes, and said no, no, he wouldn't find her there when he came back.

'I feel old,' she repeated, 'I feel old, look at me! Now I no longer have the strength to cry as much as when they brought me the news of your father and your brother. If I go to the wash place, in the evening I come home so tired I can do nothing; and it didn't used to be like that. No, my son, I'm no longer the woman I was. Then, when your father and brother died, I was younger and stronger. Your heart gets tired too, you see; and wears away piece by piece, as old dresses fall apart in the wash. Now my courage is failing me, and everything fills me with dread; I feel I'm sinking, as when a wave goes over your head, if you're at sea. Go, if you want to; but let me close my eyes first.'

Her face was all wet; but she didn't realize she was crying, and she felt as though she had her son Luca and her husband before her eyes, when they had gone away and never been seen again.

'So I'll never see you again,' she said to him. 'Now the house is gradually emptying; and when your poor old grandfather has gone too, who will look after those poor little orphans? Ah, our Lady of Sorrows!'

She held him in her arms, with his head on her breast, as though her boy wanted to run off then and there; and he couldn't bear it any longer, and began to kiss her and talk to her with his mouth against hers.

'No. No, I won't go if you don't want me to. Look! Don't talk to me like that! All right, I'll carry on like compare Mosca's donkey, to be thrown in a ditch to die when it can no longer pull his cart. Now are you satisfied? Stop crying like that. You can see how grandfather slaved away all his life? and now that he's old he's still slaving away as though it were his first day, to get himself out of the wood. That's our fate!'

'And do you think everyone doesn't have their troubles? Look at padron Cipolla running after Brasi, to see that he doesn't throw all that property into la Vespa's lap, that property he's sweated and slaved for all his life. And massaro

Filippo, who gazes up to heaven and says Hail Maries for his vines with every cloud that passes. And zio Crocifisso who has half-starved himself to set money aside, and is always quarrelling with one person or another! And do you think those foreign sailors don't have their troubles too? Who knows if they'll find their mothers at home when they get back? And if we manage to buy back the house by the medlar tree, when we've got grain in the bins and beans for the winter, and when we've married off Mena, what will we need? When I'm underground, and that poor old man is dead too, and Alessi can earn the daily bread, then go off wherever you want. But then you won't go, I'm telling you! because then you will understand what we all had within us, when we saw you stubbornly insisting that you wanted to leave your house, and yet we carried on with our usual business without saying anything to you! Then you won't have the heart to leave the village where you were born, and where you grew up, and where your dead are buried under that slab, in front of the altar of Our Lady of Sorrows, which is all smooth from so many people kneeling in front of it, of a Sunday.'

From that day onward 'Ntoni stopped talking about getting rich, and gave up the idea of leaving, and his mother kept a watchful eye on him, when she saw him gloomily sitting on the front steps; and the poor woman really was so pale, tired and haggard, that as soon as she had a spare moment she too would sit down, with her hands folded and her back already bent like her father-in-law's, so that she was a truly moving sight. But she didn't know that she too was going to have to leave when she least expected it, on a journey after which you are at rest for ever, under that smooth marble in the church; and she was to leave them all in mid-journey, those she loved, those who were so dear to her that they seemed to tear her heart from her in little pieces, now one of them and now another.

There was cholera in Catania, so that everyone who was able, left to go wherever they might in the nearby villages and countryside. This was providential for Trezza and Ognina, with all those foreigners spending. But the retailers turned up their noses if you talked of selling a dozen barrels of anchovies, and said that money had vanished, because of the cholera.

'So don't people eat anchovies any more?' Piedipapera then asked. But to padron 'Ntoni, and to anyone who had any to sell, he would say firmly that with cholera around people wouldn't want to ruin their stomachs with anchovies and such like muck, they'd rather eat pasta and meat; so you had to close your eyes, and be flexible about the price. The Malavoglia hadn't reckoned with that! and so, in order not to go sideways like crabs, la Longa went to take eggs and fresh bread here and there to the foreigners' houses, while the men were at sea, and she made a few pennies. But you had to watch out for dubious types, and not accept so much as a pinch of snuff from anyone you didn't know! Going along the street you had to walk right in the middle, well away from the walls, where you ran the risk of picking up all manner of nasty things, and not to sit down on the stones, or along the walls. Once, while she was coming back from Aci Castello, with her basket on her arm, la Longa felt so tired that her legs were shaking and seemed as if they were made of lead. So she let herself be overcome by the temptation to rest for a couple of minutes in the shade of the wild fig which is just near the little shrine, just before you enter the village; and she didn't notice at the time, but she did remember afterwards, that a stranger who seemed tired too, poor thing, had been sitting there a few moments before, and had left drops of some nasty substance which looked like oil on those stones. Anyway, she slumped down there too; she caught cholera and when she got home she was exhausted, waxen as an ex-voto tablet to the Virgin, and with dark rings round her eyes; so that Mena, who was alone in the house, began to cry just at the sight of her, and Lia went to get costmary and mallow leaves. Mena was trembling like an aspen, while she made the bed; yet the sick woman, seated on a chair, dead tired, with her yellow face and dark-ringed eyes, insisted on saying:

'It's nothing, don't be alarmed; as soon as I'm in bed, it will pass,' and she even tried to help her, but her strength failed her at every move and she went and sat down again.

'Holy Virgin,' stammered Mena. 'And the men out at sea.'

Lia took refuge in tears.

When padron 'Ntoni was coming home with his grandsons and saw the door half closed, and the light through the shutters, he dug his hands into his hair. Maruzza was already in bed, with those eyes of hers which, seen like that in the dark at that hour, looked as empty as though death had already sucked them dry, and her lips were black as coals. At that time neither doctor nor chemist were to be found about after sunset; and even the neighbourhood women had bolted their doors, for fear of the cholera, and stuck images of saints all over the cracks. For that reason Maruzza could expect help from no one except her own family, poor things, who were running through the house as though they were mad, seeing her sinking like that, in that little bed, and they were at their wits' end, and beat their heads against the walls. Then la Longa, seeing that there was no more hope, wanted them to put that pennyworth of cotton wool soaked in holy oil that they had bought at Easter on her chest, and even said that they should leave the candle alight, as they had done when padron 'Ntoni was going to die, because she wanted to see them all around the bed, and feasted her eyes on them one by one, those staring eyes of hers which could no longer see. Lia was crying fit to break your heart; and all the others, white as rags, looked at each other hopelessly; and they gritted their teeth so as not to burst out sobbing in front of the dying woman, who was quite aware of what was going on, for all she could no longer see, and what she most regretted in going her way was leaving those poor creatures so bereft. She called them by name one by one, in a hoarse voice; and wanted to raise her hand, which she could no longer lift, to bless them, as though she knew she was leaving them a treasure. ''Ntoni' she kept saying, almost inaudibly. ''Ntoni. To you, the eldest, I command these orphans.' And hearing her talk like that, while she was still alive, the others could not help bursting out crying and sobbing.

So they spent all night around the bed where Maruzza now lay motionless, until the candle began to gutter and go out, too, and the dawn came in through the window, as pale as the dead woman, whose face was haggard and sharp as a knife, with blackened lips. But Mena wouldn't stop kissing her on the mouth, and talking to her as if she could hear her. 'Ntoni beat his breast sobbing:

'Oh mother! now you have gone before me, and I wanted to leave *you*!' And that picture of his mother, with her white hair and face as yellow and sharp as a knife, remained in front of Alessi's eyes until his own hair whitened.

Later on that day they came to collect la Longa in a tearing hurry, and no one even though of the visit of condolence; everyone was thinking about their own skin, and even don Giammaria stayed on the threshold, when he sprayed the holy water with the aspergillum, holding St. Francis' tunic bunched and raised — like the truly selfish friar he was, spouted the chemist. He on the other hand, if they had brought him the doctor's prescription for some medicine or other, would open up the shop even at night, because he wasn't afraid of cholera; and he even said that it was folly to believe that they spread the cholera along the streets and into the doorways.

'That's a sign that it's him who's spreading the cholera,' hinted don Giammaria. So everyone greeted the chemist eagerly in the village, but he would cackle away, just exactly like don Silvestro, and would say:

'I'm a republican. Now if I were a clerk, or a government lackey, it might be different . . .' But the Malavoglia were left alone, in front of that empty bed.

For a time they didn't open the door, after la Longa had gone through it. It was lucky they had a few beans in the house, and wood and oil, because padron 'Ntoni had acted like the wise ant during good times, otherwise they would have died of hunger, and no one came to see whether they were alive or dead. Then, gradually, they began to put their black handkerchieves around their necks, and go out into the street, like slugs after the rain, pale-faced and still shattered. From a distance the neighbourhood women asked them how the tragedy had happened; for comare Maruzza had been one of the first to go. And when don Michele or another of the braided-hatted government shirkers passed by, they looked at them with eyes bright with hatred, and ran to lock themselves in their houses. The village was in a desolate state, and the very hens shunned the streets; even mastro Cirino was lying low, and didn't bother about ringing the mid-day or evening bell, and he ate municipal bread too, with those twelve *tari* a month they gave him to be caretaker at the town hall, and he was afraid they might give him the greeting accorded to government lackeys.

Now don Michele was Lord of the street, since Pizzuto, don Silvestro and all the others had gone to ground like rabbits, and the only person strutting in front of Zuppidda's house was him, don Michele. It was a pity that the only people to see him were the Malavoglia, who now had nothing more to lose and so would sit on their doorstep looking to see who was passing by, motionless, chins in hands. In order not to waste his strolling time, don Michele would take a look at St. Agatha, now that all the other doors were closed; and he did so partly to show that lout 'Ntoni that he wasn't afraid of anyone in the world. And then Mena, pale as she was, really did look like St. Agatha; and her little sister, with that black handkerchief, was beginning to be a fine young girl too.

Poor Mena suddenly felt as though twenty years had fallen on her back. Now she behaved with Lia as la Longa had acted with her; she felt she had to keep her under her wing like a chicken, and as though the whole weight of the house fell on her back. She had become used to being alone with her little sister when the men went to sea, and to being with that empty bed ever before her eyes. If she had nothing to do, she would sit with her hands folded, looking at it, and then she felt that her mother had left her; and when in the street they said:

'So and so is dead, or so and so,' she thought: 'That's how it must have sounded when they heard: la Longa is dead,' la Longa who had left her alone with that poor little orphan who wore a black handkerchief like herself.

Nunziata, or cousin Anna, came from time to time, with light steps and long faces, without saying a word; and they stood on the doorstep looking at the empty road, with their hands under their aprons. The people coming back from the sea walked fast, watchfully, with their nets on their shoulders, and the carts didn't even stop at the wine shop.

Where was compare Alfio's cart going now? Was he even now dying of cholera under a hedge, that poor fellow who had no one in the world? Piedipapera went by sometimes too, looking starved and peering about him; or zio Crocifisso, who had business scattered here and there, and went to feel his debtors' pulses, because if they died they were stealing his just desserts. The viaticum was also rushed by, in don Giammaria's hands, and he had his cassock tucked up, and a barefoot boy who rang the bell, because mastro Cirino was nowhere to be seen. That bell rang with a chilling sound in the empty streets, with not even a dog to be seen, and don Franco himself kept his door half-closed.

The only person who wandered about day and night was la Locca, with her tangled white hair, and she would sit outside the house by the medlar tree, or wait for the boats on the shore, and not even the cholera wanted anything to do with her, poor thing.

The foreigners too had fled, like birds when winter comes, and there were no buyers for fish. So that people said the cholera would be followed by famine. Padron 'Ntoni had had to dip into the money for the house, and he saw it being frittered away bit by bit. But all he could think of was that Maruzza had died outside her own home, and the thought obsessed him. When he saw the money being spent, 'Ntoni shook his head too.

Finally, when the cholera was over, and the money put together with so much effort had been half-spent, he went back to saying that it couldn't go on like that, with that life of small gains and small losses; that it was better to make one big effort to get out of trouble at a single blow and that he didn't want to stay there any longer, in that place where his mother had died, amidst all that filthy poverty.

'What can I do for Mena if I stay here? You tell me.' Mena looked at him timidly, but tenderly, just like her mother, and didn't dare say a word. But once, leaning shyly against the doorpost, she screwed up the courage to say:

'I don't mind about your help, provided you don't leave us. Now that mother isn't here, I feel like a lost soul and I don't care about anything any more. But I'm sorry for that poor orphan who'll be without anyone in the world, if you go, like Nunziata when her father disappeared.'

Lia and Alessi opened their eyes wide and looked at him in alarm; but his grandfather let his head fall on to his chest.

'Now you have neither father nor mother, and you can do whatever you like,' he said to him at last. 'As long as I'm alive I'll take care of these children; when I'm no longer here, the Lord will do the rest.'

Since 'Ntoni wanted to leave at all costs, Mena put his affairs in order, as his mother would have done, because after all she thought that out there, in some foreign land, her brother would no longer have anyone to think of him, like compare Mosca. And while she sewed his shirts and patched his clothes, her thoughts were far away, among so many past things, and her heart swelled with memories.

'I can't bear to pass by the house by the medlar tree,' she would say when she was sitting with her grandfather, 'I feel it in my throat, and it chokes me, what with all the things which have have happened since we left it.'

And while she was preparing her brother's things, she cried as though she were never to see him again. At last, when everything was in order, her grandfather summoned his boy to give him the final lecturings, and the last advice for when he would be alone, and would have to make capital only out of his head, without his family to tell him how to behave, or to grieve together; and he also gave him a bit of money, in case he should need it; and his fur-lined cloak, because he himself was old now, and wouldn't be wanting it.

Seeing their older brother intent on preparations for his departure, the children trailed quietly after him through the house, and didn't dare say a word to him, as though he were already a stranger.

'That's how my father went off,' said Nunziata at last, from the doorstep where she was standing, having come to say goodbye. Then no one said another word.

The neighbourhood women came by one by one to say goodbye to compare 'Ntoni, and then they stood and waited on the road to see him go. He hesitated, with his bundle on his shoulder and his shoes in his hand, as though his courage and his legs had failed him at the last minute. And he looked around him as though to engrave the house and the village and everything on his memory, and he looked as upset as everyone else. His grandfather took his stick to go with him to the city, and Mena cried quietly in a corner.

'Come now,' said 'Ntoni, 'this won't do! It's not as though I weren't ever coming back, after all. Don't forget I came back from my military service.' Then, after he had kissed Mena and Lia, and said goodbye to the women, he moved to go, and Mena ran after him with her arms outstretched sobbing aloud, almost beside herself, and saying to him:

'Now what will mother say?' for all the world as though mother had been able to see and speak. But she was repeating what had remained clearest in her mind when 'Ntoni had first said that he wanted to leave, and she had seen her mother cry every night, and had found the sheet all wet the next morning, when she was making the bed.

'Goodbye, 'Ntoni,' Alessi shouted after him as he plucked up his courage when his brother was already out of earshot, and then Lia began to scream.

'That's how my father left,' said Nunziata after a pause, from where she was still standing in the doorway.

'Ntoni turned round before he turned out of strada del Nero, and he too had tears in his eyes, and waved. Then Mena closed the door, and went to sit in a corner with Lia, who was crying out loud.

'Now another one has gone,' she said. 'And if we were in the house by the medlar tree, it would seem as empty as a church.'

Now that all those who loved her were leaving one by one, she really did feel like a fish out of water. And Nunziata, standing there with her little ones around her, kept saying:

'That's how my father left, too.'

CHAPTER XII

Now that Alessi was the only person left to help with the boat, padron 'Ntoni had to take someone by the day, either compare Nunzio, who had all those children and a sick wife, or la Locca's son, who would come whimpering outside the door that his mother was dying of hunger, and zio Crocifisso wouldn't give her anything because the cholera had ruined him, he said, what with so many people having died and cheated him of his money, so that he had caught the cholera too — though he hadn't died, added la Locca's son, shaking his head gloomily.

'My mother and I and all the family would have been able to eat now, if he had died. We spent two days with la Vespa looking after him, and he seemed to be sinking from one moment to the next, but then he didn't die!'

But what the Malavoglia earned often wasn't enough to pay zio Nunzio, or la Locca's son, and they had to dip into the hard-earned money for the house by the medlar tree. Every time Mena went to get the sock from under the mattress, she and her grandfather sighed. It wasn't la Locca's poor son's fault; he would gladly have done the work of four men to earn his day's keep; it was the fault of the fish, which weren't keen to be caught. And when they came back crestfallen, banging the oars and with the sail all slack, la Locca's son would say to padron 'Ntoni:

'I'll chop some wood or bind up vine shoots; I can work until midnight if you want, as I did with zio Crocifisso. I want to earn my day's pay.'

Then, after pondering a bit, padron 'Ntoni decided to talk to Mena about what they would do. She was as sensible as her mother, and there was now no one else in the house to discuss it with, whereas before there had been so many. The best thing was to sell the *Provvidenza*, which earned nothing, and ate up the day's pay for Nunzio and la Locca's son; otherwise the money for the house would all be frittered away. The *Provvidenza* was old and always needing more money spending on her to patch her up and keep her afloat. Later, if 'Ntoni came back and things were looking up, they would buy a new boat, when they had got the money for the house together, and would call her the *Provvidenza*, too.

One Sunday he went into the square to discuss it with Piedipapera, after mass. Compare Tino shrugged his shoulders, shook his head, said that the *Provvidenza* was just about good for firewood, and so saying he led him down to the shore; you could see the patches, under the new coat of pitch, it was like some sluts he knew, with wrinkles under their corsets; and he started kicking her in the stomach again, with his lame foot. Anyhow, business was bad; rather than buying, people would be wanting to sell their boats, and newer than the *Provvidenza*. And who would buy her? Padron Cipolla didn't want any of that old rubbish. That was zio Crocifisso's province. But at that moment zio Crocifisso had other things on his mind, what with that one-track-minded Vespa who was driving him crazy, running after all the marriageable men in the village. At last, for the sake of friendship, he agreed to go and talk to zio Crocifisso about it, at the right moment, if padron 'Ntoni was determined to sell the *Provvidenza* for a song; because he, Piedipapera, had zio Crocifisso round his little finger.

In fact, when he talked to him, leading him off towards the cattle trough, zio Crocifisso answered with a series of shrugs, and shook his head like a puppet, and showed all the signs of wanting to escape. Compare Tino, poor thing, was holding him by the jacket, so that he would be forced to listen; and he shook him; held him close so as to whisper in his ear.

'Yes, you're a fool if you let this opportunity pass you by! For peanuts! Padron 'Ntoni is selling it because he simply can't carry on, now that his grandson has left him. But you could put it in the hands of compare Nunzio, or la Locca's son, who are starving to death, and would come and work for nothing. You'd come in for everything they catch. You're a fool, I tell you! The boat is well-kept, virtually new. Padron 'Ntoni knew what he was doing when he had it mended. This is a real bargain, like the lupin business, you mark my words!' But zio Crocifisso wouldn't hear of it, and almost burst into tears, with that yellow face, now that he had had cholera; and he pulled away and almost left Piedipapera holding his jacket.

'I'm not interested,' he repeated. 'Not interested. You don't know what I suffer inwardly, compare Tino! Everyone wants to suck my blood like leeches, and take my possessions. Now there's Pizzuto too running after la Vespa, all like a pack of hunting dogs.'

'You take her then, that Vespa! Isn't she your flesh and blood, she and her smallholding? She won't be another mouth to feed, after all; that woman's hands are blessed by God, and the money you spend on the bread you give her will be well spent. You'll also have a tame servant, unpaid, and you'll get the smallholding into the bargain. Listen to me, zio Crocifisso, this is another deal as good as the lupin deal!'

Meanwhile padron 'Ntoni was waiting for an answer in front of Pizzuto's shop, and gazing like a lost soul at the two of them, who seemed to be fighting, and trying to guess whether zio Crocifisso was saying yes. Piedipapera came over to tell him what he had managed to get out of zio Crocifisso, and then went back to talk to him again; and he came and went across the square like the shuttle in the loom, dragging his twisted leg after him, until he managed to bring about an agreement.

'Excellent,' he said to padron 'Ntoni; 'it's peanuts,' he said to zio Crocifisso, and in this way he negotiated the sale of all the tackle, because the Malavoglia had no use for it, now that they didn't have their bread on the waters, but padron 'Ntoni felt as though they were hauling the bowels from within him, fish traps, nets, harpoons, fishing rods, the lot.

'I'll find you work on a day basis, for you and your grandson Alessi, don't you worry,' Piedipapera told him.

'But you'll have to be satisfied with what you get, you know! 'The strength of the young and the wisdom of the old,' as they say. And I'll rely on your goodness of heart for some consideration of my part in the deal.'

'You have to cut your coat according to your cloth,' replied padron 'Ntoni. 'Necessity lowers nobility.'

'All right, we understand one another,' concluded Piedipapera, and he went off to discuss it with padron Cipolla, in the chemist's shop, where don Silvestro had managed to lure them yet again, him, massaro Filippo and a few other big wigs, to discuss municipal affairs, because after all it was their money, and it is pure foolishness to count for nothing in the village when you are rich, and pay more taxes than others.

'You who are so rich, you could give some bread to that poor padron 'Ntoni,' added Piedipapera. 'It wouldn't harm you to take him on by the day, with his grandson Alessi; you know he knows more about the trade than anyone else, and he'd make do with very little, because they're really on the bread line; you'd make a mint, you mark my words, padron Fortunato.'

Caught like that at that moment, padron Fortunato couldn't say no; but after they had hummed and hawed a bit over the price — and since times were lean, men had no work — padron Cipolla was actually doing a charitable action in taking on padron 'Ntoni.

'Yes, I'll take him on if he comes to ask me in person! Would you believe that he has been bearing me a grudge ever since I put an end to my son's marriage with Mena? Eh! that would have been some deal! And they have the cheek to cut me, into the bargain!'

Don Silvestro, massaro Filippo and also Piedipapera all hastened to say that Piedipapera was right. Brasi wouldn't give him a moment's peace, since he had put the idea of marriage into his head, and he was running after all the girls like a cat in January, so that he was a permanent worry to his poor father. Now the Mangiacarrubbe girl had entered the fray, having taken it into her head to get her hands on him, Brasi Cipolla, since he was there for the taking; she at least was a comely girl with broad shoulders, and not old and scrawny like la Vespa; but la Vespa had that smallholding, and all the Mangiacarrubbe girl had was her black tresses, the others said. The Mangiacarrubbe girl knew what you had to do if you wanted to get Brasi Cipolla, now that his father had tethered him back at home again because of the cholera, and he no longer went hiding on the *sciara,* or in the smallholding, or with the chemist and in the sacristy. She walked briskly in front of him, with her dainty new shoes; and in passing she brushed him with her elbow, in the midst of the crowd coming back from mass; or she would wait for him at the door, with her hands on her stomach, and send him a lethal look, a look that steals the heart away, and turn round to adjust the corners of her handkerchief under her chin to see if he was following her; or run home as he appeared at the end of the little street and go to hide herself behind the basil on the window sill, with those great dark eyes which devoured him from her hiding place. But if Brasi stopped to gaze at her like the great oaf he was, she turned her back on him, with her chin on her chest, all red, eyes lowered, chewing the edges of her apron, as though butter wouldn't melt in her mouth. At last, since Brasi couldn't steel himself to take her, she had to collar him and say: 'Listen, compare Brasi, why do you torment me so? I know I'm not meant for you; and it would be better if you didn't pass by this way, because the more I see you the more I want to see you, and by now I'm the talk of the village; Zuppidda comes to the door every time she sees you pass, and then goes to tell everybody; though she'd do better to keep an eye on that flirt of a daughter of hers, Barbara, who has turned this little street into an open square, so many people come here, and she keeps quiet about how many times don Michele goes up and down, to see Barbara at the window.'

What with such natterings Brasi no longer budged from the street, in fact not even a sound thrashing could have dislodged him, and he was always hanging around, strolling about with his arms dangling, nose in the air and mouth agape, like a puppet. The Mangiacarrubbe girl for her part would be at the window, changing silk handkerchieves every day, and glass necklaces, like a queen. She put everything she had on display in that window, and that nincompoop Brasi took the lot for pure gold, and he was driven wild, to the point where he wasn't afraid even of his own father, if he had come to remove him with a thrashing.

'Here we see God's handiwork in punishing padron Fortunato's pride,' people said. 'It would have been a hundred times better for him to have given his son to the Malavoglia girl, who at least had that bit of dowry, and didn't spend it on handkerchieves and necklaces.'

Mena on the other hand didn't even put her nose to the window, because that would not have been right, now that her mother was dead, and she wore a black handkerchief; and then she had to look after her little sister, and act as mother to her, and she had no one to help her with the household chores, so that she even had to go to the wash place, and the fountain, and take the bread to the men, when they were out on a day's work; so that she was no longer like St. Agatha, as she had been, when no one saw her and she was always at her loom. From the day Zuppidda had begun to preach from the balcony, with her spindle as though she wanted to gouge out his eyes with it, don Michele, if he came to hang around those parts for Barbara, would pass along the strada del Nero ten times a day, to show he wasn't afraid of Zuppidda or of her spindle either; and when he got to the Malavoglia's house he would slow down, and look inside, to see the fine girls who were growing up in the Malavoglia household.

Of an evening, coming back from the sea, the men would find everything ready: the pan boiling and the table set; but by now that table was too big for them, and they looked quite lost around it. They closed the door and ate in peace and quiet; then they would go to sit at the doorway, clasping their knees, to rest from the day's labours. At least they lacked for nothing, and were no longer dipping into the money for the house. Padron 'Ntoni never took his gaze off that house, nearby as it was, with the windows closed and the medlar tree visible over the top of the courtyard wall. Maruzza had not been able to die there; nor perhaps would he; but the money was beginning to pile up, and his grandchildren would go back there one day, now that Alessi too was becoming a man, and was a good lad in the true Malavoglia mould. Then when they had married off the girls and bought back the house, if they could get a boat to sea as well, they would have all they wished for, and padron 'Ntoni would be able to close his eyes in peace.

Nunziata and cousin Anna too came to sit there on the stones, chatting after supper with those poor folks, who were so forsaken like themselves, so that it was almost as though they were relatives. It was almost a second home for Nunziata, and she brought her little ones with her, like a hen with her chicks. Seated by her, Alessi would say:

'Have you finished your cloth for to-day?' or: 'Will you be going to pick olives at massaro Filippo's on Monday? What with it being the olive harvest, you'll have no trouble finding work by the day, and you can take your little brother along with you, because now they'll give him a couple of pence a day too.' Nunziata gravely told him all her plans, and asked his advice, and they drew aside and talked sagely together, as though they were already full of years.

'They've learned young because they've seen so many troubles,' padron 'Ntoni would say. 'Misfortune brings sound judgement.' Alessi, with his arms round his knees just like his grandfather, would ask Nunziata:

'Will you have me for a husband when I'm grown up?'

'There's plenty of time,' she would say.

'Yes, there is time, but it's better to start thinking now, so that I'll know what I have to do. First we must marry off Mena, and Lia, when she's grown up too. Lia is beginning to want long clothes, and handkerchieves with roses, and then you've got to settle your own children. Somehow we must buy a boat; and the boat will help us to buy the house. My grandfather would like to buy back the house by the medlar tree, and I would too, because I know my way about it, blindfold, or at night; and there's a big courtyard for the tackle, and you're right near the sea. And when my sisters are married, grandfather can come and be with us, and we'll put him in the big room in the courtyard, which gets the sun; so that when he can't come down to the sea any more, poor old man, he can sit at the doorway into the courtyard, and in the summer he'll have the medlar tree to give him shade. We'll have the room overlooking the vegetable patch, if you like, and you'll have the kitchen near by, so we'll have everything to hand. Then when my brother 'Ntoni comes back we'll give it to him, and we'll go up to the attic. All you'll need to do is go down the little stairs to be in the kitchen or vegetable patch.'

'The fireplace in the kitchen needs rebuilding,' said Nunziata. 'The last time I cooked the soup on it, when poor comare Maruzza didn't feel like doing anything, you had to hold the saucepan up with stones.'

'Yes, I know,' answered Alessi with his chin on his hands, nodding. He had a look of enchantment in his eyes, as though he could see Nunziata in front of the hearth, and his grief-stricken mother beside the bed. 'You too could find your way around the house by the medlar tree in the dark, you've been there so often. Mother always said you were a good girl.'

'Now they've planted onions in the vegetable patch, and they've come up as big as oranges.'

'Do you like onions?'

'Of course, I have to. They're good with bread, and they don't cost much. When we haven't got enough money for soup, me and the little ones always eat onions.'

'That's why they sell so many. Zio Crocifisso doesn't care about having cabbages and lettuces, because he has another vegetable patch in his own house, and he's grown nothing but onions. But we'd have broccoli, and cauliflowers, wouldn't we? That'll be good, won't it?'

Squatting on the step, with her arms around her knees, the young girl too was gazing into the distance; and then she began to sing, while Alessi sat there listening intently. At last she said:

'But there's plenty of time.'

'Yes,' agreed Alessi; 'first we have to marry off Mena, and Lia too, and settle your little ones. But it's as well to start thinking about it.'

'When Nunziata sings,' said Mena, appearing in the doorway, 'it's a sign that the next day will be fine, and she'll be able to go to the wash place.' Cousin Anna was in the same position, because her smallholding and vines were at the wash place, and what was good news for her was when she had washing to do, all the more so now that her son Rocco

175

deposited himself in the wine shop from one Sunday to the next, to digest the ill-humour which that flirt of a Mangiacarrubbe girl had visited upon him.

'It's an ill wind that blows nobody any good,' padron 'Ntoni said to her. 'Perhaps this way he'll learn sense, your Rocco. It'll do my 'Ntoni good to be away from home too; then when he comes back, tired of wandering around the world, everything will seem good to him, and he won't complain about things any more; and if we manage to have boats at sea once again, and to put our beds up there, in that house, you'll see what a fine thing it will be to rest in the doorway, of an evening when you come back tired, and the day has gone well; and to see the light in that room where you've seen all the dear faces you've ever known. But now so many of them have gone away one by one, and they'll never be back, and the room is dark and the door closed, as if those who've gone away had put the key in their pockets for ever.'

''Ntoni shouldn't have left,' added the old man after a pause. 'He should have known that I'm old, and if I die these children will have nobody'.

'If we buy the house by the medlar tree while he's away, he'll hardly be able to believe it when he comes back,' said Mena, 'and he'll come looking for us here.'

Padron 'Ntoni shook his head sadly.

'But there's plenty of time,' he too said at last, like Nunziata; and cousin Anna added:

'If 'Ntoni comes back rich, he'll buy the house.' Padron 'Ntoni said nothing; but the whole village knew that 'Ntoni was to come back rich, after having been away so long seeking his fortune, and many were already envying him, and wanting to leave everything and go off in search of their fortunes, like him. And indeed they were right, because all they were leaving behind was silly whimpering women; and the only one who hadn't the heart to leave his woman was that blockhead, la Locca's son, who had the sort of mother you know her to be, and Rocco Spatu, whose heart was in the wine shop.

But luckily for those silly women, suddenly the news spread that padron 'Ntoni's 'Ntoni was back, one night, on a ship from Catania, and was ashamed to be seen without shoes. If it had been true that he was coming back rich, he wouldn't have had anywhere to put his money, so ragged was he. But his grandfather and brother and sisters greeted him warmly all the same, as though he had come back rolling in it, and his sisters hung around his neck, laughing and crying, because 'Ntoni hardly recognised Lia, she had grown so, and they said to him:

'Now you won't leave us again, will you?'

His grandfather too blew his nose, and muttered:

'Now I can die in peace, knowing that these children won't be left alone and stranded.'

But for a week 'Ntoni didn't have the courage to set foot in the street. When they saw him everyone laughed in his face, and Piedipapera went round saying:

'Have you seen the riches padron 'Ntoni's 'Ntoni has brought back with him?' And those people who had been rather slow to make up their bundles before embarking on that giddy venture, held their sides for laughing.

When someone doesn't manage to grab fortune by the tail, he is an imbecile, as is well-known. Don Silvestro, padron Cipolla and massaro Filippo weren't imbeciles, and everyone was pleased to see them, because those who have nothing stand agape looking on at the rich and fortunate, and work for them, like compare Alfio's donkey, for a handful of hay, instead of lashing out, and kicking the cart under foot, and lying down on the grass with their hooves in the air.

The chemist was right when he said that the world as it was right now needed a kick, and a fresh start. And yet he too, with his big beard, preaching about fresh starts, was one of those who had grabbed fortune by the tail, and he kept it in his glass cases, and enjoyed prosperity standing on the doorstep of his shop, chatting with this person or that, and when he had pounded away making a hole in the drop of dirty water in his mortar, his work was done. What a fine trade his father had taught him, making money with water from the water tanks! But 'Ntoni's grandfather had taught him a trade which consisted of breaking his back and arms all day long, and risking his neck, and dying of hunger, and never having a day to stretch out in the sun like Mosca's donkey. A thieving trade which destroyed your soul, by the Virgin! and he had had it up to here, so that he preferred to do as Rocco Spatu did, which at least was nothing. Already he was past caring about Zuppidda and comare Tudda's Sara, or any other girl in the world. All they did was look for a husband who would toil like a maniac to provide them with food, and buy them silk handkerchieves, while they sat out on the step of a Sunday, with their hands on their full stomachs. But in his case it was *he* who wanted to sit down with his hands on his stomach, of a Sunday and a Monday too, and all the other days, because there is no point in wearing yourself to a shadow for nothing.

So 'Ntoni too acted the preacher, like the chemist; at least he had learned this much on his travels, and now his eyes were opened, like kittens' ten days after they're born. 'The hen that leaves the coop comes home with a full stomach.' At least he had filled his stomach with good sense, and he would go into the square to tell people what he had learned, to Pizzuto's shop and to Santuzza's wine shop too. He didn't sneak off to Santuzza's on the quiet any more, now that he was a man, and his grandfather couldn't pull his ears, after all; and he could have held his own if they chided him for going after such crumbs of comfort as he could find.

Instead of seizing him by the ear, his grandfather, poor thing, approached him with kindness.

'You see,' he would say to him, 'now that you're here we'll soon make up the money for the house' — he always kept on with that refrain about the house. 'Zio Crocifisso has said that he won't give it to anyone else. Your mother, poor creature, wasn't able to die there! The house will help to provide for Mena's dowry; because at my age, you know, it's hard to go out by the day, and be at someone else's beck and call, when you've been your own master. Do you think we should buy the boat with the money for the house? Now you're a man, and you must have your say too, because you have more judgement than an old man like me. What would you like to do?'

What 'Ntoni wanted to do was nothing! What did he care about the house and the boat? Another bad year would come, another cholera epidemic, another disaster, and eat up the house and the boat, and they'd all be back to acting like ants. A fine business! And anyhow when they had got the house and the boat, did that mean an end to work? or that one could eat meat and pasta every day? While in those places where he had been, there were people who went around in carriages all day long, no more no less. People in comparison with whom don Franco and the town clerk worked like donkeys covering their reams of ridiculous paper, and making holes in the dirty water in the mortars. At least he had the wit to want to know why there were people in this world who enjoyed themselves without lifting a finger, and had been born with silver spoons in their mouths, and others who had nothing, and led lives of hopeless drudgery.

And the idea of going out by the day didn't appeal to him at all, after all he had been born his own master, even his grandfather had said as much. To have someone else call the tune, people who had come up from nothing, and everyone in the village knew how they had made their money bit by bit, sweating and straining! He would work by the day because his grandfather was forcing him to, and he hadn't the heart to say no. But when the skipper was towering over him, like a cur, and shouting to him from the stern: 'Hey, you there, what's going on?', then he felt like hitting him over the head with his oar, and preferred to stay at home mending the fish traps, and the nets, sitting on the shore with his legs outstretched, and his back to the stones; because then no one criticised you if you sat for a moment with your arms crossed.

Rocco Spatu went to stretch out there too, and Vanni Pizzuto, when he hadn't anything else to do, between one beard and the next, and even Piedipapera, because his trade was chatting with this person or that, looking for opportunities for deals. And they talked about what was happening in the village, of what donna Rosolina had told her brother, under the seal of confession, when the cholera had been raging, that don Silvestro had swindled her out of twenty five *onze,* and she couldn't call in the police, because donna Rosolina had robbed those twenty five *onze* from her brother the priest, and they would all have known the reason

179

she had given don Silvestro that money, to her shame!

'Anyhow,' observed Pizzuto, 'where did donna Rosolina get those twenty five *onze* from? 'Stolen goods are soon gone.'

'At least they were still in the family,' said Spatu; 'if my mother had twelve *tari* and I took them from her, would I rate as a thief?'

Since they were on the subject of thieves, they began to talk of zio Crocifisso, who had lost more than thirty *onze*, they said, with so many people having died of cholera, and he had been left with the pledges. Now, because he didn't know what to do with all those rings and ear-rings he'd been left, Dumb bell was marrying la Vespa; this was no rumour, because they'd even seen him going to sign on at the town hall, for the banns, with don Silvestro as witness.

'It's not true he's taking her because of the ear-rings,' said Piedipapera, who was in a position to know. 'After all, the ear-rings and necklaces are pure gold and silver, and he could have gone and sold them in the city; indeed he would have made a hundred per cent on the money he had lent. He's taking her because la Vespa has made it quite clear to him that she was about to go to the notary with the intention of marrying compare Spatu, now that the Mangiacarrubbe girl has lured Brasi Cipolla into her house. No offence, compare Rocco.'

'That's all right, compare Tino,' answered Rocco Spatu. 'I don't mind; anyone who trusts that monstrous pack of women is a fool. The one I love is Santuzza, who gives me credit when I need it; and you'd need two Mangiacarrubbe girls to make one of her! with that chest, eh, compare Tino?'

'A handsome hostess means a big bill,' said Pizzuto spitting.

'They want husbands so they can be supported by them,' added 'Ntoni. 'They're all the same.' Piedipapera continued: 'So zio Crocifisso ran panting to the lawyer, puffing like a grampus, and he's really taking la Vespa.'

'What a bit of luck for the Mangiacarrubbe girl,' exclaimed 'Ntoni.

'A few years from now, when his father dies, God forbid, Brasi Cipolla will be stinking rich,' said Spatu.

'Now his father is raising hell, but as time goes by he'll resign himself. He has no other children, and all he can do is marry, if he doesn't want the Mangiacarrubbe girl to enjoy his property against his will.'

'I'm delighted,' concluded 'Ntoni. 'The Mangiacarrubbe girl has nothing. Why should padron Cipolla be the only one who's rich?'

Here the chemist entered the discussion, having come to smoke his pipe on the shore, after lunch, and he kept harping on that the world had taken a wrong turning, and everything should be started again from scratch. But with that lot, it really was like trying to make a hole in water. The only one who had any grasp was 'Ntoni, who had seen the world, and had his eyes that bit open, like kittens; as a soldier he had been taught to read, and so he too went to the door of the chemist's shop to listen to what the papers said, and to chat with the chemist, who was good-hearted enough with everyone, and hadn't his wife's fancy ideas, so that she would scold him, asking him why he got involved in matters that didn't concern him.

'You have to let women speak on, and just do things on the quiet,' said don Franco as soon as the Signora had gone up into her room. He had no objection to mingling with people who went barefoot, provided they didn't put their feet on the chair struts; and he explained to them what the papers said word by word, stabbing the newsprint with his finger and saying that the world ought to be run just as they said there.

Arriving on the shingle where his friends were having their discussions, don Franco winked at 'Ntoni Malavoglia, who was mending the nets with his legs stretched out and his back up against the stones, and nodded in his direction, shaking his big beard in the air.

'It's a fine just world where some have their backs against stones, while others lie with their bellies in the sun, smoking their pipes, whereas all men ought to be brothers, and Christ, the greatest revolutionary of them all, said so, and to-day his priests act the policeman and the spy.' Didn't they know that don Michele's business with Santuzza had been discovered by don Giammaria, in confession?

'Don Michele indeed! Santuzza had got massaro Filippo; and don Michele is always buzzing about the strada del Nero, without the slightest fear of comare Zuppidda and her spindle. After all, he's got a pistol.'

'Santuzza has both, I tell you! Those women who confess every Sunday have a big sack to put their sins in; that's why Santuzza wears that medal on her chest, to cover all the filth beneath.'

'Don Michele is wasting his time with Zuppidda; the town clerk has said that he'll get her to fall for him like a ripe pear.'

'Oh, I know! In the meantime don Michele is enjoying himself with Barbara, and the others in the street. I know,' and he winked slyly at 'Ntoni.

'He has nothing to do, and every day he gets his four *tari* wages.'

'That's what I always say,' repeated the chemist tugging at his beard. 'The whole system is rotten; idlers are paid to do nothing, and cuckold us, who pay them, that's how it is. People get four *tari* a day to stroll under Zuppidda's windows; and don Giammaria pockets a *lira* a day to hear Santuzza's confession, and listen to all the filth she tells him; and don Silvestro . . . I know! and mastro Cirino gets paid to irritate us with his bells, but doesn't light the lamps, and pockets the oil himself, and goodness knows what other skullduggery goes on there at the town hall. My word! And they wanted to make a clean sweep of them all, but then they all came to some kind of an understanding yet again, don Silvestro and the rest, and not another word was said about it. Just like those other thieves in Parliament, who do nothing but jabber among themselves; but do you have any idea of what they say? They froth at the mouth, and seem to grab one another by the hair from one moment to the next, but they're laughing up their sleeves at those idiots who have any faith in them. It's all bluster, eyewash for the people who pay the thieves and toadies, and police spies like don Michele.'

'A fine business,' said 'Ntoni, 'four *tari* a day to stroll up and down. I'd like to be a customs guard.'

'That's it,' said don Franco with his eyes starting out of his head. 'Here you see the results of the system. The result is that everyone becomes riff-raff. No offence, compare 'Ntoni. 'The fish stinks from the head downwards.' I'd be like you too, if I hadn't studied, and didn't have this trade which earns me my daily bread.'

Indeed, they said, the trade his father had taught him was a good trade, pounding away with a pestle and making money out of dirty water; while there were people who had to roast their heads in the sun, and get cramp in their legs and backs in order to earn ten sous; and so they left the meeting and the chatting, and went off to the wine shop, spitting as they went.

CHAPTER XIII

When his grandson came home drunk of an evening, padron 'Ntoni did all he could to get him to go to bed without the others noticing, because this was one thing they had never had in the Malavoglia family, and it made the tears start in his eyes. At night, when he got up and called Alessi to go down to the sea, he let the other boy sleep; he would have been good for nothing, anyway. At first 'Ntoni had been ashamed, and had gone to wait for them on the shore, as soon as they came back, with his head bent. But gradually he became hardened, and said to himself that he would have a Sunday again, to-morrow.

The poor old man looked for all the means he could to touch the boy's heart, and even had his shirt exorcised by don Giammaria on the quiet, and spent three *tari* on it.

'You see,' he said to him, 'we've never had this in the Malavoglia family! If you start taking Rocco Spatu's path, your brother and sisters will follow. 'One bad apple infests the barrel,' and that money we've put aside with so much effort will go up in smoke. 'For a horse's nail the kingdom was lost,' and then what shall we do?'

'Ntoni kept his head bowed, and muttered to himself; but the next day he was at it again, and once he said to him: 'What do you expect? At least when I'm drunk I don't think about my troubles.'

'What troubles? You're healthy, you're young, you know your trade, what more do you ask? I am old, and your brother is still a boy, and we've pulled ourselves out of the ditch. Now if you were willing to help us we could get things back as they were, even if we no longer felt the old happiness, because the dead don't come back to life, but at least we wouldn't have other troubles; and we'd all be together, as the fingers of a hand should be, and with bread in the house. And if I die, what will become of you? Because, you see, I can't help feeling afraid every time I leave the shore. I'm old . . .'

When his grandfather succeeded in touching him, 'Ntoni began to cry. His brother and sisters, who knew everything, cowered in a corner when they heard him coming, as though he were a stranger, or as though they were afraid of him, and their grandfather, with his beads in his hands, called upon the blessed soul of Bastianazzo, or of his daughter-in-law Maruzza, to work a miracle. When Mena saw him come in with a pale face and bright eyes, she would say to him: 'Come in this way, grandfather is in there!' And she let him in through the little door into the kitchen; then she would begin to cry quietly by the hearth; so that at last 'Ntoni said: 'I won't go to the wine shop again, not even if they drag me there!' And he started to work with a will like before; indeed, he got up before the others, and went to wait for his grandfather on the shore, two hours before daybreak, when the Three Kings were still high over the village belltower, and the crickets were trilling in the small holdings as though they were right nearby. His grandfather could hardly contain himself for joy, and would chatter on to show him how much he loved him, and to himself he said that this miracle was the work of those blessed souls, 'Ntoni's parents.

The miracle lasted the whole week, and on Sunday 'Ntoni didn't even want to go out into the square, so as not to glimpse the wine shop and his friends calling him there. But he almost broke his jaw yawning during that whole day with nothing to do, and it seemed endless. He was no longer a young boy who could pass the time going for broom on the *sciara,* singing like his brother Alessi and Nunziata, or sweeping the house like Mena, but nor was he an old man like his grandfather, to enjoy himself mending broken barrels and fish traps. He sat by the door on the strada del Nero, and not even a hen passed by, and he heard the voices and laughter from the wine shop. And he actually went off to bed out of sheer idleness, and on Monday he started to sulk again. His grandfather said to him: 'For you it would be better if there were no Sundays; because the next day you're like one possessed.' So that was what would have been better for him, that there should never be any Sundays, and his heart sank to think that all days should be Mondays.

So that when he came back from the sea, of an evening, he didn't even feel like going to sleep, and vented his feelings by roaming about with his miseries, until at last he went back to the wine shop.

At first, when he came home unsteady on his feet, he would go in shame-facedly, making himself small and muttering excuses, or at least holding his tongue. But now he would raise his voice, pick a quarrel with his sister if she was waiting for him at the door, pale-faced and swollen-eyed, and if she told him in a low voice that his grandfather was there, he would answer that he didn't care. The next day he would get up upset and ill-tempered, and begin to shout from morning till night.

Once there was a nasty scene. No longer knowing how to appeal to him, his grandfather had pulled him into a corner of the little room, with the doors closed, so that the neighbours wouldn't hear, and said to him, weeping like a child, the poor old man: 'Oh 'Ntoni! Have you forgotten that your mother died here? why do you want to give your mother the pain of seeing you turn out like Rocco Spatu? Can't you see how poor cousin Anna sweats and strains for that drunkard of a son of hers? And how she cries, at times, when she has no bread to give her other children, and hasn't even the heart to laugh at anything? 'Bad company will teach you bad ways' and 'who keeps company with the wolf will learn to howl.' Don't you remember that night when we were all here round that bed, and she put Mena and the little ones in your care, when she had the cholera?' 'Ntoni was crying like a newly weaned calf, and said that he too wanted to die; but then gradually he went back to the wine shop, and at nights, instead of coming home, he would wander the streets, stopping in front of doorways, with his shoulders against the wall, dead tired, along with Rocco Spatu and Cinghialenta, and he began to sing with them, to ward off desperation.

At last poor padron 'Ntoni no longer dared show himself in

186

the streets for very shame. Whereas his grandson, to avoid sermonising, came home looking black; so that they no longer spoiled his fun with the usual preachings. In fact he did his own sermonising himself, under his breath, and everything was the fault of the misfortune which had caused him to be born in that lowly state.

And he went to let off steam with the chemist and those others who had a bit of time to spare, to chat about the undeniable injustice that there is in all things in this world; because if you go to Santuzza's to forget your troubles, you are called a drunkard; while so many others who get drunk at home on good wine have no troubles at all, nor anyone to reproach them or preach at them to go to work, since they have nothing to do and are rich enough for two; and yet we are all sons of God in the same fashion, and everyone ought to have their share equally.

'That boy has talent,' the chemist would say to don Silvestro, and to padron Cipolla, and to anyone who would listen. 'His views are rough and ready, but he gets the point; it's not his fault if he can't express himself better; it's the government's fault, because it allows him to remain in ignorance.'

To educate him, he would bring him the *Secolo* and the *Gazzetta di Catania*. But 'Ntoni found reading boring; firstly because it was an effort, and when he was in the navy they had taught him to read whether he wanted to or not; but now he was free to do whatever took his fancy, and he had somewhat forgotten how the words ended up as the writing. And then all that printed chatter didn't earn him a penny. What did it all matter to him? Don Franco explained to him why it should matter to him; and when don Michele walked through the square, he pointed to him with his beard, winking, and he blurted out in a low voice that he too was passing by on account of donna Rosolina, now that he had heard that donna Rosolina had money, and gave it to people so that they would marry her.

'To begin with, you'd have to get rid of all those braided caps. What we need is revolution. Revolution is what we must have!'

'And what will you give me to revolt?'

Then don Franco would shrug, and go off in irritation to pound his dirty water in his mortar. Because that was what it amounted to, he said, with people like that — making a hole in water. And as soon as 'Ntoni had turned his back, Piedipapera added in a low voice:

'If he wanted to kill don Michele, he ought to kill him for something else; because don Michele wants to steal 'Ntoni's sister; but 'Ntoni is worse than a pig, and is getting himself kept by Santuzza.' Piedipapera felt don Michele weighing heavy on his stomach, since don Michele looked at him and Rocco Spatu and Cinghialenta grimly when he met them; that was why he wanted him out of the way.

Those poor Malavoglia were now at the point where they were the talk of the village, on account of the brother, so low had the family fallen. Now the whole world knew that don Michele was walking up and down the strada del Nero, to irritate Zuppidda, who was mounting guard over her daughter with her spindle in her hand. Meanwhile, in order not to waste his walking time, don Michele had cast his eyes on Lia, who had grown up a fine young girl too, and there was no one to mount guard over her, except her sister who blushed for her, and said: 'Let's go back inside, Lia. It's not right for orphans like us to sit at the door.'

But Lia was vainer than her brother 'Ntoni, and she liked sitting at the door and showing off her handkerchief with the roses, so that everyone told her how fine she looked with that handkerchief, and don Michele devoured her with his gaze.

Poor Mena, while she was there in the doorway waiting for her brother to come home drunk, felt utterly tired and disheartened, when she tried to drag her sister indoors because don Michele was passing by, and Lia would say:

'Are you afraid he'll eat me? Anyway, no one wants anything to do with us, now that we have nothing. You see how my brother has ended up, not even the dogs want him!'

'If 'Ntoni had any guts,' Piedipapera would say, 'he'd get rid of that don Michele.'

But 'Ntoni had another reason for wanting to get rid of don Michele. After she had broken with don Michele, Santuzza

188

had begun to be sweet on 'Ntoni, because of that way he had of wearing his cap pulled down over his ear, and of rolling his shoulders, which he had picked up as a sailor; and she put aside all the plates with the remains which the customers left for him under the counter; and she also filled up his glass for him now and again. In this way she kept him around the wine shop fat and satisfied as the butcher's dog. And then 'Ntoni did his bit, fighting with those customers obliged by misfortune to quibble over details and who shouted and swore before paying. But with his tavern friends he was cheerful and talkative, and he also kept an eye on the counter, when Santuzza went to confession. So that everyone there was as fond of him as if he were in his own house; except for zio Santoro who looked at him with dislike and grumbled, between one Hail Mary and the next, that he was living off his daughter, like a cleric; Santuzza replied that she was the boss, if she wanted 'Ntoni to live off her, fat as a cleric; a sign that he served her purpose, and she had no need of anyone.

'Oh yes you do,' muttered zio Santoro when he could get her for a moment on his own. 'You still need don Michele. Massaro Filippo has told me ten times that it's time to stop this nonsense, that he can't keep the new wine in the cellar any longer and it will have to be smuggled into the village.'

'Massaro Filippo is thinking of his own interests. But even if I had to pay the tax twice over, and the fine for smuggling, I still wouldn't want anything more to do with don Michele, and that's final.'

She refused to forgive don Michele for that dirty trick he had played her with Zuppidda, after she had treated him like a cleric so long in the wine shop, for love of his braided cap; and 'Ntoni Malavoglia, all non-uniformed as he was, was worth ten don Micheles; and what she gave him, she gave him with all her heart. That was how 'Ntoni earned his bread, and when his grandfather reproached him for doing nothing, he would say: 'Do I cost you anything? I don't spend any of the money for the house, and I earn my daily bread.' 'It would be better that you should die of hunger,' his grandfather told him, 'and that we should all die this very day!' Finally everyone fell silent where they were sitting, turning their backs on each other. Padron 'Ntoni's only resort was not to open his mouth, so as not to quarrel with his grandson; and when he was tired of the preaching, 'Ntoni left the whole crew sitting there, whimpering, and went off to find Rocco and compare Vanni, with whom you could have a good time and always find some new lark to get up to.

Once they had the bright idea of serenading zio Crocifisso, on the night of his wedding with la Vespa, and they took everyone to whom zio Crocifisso would no longer lend money, to gather under his window, with bits of broken pots and pans, and the butcher's cowbells, and reed pipes, making a din and a racket until midnight, so that la Vespa got up the next day greener than ever, and lost her temper with the odious Santuzza, in whose tavern they had cooked up the dirty deed, out of jealousy because she had found herself a husband, so as to be in God's grace, while the others were always in mortal sin, and got up to all kinds of tricks, under the Virgin's scapular.

People laughed in zio Crocifisso's face, when they saw him on the square, a husband, dressed in his new clothes, and yellow as a canary with the fright la Vespa had given him with that new dress which cost money. La Vespa spent money like water, and if he had let her she would have spent his entire fortune within a week; and she said that now she was in charge, so that every day there was a frightful shindy at zio Crocifisso's. His wife sunk her nails into his face, and screamed that she wanted the keys, and didn't want to carry on being in the position of going short of the odd piece of bread and a new handkerchief worse than before; because if she had known what that marriage would lead to, with that fine husband she had landed, she would rather have kept the smallholding and the medal of the daughter of Mary; indeed, for all the good it did her, she could have been wearing it still. And he shrieked that he was ruined; that he was no longer master in his own house, which was still cholera-ridden, and they wanted to make him die of heartbreak before his time, cheerfully to squander the possessions he had so laboured to put together! He too, if he had known all this, would have said to the devil with wife and smallholding; because he had no need of a wife, and they had got him by the scruff, making him believe that la Vespa had got her hands on Brasi Cipolla and that she was just about to slip out of his grasp together with the smallholding, that damned smallholding!

Just as the time it became known that Brasi Cipolla had let the Mangiacarrubbe girl persuade him to elope with her, like a fool, and padron Fortunato was looking for him everywhere all over the *sciara*, and in the ravine, and under the bridge, foaming at the mouth, swearing and cursing that if he found them he would give them right royal kicks, and tear off his son's ears. On hearing such talk zio Crocifisso too thrust his hands into his hair, and said that the Mangiacarrubbe girl had ruined him by not laying her hands on Brasi a week earlier.

'It's the will of God,' he would say, beating his breast; 'it was God's will that I should take la Vespa as punishment for my sins!' And his sins must have been black indeed, because la Vespa poisoned the very bread in his mouth, and made him suffer the pains of Purgatory, day and night. In addition she boasted that she was faithful to him, that she wouldn't look another mortal in the eye, be he as young and handsome as 'Ntoni Malavoglia or Vanni Pizzuto, for all the gold in the world; while the men continued to buzz around her, proffering temptation as if she had honey in her skirts.

'If it were true, I'd go and get her one myself,' muttered zio Crocifisso, 'on condition he got her out of my hair!' And he also said that he would pay Vanni Pizzuto or 'Ntoni Malavoglia something for them to cuckold him, since 'Ntoni was in that business.

'Then I could send her away, that witch I've brought into my house!'

But 'Ntoni was into richer pickings, and ate and drank, so that he was a joy to behold. Now he held his head high and laughed if his grandfather said something to him in a low voice; now it was his grandfather who made himself small, as though the fault were his. 'Ntoni said that if they didn't want him in the house he knew where to go to sleep, in Santuzza's stable; and anyway they weren't spending anything on him for food. Padron 'Ntoni and Alessi and Mena could put aside everything they earned with fishing, and weaving, and at the wash place, for that miraculous boat of St. Peter's, with which you had the privilege of half breaking your arms every day for a few ounces of fish, or for the house by the medlar tree, which they would finally repurchase, cheerfully to die of hunger in! Anyway, he didn't want a penny; since he was a poor devil in any case, he preferred a bit of rest, while he was young, and not yet barking at night like his grandfather. The sun was there for everyone, and the shade of the olive trees for a bit of relief, and the piazza to stroll in, and the steps of the church to chat on, and the main street to see people pass by and hear the news, and the wine shop to eat and drink with your friends. Then when you felt another jaw-breaking attack of boredom coming on you could play *mora*, or *briscola*; and at last when you were tired, there was the smallholding where compare Naso's sheep grazed, and you could stretch out and sleep during the day, or comare suor Mariangela's stable for the night.

'Aren't you ashamed of the life you lead?' his grandfather asked him at last, having come to look for him specially with his head bowed and his back all bent; and he wept like a child as he said it, tugging him by the sleeve behind Santuzza's stable, so that no one should see them.

'Don't you ever think about your house? If only your father were here, and la Longa! Oh 'Ntoni, 'Ntoni!'

'But are you lot any better off than me, working and slaving for nothing? We're cut out for misery, that's what it is! Look what it's done to you, you're like a violin bow and you've always lead the same life, right until your old age. And where has it got you? You lot don't know the world, and you're like kittens with your eyes still closed. Do you eat the fish you catch? Do you know who you're working for, from Monday to Saturday, worn away to such a state that not even the hospital would want you? You're working for people who don't do anything, and have money by the spadeful!'

'But you haven't any money, and nor have I! We've never had any, and we've always earned our bread as God has willed it; that's why you have to buckle to, earning it, if you don't want to die of hunger.'

'As the devil has willed it you mean! Our misfortune is all

the work of the devil! Now you know what's awaiting you, when you can no longer buckle to, because rheumatism has turned your hands into a vine root — the ditch under the bridge, that's what's waiting for you, to die there!'

'No, no,' exclaimed the old man suddenly joyful, and throwing his vine root arms round his grandson's neck. 'We've got the money for the house, and if you help us . . .'

'Ah, the house by the medlar tree! Do you think it's the finest dwelling in the world, all of you who haven't seen anything else?'

'I know it's not the finest dwelling in the world. But you shouldn't say that, because you were born there, and all the more so since your mother couldn't die there.'

'Nor could my father. Our trade is to leave our skins on the bottom, for the sharks. And at least, until that day comes, I want to enjoy whatever bit of good luck I can find, since it's pointless to wear one's fingers to the bone for nothing. Anyway, when you've got the house, and the boat, and Mena's dowry, and Lia's? Ah, by the blood of the thieving Judas, what a life!'

The old man went off disconsolately, shaking his head, with his back bent, because his grandson's bitter words had crushed him worse than any piece of rock. Now he lacked the courage for anything and was truly downhearted, and wanted to weep. He could think of nothing except that Bastianazzo and Luca had never been possessed by those things which possessed 'Ntoni, and they had always done what they had to do without complaining; and he even began to tell himself that it was pointless to think about Mena's dowry, since they would never manage to get it.

Poor Mena seemed to know this too, she was so downcast. Now the neighbourhood women went straight by the Malavoglia's door, as though they still had cholera, and left her alone, she and her sister with her handkerchief with the roses, or with Nunziata or cousin Anna, when they were kind enough to go and chat for a bit; because cousin Anna too, poor thing, had her own drunkard of a Rocco, and by now everyone knew it; and Nunziata had been too small, when that fine father of hers had walked away to go and seek his fortune elsewhere. The poor things got on so well for that very reason, when they talked in low voices, with their heads bent, and their hands under their aprons, and even when they were silent, without looking at each other, each thinking about their own affairs.

'When you're reduced to the state we're in,' said Lia, who talked like a grown woman, 'you have to fend for yourself, because that's what everyone else does.'

Sometimes don Michele would stop to greet them and tell the odd joke; so that the girls had become quite used to his braided cap, and weren't alarmed by him any more; indeed Lia actually told some jokes herself, and laughed at them; nor did Mena dare to scold her, or go off into the kitchen and leave her alone, now that their mother was no longer there; and she too sat there huddled in on herself, looking up and down the roadway with tired eyes. Now as it became clear that the neighbours had abandoned them, her heart swelled with gratitude every time don Michele deigned to stop at their door to have a chat, with that impressive braided cap of his. And if don Michele found Lia alone, he looked her straight in the eye, pulling on his moustache, with his braided cap so boldly set, and said to her: 'What a fine girl you are, comare Malavoglia!'

No one had ever said that to her; so she turned as red as a tomato.

'How come you're not married yet?' don Michele also asked.

Lia shrugged, and said that she didn't know.

'You ought to wear a dress of silk and wool, and long ear-rings; then you'd outshine many a city lady, my word of honour.'

'Dresses of silk and wool are not for me, don Michele,' answered Lia.

'Why not? Hasn't Zuppidda got one, and won't the Mangiacarrubbe girl be getting one, now that she has landed Brasi Cipolla? and if she wants, won't la Vespa be able to have one like the rest?'

'They're rich!'

'What a wretched life,' exclaimed don Michele bringing

194

his fist down on his sabre. 'I'd like to get a winning ticket in the state lottery, indeed I would, and show you what I'm capable of!'

Sometimes don Michele added: 'May I?' with his hand on his cap, and came and sat right there on the stones, when he had nothing to do. Mena thought he was there because of comarè Barbara, and didn't say anything. But don Michele swore to Lia that it wasn't for Barbara, and he had never even thought of her, on his holy sword of honour. He was thinking of something quite different, if comare Lia didn't know . . .

And he rubbed his chin, or pulled at his moustache, staring at her like the basilisk. The girl turned all the colours of the rainbow and stood up to go. But don Michele took her by the hand, and said to her: 'Why do you do me this wrong, comare Malavoglia? Stay there, no one is eating you.'

And this was how they passed the time, while they were waiting for the men to come home from the sea; she on the doorstep, and don Michele on the stones, whittling away at some twig out of sheer awkwardness, and asking her whether she would like to live in the city.

'What would I do in the city?'

'That's the place for you! You're not made to live here, among these yokels, my word of honour! You're made of finer clay, top quality goods, and you should be living in a pretty little house, and go walking along the Marina and in the Villa gardens, where there's music, and you all dressed up — I know all about it. With a fine silk handkerchief on your head, and an amber necklace. Here it's like being among swine, word of honour, and I can't wait to be transferred, because they promised me they'd have me back in the city in the new year.' Lia began to laugh at the jest, and shrugged her shoulders, because she scarcely knew what amber necklaces and silk handkerchieves were. Then once with a mysterious flourish don Michele pulled out a lovely red and yellow handkerchief, in all its special paper, which he had got from a smuggler, and he wanted to give it to comare Lia.

'No, no,' she said, all flushed. 'I wouldn't take it if you killed me.'

And don Michele insisted: 'I didn't expect that of you,

comare Lia. I don't deserve it, really I don't.' And he had to roll the handkerchief up again in its paper and put it away in his pocket.

From then onwards, when she saw don Michele's nose rounding the corner, Lia ran to shut herself indoors for fear he wanted to give her the handkerchief.

Don Michele walked up and down in front of the house in vain, making Zuppidda foam at the mouth, and crane his neck towards the Malavoglia's front door though he might, there was no longer anyone to be seen so that finally he decided to go in. When they saw him before them, the girls were open-mouthed and trembling as though they had the tertian fever, and didn't know what to do.

'You wouldn't accept the silk handkerchief, comare Lia,' he said to the girl, who had turned red as a poppy, 'but I've come back because of the affection I feel for you and your family. What's your brother 'Ntoni doing?'

Then Mena turned red, too, when they asked what her brother 'Ntoni was doing, because he wasn't doing anything. And don Michele went on: 'I'm afraid he may cause you all some trouble, your brother 'Ntoni. I'm a friend, and I shut my eyes; but when another sergeant comes in my place, he'll want to know what your brother does with Cinghialenta, of an evening, towards the Rotolo, and that other down and out Rocco Spatu, when they walk over the *sciara,* as if they had shoe leather to waste. You would do well to open your eyes to what I'm saying to you now, comare Mena; and also tell him that he shouldn't hang around with that troublemaker Piedipapera, in Pizzuto's shop, because everyone knows everything that goes on, and it'll be him who lands up in trouble. The others are crafty old foxes, and your grandfather would be well advised not to let him go walking over the *sciara,* because the *sciara* is no place for walking, and the rocks of the Rotolo can hear things just as though they had ears, tell him, and they don't need a telescope to see the boats which go creeping quietly round the coast towards dusk, as if they were going to catch bats. Tell him this, comare Mena, and also tell him that the person giving him this warning is a friend who wishes him well. As for Cinghialenta and Rocca

196

Spatu, and Vanni Pizzuto too, they're being watched. Your brother trusts Piedipapera, and what he doesn't understand is that the customs guard gets a percentage on contraband, and that to catch them you give a share to one of the gang, and make him squeal. And only tell him this about Piedipapera: Christ said to St. John, 'Take heed of a person marked.' The proverb says so too.'

Mena opened her eyes wide, and paled, without really understanding what she was hearing; but she already felt alarm that her brother should have dealings with people in uniform. Then don Michele took her by the hand, to give her courage, and continued:

'If anyone knew that I had come to tell you this, I'd be done for. I'm risking my braided cap, for the good will I feel for you and the other Malavoglia. But I don't want your brother to get into any trouble. And I don't want to come upon him at night somewhere he shouldn't be, not even if it means getting a smuggling fine of a thousand *lire,* my word of honour!'

The poor girls were worried silly, since don Michele had started them thinking along these lines. They couldn't sleep at night, and waited up for their brother behind the door until late, trembling with cold and fear, while he went singing through the streets with Rocco Spatu and other members of the gang, and the poor girls thought they heard shots and shouts, as there had been on the night of the hunt for the two-legged quails.

'You go to bed,' Mena kept saying to her sister. 'You're too young, there are some things you shouldn't know.'

They said nothing to their grandfather, not wanting to give him this last heartbreak; but when they saw 'Ntoni in a somewhat calmer mood, sitting glumly at the doorway, with his chin in his hand, they plucked up courage and asked him: 'What are you doing all the time with Rocco Spatu and Cinghialenta? watch out, because you've been seen on the *sciara* and towards the Rotolo. You know the old saying which Christ said to St. John: 'Take heed of a person marked.' '

'Who told you?' asked 'Ntoni, leaping up like a fiend. 'Tell me who told you.'

'Don Michele told me,' she answered with tears in her eyes. 'He told me that you should beware of Piedipapera, because to catch a smuggler you have to give a share to one of the gang.'

'Is that all he said?'

'Yes, that's all.'

Then 'Ntoni swore it wasn't true, and she shouldn't tell their grandfather. And he got up hurriedly, and went off to the wine shop to cool off, and if he met anyone in uniform he went the long way round, so as not to catch even a glimpse of them.

Actually don Michele knew nothing, and was talking at random, to frighten him, because of the tantrum he'd had after the business with Santuzza, who had thrown him out like a mangy dog. When all was said and done he wasn't afraid of don Michele and his braid, well-paid as he was to suck the blood of the poor. A fine business! Don Michele had no need to put himself out in any way at all, so fat and well-fed was he! and all he had to do was to get his hands on some poor devil, if someone made an effort to earn a twelve *tari* piece as best they could. And then there was that other outrage, which meant that to land foreign goods you had to pay a tax, and don Michele and his policemen had to stick their noses in! They could lay their hands on everything, and take what they wanted; but the others, if they risked their lives trying to land their goods, were regarded as thieves, and were hunted down worse than wolves with pistols and rifles. But robbing thieves has never been a crime. Even don Giammaria said so in the chemist's shop. And don Franco approved with his head and his whole beard, smirking, because when they brought in the republic you wouldn't be seeing any more of these dirty dealings.

'Or those devil's employees,' added the priest. Don Giammaria was still smarting from the twenty five *onze* which had disappeared from his house.

Now donna Rosolina had lost her head along with the twenty five *onze*, and was running after don Michele, to make sure of losing the remainder. When she saw him going down the strada del Nero, she thought he was coming to see her on the little terrace, and she would stand at the parapet with her tomato preserve, and jars of peppers, to demonstrate her capabilities; since it was now quite impossible to drum it into her head that don Michele, with his stomach, now that he had emerged from a period of mortal sin with Santuzza, was not looking for a judicious housekeeper with good sense, and she knew what that meant; so she defended him, if her brother said a word against the Government and its paid shirkers, and would reply: 'Shirkers like don Silvestro do indeed suck a place dry without doing anything; but you need the taxes to pay the soldiers, who cut such a dash with their uniforms, and we'd devour each other like wolves if we didn't have soldiers.'

'Layabouts who are paid to carry guns, and nothing more,' snarled the chemist; 'like priests, who take three *tari* per mass. Tell the truth, don Giammaria, what capital do you put into your mass that they pay you three *tari* for it?'

'And what capital do you put into that dirty water that you make people pay through the nose for?' snapped back the priest, foaming at the mouth.

Don Franco had learned to laugh like don Silvestro, to drive don Giammario crazy; and he carried on taking no notice of him, because he had come upon the best means to bamboozle him.

'They earn their day's keep in half an hour and then they can idle around all day; just like don Michele who cuts the figure of a complete fool and timewaster, always there under your feet, even since he stopped warming Santuzza's benches.'

'That's why he had it in for me,' 'Ntoni intervened to say; 'he's as mad as a rabid dog, and comes on heavy-handed because he's got a sabre. But by the blood of the Virgin, one of these days I'll slash his face with his own sabre, to show him I don't give a hang, myself!'

'Well said,' exclaimed the chemist, 'that's the spirit! The people must show their teeth. But not here, because I don't want trouble in my shop. The Government wouldn't be able to believe its luck at being able to embroil me good and proper; but I don't like dealings with judges and all the rest of the rotten mob.'

'Ntoni Malavoglia raised his fists to the skies, and swore black and blue by Christ and the Virgin that he wanted to put an end to it, even if it meant going to prison; anyhow, he had nothing to lose. Santuzza no longer doted on him in the same way, so much had that useless old father of hers said to her about him, whinging between one Hail Mary and the next after massaro Filippo was no longer sending the wine to the wine shop! He told her that customers were beginning to drop off like flies on St. Andrew's Day, now that they couldn't get massaro Filippo's wine any more, since they'd all become as used to it as children to their mother's milk. Each time, zio Santoro would say to his daughter: 'What do you want with that dead beat 'Ntoni Malavoglia? Can't you see he's eating you out of house and home to no end? You're fattening him up better than a prize pig, and then he goes off and plays the lover with la Vespa and the Mangiacarrubbe girl, now that she's rich.' And he also told her: 'The customers are leaving because he's always hanging around your apron strings, without leaving you a free moment to tell a joke.' Or: 'Ragged and filthy as he is, it's disgusting having him in the shop; it's like a stable, and people can't even bear the idea of drinking out of the glasses.

It was fine having don Michele at the door, with all that uniform. People who pay for wine want to drink it in peace and quiet, and they like seeing a man with a sabre there in front of them, and everyone would doff their caps, and pay up what they owed without a murmur, because it was marked up there on the wall in charcoal. Now he's no longer there, not even massaro Filippo comes. He passed by recently, and I tried to get him to come in; but he says it's pointless coming here, since he can't smuggle in his wine must any more, now that you've quarrelled with don Michele. And that's no good for man or beast. People are beginning to say that your charity to 'Ntoni isn't totally disinterested, since massaro Filippo doesn't come here any more, and you'll see how it will end! The priest will get to hear of it, and they'll take away your Daughter of Mary medal!'

But Santuzza held out, because she still wanted to be mistress in her own house; and her eyes were opened, too, since everything her father told her was holy writ, and she no longer treated 'Ntoni as she had previously. She no longer kept him the leftovers, and she put dirty water in the remains of other people's drinks when she gave them to him; so that finally 'Ntoni began to sulk, and Santuzza told him she didn't like layabouts, and she and her father earned their daily bread, and so should he, and help a bit around the house, instead of hanging around there like a beggar, bawling and snoozing with his head on his arms, or spitting all over the floor, so that it was all wet and you no longer knew where to tread.

For a bit 'Ntoni went to chop wood, grumbling, or to blow on the fire, to avoid trouble. But he found it hard working all day like a dog, worse than he had once done in his own home just to be treated worse than a dog with rudeness and rough words, for the sake of those dirty dishes they gave him to lick. At last, once while Santuzza was coming back from confession with her rosary in her hand, he made a scene, complaining that this was happening because don Michele had started hanging around in front of the wine shop again, and was also waiting for her there on the square, when she went to confession, and zio Santoro shouted after him to greet him, when he heard his voice, and even went looking for him in Pizzuto's shop, feeling his way along the walls with his stick. Then Santuzza flared up, and told him that he had come on purpose to make her sin, while she had the host in her mouth, and to waste her communion.

'If you don't like it, you can leave,' she shouted to him. 'I don't want to damn my immortal soul for you; and I didn't say anything to you when I learned that you were running after sluts like la Vespa or the Mangiacarrubbe girl, now that they're unhappily married. Go and see them, now that they've got a trough in the house and are looking for a pig.' But 'Ntoni swore that it wasn't true, and he didn't care a hang about those things; he didn't think about women any more, and she could spit in his face if she ever saw him talking with another one.

'No, you won't get rid of him that way,' zio Santoro repeated the while. 'Can't you see how much he cares about the bread he steals from you? You'll have to break the pan in order to mend it. You'll have to kick him out bodily. Massaro Filippo told me that he can no longer keep the wine must in the barrels, and he'll sell it to others if you don't make your peace with don Michele and can't get it smuggled in as you used to!' And he went off again to look for massaro Filippo in Pizzuto's shop, feeling the walls with his stick. His daughter was acting all haughty, protesting that she would never bow her head to don Michele, after that dirty trick he'd played on her.

'Leave him to me, I'll see to him,' zio Santoro assured her. 'I'll do things discreetly, I wouldn't let you seem to be going back to lick don Michele's boots; am I your father or not, by heavens?'

Since Santuzza had been treating him so rudely, 'Ntoni had to think up ways of paying for the bread they gave him at the wine shop, because he didn't dare appear at home, and meanwhile those poor people were thinking of him as they ate their soup listlessly, as though he were dead, and they didn't even put on the tablecloth, but ate scattered about the house, with their bowls on their knees.

'This is the final straw, for me in my old age,' their grandfather would repeat; and those people who saw him with his nets on his shoulders, going out to work by the day, would say: 'This is the last winter for padron 'Ntoni. Soon those orphans will be left all alone.' And if Mena told her to go indoors when don Michele came by, Lia would answer brazenly: 'Oh yes! I have to go indoors as though I were some sort of treasure! Don't you worry, even the dogs can resist treasures like us!'

'Come now! If your mother were here you wouldn't talk like that,' murmured Mena.

'If my mother were here I wouldn't be an orphan and I wouldn't have to think about fending for myself. 'Ntoni wouldn't be wandering around the streets either, so that you feel ashamed to hear yourself called his sister; and no one will come and take 'Ntoni Malavoglia's sister to wife.'

Now that he was penniless, 'Ntoni no longer showed caution about appearing together with Rocco Spatu and

Cinghiaenta on the *sciara*, and towards the Rotolo, and talking in low voices among themselves, with black expressions, like starving wolves. Once more don Michele warned Mena: 'Your brother will give you trouble, comare Mena!'

Mena was obliged to go and look for her brother on the *sciara* too, and towards the Rotolo, or at the door of the wine shop; and she cried and wept, pulling him by his shirt sleeves. But he replied: 'No! It's don Michele who wishes me ill, I've told you. He's always cooking up tricks against me with zio Santoro. I heard them myself in Pizzuto's shop, and don Michele was telling him: 'And if I went back to your daughter, what sort of a figure would I cut?' And zio Santoro answered: 'That's a good one! The whole village would be gnawing their elbows in envy, I tell you!' '

'But what will you do?' asked Mena, pale-faced. 'Think of mother, 'Ntoni, and remember we have nobody any more.'

'Nonsense! I want to put him and Santuzza to shame in front of the whole village, when they go to mass. I want to give them a piece of my mind, and make people laugh. I'm not afraid of anyone in the world; and the chemist will hear me too.'

For all Mena's begging and beseeching, he just repeated that he had nothing to lose, so that other people should be on their guard, because he was tired of that life, and wanted to be done with it — as don Franco said. And since he was out of favour at the wine shop, he would hang around the square, especially on Sundays, and sit down on the church steps to see what sort of face those brazen people who went there to hoodwink the world would make, and to cock a snook at the Signora and Madonna under their very eyes.

When she saw 'Ntoni playing the sentinel on the door of the church, Santuzza would go to Aci Castello to mass, early in the morning, to avoid all temptation to sin. 'Ntoni saw the Mangiacarrubbe girl go past, with her nose in her shawl, not looking at anyone any more, now that she had got her man. La Vespa, all in finery and with a whole handful of rosary, went to pray to the Lord to set her free of her husband, that punishment sent by God; and 'Ntoni sniggered after them:

'Now that they've landed a husband they don't need anything any more. There's someone who's duty it is to provide them with food.'

Zio Crocifisso had to say goodbye to his devotions, since he had lumbered himself with la Vespa, and he didn't even go to church, so as to be away from his wife at least for the length of a mass; that way he was driven along the road to perdition.

'This will be my last year,' he would whimper; and now he would run in search of padron 'Ntoni, and other equally unfortunate folk. 'It's hailed in my vineyard and I'll never make it to the wine harvest.'

'See here, zio Crocifisso,' padron 'Ntoni would reply; 'I'm ready to go the to the notary for the house whenever you like, and I've got the money here.' He thought of nothing but his house, and didn't give a hoot about other people's affairs.

'Don't talk to me about notaries, padron 'Ntoni; when I hear the word notary I remember the day I allowed myself to be dragged there by la Vespa, and I curse the day I set foot there!'

But compare Piedipapera, who sniffed possibilities for the go-between, said to him: 'When you die, that witch la Vespa is quite capable of giving away the house by the medlar tree for a song and it would be better if you looked after your affairs yourself, as long as you're alive to do so.'

Then zio Crocifisso said yes, they would go to the notary, but he had to gain something on this deal, as anyone could see how many losses he'd made. And pretending to talk with him, Piedipapera added: 'If she hears that you've got back the money for the house, that witch of a wife of yours is quite capable of throttling you to buy herself so many necklaces and handkerchieves.' And he also said: 'At least the Mangia-carrubbe girl doesn't buy necklaces and silk handkerchieves any more, now that she's landed a husband. See how she comes to mass in a little cotton frock.'

'I don't care what the Mangiacarrubbe girl does, but they ought to have burned her alive too, along with all other women who are in this world to drive you crazy. Do you really believe she doesn't buy anything any more? It's all a deception, to gull padron Fortunato, who is going around bawling that he wants to grab himself any wife in the middle of the street, rather than have his property enjoyed by that wretch who has robbed him of his son. Personally I'd give him la Vespa, if he would have her. They're all the same! And God help anyone who falls for them, completely blinded as you have to be to do so. Look at don Michele, who goes to the strada del Nero to make eyes at donna Rosolina; he's got everything he needs. Respected, well paid, a healthy stomach . . . even he runs after women, troubling trouble; all in the hope of a few pence from the priest.'

'Oh no, he doesn't go there for donna Rosolina, oh dear no!' said Piedipapera winking at him slyly. 'Donna Rosolina can make sheep's eyes at him until she takes root on the spot, on the terrace among all her tomatoes. Don Michele doesn't give a hoot about the priest's money. I know what he's up to in the strada del Nero!'

'So what do you want for the house?' resumed padron 'Ntoni.

'We'll talk about it when we're at the notary's,' answered zio Crocifisso. 'Now let me hear holy mass in peace'; and he sent him away quite crestfallen.

'Don Michele has other things on his mind,' repeated Piedipapera, sticking a healthy length of tongue out behind padron 'Ntoni's back, and casting a look in the direction of his grandson, who was going to perch on the wall, with that rag of a jacket on his shoulders, darting poisonous looks at zio Santoro, who had taken to coming to mass, to hold out his hand to the faithful, muttering Hail Maries and Gloria Patris, and he knew everyone individually, as the crowd came out of the church, and would say to each of them: 'May the good Lord send you luck,' and to another: 'Your good health,' and as don Michele passed in front of him, he even said: 'She's there waiting for you in the vegetable patch behind the shed. Holy Mary Mother of God, ora pro nobis. Oh Lord God forgive me!'

As soon as don Michele went back to hanging around Santuzza, people said: 'The cats and dogs have made it up! That means they must have been sulking at each other with good reason!'

And as massaro Filippo too had gone back to the wine shop: 'Him too! Can't he live without don Michele? That's a sign he's in love with the sergeant, rather than with Santuzza. Some people wouldn't know how to be alone even in paradise!'

Then 'Ntoni Malavoglia seethed, kicked out of the wine shop as he was, worse than a mangy dog, without a penny in his pocket to go and drink under don Michele's nose, and seat himself down there all day, with his elbows on the table, and make them all fume. Instead he had to stay out on the street like a stray dog, with his tail between his legs and nose to the ground, muttering: 'By the blood of Judas! one of these days something serious will happen, that's for sure!'

Rocco Spatu, and Cinghialenta, who always had a bit of money, laughed in his face, from the door of the tavern, making gestures of contempt, and then they came to talk to him in low voices, pulling him by the arm towards the *sciara* and whispering in his ear. He kept on nodding assent, like the dolt he was. Then they told him sharply: 'It serves you right to die of hunger in front of the wine shop, watching don Michele giving you horns by the minute, swine that you are!'

'By the blood of Judas, don't say that,' shouted 'Ntoni, fists flailing, 'or one of these days something serious will happen, you see if it doesn't!'

But the others left him there, shrugging their shoulders, and sneering; so that at last they got him really rattled; and he went and stood himself right in the middle of the wine shop, waxen as a corpse, with his hand on his hip and his old jacket on his shoulder, as brave as if it were made of velvet, casting vicious looks around to fall upon certain people he knew. Don Michele pretended not to see him, for love of his braided cap, and tried to leave; but now that don Michele was playing the goat, 'Ntoni felt his hackles rise, and laughed and sneered in their faces, at him and Santuzza; and he spat in the wine he was drinking, saying it was as poisonous as that they had given to Christ on the cross! And baptised into the bargain, because Santuzza had put water in it, and it was real idiocy to come and let oneself be robbed in that tavern; and that was why he wasn't coming any more! Touched to the quick,

Santuzza couldn't contain herself any longer, and told him that if he didn't come there any more it was because they were tired of supporting him on charity and that they had been obliged to drive him out of the door with a broom, he was so hungry. Then 'Ntoni began to raise merry hell, shouting and breaking glasses, saying that they had driven him out to bring in that other dolt with the braided cap; but he was man enough to bring the wine out of his nose, if he wanted to, because he wasn't afraid of anyone. Equally yellow, don Michele, with his cap askew, stammered: 'Word of honour, this time it will end badly,' while Santuzza sent glasses and jugs flying at both of them. So at last they came to blows, and rolled under the benches, vicious as cats, while people kicked and punched them to get them apart; and at last Peppi Naso succeeded with the leather belt he took off his trousers, which skinned you where it touched you.

Don Michele brushed down his uniform, went to retrieve the sabre he'd lost in the fray and went out muttering between his teeth, without further ado, for love of his braided cap. But 'Ntoni Malavoglia, whose nose was pouring blood, seeing him sneak off like that, couldn't restrain himself from mouthing a sea of curses after him from the door of the wine shop, showing him his fist, and using his sleeve to wipe away the blood from his nose; and he promised he'd give him his come-uppance next time he met him.

CHAPTER XIV

When 'Ntoni Malavoglia met don Michele to give him his come-uppance it was a nasty business, and at night, and pouring with rain, and so dark a cat would have stumbled, on the part of the *sciara* towards the Rotolo, where the boats which pretended to be fishing for cod at midnight tacked stealthily by, and where 'Ntoni went to doze, with Rocco Spatu and Cinghialenta and other down-and-outs, with their pipes in their mouths, so that the guards knew them one by one by those dots of fire from their pipes, while they were hiding among the rocks with their rifles in their hands.

'Comare Mena,' don Michele began again, as he went down the strada del Nero, 'tell your brother not to go to the Rotolo at night, with Rocco Spatu and Cinghialenta.'

But 'Ntoni turned a deaf ear, because 'a starving stomach knows no reason' and don Michele didn't alarm him any more, after they had rolled together sprawling and brawling under the benches in the wine shop; and furthermore he had promised to give him his come-uppance when he met him, and he didn't want to look a blusterer and braggart in the eyes of Santuzza and all those who had been present at the threat.

'I told him I'd give him his come-uppance wherever I met him; and if I meet him on the Rotolo I'll be giving it him at the Rotolo!' he repeated with his friends, and they'd even dragged la Locca's son along with them. They had spent the evening in the wine shop, drinking and cackling, because a tavern is like a sea port, and Santuzza couldn't send him away, now that he had money in his pocket and jangled it in his hand. Don Michele had been on his rounds, but Rocco Spatu, who knew the law, said, spitting, that as long as there was a light at the door, they had a right to be there, and he leant up against the wall to feel more at ease. 'Ntoni Malavoglia was relishing making Santuzza yawn as she dozed behind the glasses, with her head resting on those cushions which bore the medal of the Daughter of Mary.

'What she's lying on is softer than a bundle of fresh grass,' said 'Ntoni, whom wine made forthcoming; whereas Rocco, tight as a tick, didn't utter a word, with his shoulders to the wall.

Meanwhile zio Santoro, groping his way, had removed the light and closed the door.

'Go away now, I'm sleepy,' said Santuzza.

'Well, I'm not. Massaro Filippo doesn't bother *me* of a night.'

'I don't care whether he bothers you or not; but I don't want to get a fine on your account, if they find me with the door open at this hour.'

'Who will fine you? that prying don Michele? Get him to come here and I'll fine him! Tell him that 'Ntoni Malavoglia is here, by Christ!'

Meanwhile Santuzza had taken him by the shoulders and was pushing him out of the door.

'Go and tell him yourself; and go and look for trouble elsewhere. I don't want chats with the police on account of your charms.'

Seeing himself thrown out on the street like that, in the mud, with the rain coming down in torrents, 'Ntoni pulled out a good solid knife, and swore black and blue that he'd stab the pair of them, her and don Michele both! Cinghialenta was the only one in a position to use his wits for all of them, and he was pulling 'Ntoni by the jacket, and saying: 'Let it drop for now! Don't you know we've work to do?'

Then la Locca's son felt a great desire to cry, there in the dark.

'He's drunk,' observed Rocco Spatu, standing under the eaves. 'Bring him here, it'll do him good.'

Slightly calmed by the water which was pouring from the eaves, 'Ntoni allowed himself to be led away by compare Cinghialenta, still fuming, while he splashed in the puddles, and swore that if he met don Michele he would give him what he had proposed. And then suddenly indeed he did find himself nose to nose with don Michele, who was buzzing around there as well, with his pistol on his stomach and his trousers tucked into his boots. Then 'Ntoni calmed down suddenly, and all three of them tiptoed towards Pizzuto's shop.

On arriving at the door, now that don Michele was safely some way off, 'Ntoni wanted them to stop to hear what he was saying.

'You see where don Michele was going? and Santuzza saying she was sleepy! Now what will they do if massaro Filippo is still in the stable?'

'You leave don Michele be,' Cinghialenta told him, 'things being as they are, he'll let us go about our business.'

'You're a fine lot' said 'Ntoni, 'to be afraid of don Michele.'

'To-night you're drunk! otherwise I'd show you if I'm afraid of don Michele! Now that I've sold my mule I don't want anyone coming around to see how I earn my daily bread, blood of a dog!'

Then they began to murmur in low voices up against the wall, while the roar of the rain covered their words. Suddenly the bell struck the hour, and all four of them fell silent to listen.

'Let's go to Pizzuto's place,' said Cinghialenta. 'He can stay open as late as he likes, and with no light outside.'

'It's so dark you can't see to get there,' said la Locca's son.

'We need a drink, in this weather,' replied Rocco Spatu. 'Otherwise we'll come a cropper on the *sciara*.'

Cinghialenta began to grumble that they weren't going there for the sheer joy of the outing, and he said he'd get them some lemon water at mastro Vanni's.

'I don't need lemon water,' snapped 'Ntoni, 'and you'll see that I can look after my affairs better than you lot!'

Compare Pizzuto didn't want to open up at that hour, and told them that he was in bed; but as they carried on knocking, and threatening to wake up the whole village and get the customs guards to come and poke their noses into their affairs, he asked them for the password and came to open up in his underclothes.

'Are you mad, knocking like this at this hour?' he exclaimed. 'I've just seen don Michele go by.'

'Yes, we saw him too; and now he's telling his beads with Santuzza.'

'Do you know where don Michele has just been?' Pizzuto asked him looking him straight in the eye; 'Ntoni shrugged; and Vanni, while he stood aside to let them in, winked at Rocco and Cinghialenta.

'He's been to the Malavoglia's,' he whispered in their ear. 'I saw him come out!'

'Much good may it do him,' replied Cinghialenta; 'but we ought to tell 'Ntoni to ask his sister to keep don Michele busy all night, when we've got work to do!'

'What's that you're going to ask me?' asked 'Ntoni thickly.

'Nothing, nothing to do with to-night.'

'If it's nothing to do with to-night, why did you make me leave the wine shop so I could get all soaking wet?' asked Rocco Spatu.

'It's something else, something we were talking about with Cinghialenta.'

And Pizzuto added: 'Yes, the man from Catania came, and said that the goods would be there this evening, but it will be quite a job unloading it in this weather.'

'All the better; no one will see us.'

'Yes, but the guards have sharp ears; and I thought I saw them hanging around here, and looking into the shop.'

Then there was a moment of silence, and to get them moving, compare Vanni went to fill up three glasses of absinthe.

'I don't give a hang about the guards,' exclaimed Rocco Spatu after he had drunk his down. 'So much the worse for them if they come sticking their noses into my affairs: I've got my jacknife, and it doesn't make as much racket as their pistols.'

'We earn our bread as best we can, and we don't want to harm anyone,' added Cinghialenta. 'Can't a person unload his goods where he chooses anymore?'

'They stroll around like thieves, to earn themselves the tax on every pocket handkerchief you want to unload, and no one shoots at them,' added 'Ntoni Malavoglia. 'You know what don Giammaria said? He said that robbing thieves is no sin. And the greatest thieves are those braided men, who eat us alive.'

'Let's make mincemeat of them,' said Rocco Spatu, his eyes glinting like a cat's.

But at such talk la Locca's son put down his glass, before having even put it to his mouth, yellow as a canary.

'Are you drunk already?' asked Cinghialenta.

'No,' he answered, 'I haven't been drinking.'

'Let's go outside, the fresh air will do us all good. And goodnight to the rest.'

'One moment,' shouted Pizzuto with his hand on the door.

'It's not the money for the absinthe; I gave it you for nothing, because we're friends; but one thing I do ask you. My house is here for you to use, if things go well. As you know, I've got a back room which could house a shipful of stuff, and no one ever looks into it, because don Michele and his guards and I are thick as thieves. But I don't trust Piedipapera, because the other time he pulled a fast one and took the stuff to don Silvestro's house. Don Silvestro would never be satisfied with what you'd give him as his cut, because he'd say that he was risking his job; but you wouldn't have that worry with me, and you'll give me a fair deal. And in fact I've never refused Piedipapera his cut, and I give him a glass of something every time he comes, and I shave him for nothing. But by Christ! if he double-deals me another time I won't be made a fool of, and I'll go and tell don Michele about all these dirty goings on!'

'No, no, compare Vanni; there's no need to go and tell don Michele. Have you seen Piedipapera this evening?'

'He hasn't even been out on the square; he was there in the chemist's shop playing at republicans with the chemist. Every time there's any action he lies low, to prove he isn't involved in anything that might be going on. He's a canny old hand, and he'll never be bullet fodder for the customs guards, even though he's as lame as the devil. But he leaves the bullets for the others.'

'It's still raining,' said Rocco Spatu. 'Isn't it ever going to stop to-night?'

'There won't be anyone at the Rotolo with this awful weather,' added la Locca's son, 'and we'd do better all to go home.'

'Ntoni, Cinghialenta and Rocco Spatu, who were at the doorway, looking out at the rain which was sizzling like fish in a frying pan, were quiet for a moment, gazing out into the darkness.

'What a dolt you are,' exclaimed Cinghialenta to give him courage; and Vanni Pizzuto slowly shut the door, after saying in a low voice: 'Listen, will you? If anything were to happen to you, you didn't see me this evening! I gave you the drink out of friendship, but you didn't come to my house. I count on you to keep your side of the bargain — I've no one in the world, you know.'

The others went off dejectedly into the rain, hugging the walls.

'Now he's starting,' muttered Cinghialenta, 'speaking ill of Piedipapera, and saying he has no one in the world. At least Piedipapera has a wife. And so have I. But I'm bullet fodder.'

At that moment they were creeping past Cousin Anna's door, and Rocco Spatu said he had a mother too, and at that moment she was lucky enough to be fast asleep in bed.

'Anyone who can be between the sheets, in this weather, certainly won't be wandering the streets,' said compare Cinghialenta.

'Ntoni motioned to them to be quiet, and to turn into the side street, so as to avoid going in front of his house, because Mena or his grandfather might be waiting for them, and would hear them.

'Your sister isn't waiting for you, I can assure you,' that drunkard Rocco Spatu said to him. 'If anything, she's waiting for don Michele.'

Then 'Ntoni felt a murderous rage against don Michele, while he felt for the knife in his pocket, and Cinghialenta asked them if they were drunk, to quarrel over trifles like that, while certain matters were under way.

In fact Mena was waiting for her brother at the door, with her beads in her hand, and Lia too, without saying a word of

213

what she knew, but as pale as a corpse. And it would have been better for everyone if 'Ntoni had gone down the strada del Nero, instead of turning off into the side road. Don Michele had indeed been there just after sunset, and had knocked on the door.

'Who is it at this hour?' asked Lia, who on the sly was hemming a silk handkerchief which don Michele had at last persuaded her to accept.

'It's me, don Michele; open up, I've something urgent to say.'

'I can't, because everyone is in bed and my sister is in the next room, waiting for 'Ntoni at the door.'

'It doesn't matter if your sister hears you opening up. It's 'Ntoni I've come to talk about, and it's urgent. I don't want your brother to go to prison. But open up, because if they find me here I'll lose my job.'

'Oh holy Virgin,' the girl exclaimed. 'Oh holy Virgin!'

'Shut your brother in the house this evening, when he gets back. But don't tell him I've been by. Tell him it would be better if he stayed at home. Make sure you tell him.'

'Oh holy Virgin,' the girl repeated, her hands clasped.

'Now he's at the wine shop, but he'll have to pass this way. You wait for him at the door, it'll be the better for him.'

Lia cried quietly, so that her sister should not hear, and don Michele saw her cry, with his pistol on his stomach and his trousers in his boots.

'There's no one worrying about *me* this evening, comare Lia, but I'm in danger too, like your brother. So, if anything happens to me, remember that I came to warn you, and risked losing my position in the process.'

Then Lia lifted her face from her hands with her eyes full of tears.

'May God reward you for your kindness, don Michele.'

'I don't want to be rewarded, comare Lia; I did it for you and for the good will I bear you.'

'Go away now, everyone is asleep. Go away, for the love of God, don Michele.'

Don Michele went, and she stayed behind the door telling her beads for her brother; and she prayed that the Lord would send him in that direction.

But the Lord did not send him in that direction. All four of them, 'Ntoni, Cinghialenta, Rocco Spatu and la Locca's son were creeping off hugging the walls of the little lane, and when they got to the *sciara* they took their shoes off, and listened for a bit, feeling nervous and holding their shoes in their hands.

'I can't hear anything,' said Cinghialenta.

The rain carried on falling, and all you could hear from the *sciara* was the rumbling of the sea below.

'It's as dark as the inside of a cow,' said Rocco Spatu. 'How will they get to the *scoglio dei colombi* in this darkness?'

'They're all used to it,' replied Cinghialenta. 'They know every inch of the coast, with their eyes closed.'

'But I can't hear a thing,' observed 'Ntoni.

'It's true, you can't hear a thing,' added Cinghialenta. 'But they must have been down there for some time now.'

'Well then, we'd better go home,' said la Locca's son.

'Now you've eaten and drunk, all you can think about is going home; and if you don't shut up, I'll kick you straight into the sea,' Cinghialenta told him.

'The fact is,' grumbled Rocco, 'that I don't like the idea of spending the night here, with nothing doing.'

'Now we'll know if they're there or not;' and they began to hoot like owls.

'If don Michele's guards hear us,' added 'Ntoni, 'they'll come running straight away, because owls aren't abroad on nights like this.'

'Then we'd better leave,' whimpered la Locca's son, 'because nobody's answering.'

All four looked at each other, even though it was black as pitch, and considered what padron 'Ntoni's 'Ntoni had said.

'What shall we do?' la Locca's son asked yet again.

'Let's get down on the road,' suggested Cinghialenta; 'if there's no one there, it means they haven't come.'

While they were going down on to the road, 'Ntoni said that Piedipapera was quite capable of selling them all for a glass of wine.

'Now that you haven't got a glass in front of you,'

Cinghialenta said to him, 'you're afraid too.'

'Come now, blood of the devil! I'll show you if I'm afraid!'

As they picked their way gingerly among the rocks, moving cautiously so as not to break their necks, Spatu observed quietly: 'Vanni Pizzuto got so angry about Piedipapera getting a cut without doing anything, but even he is in his bed right now.'

'Well,' concluded Cinghialenta, 'if you don't want to risk your skin, you ought to have stayed at home and slept.'

No one said another word, and 'Ntoni, putting his hands in front of him to see where he was putting his feet, reflected that compare Cinghialenta needn't have said that, because in such predicaments everyone sees their own homes before their eyes, with their beds and Mena cat-napping behind the door.

At last that drunkard Rocco Spatu said: 'Our skins aren't worth a penny.'

Suddenly, from behind the street wall, they heard a shout of 'Who goes there? Halt. Everybody halt.'

'We've been betrayed,' they began to shout, and ran off over the *sciara,* without caring where they put their feet.

But 'Ntoni, who had already scaled the wall, found himself nose to nose with don Michele, who had his pistol in his hand.

'By the blood of the Virgin,' shouted Malavoglia pulling out his knife; 'I'll show you if I'm afraid of a pistol!'

Don Michele's pistol went off, but he slumped like a felled ox, stabbed in the chest. Then 'Ntoni tried to run away, leaping higher than a goat, but the guards were on to him, while gunshots rained down like hail, and they threw him to the ground.

'Now what will my mother do?' wailed la Locca's son, while they were trussing him up tighter than a pig for market.

'Don't tie me so tight, blood of the Virgin,' shrieked 'Ntoni; 'you can see that I can't move!'

'Come on, Malavoglia,' they answered him. 'Your goose is well and truly cooked,' and they pushed him forwards with the muzzles of their rifles.

While they were taking him to the barracks, trussed up tighter than a pig for market, with don Michele behind him

216

on the guards' shoulders, he was peering round to see where Cinghialenta and Rocco Spatu were.

'They've got away,' he said to himself; 'they have nothing to worry about now, like Vanni Pizzuto and Piedipapera who are asleep between the sheets at this hour. My house is the only place where they won't have been sleeping, since they heard the pistol shots.'

And indeed those poor folk were not asleep, and were standing at the door, in the rain, as if they had had a premonition; while the neighbours turned over and went back to sleep, yawning and saying that they would hear what had happened to-morrow.

Later on, just as dawn began to break, people crowded in front of Pizzuto's shop, where the light was still on; and there was a great chattering about what had happened, in the pandemonium of that night.

'They caught both the smugglers and their goods,' Pizzuto told people, 'and don Michele got himself stabbed.' People looked towards the Malavoglia's doorway, and pointed. At last cousin Anna came out, all unkempt, white as a rag and at a loss for words. Suddenly, as if scenting disaster, padron 'Ntoni asked: 'And 'Ntoni? where is 'Ntoni?' 'They arrested him last night for smuggling, along with la Locca's son!' answered cousin Anna, all judgement gone. 'They killed don Michele!'

'Ah, mamma mia,' shrieked the old man thrusting his hands into his hair; and Lia did the same. Still with his hands to his head, padron 'Ntoni could only say, 'Ah mamma mia. Mamma mia.'

Later on Piedipapera came, looking distressed and striking his forehead: 'I was dumbfounded when I heard. What a disaster, padron 'Ntoni.' Comare Grazia, his wife, was positively weeping, poor thing, seeing how disasters rained down on the Malavoglia household.

'What are you here for?' her husband asked her under his breath, pulling her over to the window. 'You've nothing to do with all this. Now even showing your face in this household means attracting the attention of the police.'

And that was why people didn't even come to the

217

Malavoglia's doorstep. Only Nunziata, as soon as she heard the news, had put her little ones into the care of the least small, and asked her neighbour to keep an eye on the house, and had run to comare Mena's, to weep with her, which was the action of someone who hadn't yet reached the age of judgement. The others stood looking on, enjoying the sight from a distance, on the road, or crowded like flies around the front of the barracks, to see how padron 'Ntoni's 'Ntoni looked behind bars, after that knifing he had given don Michele; or they ran to Pizzuto's shop, where he was selling absinthe, and shaving people, and telling everyone how everything had happened, word for word.

'The idiots,' pronounced the chemist. 'So now who's got caught then? The idiots.'

'It'll be a bad business,' added don Silvestro; 'there'll be no getting him off a prison sentence.' 'The people who ought to go to prison never do,' don Giammaria told him to his face.

'No, that's quite true,' answered don Silvestro brazenly.

'In this day and age,' added padron Cipolla, yellow with gall, 'the real thieves steal your property in broad daylight, and in the public square. And they can enter your house without breaking either doors or windows.'

'As 'Ntoni Malavoglia wanted to do with mine,' added Zuppidda, joining the group as she spun her flax.

'By heaven, I always told you so,' began her husband.

'You be quiet, you know nothing about it! What a day this would have been for my daughter Barbara, if I hadn't kept my eye on things.'

Her daughter Barbara was at the window, all ready to see padron 'Ntoni's 'Ntoni go by between the policemen when they took him to the city.

'There he'll go and there he'll stay,' they all said. 'You know what it says over the law courts in Palermo? 'Run as far as you like, I'll wait for you here,' and 'the whetstone eats up rusty iron.' Poor devils.'

'Decent folk don't set their hands to that sort of thing,' shrieked la Vespa. 'People who look for trouble get it. Look at the kind of people who do such things — people who haven't got other jobs, good for nothings, like Malavoglia, and la

Locca's son.' Everyone said yes, that when a son of that sort turned up, it would be as well that the house should collapse about his ears. Only la Locca went looking for her son, and stood outside the barracks, screaming for them to hand him over, refusing to listen to reason; and when she went to irritate her brother Dumb bell, and settled firmly on the steps of the balcony for hours on end, with her white hair swirling, zio Crocifisso would say: 'I've got my own prison here at home! I'd like to be in your son's position! What do you want from me? He didn't earn a penny for you anyway!'

'This is a positive advantage for la Locca,' observed don Silvestro. 'Now that she hasn't got that excuse of having someone to look after her, they'll put her in the poorhouse, and she can eat meat and pasta every day. Otherwise she'd be the responsibility of the Town Council.'

'And it's a good thing for padron 'Ntoni too. Do you suppose that loafer of a grandson of his didn't cost him money? I know what a son like that costs a person. Now the king will be shouldering the burden.'

But instead of being relieved at saving that money, now that his grandson was no longer devouring it, padron 'Ntoni carried on throwing it after him with pettyfogging lawyers, that money which had cost them so dear, and which was intended for the house by the medlar tree.

'Now we don't need the house any more, or anything else!' he would say, his face as white as 'Ntoni's own, when they had taken him into town between the policemen, and the whole village had gone to see him with his hands tied and his bundle of shirts under his arm, which Mena had taken to him weeping, in the evening, when no one could see her. His grandfather had gone looking for a lawyer, the one with the patter, because now, after having seen don Michele go by in a carriage, while they were taking him to hospital, with his face yellow and his uniform all unbuttoned, the poor old man was afraid, and didn't stop to quibble about the lawyer's talkative nature, provided they got his boy's hands untied and had him brought home; because it seemed to him that after that upheaval, 'Ntoni ought to come back home and be with them for ever, like when he was a boy.

219

Don Silvestro did him the kindness of going with him to the lawyer, because he said that when one of your fellow men is in trouble, as was the case with the Malavoglia, you have to help them as best you can, even if he is a gaol bird, and do your utmost to get him out of the hands of the law, that's what we're Christians for, to help our neighbours. After he'd heard the whole story, and had it summed up for him a second time by don Silvestro, the lawyer said it was a fine case, and would certainly merit a life sentence, were he not involved, and he rubbed his hands. Padron 'Ntoni became as soft as a sponge at talk of a life sentence; but doctor Scipioni slapped him on the shoulder, and told him he wasn't a man of learning if he couldn't get him off with four or five years inside.

'What did the lawyer say?' asked Mena as soon as she saw her grandfather reappear looking as he did; and she began to cry before she heard the answer. The old man was tearing his few remaining white hairs, and went around the house like a madman repeating that it would be better if they were all dead. Lia, white as a sheet, stared wide-eyed at whoever was talking, unable to open her mouth. Soon afterwards the subpoena appeared, for Barbara Zuppidda, Grazia Piedipapera, don Franco the chemist and everyone who had been in the square and in Pizzuto's shop; so that the whole village was in turmoil and people panicked with the official documents in their hands, and swore they knew nothing so help them God! Because they didn't want to get involved with the law. And they cursed 'Ntoni Malavoglia and all the rest of them who embroiled people in their affairs whether they liked it or not. Zuppidda was shrieking like one possessed: 'I know nothing; I shut myself in my house at dusk and I'm not the sort who goes wandering around to get up to this sort of trick, or standing at doorways gossiping with spies.'

'I like to keep the Government at a distance,' added don Franco. 'They know I'm a republican, and they'd be delighted to have an excuse to get me to disappear from the face of the earth.'

People racked their brains to know what Zuppidda and comare Grazia and the others might say in evidence, because they had seen nothing, and had heard the shots from their beds, while they were asleep. But don Silvestro rubbed his hands like the lawyer, and said he knew why they had been summoned, and so much the better for the accused. Each time the lawyer went to talk with 'Ntoni Malavoglia, don Silvestro went with him to the prison, when he had nothing to do; and now no one was going to the Town Council and the olives were gathered. Padron 'Ntoni too made an attempt to go two or three times; but when he arrived in front of those barred windows, and the soldiers with the guns who looked at him and all the people who went in, he had felt sick and had stayed waiting outside, sitting on the pavement, among all the people selling chestnuts and prickly pears, and he couldn't believe that his 'Ntoni was in there, behind those bars, with those soldiers mounting guard. Then the lawyer came back from his chats with 'Ntoni fresh as a daisy, rubbing his hands; and he told him that his grandson was well, indeed he had put on weight. Now the poor old man felt as if his grandson were just one of the soldiers.

'Why don't they let him come back to me?' he asked each time like a parrot, or a child which won't listen to reason, and he also wanted to know if they were keeping him with his hands tied.

'You leave him be,' doctor Scipioni would say to him, 'in such cases it's better to let a little time go by. Anyway he's got everything he needs, as I told you, and he's fattening up like a capon. Things are going well. Don Michele has almost recovered from his wound, and that's a good thing for us too. Don't you worry, I tell you, and go back to your boat, because this is my business.'

'I can't go back to my boat now that 'Ntoni is in prison; I can't. Everyone would stare at us as we passed, and I can no longer think straight, now that 'Ntoni is in prison.'

And he would constantly repeat the same thing, while the money went though his fingers like water, and his family spent their days holed up in the house, with the door closed.

At last the day of the summons came, and those involved had to go to the law courts on foot, if they didn't want to go with the policemen. Even don Franco went, and took off his

221

awful old black hat to appear in front of the law, and he was paler than 'Ntoni Malavoglia, who was like a wild beast behind the bars, with the policemen beside him. Don Franco had never had any dealings with the law, and it annoyed him to have to appear for the first time in front of that handful of judges and policemen who can stick you behind bars in the twinkling of an eye, as they had done with 'Ntoni Malavoglia.

The whole village had gone to see how padron 'Ntoni's 'Ntoni looked behind bars, between the policemen, as yellow as tallow, not daring to blow his nose so as not to catch the eyes of all those friends and acquaintances devouring him, and he twisted his cap in his hands, while the judge, with his black robe and napkin under his chin, came out with a merciless list of the dirty deeds he'd performed, all written down there on papers down to the last word. Don Michele was there, as yellow as 'Ntoni, seated on a chair, opposite the jury who were yawning and fanning themselves with their handkerchieves. Meanwhile the lawyer was chatting in a low voice with his neighbour, as though the whole thing were nothing to do with him.

'Listen to what they're asking Santuzza,' murmured Zuppidda. 'I'm curious to hear how she'll answer so as not to blurt out all her personal affairs to the law.'

'But what do they want from us?' asked comare Grazia.

'They'll want to know if it's true that Lia was carrying on with don Michele, and if her brother 'Ntoni wanted to kill him to avenge his honour; the lawyer told me.'

'I hope the cholera strikes you,' the chemist hissed at them, glaring. 'Do you want us all to go to prison? Don't you know that you always have to deny everything with the law, and say that we know nothing?'

Comare Venera shrank into her shawl, but carried on muttering: 'This is the truth. I saw them with my own eyes, and the whole village knows it.'

That morning there had been a tragedy in the Malavoglia household, because, when he had seen the whole village move off to go and see 'Ntoni convicted, their grandfather had wanted to go along with the others, and Lia, her hair tangled and her eyes wild and chin trembling, had wanted to go along too, and was looking all through the house for her shawl without saying a word, looking all distraught, and her hands trembling. But Mena seized her, pale as her sister, and had said to her: 'No, you can't go, you can't go,' and that was all she would say. Her grandfather added that they should stay at home, to pray to the Virgin; and the wailing could be heard all up and down the strada del Nero. As soon as he was in the city, hiding behind a stretch of wall, the poor old man saw his grandson go by between two policemen, and though his legs almost gave way beneath him at each step, he went to sit on the steps of the law courts, among the people coming and going about their own business. Then at the thought that all those people were going to hear his grandson being convicted, amidst the soldiers, in front of the judges, it seemed to him as though he had abandoned him in the middle of the square, or at sea in a storm, and he too went with the crowd, and stood on tiptoe, to see the bars at the top, with the hats of the *carabinieri,* and the bayonets glinting. But there was no sign of 'Ntoni, in the midst of all those people, and the poor old man continued to think that now his grandson was one of the soldiers.

Meanwhile the lawyer nattered and chattered, droning on with his words like the endless pulley from a well. He said no, it wasn't true that 'Ntoni Malavoglia had done all those dirty deeds. The judge had dug them up to land a poor son of toil in trouble, because that was his job. Anyway, how could the judge state such things? Had he perhaps seen 'Ntoni Malavoglia that night, dark as it was? 'Losers are always in the wrong,' and 'the gallows are made for the luckless.' Turning a deaf ear the judge looked at him through his glasses, with his elbows set among those horrible books. Doctor Scipioni repeated that what he would like to know was where the contraband was; and since when couldn't a decent fellow go out for a walk at whatever hour he pleased, particularly if he'd had a drop to drink, to walk it off. Then padron 'Ntoni nodded, and said yes, yes, with tears in his eyes, because at that moment he could have hugged the lawyer who was saying that 'Ntoni was a drunkard. Suddenly he raised his head. That was good stuff! What the lawyer was saying right now alone was worth fifty *lire*; he was saying that they wanted to get him with his back to the wall, and to prove that 'Ntoni had been caught red-handed with the knife in his hand, and they had wheeled on don Michele, with the stuffing knocked out of him because of that knife wound to his stomach: 'Who says that 'Ntoni Malavoglia gave it to him?' spouted the lawyer, 'Who can prove it? and who knows whether don Michele might not have inflicted that wound on himself, just to get 'Ntoni Malavoglia sent to prison?' Well, if they were interested, they should know that smuggling had nothing to do with it. There was long-standing bad feeling between don Michele and 'Ntoni Malavoglia concerning women. And padron 'Ntoni nodded again, and if they had made him swear solemnly before the Cross he would have sworn, and the whole village knew about it, that business of Santuzza and don Michele, who was gnawing his fists from jealousy, after Santuzza became sweet on 'Ntoni, and they had met up with don Michele at night, and after the boy had drunk; everyone knows what happens when you're blind drunk. The lawyer continued: they could ask Zuppidda, and comare Venera, and a hundred thousand witnesses, again, whether don Michele was carrying on with Lia, 'Ntoni Malavoglia's sister, and he hung around the strada del Nero every evening for the girl. They'd even seen him on the night of the knife wound!

Then padron 'Ntoni heard no more, because his ears began to buzz, and for the first time he saw 'Ntoni, who had stood up in his cage, and was tearing at his cap, pulling faces like one possessed, eyes starting from their sockets, and saying no, no! His neighbours took the old man away, thinking he'd been taken ill; and the *carabinieri* laid him down in the witness room on the bunk bed there, and threw cold water in his face. Later, when they brought him lurching down the stairs, holding him under the armpits, the crowd too was streaming out like a river, and he heard them say that they had condemned him to five years hard labour. At that moment 'Ntoni too was coming out through the other little door, pale, between two policemen and hand-cuffed like Christ.

Gnà Grazia began to run in the direction of the village, and arrived before the others, with her tongue hanging out, because bad news travels fast. As soon as she saw Lia who was waiting at the door, like a soul in purgatory, she took her by the hand and said to her, as upset as the girl herself: 'What have you been doing, you wretched child, for them to tell the judge that you'd been carrying on with don Michele, and your grandfather has been taken ill!'

Lia said nothing, as though she had not heard, or didn't care. She just stood there staring at her, wide-eyed and open-mouthed. At last, slowly, she sat down on the chair, heavily, as though both her legs had been broken at a blow. Then, after she had sat like that for a long time, without moving and without saying a word, so that comare Grazia felt the need to dash water in her face, she began to stammer: 'I want to go away. I don't want to stay here any more!' and she said it to the chest of drawers, and to the chairs, like a mad woman, so that her sister ran vainly behind her weeping: 'I told you so, I told you so!' and tried to seize her once more. That evening, when their grandfather was brought home on the cart, and Mena had run out to meet him, because by now she no longer felt any sense of shame in front of people, Lia went out into the courtyard and then into the street, and went off in earnest, and no one saw her again.

CHAPTER XV

People said that Lia had gone to be with don Michele; by
now the Malavoglia had nothing to lose, and don Michele at
least would have seen that she didn't starve. Padron 'Ntoni
was virtually food for carrion by now, and did nothing but
wander round, bent double, like a face on an old pipe,
uttering meaningless proverbs; 'Everyone calls for an axe to
be taken to a fallen tree,' 'if you fall in the water you're bound
to get wet,' and 'to the lean horse, flies.' And to anyone who
asked him why he was always wandering around, he would
say that 'hunger drives the wolf from the wood,' and 'a
starving dog fears not the stick.' But people didn't take any
notice, now that he was reduced to that state. Everyone gave
their own piece of advice, and asked him what he was waiting
for with his back to the wall, there under the bell-tower, so
that he looked like zio Crocifisso when he was waiting to lend
money to people, sitting up against the boats pulled up on the
beach, as if he had padron Cipolla's fishing boat; and padron
'Ntoni would answer that he was waiting for death, which
was slow in coming for him, because 'a luckless man has long
days.' No one talked of Lia any more in the household, not
even St. Agatha, and for comfort she would go off and cry in
private, in front of her mother's little bed, when there was no
one in the house. Now the house seemed as vast as the sea,
and they felt quite lost in it. The money had gone off with
'Ntoni; Alessi was still away, finding work here and there;
and Nunziata did them the kindness of coming to light the
fire, when Mena had to go and take her grandfather by the
hand, towards dusk, like a child, because he was worse than a
hen and couldn't see in the dark any more.

Don Silvestro and the other people in the village said that

Alessi would have done better to send his grandfather to the poorhouse, now that he was good for nothing; and this was the only thing the poor old man was afraid of. Every time that Mena went to put him out in the sun, leading him by the hand, so that he could spend the whole day waiting for death, he thought they were taking him to the poorhouse, such an old dodderer had he become, and he mumbled that death was slow in coming, so that some people fell into the habit of asking him laughingly how far death had got on its road.

Alessi came home on Saturdays, and counted out the week's money for him, as though his grandfather still had all his wits about him. He carried on nodding his head; and then he had to go and hide the bundle under the mattress, and to please him, Alessi told him that they had nearly got together the money for the house by the medlar tree once again, and in a year or two they would have the whole sum.

But the old man shook his head, stubbornly, and retorted that now they didn't need the house any more; and it would have been better had there never been a Malavoglia family, now that the Malavoglia were scattered here and there.

Once he called Nunziata aside, under the almond tree, when there was no one around, and it seemed as though he had something serious to say; but he moved his lips without talking, and was seeking the words looking this way and that.

'Is it true what they say of Lia?' he said at last.

'No,' said Nunziata, with her hands solemnly crossed. 'No, by the Virgin of Ognina, it's not true.'

He began to nod, with his chin on his chest.

'So why did she run away too?' he asked, 'why did she run away?'

And he would look for her all through the house, pretending he'd lost his cap; he touched the bed and the chest of drawers, and seated himself at the loom, without a word. 'Do you know?' he asked at last. 'Do you know why she left?' But he said nothing to Mena.

Nunziata did not know, in all conscience, nor did anyone else in the village.

One night Alfio Mosca drew up in the strada del Nero, with his cart, which was now drawn by a mule, and that was

227

why he had caught the fever at Bicocca, and had almost died, so that his face was all yellow and his stomach as swollen as a gourd; but the mule was fat and sleek.

'Do you remember when I set out for Bicocca?' he said, 'when you were still at the house by the medlar tree? Now everything is changed, because 'the world is round, and some boats sail well and some run aground.' ' This time they couldn't even offer him a glass of wine, to welcome him back. Compare Alfio knew where Lia was; he had seen her with his own eyes, and it was as if he had seen comare Mena when they were chatting from one window to the other. That was why he moved his eyes hither and thither, from the furniture to the walls, heavy as if he had his own cart lying on his stomach, and he sat without a word, near the table which had nothing on it and where no one sat any more to eat of an evening.

'I'm off now,' he repeated, seeing that they had nothing to say to him. 'When a person leaves their villages, they'd do better not to return, because everything changes when they're away, even the expression on people's faces when they look at him, and it's as though he had become a stranger.'

Mena kept silent. Meanwhile Alessi told him that he wanted to marry Nunziata, when they had got a bit of money together, and Alfio told him he was right to do so, if Nunziata had a little money herself, because she was a good girl, and everyone in the village knew her. So it seems that even their relatives forget people who are no longer there and everyone in this world has to pull their own cart, like compare Alfio's donkey, though goodness knows what life that donkey was leading, now that it had passed into other hands.

Nunziata too had her dowry, since her little brothers were beginning to earn the odd penny, and she hadn't wanted to buy either gold or linen, because she said that such things were for the rich, and there was no point in getting linen while she was still growing.

She had indeed grown into a tall girl, slight as a broomstick, with black hair, and kind eyes, and when she sat down at the doorway, with all those children swarming round her, she looked as though she were still thinking of her father on the day he had left them, and of the troubles amidst which she

228

had picked her way ever since, with her little brothers clinging to her skirts. Seeing how she had pulled herself out of trouble, herself and her little brothers, weak and thin as a broomstick as she was, everyone greeted her and gladly stopped to have a word with her.

'We've got the money,' she said to compare Alfio, who was almost a relative, they had known him for so long. 'At All Saints' my brother is starting as apprentice with padron Cipolla. When I've settled Turi too, then I'll marry; but I'll have to wait until I'm of age, and for my father to give his consent.'

'Your father has forgotten your existence,' said Alfio. 'If he were to come back now,' replied Nunziata in her soft voice that was so calm, with her arms on her knees, 'he wouldn't go away again, because now we've got money.'

Then compare Alfio repeated to Alessi that he was doing right to take Nunziata, if she had that bit of money.

'We'll buy the house by the medlar tree,' added Alessi; 'and grandfather can stay with us. When the others come back they can stay there too; and if Nunziata's father comes back there'll be room for him as well.'

They didn't speak of Lia; but they were all three thinking about her, while they sat gazing at the lamp, with their elbows on their knees.

At last compare Mosca got up to go, because his mule was shaking the bells on its collar, as though it too knew the person whom compare Alfio had met on the way, someone who was no longer expected back at the house by the medlar tree.

Zio Crocifisso on the other hand had been expecting to hear from the Malavoglia for some time about that house, because no one wanted it, for all the world as though it brought bad luck, and it was still on his hands; so that as soon as he heard of the return of Alfio Mosca, whose bones he had wanted to have broken when he was jealous of la Vespa, he went to beseech him to play the go-between with the Malavoglia to conclude the deal. Now when he met him on the road he greeted him, and even tried sending la Vespa to talk to him about that business, after all perhaps they might remember their old love, at the same time, and compare Mosca might be able to relieve him of that cross which he was bearing. But that bitch of a Vespa didn't want any mention of compare Alfio, or of anyone else, now that she had a husband and was mistress in her own house, and she wouldn't have exchanged zio Crocifisso for Victor Emanuel himself, not even if they dragged her by the hair.

'I have to have all the bad luck,' zio Crocifisso complained; and he went to unburden himself with compare Alfio, and beat his chest as though he were with his confessor, for having even thought of paying ten *lire* to get his bones broken.

'Ah, compare Alfio! If you knew the disasters that have rained down upon my house, so that I can no longer eat or sleep, and I'm eaten up with rancour and I'm no longer master of a penny of my own, after having sweated all my life and deprived myself of my own bread, to pile it up penny by penny. Now I'm fated to see it in the hands of this serpent, to do as she pleases with! And I can't even get rid of her legally, because she wouldn't be tempted by Satan himself! and she loves me so much that I'll never get her off my back before I croak, if I don't die early from sheer desperation!'

'That's what I was saying to compare Alfio,' continued zio Crocifisso seeing padron Cipolla come by, and he had been in the habit of sauntering round the square like a butcher's dog, since that other wasp of a Mangiacarrubbe girl had entered his house.

'We can't even stay in our own houses for fear of exploding from ill-temper! They've driven us out of our own houses, those carrion! like ferrets do with rabbits. We'd be better off without them. Who would have believed it, eh, padron Fortunato? And to think we were living in blessed peace! That's how the world goes! Some people are seeking marriage all over the place, while those who are married are looking for a way out.'

Padron Fortunato stood for a bit rubbing his chin, and then said that marriage was a bit like a mouse trap, those who were caught in it were struggling to escape, while the others were prowling around trying to get in.

'I think they're mad! Look at don Silvestro, he lacks for

nothing, and yet he's got it into his head to try and get Zuppidda to drop into his arms, they say; and if comare Venera finds nothing better, she'll have to let her drop.'

Padron Cipolla continued rubbing his chin and said nothing more.

'Listen, compare Alfio,' continued Dumb bell, 'get this deal with the Malavoglia's house concluded, while they've got the money, and I'll give you the wherewithal to buy some shoes, for your comings and goings.'

Compare Alfio went back to talk to the Malavoglia; but padron 'Ntoni shook his head, and said no.

'We wouldn't know what to do with the house now, because Mena can't get married, and there are no Malavoglias left! I'm still here because unlucky people have long lives; but when I've closed my eyes, Alessi will take Nunziata and leave the village.'

He too was on the point of departure. He spent most of the time in bed, like a crab under the rocks, barking worse than a dog: 'I've no place here,' he would mutter; and he felt as though he were stealing the soup from their very mouths. In vain Alessi and Mena tried to convince him. He replied that he was robbing them of their time and soup, and wanted them to count out the money under the mattress for him, and if he saw it going down bit by bit, he would murmur: 'At least if I weren't here you wouldn't spend so much. I've no place here.'

Don Ciccio, who came to feel his pulse, confirmed that it would be better to take him to the hospital, because here he was eating his own meat and that of others, to no purpose. Meanwhile the poor man listened to what other people were saying, and was afraid they would send him to the poorhouse. Alessi wouldn't hear of such a thing, and said that as long as there was bread, there was enough for everyone; and Mena, for her part, said so as well, and took him out into the sun, on fine days, and sat down beside him with her spindle, telling him fairy stories, as one does to children, and spinning, when she didn't have work to do at the wash place. She even talked to him of what they would do when a bit of luck came their way, to cheer him up; she said that they would buy a young

231

calf at the market on St. Sebastian's Day, and she herself would get it grass and feed for the winter. In May they would sell it at a profit; and she also showed him the brood of chicks she had got, and which came cheeping round their feet in the sun, sneezing in the dusty roadway. With the money from the chickens they would buy a pig, so as not to waste the prickly pear skins, and the vegetable water, and by the end of the year it would be tantamount to having put money in the money box. The old man, with his hands on his stick, nodded his head, looking at the chicks. He was paying such close attention, poor fellow, that he even managed to say that if they had had the house by the medlar tree they would have been able to rear it in the courtyard, the pig that is, since they could definitely sell it at a profit to compare Naso. In the house by the medlar tree there was even a stable for the calf, and a shelter for the feed, and everything; he remembered it inch by inch, looking here and there with his dull eyes and his chin on his stick.

Then he asked his granddaughter in a low voice what don Ciccio had said about the hospital. Then Mena would scold him as though he were a child, and ask him why he was thinking of such things. He was silent, and listened quietly to everything the girl said. But he would always go back to entreating her not to send him to the hospital, because he wasn't used to it.

At last he no longer even got out of bed, and don Ciccio said that it was all over, and there was no more need for a doctor, because padron 'Ntoni could stay in that bed for years, and Alessi and Mena and even Nunziata would have to waste their time keeping an eye on him; otherwise the pigs would eat him, if they found the door open.

Padron 'Ntoni heard everything that was being said quite well, because he looked them in the eye one by one, and his expression hurt you to look back at him; and as soon as the doctor had gone, while he was still standing talking at the doorway to Mena who was crying, and Alessi who was saying no and stamping his feet, he gestured to Nunziata to come to the bed, and said to her quietly: 'It would be better for you to to send me to the hospital; here I eat up all the money you

232

make in the week. Send me away when Alessi and Mena aren't at home. They'd refuse, because they are true good-hearted Malavoglias; but I'm using up the money for the house, and anyway the doctor said that I might be here for years like this. And I've no place here, though I wouldn't want to hang on for years there at the hospital, either.'

Nunziata too began to cry and said no, and now the whole neighbourhood was speaking ill of them, for wanting to act so haughty when they didn't even have the bread for their supper. They were afraid to send their grandfather to the hospital, while the rest of the family were already scattered here and there, and in equally undesirable places too.

And Santuzza kissed the medal she wore on her chest, to thank the Virgin for protecting her from the danger into which St. Agatha's sister had fallen, like so many others.

'They ought to send that poor old man to the hospital, so as not to put him through purgatory even before he dies,' she said. At least she didn't allow her father to lack for anything, now that he was an invalid, and she kept him conveniently manning the door.

'Indeed, he's actually a help to you,' added Piedipapera. 'That invalid is worth his weight in gold! You'd think he'd been made specially to hold open the door of the wine shop, all blind and wizened as he is! And you ought to pray to the Virgin to spare him for you for a hundred years. And anyway, what does he cost you?'

Santuzza was right to kiss the medal; no one could make any comments about her affairs; since don Michele had gone, massaro Filippo had disappeared too, and people said he couldn't manage without don Michele's help. Now Cinghialenta's wife sometimes came to raise hell outside the wine shop, with her hands on her hips, shrieking that Santuzza was stealing her husband, so that when he came home she got swiped with the halter reins, after Cinghialenta had sold the mule, and didn't know what to do with the reins, so that the neighbours couldn't sleep at night for the din.

'This isn't right,' said don Silvestro, 'a halter is made for a mule. Compare Cinghialenta is uncouth.' He would say such things in the presence of comarc Venera la Zuppidda, because after conscription had taken off the young men of the village, she had ended up being a bit friendlier towards him.

'Everyone knows what goes on in their own house,' answered Zuppidda; 'if you're saying that because of the rumour some gossips are spreading about, that I lay about my husband, I'm telling you that you know nothing about it, although you know all about book learning. Anyhow everyone can do what they want in their own house. My husband is the boss.'

'You let them talk,' replied her husband. 'Anyhow, they know that if they came anywhere near me, I'd make mincemeat of them.'

Zuppidda now asserted that her husband was the head of the household, and he could marry off Barbara with whomsoever he pleased, and if he wanted to give her to don Silvestro that meant he had promised her to him, and had bowed his head and given his assent; and when her husband bowed his head, he was worse than an ox.

'Quite so,' pronounced don Franco with his beard in the air, 'he's bowed his head because don Silvestro is someone to be reckoned with.'

Since he had been in the law courts among all those policemen, don Franco was angrier than before, and swore he would not go back, even between two *carabinieri*. When don Giammaria raised his voice to argue, he flew at him, standing bolt upright on his little legs, red as a cockerel, and drove him to the back of the shop.

'You do it on purpose to compromise me!' he spat into his face, foaming at the mouth; and if two people were arguing on the square, he would run to close the door so that no one could call him to witness. Don Giammaria was triumphant; that gangling idiot had the courage of a lion, because he had a cassock on his shoulders, and spoke ill of the Government, calmly pocketting a *lira* a day, and said that they deserved the Government they had, since they had brought about the Revolution, and now foreigners came in to steal women and people's money. He knew who he was talking about, because he'd got jaundice from the cholera, and donna Rosolina had lost weight from sheer gall, particularly after don Michele

234

had gone off, and all his dark deeds had come to light. Now all she did was rush about after masses and confessors, this way and that, right to Ognina and Aci Castello, and she neglected her tomato preserve and tunny fish in oil, to devote herself to God.

Then don Franco gave vent to his anger by cackling like don Silvestro, rising up on to the tips of his toes, with the door wide open, because there was no danger of going to prison for that; and he said that as long as there were priests, it would always be the same story, and what was needed was a clean sweep, he understood these things, and he made a sweeping gesture with his arms.

'I'd like them all burnt alive,' answered don Giammaria, who also knew who he was talking about.

Now the chemist no longer held forth, and when don Silvestro came, he went to pound his unguents in the mortar, so as not to compromise himself. Anyhow all those who hob nob with the Government, and loaf around at the king's expense, are people to watch out for. And he unburdened himself only to don Giammaria, and don Ciccio the doctor, when he left his little donkey at the chemist's to go and feel padron 'Ntoni's pulse, and he didn't write out prescriptions, because he said they were pointless, for those poor people who didn't have money to burn.

'Then why don't they send the old man to the hospital?' the others kept saying, 'and why do they keep him at home to be eaten by the fleas?' So that time and again the doctor repeated that he was coming and going for nothing, casting water into the sea, and when the neighbourhood women were at the ill man's bedside, comare Piedipapera, cousin Anna and Nunziata, he kept on declaring that the fleas were eating the old man alive. Padron 'Ntoni no longer dared even draw breath, with his face white and ravaged. And as the neighbourhood women were chattering among themselves and even Nunziata was downcast, one day when Alessi wasn't there, he said at last: 'Call compare Mosca, he'll do me the kindness of taking me to the hospital on the cart.'

So padron 'Ntoni went to the hospital on Alfio Mosca's cart, where he'd put the mattress and the pillows, but although he didn't say anything, the poor ill fellow was looking all around him, while they were taking him outside holding him under the armpits, on the day when Alessi had gone to Riposto, and they had sent Mena away on some pretext, otherwise they would never have let him go. On the strada del Nero, as they passed in front of the house by the medlar tree, and as they crossed the square, padron 'Ntoni carried on looking this way and that, to impress everything on his mind. Alfio led the mule on one side, and Nunziata, who had left the calf and the turkeys and pullets in Turi's charge, was on foot on the other, with the bundle of shirts under her arm. Seeing the cart go by, everyone came out on their doorsteps, and stood to stare; and don Silvestro said that they had done right, that was what the municipality paid its rates for to the hospital; and don Franco would have blurted out his offering, because he had it absolutely off pat, if don Silvestro hadn't been there.

'At least that poor devil will get a bit of peace,' concluded zio Crocifisso.

'Need lowers nobility,' replied padron Cipolla; and Santuzza said a Hail Mary for the poor fellow. Only cousin Anna and comare Grazia Piedipapera dried their eyes on their aprons, as the cart went slowly by, jolting on the stones. But compare Tino said shortly to his wife:

'Why are you making that wailing? have I died, maybe? What's it to you?'

While he was leading the mule, Alfio Mosca was telling Nunziata how and where he had seen Lia, who looked just like St. Agatha, and he still couldn't believe that he had seen her with his own eyes, so that his voice failed in his throat, while he talked about it to pass the time, along the dusty road.

'Ah, Nunziata, who would have thought it, when we used to chat from one doorway to the next, and the moon was up, and the neighbours would be talking, and you could hear that loom of St. Agatha's clattering all day long, and those chickens who knew her just from the sound the gate made when she opened it, and la Longa called her from the courtyard, because I could hear everything from my house just as if I were in there! Poor Longa! Now, you see, I've got

236

my mule, and everything I wanted, and if an angel from heaven had come to tell me as much I'd never have believed him — now I'm always thinking of those evenings, when I heard your voices, while I was seeing to the donkey, and I could see the light in the house by the medlar tree, which is shut now, and when I came back I didn't find anything I had left, and comare Mena seemed a changed person. When a person leaves their village, they'd do better not to return. You see, now I even think of that poor donkey which worked for me for so long, and always plodded on with its head down and its ears back, rain or shine. Who knows where they're driving it now, and with what loads, and along what roads, with its ears even lower, because it goes along sniffing the earth which will receive it, when it gets old, poor creature!'

Stretched out on the mattress, padron 'Ntoni heard nothing, and they had put a cover with canes on the cart, so that it seemed as if they were carrying a corpse.

'It's just as well he shouldn't hear anything any more,' continued compare Alfio, 'He knows about 'Ntoni's situation and one day or the next he's bound to hear about Lia.'

'He often used to ask me, when we were alone,' said Nunziata. 'He wanted to know where she was.' 'She's following her brother. We poor creatures are like sheep, and we always follow others with our eyes closed. Don't tell him, nor anyone else in the village, where I saw Lia, because it would be a knife wound for St. Agatha. She certainly recognised me, while I was walking past the door, because she went all white and then red in the face, and I whipped the mule to go faster, and I'm sure that that poor creature would rather that the mule had walked over her stomach, and that they had carried her away as we are now carrying her grandfather. Now the Malavoglia family is destroyed, and you and Alessi must start it again from scratch.'

'We've already got the money for our needs. On St. John's Day we'll sell the calf, too.'

'Good. That way, when you've put the money aside there's no danger that it will vanish away, as would happen if the calf died, God forbid. Here we are on the outskirts of town, and you can wait for me here, if you don't want to come to the

237

hospital.'

'No, I want to come too; then at least I'll see where they're putting him, and he can see me till the last moment.'

Padron 'Ntoni was able to see her until the last moment, and while Nunziata was going off with Alfio Mosca, slowly, through the great room which made you think you were in church, it was so long in the walking of it, he followed them with his eyes; then he turned away and didn't move. Compare Alfio and Nunziata climbed back on to the cart, rolled up the mattress and cover, and set off without a word, along the dusty road.

Alessi beat his head and tore his hair, when he found his grandfather no longer in his bed, and saw that they had brought the mattress back rolled up. And he took it out on Mena, as though it had been she who had sent him away. But compare Alfio said to him: 'What could you do? Now the Malavoglia family is ruined, and you others must start it off again from scratch!'

He wanted to carry on talking about the money they'd saved and the calf, which he and Nunziata had been talking about along the way; but Alessi and Mena paid no heed, with their chins in their hands and their eyes fixed and bright with tears, sitting at the door of the house where they were now alone. Meanwhile compare Alfio tried to comfort them by reminding them what the house by the medlar tree used to be like, when they used to sit and chat from one doorway to another, in the moonlight, and all day long you could hear St. Agatha's loom going, and the hens clucking, and the voice of la Longa who was always busy. Now everything was changed, and when someone leaves their village, they would do better never to return, because the very road seems to have altered, since people no longer passed by to see the Mangiacarrubbe girl and don Silvestro didn't seem to be around either, waiting for Zuppidda to drop into his arms, and zio Crocifisso had locked himself into his house to keep an eye on his possessions, or to row with la Vespa, and there was no longer so much quarrelling in the chemist's shop, since don Franco had come face to face with justice, and now he crept off quietly to read the paper, and found his relief by pounding things in the mortar all day long to pass the time. Even padron Cipolla was no longer to be found wearing down the steps in front of the church, since he had lost his peace of mind.

One day the news went round that padron Fortunato was getting married, so that the Mangiacarrubbe girl couldn't enjoy his possessions at his expense; that was why he no longer wore down the steps, and was taking on Barbara Zuppidda.

'And he was telling me marriage was like a mouse trap,' zio Crocifisso mumbled. 'Trustworthy creatures, men.'

The envious girls said that Barbara was marrying her grandfather. But people of importance, like Peppi Naso, and Piedipapera, and even don Franco, murmured: 'This is a victory for comare Venera over don Silvestro; and it's a blow for don Silvestro, and he should leave the village. In any case foreigners should be drummed out of town, and they've never put down roots here. Don Silvestro won't dare confront padron Cipolla face to face.'

'What do you think?' shrieked comare Venera with her hands on her hips, 'that he could take my daughter all penniless as he was? This time I'm in charge! and I've let my husband know as much! The good dog eats in the trough; I don't want foreigners about the house. We used to be much better off in this village, before people came from outside to note down the mouthfuls you eat, like don Silvestro, or to pound mallow flowers in the mortars, and get fat on the blood of the villagers. Then everyone knew everyone else, and what they were doing, and what their father and grandfather had always done, and even what they ate and when someone went by you knew where they were going, and the smallholdings belonged to those who were born here, and the fish were choosy about who caught them. Then people didn't roam all over the place, and they didn't go to hospital to die, either.'

Since everyone was getting married, Alfio Mosca would have liked to take comare Mena, because no one else wanted her now, since the collapse of the Malavoglia household, and compare Alfio could have been regarded as a good match for her, what with his mule; so on Sunday he pondered over all

239

the reasons that might give him hope, while he sat beside her, in front of the house, with his shoulders to the wall, whittling away at twigs from the hedge to pass the time. She too watched the people go by, and thus they spent their Sunday: 'If you still want me, comare Mena,' he said at last, 'I'm here for the taking.'

Poor Mena didn't even blush, hearing that compare Alfio had guessed that she had wanted him, when they were about to give her away to Brasi Cipolla, so far away did that time seem, and she herself didn't seem like the same person.

'Now I'm old, compare Alfio,' she replied, 'and I shan't be getting married.'

'If you're old, then I'm old too, because I was older than you when we used to chat from the window, though it feels to me as if it were yesterday, it's still so alive in my heart. But more than eight years must have gone by. And when your brother Alessi gets married, you'll be on your own.'

Mena shrugged and said she was used to doing God's will, like cousin Anna; and seeing her like that, compare Alfio continued: 'Then that means you don't care about me any more, comare Mena, and please forgive me for having said I would marry you. I know that you are better born than me, and you're the daughter of people with property; but now you have nothing, and if your brother Alessi marries, you'll be left all alone. I have my mule and my cart, and I'd never leave you short of food, comare Mena. Forgive my boldness!'

'You haven't offended me, compare Alfio; and I would have said yes when we had the *Provvidenza*, and the house by the medlar tree, if my parents had been willing, because God knows how I felt when you went off to Bicocca with your donkey cart, and I can still see that light in the stable, and you putting all your things on the cart, in the courtyard; do you remember?'

'Do I remember? So why are you saying no, now that you have nothing, and I have the mule instead of the donkey, and your parents couldn't say no?'

'Now I'm not marriageable,' Mena repeated with her face lowered, whittling twigs as well. 'I'm twenty seven, and the time for marriage has passed.'

240

'No, that's not the reason you're saying no,' repeated compare Alfio, his face lowered too. You're not telling me the reason.' And so they stayed in silence, whittling sticks without looking at each other. After he got up to leave, with his shoulders hunched, and his head down, Mena followed him with her gaze until she could see him no longer, and then she looked at the opposite wall, and sighed.

As Alfio Mosca had said, Alessi had taken Nunziata as his wife, and had bought back the house by the medlar tree.

'I'm no longer marriageable,' Mena repeated; 'you get married, you're still young enough;' and so saying she had gone up into the attic of the house by the medlar tree, like the old saucepans, and she had resigned herself, waiting for Nunziata's little ones so that she could play mother to them. Then there were hens in the hen-run, and the calf in the stable, and wood and feed under the shelter, and nets and all sorts of tackle hanging up, just as padron 'Ntoni had said; and Nunziata had planted broccoli and cauliflowers in the vegetable patch, with those delicate arms of hers, so that you could hardly imagine how so much linen for bleaching could have passed through them, and how she had brought up those fat, pink children whom Mena carried through the neighbourhood in her arms, when she played mother to them.

Compare Mosca shook his head, when he saw her pass, and turned the other way, shoulders hunched.

'You didn't think me worthy of that honour,' he said to her at last, his heart heavier than his shoulders. 'I wasn't worthy of your acceptance.'

'No, compare Alfio,' replied Mena, who felt the tears rising. 'I promise, by this pure creature I have in my arms, that that wasn't the reason. But I'm no longer marriageable.'

'Why are you no longer marriageable, comare Mena?'

'No, no,' repeated comare Mena, who was almost crying. 'Don't force me to speak, comare Alfio. Now if I married, people would start to talk about my sister Lia again, because no one would dare to take a Malavoglia, after what has happened. You'd be the first to regret it. Leave me be, I'm no longer marriageable — just resign yourself.'

241

'You're right, comare Mena!' replied comare Mosca, 'I'd never thought of that. But I can't help cursing the fate which has brought us so many sorrows.'

In this way compare Alfio resigned himself, and Mena continued to carry her nephews in her arms as though she had resigned herself too, and to sweep the attic, for when the others would come back, because they had been born there too, 'as though they were on a journey, and would be coming back,' said Piedipapera.

Whereas padron 'Ntoni had made that long journey, further than Trieste or Alexandria in Egypt, from which no traveller returns; and when his name cropped up in conversation, while they were resting, working out the week's accounts and making plans for the future, in the shadow of the medlar tree and with their bowls between their knees, the chatter would suddenly die down, because everyone felt as if the poor old man were there before their eyes, as they had seen him the last time they had gone to visit him in the great barracks of a room with its rows of beds, so that you had trouble finding him, and their grandfather was waiting for them like a soul in purgatory, with his eyes on the door, although he was almost blind, and he felt them all over, to make sure it was really them. And then he didn't say anything, while you could tell from his face that he had so many things to say, and he was a heart-rending sight with that pain in his face which he couldn't express. Then they told him that they had got back the house by the medlar tree, and wanted him to come back to Trezza again, and he said yes, yes, with his eyes, which started to shine again, and his mouth almost formed a smile, the sort of smile of people who no longer laugh, or are laughing for the last time, and which stays planted in your heart like a knife. So it was with the Malavoglia when, on Monday, they went back with Alfio Mosca's cart to fetch their grandfather, and found him gone.

Remembering all those things, they left their spoons in their bowls, and thought and thought about everything that had happened, which all seemed so dark, as though the shadow of the medlar tree had fallen upon it. Now, when cousin Anna came to spin for a while with the neighbourhood women, she had white hair, and said that she had lost the knack for laughter because she hadn't time to be happy, with the family she had on her hands, and Rocco who had to be looked for all over the place, along the road or in the wine shop, and then driven homeward like a stray calf. In the Malavoglia family too there were two strays; and Alessi racked his brains wondering where they could be, along the roads parched with sun and white with dust, because they would never come home to the village, after so long.

One night, late, the dog began to bark behind the courtyard door, and Alessi himself who went to open it, did not recognise 'Ntoni coming back with his bundle under his arm, he was so changed, covered in dust, and with a long beard. When he came in and sat in a corner, they almost didn't dare to greet him. He seemed so changed, and went peering round the walls, as though he had never seen them before; even the dog barked at him, because it had never known him. They gave him a bowl of soup because he was hungry and thirsty, and he ate as though he hadn't had a bite to eat in a week, with his nose in the dish; but the others weren't hungry, so stricken did they feel. Then when he had eaten and rested a bit, 'Ntoni took up his bundle and made as if to leave.

Alessi didn't dare to say anything to him, so changed was his brother. But seeing him pick up the bundle, he felt his heart leap out of his breast, and Mena, all bewildered, asked: 'Are you going?'

'Yes,' replied 'Ntoni.

'But where?' asked Alessi.

'I don't know. I came to see you. But since I've been here the soup has turned to ashes in my mouth. Anyhow, I can't stay here, because everyone knows me, and that's why I came at night. I'll go a long way off, where I can find a way to earn a living, and no one knows who I am.' The others didn't dare breathe, because they felt their hearts gripped as if in a vice, and they understood that he was doing right to speak like that. 'Ntoni continued to look all around, and stood at the doorway, and couldn't make up his mind to go.

'I'll let you know where I am,' he said at last, and when he was in the courtyard, under the medlar tree, and it was dark, he also said:

'And grandfather?'

Alessi didn't answer; 'Ntoni too fell silent, and said after a while:

'And Lia, I didn't see her?'

And since he waited in vain for the answer, he added with a shaking voice, as though he were cold: 'Is she dead too?'

Alessi didn't even answer; then 'Ntoni, who was under the medlar tree with his bundle in his hand, made as if to sit down, because his legs were trembling, but he straightened up suddenly, stammering: 'Goodbye, all of you. You see that I must go?'

Before going he wanted to take a turn round the house, to see if everything was as before; but now 'Ntoni, who had had the courage to leave the house and pull a knife on don Michele, and to be in all kinds of trouble, had not the courage to walk from one room to another without prompting. Seeing the desire in his eyes, Alessi had him go into the stable, with the excuse of the calf Nunziata had bought, and which was fat and glossy; then he took him into the kitchen, where they had made a new hearth, and into the next room, where Mena slept with Nunziata's children, as though they were her own.

'Grandfather would have liked to put the calf here; the hens sat in here, and the girls slept here, when *she* was here too . . .' But then he said no more, and fell silent, looking around, with his eyes bright. At that moment the Mangiacarrubbe girl passed by, scolding Brasi Cipolla down the street, and 'Ntoni said: 'She's found a husband; and now, when they've finished their quarrel, they'll go to sleep in their own home.'

The others were quiet, and there was a great quietness throughout the whole village, and all you could hear·was the occasional door banging; and at those words Alessi found the courage to say: 'If you wanted, you too could have a home of your own. There's a bed for you, in there.'

'No,' answered 'Ntoni, 'I must leave. That's where mother's bed was, which she soaked with tears when I wanted to leave. Do you remember the chats we used to have of an evening, when we were salting the anchovies, with Nunziata

244

explaining the riddles? and mother, and Lia, all there, in the moonlight, and you could hear the whole village chattering, as if we were one big family. I didn't know anything then, either, and I didn't want to stay here; but now that I know everything, I have to go.'

At that moment he was speaking with his gaze on the ground, and his head sunk into his shoulders. Then Alessi threw his arms around his neck.

'Goodbye,' repeated 'Ntoni. 'You see I was right to leave! I can't stay here. Goodbye, and forgive me, all of you!'

And he went off with his bundle under his arm; then, when he was some way off, in the middle of the square which was dark and empty because all the doorways were closed, he stopped to hear whether they were closing the door to the house by the medlar tree, while the dog barked after him, telling him with his bark that he was alone in the village. Only the sea grumbled its usual tale down below, amid the sharp rocks, because the sea is a wanderer too, and it belongs to everyone who pauses to listen to it, here and there where the sun rises and sets, and indeed at Aci Trezza it has a way of grumbling all of its own, and can immediately be recognised by its gurglings among those rocks on which it breaks, and it sounds like the voice of a friend.

Then 'Ntoni stopped in the middle of the road to look at the village, all black as it was, as though he hadn't the heart to leave it, now that he knew everything, and he sat down on the wall of massaro Filippo's vineyard.

He stayed there a long time thinking of many things, looking at the dark village, and listening to the sea rumbling to him down below. And he stayed until he began to hear certain familiar noises, and voices calling from behind closed doors, and a banging of shutters, and steps down the dark streets. On the sea shore, at the end of the square, lights began to proliferate. He lifted his head to look at the Three Kings twinkling, and the Pleiades which meant dawn, as he had seen it so many times. Then he hung his head, and began to think of his whole story. Gradually the sea began to whiten, and the Three Kings to pale, and the houses emerged one by one in the dark streets, and he knew each one of them, and the only one with a light outside it was Pizzuto's shop, and there was Rocco Spatu with his hands in his pockets, coughing and spitting.

'Soon zio Santoro will open the door,' thought 'Ntoni, 'and will squat down at the doorway to begin his day too.' Then he looked back at the sea, which had become amaranth, all dotted with boats which had begun their day too, and he picked up his bundle and said: 'Now it's time to go, because soon people will be going by. But the first person to start his day is Rocco Spatu.'

CHRONOLOGY

1840	2 September. Giovanni Verga was born in Catania, Sicily. His family were landowners and members of the minor nobility.
1848/9	Year of Revolutions in Italy.
1857	Wrote his first novel, "Amore e Patria" (unpublished).
1858	Enrols as a student of law at Catania University.
1859	Beginning of the Italian War of Independence.
1860	Insurrections in Sicily in April are followed by the arrival of Garibaldi and his volunteers who take Sicily from the Bourbons. Verga joins the National Guard founded after the arrival of Garibaldi. He is one of the founders and the editor, of the weekly political magazine, Roma degli Italiani.
1861	The Bourbons are forced out of Naples, and Garibaldi surrenders Naples and Sicily to Victor Emanuel, the Piedmontese king. In plebiscites the people of Southern Italy vote to be part of the newly formed Italian Kingdom under Victor Emanuel. Verga abandons his legal studies and publishes his first novel, "I Carbonari della Montagna," at his own expense.
1863	His patriotic novel, "Sulle lagune", is published in a magazine. His father dies.
1864	Florence becomes the new capital of Italy, replacing Turin.

1865	Verga's first visit to Florence. He becomes a frequent visitor and takes up permanent residence in 1869.
1866	20 July, naval battle at Lissa. The Austrians retreat from Venice which becomes part of Italy. His novel, "Una Peccatrice" is published.
1869	Settles in Florence, where he meets Luigi Capuana, the realist writer and theorist. Begins an affair with the 18 year old, Giselda Foljanesi.
1870	Rome is taken, and becomes the Italian capital in 1871.
1871	Zola's "La Fortune de Rougon", the first book in the Rougon-Macquart cycle, is published. Zola's theories and Naturalism become increasingly important and controversial in Italy. Verga publishes "Storia di una capinera", which is an immediate success.
1872	Goes to live in Milan, where he spends most of the next 20 years. Frequents the literary salons of the city, making a name for himself in the capital of Italian publishing. Giselda Foljanesi marries the Catanese poet Mario Rapisardi.
1873	"Eva" is published, and is criticized for its immorality.
1874/6	"Tigre Reale", "Eros", and the novella "Nedda" are published.
1877	"L'Assommoir" of Zola is published and has an overwhelming influence in Italy. Verga publishes his collected short stories, "Primavera e altri racconti."

1878	His mother dies, to whom he was greatly attached.
1880	"Vita dei Campi" is published. Visits Giselda Foljanesi.
1881	"I Malavoglia" is published. Verga is disappointed by its lack of success. Begins an affair with countess Dina Castellazi, who is married and in her twenties. It lasts most of his life.
1883	Goes to Paris, and visits Zola at Médan. Also goes to London. Publishes "Novelle Rusticane" and the novel "Il Marito di Elena", and "Per le Vie". Visits Catania where he sees Giselda Foljanesi. In December Rapisardi discovers a compromising letter from Verga to his wife, and so Giselda is forced to leave and settle in Florence.
1884	The play of "Cavalleria Rusticana" is put on with great success in Turin, with Eleonora Dusa playing Santuzza. The end of Verga's affair with Giselda Foljanesi.
1886-7	Passes most of his time at Rome. The publication of a French translation of "I Malavoglia" is without success.
1888	Returns to live in Sicily.
1889	"Mastro-don Gesualdo" is published and is an immediate success. D'Annunzio publishes his novel, "Il Piacere".
1890	Mascagni's one act opera of "Cavalleria Rusticana" is put on and enjoys an overwhelming success. Verga sues Mascagni and Sonzogno for his share of the royalties. First English translation of "I Malavoglia".

1891	Publishes a volume of stories, "I Ricordi del capitano d'Arce". Wins his case in the Court of Appeal, getting 143,000 lire, (which was a large sum then and put an end to the financial problems which had beset him).
1895	Goes with Capuana to visit Zola in Rome.
1896	The defeat at Adua puts an end to Italy's colonial expansion. Verga criticizes the demonstrations against the war. Begins writing the third novel in his "I Vinti" cycle, "La Duchessa di Leyra", but never completes it.
1898	There are riots in Milan, after the price of bread is increased, which are violently put down by the army. Verga applauds their actions as a defence of society and its institutions.
1900-3	Various of his plays are put on, but Verga's energies turn away from his writing to managing his business interests and living quietly in Sicily.
1915	Declares himself in favour of Italian involvement in WW1, and anti-pacificism.
1920	His eightieth birthday is celebrated in Rome and Catania. In November he becomes a senator.
1922	27 January Verga dies in Catania. Mussolini comes to power.
1925/8	D.H. Lawrence translates "Mastro-don Gesualdo" and "Novelle Rusticane" into English.
1950	Eric Mosbacher's translation of "I Malavoglia".